OYSTER BAY
BOOGALOO

Eric Wiilder

Gondwana Press

ASIN: B0G1VMZ3HM
ISBN-13: 9781946576279
ISBN-10: 1946576271

Cover design by: Gondwana Graphics
Printed in the United States of America

For Anne

CHAPTER 1

The bungalow cowered against the storm like an old sailor bracing for a heavy wave. Its cedar planks, tarnished with salt and age, groaned under the gale's strike, shutters rattling as the wind clawed at them. Inside, the fire in the stone hearth roared, its flames licking at the chimney, sending sparks dancing into the dim room. The air was thick with the smell of smoke, damp wool, and the salty tang of the sea that seeped through every crack on Oyster Island.

Rain battered the roof in relentless sheets, a percussion that drowned out all but the loudest thoughts. Alex Pavlovic leaned forward in his chair, his dark eyes narrowing at the chessboard between him and John Pierre Saucier, known to all as J.P. Alex was a man shaped by harsher winters than this island could summon; his posture was stiff, his hands calloused from years of labor and survival. A glass of vodka gleamed in the firelight, half-drained, its sharp clarity reflecting his intense focus.

The chess set, an antique with ivory pieces worn smooth by decades of play, was his pride, scavenged from a forgotten estate sale in Mobile, Alabama. Each piece carried a weight of history, much as the man who moved them did. J.P. sprawled opposite him, his ease a stark contrast to Alex's intensity. His sleeves were rolled to the elbows, dark hair damp from the humidity, and his rum glass—etched with a faded schooner—never strayed far from his hand.

By the fire, Lucky, J.P.'s chocolate Lab, graying at the muzzle, snored with the patience of an old priest. His paws twitched in a dream of chasing rabbits or gulls across the island's dunes, his warmth a quiet anchor in the room.

The bungalow, perched on Oyster Island's far side near the ruins of an old sugar plantation and its derelict distillery, was Alex's weathered but cozy retreat. The fire cast flickering shadows across an ornate rug—a thrift store treasure from Chalmette, its threads worn but vibrant, a steal at ten dollars. Built-in bookshelves sagged under the weight of Alex's collection: Faulkner's humid prose, Dostoevsky's brooding tomes, and obscure volumes from estate sales, their spines cracked from late-night reading.

A chipped but exquisite China set, pieced together from thrift stores across the Gulf, sat on a shelf, each piece a testament to Alex's knack for spotting quality in the overlooked. A brass barometer, salvaged from a wrecked shrimp boat, hung on the wall, its needle trembling in the storm's pressure.

Alex, short and stocky with a receding hairline, studied the chess pieces as thunder shook the roof, his glass of vodka never far from his hand. His gruff demeanor and his rugged masculinity—almost primal—hid a loneliness he'd never admit. A former Russian Army officer turned deserter, he'd fled to the U.S. as an illegal immigrant, working first as a roughneck in South Dakota before meeting J.P. and landing a job as concierge at the Majestic Hotel and Casino, a Prohibition-era relic on stilts over Oyster Bay.

His past as a liquor distributor fueled his obsession with the island's dormant Batiste Distillery, its crumbling brick walls a siren call to his ambitions. The island's water, filtered through ancient limestone, was geologically unique—perfect for rum. Alex had spent months researching its potential, poring over old plantation records and chemical analyses in his bungalow's cramped study. He'd convinced Jake Huntington, billionaire and star of the TV reality show, Cryptid Hunter, to bankroll the distillery's revival, a gamble that wouldn't make or break him. Like Alex, Jake liked challenges. The bungalow's proximity to the distillery suited his control-freak tendencies; he could walk the overgrown path to the site in minutes, checking equipment or dreaming of copper stills under the stars.

J.P., by contrast, was a man of the Gulf, born to its rhythms. He sprawled in his chair, sipping rum, his Stetson tilted back. A retired St. Bernard Parish deputy sheriff and former Army captain, he had a cowboy swagger, dark Cajun features, and a movie-star charm that made women swoon. Like Alex, he'd never married, though his Labrador, Lucky, snoring by the fire, was his constant companion. J.P. co-owned the island's dog training facility; his psychology degree from U.S.L. was long buried under years of service in law enforcement and the military. The two men bantered over chess, their voices competing with the storm's howl.

"Distillery's going to be a goldmine," J.P. said, moving a knight. "Once it's up, you'll be the rum king of the Gulf."

Alex snorted, swirling his vodka. "Weeks away. The arrival of our copper kettles is delayed once again."

"Why don't you go with stainless steel?" J.P. asked. "You told me yourself stainless steel kettles are stronger and last longer than copper, not to mention you could have them installed as early as later this week."

"There are reasons," Alex said.

"Like what?" J.P. asked.

"Copper interacts chemically with the spirit as it's being distilled, scrubbing sulfur out of the fermented liquid and vapor. You want your rum tasting like a swamp?"

"Why hell no," J.P. said with a grin.

"Neither does anyone else," Alex said. "You can't make good spirits without it. Copper is essential."

J.P. swirled his glass of rum and said, "You mean there's copper in this swill?"

When Alex reached for the glass, J.P. yanked it away. "Just kidding," he said. "I've never tasted better rum than this."

"Then stop calling it swill," Alex said.

"I said I was kidding. Is it the copper that makes it taste so good?"

"Among other things," Alex said. "There are minerals in everything we eat or drink. In rum, there are trace amounts of iron, potassium, zinc, copper, and manganese. Most of the trace elements come from sugarcane. They are present in such minute quantities that they don't affect your nutrition, only the taste of the rum."

"What about the water?" J.P. asked.

"There's no better water on earth for distilling rum than right here on Oyster Island," Alex said.

"How the hell do you know so much about everything?"

J.P. laughed and shook his head when Alex said, "In Russia, you have to show up for classes and do your homework."

"Touché," J.P. said.

When thunder rattled the window panes, Alex topped up their glasses as J.P. studied his next move on the chessboard.

"Exactly what are you doing?" he asked.

J.P. glanced up from the board and said, "I didn't realize we had a time limit on our moves."

"It isn't chess I'm talking about," Alex said.

"What are you talking about?"

"You. It's Friday night, and you're here playing chess with me?"

"What am I supposed to be doing?" J.P. asked.

"Wining and dining some beautiful and bewitching woman," Alex said.

"I could say the same thing about you. You haven't had a girlfriend since you moved to Oyster Island. Something you want to tell me?"

Alex's eyes flicked to the board, avoiding the jab. "Check. And no. Women are trouble. Like this storm."

The low-water creek J.P. had crossed to get to Alex's bungalow was now a raging stream. The storm's intensity had turned it into a powerful torrent, nearly impassable.

"Speaking of the storm, Lucky and me are stuck here for the night. No one was expecting this storm, and even my ATV can't make it across the low-water crossing," J.P. said.

"You and Lucky are always welcome here," Alex said. "You know that."

"At least I have Lucky," J.P. said. "You don't even have a dog."

"I'm happy the way I am and need no one except myself," Alex said.

"Yeah, yeah," J.P. said. "I've heard it all before."

Thunder rattled the roof, lightning strobing through the windows. Lucky's ears twitched, but he stayed put, a brown heap of fur by the hearth. The men fell silent, focused on resetting the board for another game, until a sound pierced the storm's din—a distant, chilling scream.

J.P. froze, his glass halfway to his lips. "Hear that?"

Alex was already on his feet. The chessboard toppled, pawns and knights scattering across the rug as he pulled on his rain slicker with practiced speed, jaw set, eyes narrowed. Without a word, he strode to the door. Lucky was up in an instant, tail stiff, ears pricked. J.P. cursed under his breath, tossed back the last of his rum, pulled on his raincoat, and followed.

The storm hit them like a wall. Wind clawed at their clothes, rain stung their faces, and the surf roared like a living thing. Lightning split the sky in jagged veins of white, illuminating the beach in violent flashes. The three figures—man, man, and dog—pushed forward against the wind, boots sinking into wet sand as the waves licked at their ankles. The beach sat about a hundred yards from Alex's bungalow, the squall blowing at a gale force, churning up the waves into chest-high white caps.

Then the light changed.

Above the water, a shimmer gathered, initially unfocused, like heat rising from stone. It resembled a mirage in the sky, an image so real it seemed a motion picture projected onto nature's canvas. A sailboat, with its sails furled and tightly wrapped as if the owner were asleep, floated nearby. The only trouble was that it wasn't anchored; the craft was drifting in the choppy Gulf of Mexico with no land in sight.

J.P. and Alex watched the scene unfold, their attention fixed on the image before them. As the sea grew more turbulent, waves rocked the sailboat and sent foamy water crashing over the bow. A young woman in a white nightgown appeared on

5

deck, frantic as she grasped the railings, trying to unfurl the canvas, raise the sails, and point the sailboat into the wind. For a moment, a wave masked the boat. When it cleared, the woman was gone, apparently washed overboard.

The image of the sailboat and the stormy seas evaporated, then coalesced into a figure cloaked in shadow, its face hidden beneath a cowl, but its eyes—two burning coals—pierced the storm. The apparition flickered in and out, as though the storm itself resisted its presence.

"What the hell!" J.P. said.

Alex saw it too—the flickering image of a man dressed in a dark robe, his face shrouded in shadows from the draping cowl over his head. When the being's image spoke, the voice was guttural and ancient, seeming to vibrate in their bones.

Beware the tides of January. They carry both good and evil. You must choose. The wrong choice leads to a horrible death.

The figure wavered, dissolved into lightning, and was gone. Before they could process it, another scream split the air— human, desperate. For a moment, only the storm remained. Then the scream came again—closer, sharper, frantic.

A pale shape thrashed in the surf: a young woman, her long blond hair plastered to her face, her white nightgown clinging to her as the riptide dragged her under. J.P. didn't have to point; Alex was already racing into the surf. Lucky bolted past him, plunging into the waves with a bark that was swallowed by the wind. He reached the struggling woman, teeth gripping the fabric of her gown, but the current seized them both, dragging them sideways into deeper water. When Alex charged after them, J.P. caught his arm.

"We'll all drown if we don't work together. Pull off your slicker!" Alex obeyed, stripping the heavy coat and thrusting one sleeve into J.P.'s hands. "Don't let go!"

Alex clasped the sleeve of the slicker and waded forward, the surf battering his chest, until his fingers closed around Lucky's collar. The big dog didn't struggle; it simply refused to release the woman, even as the tide pulled them both under.

"Hang on, Russkie!" J.P. shouted, bracing himself on the shore, the slicker stretched taut between them.

Inch by inch, with the storm raging around them, J.P. dragged the trio back to land. By now, the rain was coming down in bucketloads. They were already soaked to the bone, and the driving rain made little difference. Lightning struck the ground so close that the explosion of thunder was almost simultaneous.

"Mother Mary!" Alex said.

"Too damn close!" J.P. said. "Thought I was back in Afghanistan for a second."

"Take her back to the bungalow before the next one hits and turns us into toasted marshmallows," Alex said.

"She'll never make it if I do," J.P. said. "She ain't breathing."

J.P. lay the woman on the sand, her body limp and lifeless, and began mouth-to-mouth, his hands steady despite the storm's fury. He dropped to his knees beside her, pressing his mouth to hers, forcing air into her lungs. Water spilled from her lips, and then—at last—she coughed, gasped, and her chest heaved with life. Lucky shook himself violently, spraying seawater in every direction, then pressed his wet body against her side as if to guard her.

J.P. scooped the woman into his arms, her head lolling against his shoulder. "Back to the bungalow before we all drown right here on the beach."

The storm had only intensified, and Alex barely heard what J.P. had said.

"Or get struck by lightning," he said.

Alex lingered a moment, the storm still howling. He started after J.P., but something rustling in the brush at the edge of the beach caused him to come to an abrupt halt. He turned, half-expecting another vision, but instead found a trembling shape: a solid white cat, her belly swollen with kittens, eyes wide with fear.

"Ah, little mother," he said, crouching low. He gathered her gently into his arms, tucking her against his chest. She pressed her face into his shirt, shivering. "Tonight, we save two damsels in distress."

CHAPTER 2

Alex cradled the frightened animal and turned back toward the glow of the bungalow's windows. The cat, feeling Alex's warmth and the brief lull in the wind as he moved away from the water, began to purr softly against his soaked shirt. He adjusted his grip on her, noting the almost frantic rhythm of her small heart against his ribs.

It was an almost domestic feeling to hold a creature so fragile while the world around him was tearing itself apart. The storm's howl was a living thing, clawing at the dunes, spitting salt and sand into his face. Each gust felt personal, as if the Gulf itself resented his intrusion.

Alex had seen battlefields less chaotic than this storm-whipped stretch of sand, yet here he was, playing rescuer to a pregnant feline. The irony didn't escape him. He was a man who preferred order, a ledger of pros and cons, yet he was now fully immersed in the raw chaos of the Gulf. His mind flickered to the ledgers he kept for his rum distillery—precise measurements of molasses, yeast, time. Out here, there was no such control. The sea dictated terms, and tonight, it was a tyrant.

J.P. was already a dark silhouette pushing through the dunes, his broad shoulders shielding the woman's inert form. Even at a distance, Alex could see the deliberate strength in his friend's stride. J.P. was a man built for emergencies, with his law enforcement training running like a deep current beneath the easygoing Cajun charm. He was the counterpoint to Alex's coiled intensity—the reliable anchor in the storm. Yet even J.P.'s steady presence couldn't quell the unease gnawing at Alex's gut, the memory of that spectral figure lingering like damp rot.

"What's your problem, Pavlovic? Double time!"

J.P.'s voice, though strained by the wind, carried a clear note of command, and Alex broke into a run, the deep sand pulling at his boots and soaked socks. The beach behind them was now completely swallowed by the churning tide, the waves licking violently at the edge of the low-slung dunes. He thought of the apparition again—the chilling voice, the burning eyes. "Beware the tides of January. They carry both good and evil." Was the woman the 'good'? Was the specter the 'evil'? Or was it more complicated?

The words echoed in his skull, sharp as shrapnel, stirring memories of frostbitten nights in Chechnya, where shadows whispered truths no sane man would heed. The logical part of his mind, which handled balance sheets and chemistry, argued that it was just an optical illusion caused by lightning and rain— a trick of his overstressed mind.

But the primal fear, the one he'd learned to trust in the Russian winter, told him he'd seen something ancient and dangerous. And J.P. had seen it too, his wide eyes betraying the same dread before he'd masked it with action. Whatever it was, it wasn't just in Alex's head.

That shared glance on the beach had confirmed it—a silent pact that something unnatural stalked this night. Reaching the bungalow, Alex kicked the door open. The fire, thankfully, was still roaring, the warm air a shock after the freezing rain.

J.P. was already in action, laying the woman gently on the ornate rug near the hearth. He stripped the wet nightgown from her, revealing a slender body marked with faint bruises. Her skin was deathly pale, her lips a blueish hue. Lucky immediately curled up next to her, a warm sentry, as if he sensed the woman's fragility.

"Grab some blankets," J.P. barked, his face grim. "And rum. She needs internal heat."

Alex nodded, his mind now fully operational as military discipline took over. The cat, sensing the shift in focus, darted from his arms to hide under the nearest chair. Alex retrieved a woolen blanket from his bedroom and poured two generous mugs of rum, one for the patient and one for himself.

The burn of the liquor grounded him, a tether to the tangible amid the night's madness. He watched J.P. carefully cover the young woman, then hold the mug to her lips, coaxing her to take a tentative sip. Her eyes fluttered, still unfocused, like a radio struggling to find a signal.

"Any identification?" Alex asked, handing J.P. a towel.

"Where would it have been in that little bit of nothing nightgown she was wearing?" J.P. said, shaking his wet hair.

"Where the hell did she come from?" Alex asked.

"Out of the storm like a ghost. No boat, no house nearby, just... her." He looked at Alex, the familiar movie-star charm absent, replaced by a troubled intensity. "But she ain't no ghost. Can't say the same about that spook we saw in the sky."

"Amen to that," Alex said.

J.P. glanced at the woman's bruises. "One thing I know for sure, this little lady was the person on the boat in the mirage we saw."

"But how...?" Alex asked, his voice low, as if speaking too loudly might summon the specter back.

"Don't know," J.P. said with a shake of his head.

As J.P. worked to wrap the woman in thick wool, her eyes, previously unfocused, snapped open. They were the color of storm-churned water—deep blue-gray and utterly wild. The firelight danced in them, turning her gaze into something feral, untamed.

"No! Don't let them..." she gasped, her voice a reedy whisper. She tried to fight the blanket, her arms flailing against J.P.'s chest. "The salt... the sugar... they hate the sugar!"

"What are you talking about?" J.P. asked, his tone steady but urgent. "What's your name?"

It was as if she didn't hear his question. She thrashed again, her gaze fixed on the firelight reflected in Alex's mug of rum. With surprising strength, she pointed a trembling finger past them, toward the storm-lashed window. The glass rattled in its

11

frame, as if the storm itself were trying to claw its way inside.

"He told me to choose!" she said, her voice rising to a frantic pitch. "The tides of January are hungry, and the reef is singing. You have to burn the reef before it takes them all!"

Alex and J.P. exchanged a glance over her head, the easy camaraderie of their chess game utterly gone. The woman's words mirrored the apparition's warning too closely, each syllable a hammer against Alex's carefully constructed rationality. His distillery, his rum, salt, and sugar were its lifeblood. Was this a coincidence, or something darker tying her delirium to his world?

"She's in shock," J.P. said, his voice clipped, professional.

Alex shook his head, his knuckles white around the mug.

"Not shock," he said. "The nonsense she's babbling is high-grade terror bordering on psychosis."

J.P. gave Alex a look, then gently held the woman down, his former deputy sheriff authority softening with compassion.

"It's okay. You're safe here. There's no reef. You're on dry land, in a house that's sheltered from the storm."

She ignored him, struggling, her eyes searching the room, fixating on the chipped China set on the shelf—a thriftstore relic from someone's mother, incongruous in this rugged outpost.

"The queen is a lie. The pawns... They all follow her into the water. Your silver planks are sinking!"

Her chest heaved, and she slumped back against the rug, eyes closed, arms flailing, a trickle of spittle coming from her mouth. Her mental condition left the two men standing over her with the unsettling realization that they hadn't just saved a drowning victim; they had invited a tempest of madness and mystery into Alex's controlled world.

The mention of "tides of January" and the apparent mental distress confirmed to Alex that she saw the same apparition he did. The words 'salt' and 'sugar' now rang in his head, a grotesque counterpoint to his obsession with making rum. The warning wasn't abstract; it was personal and concerned the island. The storm outside seemed to pulse in rhythm with her words, as if the Gulf itself were listening. J.P. reacted instantly to the woman's frantic outburst, speaking in the low tone he'd used a thousand times to talk down a suspect or calm a trauma victim.

"It's all right. Deep breaths."

"She needs a doctor," Alex said, his voice tight, his mind racing through logistics—tides, roads, and the flooded creek cutting them off from the populated part of the island.

"You planning to swim her across the creek on your back?" J.P. shot back, his tone dry but not unkind. "No one's going anyplace until the rain stops and the water in the creek recedes."

"She'll hurt herself before then," Alex said, watching her trembling form. "We must restrain her."

J.P. knew better than to physically restrain a person in her mental state, at least for any length of time.

"You ever tried to restrain a crazy person?" he asked, his eyes narrowing.

Alex didn't answer, his silence heavy with memories of comrades lost to their own mental demons in war's crucible.

J.P. continued trying to calm the woman, his soothing words having no effect. She was thrashing and flailing her arms, her eyes wide with a terror that transcended the storm. He reached inside the breast pocket of his sodden jacket and pulled out a sealed plastic pouch.

"What is that?" Alex asked, his tone sharp, suspicious.

"Old habits die hard. I still keep a couple of things close by," J.P. said, pulling out a small vial and a syringe.

"A sedative?" Alex asked.

J.P. nodded. "Police work isn't always about bullets. Sometimes it's about chemistry."

With practiced efficiency, he administered a mild sedative into her arm, the action precise and professional. Her struggles subsided almost immediately, her body relaxing into a deep sleep, her chest rising and falling in shallow breaths.

Together, they moved her. Alex threw open the door to his spare bedroom, the air inside cool and musty, untouched by the fire's warmth. They laid her gently on the bed and covered her with the woolen blanket, tucking the edges around her slender form as the rain drummed an incessant rhythm on the roof.

J.P. extinguished the bedside lamp, leaving her to the darkness and the sedative's grip. Once the young woman was asleep, J.P. and Alex realized they were both dripping wet, their clothes heavy with seawater and rain.

"There are robes in the sanuzel," Alex said, catching himself with a wry grin. "The bathroom. Like you said, old habits die hard."

They gathered back in the den, their hair damp but their bodies dry, covered in plush terrycloth bathrobes. The fire crackled, and the overturned chessboard sat as a scattered reminder of the night's disruption. The air was thick with smoke, damp wool, and an unsettling silence.

Alex stood staring into the flames, swirling the mug of rum he hadn't yet drunk. He ran a hand over his smoothly shaven face. The mew of the little white cat captured his attention.

"There's my little lady," he said, lifting her gently off the floor.

Her fur was still damp, her body light as a shadow. Taking her to his tiny kitchen, he poured her a bowl of milk and placed the sardines from a can he opened beside it. The cat wasn't just hungry; she was starving and didn't have to be coaxed. Her delicate bites were desperate, her eyes darting as if expecting the food to vanish.

"She belongs to somebody," J.P. said, leaning against the counter, his arms crossed.

Alex shot him a skeptical look. "How do you know?"

"Oyster Island is rife with wildlife. If little mama had grown up in the wild, she wouldn't be so skinny. She's someone's cat."

"How did she get on the island?" Alex asked, his mind turning to the woman in the next room, another stray washed up by the storm.

"No idea, but if I were you, I'd give her another can of those sardines."

When the cat finished eating, she licked her paws with satisfaction. Alex made a bed for her in front of the fire. Lucky snuggled closer to her, and they were both soon asleep, a small island of calm amid the chaos. The wind outside the bungalow had abated, though the rain continued to pound the roof, a relentless tattoo that mirrored Alex's racing thoughts.

"Sounds like an all-nighter," J.P. said, his voice heavy with fatigue.

"Another game?" Alex asked, nodding to the chessboard, though his heart wasn't in it.

J.P. shook his head, pouring himself more rum. "Neither of us can focus now."

He settled into his chair, the easy slouch replaced by a taut posture. His eyes were dark, serious.

"She's in extreme psychosis," Alex said, not a question but a clinical observation.

"That wasn't just adrenaline and hypothermia, Alex. She's been traumatized for a long time. The stress... It can break down the mind faster than any physical torture." He took a slow sip of rum. "She almost drowned, but the real enemy now is in her head."

Alex nodded slowly, his eyes reflecting the fire. "I have seen this—weeks on the front line, cold, no sleep. Soldiers start to see things. They are fine shooters, disciplined, but they whisper about spirits, about shadows. I saw a good soldier try to shoot a tree because he said it was the devil. This is that kind of broken. Crazy, psychotic shit caused by endless danger."

His voice was low, the memories surfacing like bodies in a flooded trench.

"One thing I know," J.P. said, setting his rum down with a decisive click. "She must have seen the same dark dude that we did. Maybe it was him, or the storm, whatever put that deep terror in her eyes." He leaned forward, his voice dropping to a whisper. "And if she truly saw the same thing we saw, Alex, then what the hell was it trying to tell us?"

Alex turned from the fire, his gaze intense. "The girl, the cat, the specter, the sinking boat… It's all connected to the water, to this island."

His fingers tightened around the glass, the vodka catching the firelight like a warning.

"Why the hell do you say that?" J.P. asked.

"Salt and sugar. She said it, just like the apparition. My rum, my distillery—it's all tied to this place. What if the danger isn't just her? What if it's here, in the ground we're standing on?"

Alex laughed when J.P. said, "You never struck me as the superstitious type."

"I'm Russian," he said. "It comes with the territory."

J.P. sighed, running a hand over his face, his stubble rasping against his palm.

"Nothing we can do tonight but dry out and wait. That sedative will keep her down until morning. Trying to get a coherent story from her now would break her further. Tomorrow," he said, a hard certainty entering his voice, "we'll run a tracer on her. Find out who she is and what she was doing out here alone."

Alex looked toward the spare bedroom, the darkness a heavy cloak. The woman's words—the reef is singing, burn the reef—twisted in his mind, coiling around his memories of the apparition's burning eyes.

"And if she's right about the danger?" he asked, his voice barely above a whisper. J.P. met his gaze, the glint in his eye cold and sharp. "Then whatever put the fear of God into her will have to go through a former St. Bernard Parish deputy sheriff and a former Russian officer to get her."

He raised his glass, a grim toast to the unknown.

"To surviving the night, comrade."

Alex clinked his glass against J.P.'s, but the gesture felt hollow. Outside, the storm roared on, and the island seemed to hold its breath, waiting for the tides of January to reveal their secrets.

CHAPTER 3

The morning broke over Oyster Island like a painter's afterthought, the sky a brazen blue, scrubbed clean by the storm's retreat. Sunlight spilled through the bungalow's salt-streaked windows, gilding the worn oak of the kitchen table where Alex and J.P. sat, cradling mugs of coffee laced with Dominican rum. The air was thick with the bitter tang of roasted beans and the sweet burn of liquor, a makeshift ritual to steady their nerves after the night's madness.

Outside, the Gulf's waves lapped at the shore with a rhythm that felt almost harmonious, a stark contrast to the feral roar of the previous night. Yet the calm was uneasy, as if the island itself were holding its breath, waiting for the other shoe to drop. The dunes, reshaped by the storm, glittered with flecks of shell and seaweed, last night's battlefield now posing as a postcard, its deceptive serenity hiding the churn of secrets beneath.

Alex's fingers traced the rim of his mug, his eyes fixed on the horizon where the sea met the sky. The serenity felt like a lie, a thin veneer over the apparition's warning and the young woman's frantic ravings. The overturned chessboard still lay in the den, a silent testament to the night's upheaval, its scattered pieces catching glints of sunlight like tiny omens. The fire had died to embers, leaving a faint smokiness that clung to the air, mingling with the briny scent of the tide. Every creak of the bungalow's timbers felt like a whisper, urging vigilance.

J.P., slouched in his chair, seemed less troubled, his slender frame relaxed, but his gaze sharp, scanning the room as if expecting a specter to materialize from the shadows. His deputy's badge, still tucked in his pocket, weighed heavier today, the metal warm against his thigh, a reminder of duty in a place that felt increasingly untethered from reason.

The door to the spare bedroom creaked open, a deliberate groan that sent a shiver down Alex's spine. The woman emerged, wrapped in the woolen blanket, her long blond hair a tangled mess that framed her pale face. Her eyes, still that storm-churned blue-gray, were wide but less wild, as if the sedative had dulled the edge of her terror. She moved slowly, her bare feet silent on the hardwood, the blanket trailing like a cloak, its frayed edges brushing the floorboards. Her presence seemed to shift the room's gravity, drawing the air tighter, as if the bungalow itself were bracing for what she might say or do.

A soft mew broke the silence, and the cat darted from her makeshift bed by the hearth, a blur of white leaping into the woman's arms. The blanket slipped to the floor, pooling around her ankles as she held the cat close to her chest, her slender frame trembling. For a moment, the two men stared, caught off guard by the young woman's toned body, which, due to the past night's chaos, neither of them had noticed.

Her skin was sun-kissed, marked by the faint lines of a bikini, a testament to days spent under the Gulf's relentless sun. The bruises on her arms stood out like storm clouds against her fairness, hinting at a struggle that went beyond the waves. She seemed unruffled by her nudity, more interested in the purring cat in her arms.

"Squeaky, you're alive," she said, her voice cracking with raw emotion. "I was afraid a shark had eaten you."

Tears streaked her face, and she buried her nose in the cat's fur, oblivious to her own exposure. Alex rose swiftly, his chair scraping the floor, and retrieved a terrycloth robe from the bathroom. He draped it over her shoulders with a gentleness that belied his soldier's build, his hands steady but his eyes searching her face for answers. The robe smelled faintly of cedar and salt, a grounding scent that seemed to anchor her as she pulled it closed. She didn't seem to notice; her sobs muffled against Squeaky's purring form, the cat's warmth anchoring her to the moment.

J.P. leaned forward, his mug forgotten, his deputy's instincts kicking in at the bruises on her arms, her fragility a stark contrast to the ferocity of her words the night before. The room felt larger now, charged with the weight of her presence, as if she carried the storm's residue within her. The sunlight streaming through the windows seemed to bend around her, casting her shadow long and jagged across the floor, a silhouette that hinted at something larger, something unresolved.

Outside, a gull's cry pierced the morning, sharp and accusing, and Alex's grip tightened on the robe, his mind flashing to the apparition's burning eyes and the cryptic words tides of January. The phrase echoed in his skull, a warning he couldn't shake, like a bell tolling in the distance.

He exchanged a glance with J.P., who gave a subtle nod, both men silently agreeing that the calm of the morning was a fragile illusion.

"Miss," J.P. said, his voice low and measured, the same tone he'd used on countless rattled witnesses in his years as a deputy. "You and your cat are safe here. Can you tell us your name?"

She lifted her head, her eyes darting between them, clutching Squeaky tighter. "I... I'm Trixie Kettler," she said, her voice a hesitant thread, as if she were testing the words to see if they still belonged to her. "Where am I?"

"Oyster Island," Alex said, his Russian accent clipped but soft, a remnant of a life he rarely spoke of. "You washed up on the beach last night. We heard your screams and dragged you out of the water.

Trixie's gaze flickered to the window, fear flaring briefly in her eyes, like a spark catching dry tinder.

"I was anchored in a sheltered cove. When I awoke, I was out in the Gulf, the storm lashing my boat and the sails furled. The waves flipped the boat and sent me overboard. I was almost to shore when I got caught in a damn riptide."

Her voice trembled, but there was steel beneath it.

She gave J.P. a confused look when he said, "We know."

"How do you know?" she asked, her eyes narrowing, a flicker of suspicion crossing her face, as if she wondered if it was they who had cut her anchor line.

Sensing her thoughts, Alex raised a hand, his voice calm but firm. "We have no idea why your boat drifted into the storm. Sit with us. You look as if you need a cup of coffee, and I'll cook you an omelet."

Trixie smiled, the first crack in her guarded expression, and she joined them at the table, Squeaky still nestled in her arms. Alex poured a mug of coffee—the steam curling upward like a ghost—and slid it across the table. She took a sip, her eyes closing briefly as the warmth hit her tongue.

"This is good," she said, her voice steadier now. "Strong and black. Just the way I like it, though I'd like it even better with a little rum in it."

"Dominican rum," Alex said, topping up her mug with a generous pour. "Best in the world."

"Until you get the old Baptiste distillery back up and running," she said, her tone teasing but her eyes sharp, as if testing him.

Alex froze, his hand hovering over the bottle. "How do you know about the Baptiste Plantation?"

His voice was quiet, but there was an edge to it, a sudden wariness that made the room feel smaller. Trixie met his gaze, unfazed.

"I'm a doctoral candidate at L.S.U. Research is my passion."

"Oh yeah?" J.P. said, leaning back in his chair, his curiosity piqued. "What's your major?"

"Oceanography and Coastal Sciences," Trixie said, her voice gaining confidence as she spoke. "I study the Gulf, its ecosystems, and the way human interference shapes the coastline. Louisiana's shoreline is measured in thousands, not hundreds of miles."

"Impossible," Alex said, his skepticism betraying his unfamiliarity with the region.

Trixie grinned, a spark of her former fire returning. "You

wouldn't be very good at Jeopardy. Louisiana's shoreline along the Gulf of Mexico is exceptionally long because of the many marshes, swamps, and bayous that form a highly indented and complex coast. It's a labyrinth of water and land, constantly shifting."

"I stand corrected," Alex said, a wry smile tugging at his lips. "I'll cook your omelet and shut up for a while."

As Alex stepped away to the kitchen, Trixie leaned toward J.P., her voice low.

"He's cute. Where's he from?"

"Russia," J.P. said, his tone neutral but his eyes glinting with amusement.

"Sounds like a story there," she said, her curiosity evident. "You'll have to tell me sometime."

"Alex's story is almost unbelievable. Let him tell it," J.P. said, his voice carrying a note of respect for his friend.

Alex returned with a steaming plate, presenting it with a flourish that seemed almost theatrical. The omelet was golden, flecked with herbs, accompanied by slightly sweet pancakes. Trixie attacked the food with a hunger that matched Squeaky's the previous night, the cat now curled contentedly in her lap.

"This is wonderful," she said between bites, her words muffled by a mouthful of omelet. "The omelet is tasty, and these little pancake-like things are to die for. What are they?"

"Syrniki," Alex said. "Slightly sweet pancakes made from tvorog, flour, and eggs."

"Tvorog?" she asked, her brow furrowing.

"A type of Russian cottage cheese," Alex said, a hint of pride in his voice.

Trixie's eyes widened when J.P. added, "Alex made it himself."

"You make your own cottage cheese?" she said.

"Yes," Alex said, warming to the subject. "You start by curdling milk with an acid, such as vinegar or lemon juice, then straining the curds. It takes about an hour—"

"Stop," J.P. said, holding up a hand, his tone playful but firm. "How you make Russian cottage cheese isn't on my need-to-know list."

Trixie laughed, a bright sound that cut through the room's lingering tension. "The mayhaw jelly you served with the Syrniki is tasty. Did you make that yourself, too?"

Alex nodded. "Gathered the berries down by the swamp. Would you like a jar of my homemade mayhaw jelly?"

"You kidding? I grew up on mayhaw jelly," Trixie said, her voice softening with nostalgia. "My grandmother used to make it every spring, the kitchen smelling like sugar and tart fruit."

"Sounds like a Cajun thing," J.P. said, his grin teasing, "though you aren't a Cajun with a last name like Kettler."

Trixie's eyes flashed with mock indignation. "Hell, J.P.! I take offense to that statement. I'm a third-generation German living in Louisiana. There are probably as many Germans in this state as there are Cajuns."

"You're right about that," J.P. said, chuckling. "My aunt Hilda would spank my skinny ass if she ever heard me disparaging my German relatives."

"And I'd be right there to help her," Trixie said with a grin, her spirit visibly returning."

Are you still hungry?" Alex asked, watching her closely, as if gauging her strength.

"Your omelet and Syrniki with mayhaw jelly were so tasty, I could eat more, though my appetite is satisfied. I'll take more coffee and rum, though."

"There's plenty of both," Alex said, topping up her mug and starting a fresh pot. The scent of coffee filled the room, grounding them in the moment, but the weight of the night's events lingered like a storm cloud on the horizon.

J.P. leaned forward, his deputy's instincts taking over. "What were you doing anchored off Oyster Island in a small sailboat, if you don't mind me asking?"

"Working on my dissertation," Trixie said, her tone matter-of-fact. "There's a man-made reef about a mile out in the Gulf where they dump old cars, appliances, and such. An entire biological ecosystem has developed around it. I'm studying the effects man-made reefs have on the coastline—how they protect it, how they change it."

"Sounds like important work," J.P. said, nodding. "Is that what you were babbling about last night?"

Trixie's expression clouded, her fingers tightening around her mug. "There's not much about last night I remember. What did I say?"

J.P. hesitated, glancing at Alex, who met his gaze with a grim nod. "I don't remember, exactly," J.P. said, hedging.

Alex didn't. He leaned forward, his voice low, each word deliberate. "I do. You said, 'The tides of January are hungry, and the reef is singing. You have to burn the reef before it takes them all!' What did you mean?"

Trixie shook her head, her eyes wide with confusion. "No earthly idea. It sounds like something I'd say if I was delirious, which I probably was." She paused, her gaze drifting to the window, where the Gulf sparkled under the morning sun. "Whatever it was, it felt... real. Like something was pulling me toward it, out there in the water."

The room fell silent, the weight of her words settling over them like a fog. Outside, the waves continued their rhythmic dance, but now they seemed to carry a faint undertone, a low hum that wasn't quite natural. Alex's hand tightened around his mug, the apparition's warning echoing in his mind. Tides of January. The phrase felt like a key, but to what lock?

"I need to find my boat," Trixie said, breaking the silence. "If it hasn't sunk. Will you help me?"

"After you see a doctor," J.P. said firmly, his deputy's tone returning.

"For what?" Trixie said, her voice sharp with defiance.

"To make sure you're okay," J.P. said. "You have bruises all over."

Trixie laughed, a brittle sound that held more bravado than humor. "You've both seen me naked, so I know you realize I'm fit. I ran the Louisiana Marathon last weekend in under four hours. If I needed to see a doctor, believe me, I'd know it."

"If you're sure," J.P. said.

She stood, setting Squeaky gently on the floor, and tightened the robe around her. "What I need is to get back out there, find my boat, and figure out what the hell happened last night."

Alex and J.P. exchanged another glance. "All right," Alex said, standing, his voice resolute. "We'll help you find your boat."

Trixie nodded, her eyes meeting his with a mix of gratitude and determination. "Deal. But don't expect me to stay on shore while you two play hero."

J.P. chuckled. "Wouldn't dream of it."

As they packed up, the Gulf outside seemed to watch, its surface calm but its depths hiding something old and hungry. The January tides were coming, their shadow already cast, and the reef, somewhere out there, was singing.

CHAPTER 4

Alex cracked open the door of his weathered bungalow, his eyes scanning the sky above Oyster Island. The storm that had battered the coast all night had finally relented, leaving a bruised horizon streaked with violet and gold. The air smelled of salt and damp earth, and the distant cry of a gull pierced the quiet.

"The storm has passed," he said, his voice low but firm. "Let's head out before old Mother Nature changes her mind."

J.P. and Alex drained the last of their coffee, the bitter dregs grounding them for the task ahead. They were halfway to the door when Trixie's voice, sharp and laced with exasperation, froze them in place.

"I can't go dressed in a bathrobe," she said, gesturing to the oversized terrycloth garment cinched around her waist. "Do you have anything I can wear?"

Alex and J.P. exchanged a glance, a flicker of amusement passing between them. "All I have is what I'm wearing," J.P. said, spreading his hands to indicate his faded jeans and flannel shirt, still damp from the morning's humidity.

"I've got clothes," Alex offered, scratching the back of his neck. "Though nothing your size."

Trixie arched an eyebrow. She and Alex were roughly the same height, but the resemblance ended there. Trixie was svelte, her frame honed by years of long-distance running, with a wiry strength that belied her delicate appearance. Alex, on the other hand, was built like a professional wrestler—broad shoulders, muscular arms, and a barrel chest that strained the seams of his shirt.

The mental image of Trixie in his clothes was almost too much for J.P., who bit the inside of his cheek to keep from grinning. Alex disappeared into his bedroom and returned with a folded stack of clothes: a gray sweatshirt with frayed cuffs and a pair of cargo pants that looked like they'd seen better days. Trixie took them with a skeptical look and vanished into the bathroom.

When she emerged, the sweatshirt hung off her like a sail, the sleeves swallowing her hands, and the pants were cinched tight with a belt looped twice around her waist. She looked like a kid playing dress-up in her father's closet.

J.P. coughed into his fist, and Alex's lips twitched. Trixie's eyes narrowed as she caught their expressions, her fist rising in mock threat.

"First one of you yahoos who laughs is getting slugged," she said, her voice carrying the edge of someone who meant it.

"Never once thought of it," J.P. said, raising his hands in surrender.

"Or I," Alex added, his face a mask of innocence.

"Yeah, yeah," Trixie said, brushing past them to the door, her borrowed outfit rustling with every step.

"Let's move."

Oyster Island had no paved roads, just sandy trails and muddy ruts carved by years of use. Everyone got around on ATVs, and J.P.'s was a beast of a machine—a fully enclosed, custom job painted in the vibrant purple, green, and gold of the Oyster Bay canine training facility. The colors, a nod to Mardi Gras, stood for justice, faith, and power, though J.P. liked to joke they also meant "party, party, and more party."

The ATV could carry five passengers comfortably—six in a pinch—and had enough cargo space for supplies or equipment. It was the pride of the island, and Trixie's mood visibly lightened when she saw it parked outside.

"Nice ride," she said, running a hand along the sleek siding.

"Get you most anywhere on the island," J.P. said with a grin, climbing into the driver's seat. "Hop in."

Alex and Lucky took the backseat, their bulk filling the space, while Trixie sprawled in the passenger seat, her legs stretched out as if she owned the place. J.P. gunned the engine, and the ATV roared to life, bouncing over the uneven terrain. The low-water creek crossing was still slick from the storm, and brackish water sprayed the sides of the vehicle as J.P. powered through, kicking up mud and shells with the tires.

Trixie braced herself against the dashboard, her eyes scanning the landscape as they trundled along the beachfront path. The island unfolded around them in a blur of wild beauty— windswept dunes, patches of sea oats swaying in the breeze, and the endless expanse of the Gulf shimmering under the morning sun. J.P.'s knuckles whitened as he navigated shallow ruts carved by the storm, his focus split between the path and the occasional glance at Trixie. She pointed out an egret standing on one leg in a swampy slough beside the trail, its white feathers stark against the murky water.

"Where are we going?" she asked, her voice cutting through the hum of the engine.

"My place," J.P. said.

Trixie's lips twitched. "You and Alex don't live together?"

J.P. let out a bark of laughter. "No ma'am. Lucky and I live in an Airstream trailer parked beside the old lighthouse."

"Why are we going there?" she asked, her curiosity relentless.

"To get you some clothes that fit," J.P. said. "I have a trunk full of women's stuff that's collected over the years."

Alex snorted from the backseat. Trixie shot J.P. a sidelong glance, her tone teasing. "I'll bet you do."

J.P. just grinned, unfazed, as the ATV crested a low rise, revealing the old lighthouse on its promontory. The structure was a relic of the Prohibition era, its weathered brick tower standing sentinel over the Gulf to the south and the glittering Majestic Hotel and Casino to the north.

The hotel was a recent acquisition by Eddie Toledo, a former Federal D.A. who'd tangled with Frankie Castellano, the Don of the South, to secure it. Their deal had been messy—full of threats and double-crosses—but they'd patched things up, at least for now. The lighthouse, though, was the island's true heart, its beacon still functional thanks to Jack Wiesinski, the keeper who lived in the stone cottage nearby.

Jack was also a partner in the canine training facility, a modern complex near the lighthouse with a kennel, training pens, exercise yards, and a full-time vet. J.P. pulled the ATV to a stop beside his Airstream, a gleaming stainless steel trailer that looked like a silver bullet against the rugged landscape. It was outfitted with every comfort—solar panels, a compact kitchen, even a tiny porch strung with fairy lights.

"Love it," Trixie said, her eyes sweeping over the trailer's retro charm as she stepped out of the ATV.

"My bedroom's through that door," J.P. said, pointing. "Trunk's in there. Take your time and find something that suits you. Alex and I will wait out here."

Inside, J.P.'s den was a cozy haven—two worn recliners, a coffee table cluttered with fishing magazines, and a faded rug where Lucky promptly flopped down. J.P. and Alex settled into the chairs, the morning's events catching up with them. The hum of the island—distant waves, the occasional squawk of a seabird—lulled them into a half-doze, with Lucky's soft snores adding to the rhythm.

The bedroom door swung open, and Trixie strutted out in a polka dot bikini so tiny it barely qualified as clothing. "Ta da!" she said, striking a pose with her arms spread wide. The bikini left little to the imagination, and a scrollwork tattoo peeked out from the small of her back, curling like a secret signature.

J.P.'s jaw dropped. "Damn, girl! You're rocking it."

Trixie spun, giving them a view of the tattoo and the bikini's precarious fit. J.P. let out a low whistle, and Alex's eyes widened, though he tried to play it cool. "You think it shows too much skin?" she asked, her tone daring them to say yes.

"No way," they said in unison, their voices a mix of awe and amusement.

Trixie smirked and disappeared back into the bedroom. J.P. leaned over and nudged Alex.

"Damn, that girl has a body."

"And she knows it," Alex replied, shaking his head.

When Trixie returned, she'd traded the bikini for a pair of jeans that hugged her curves like they'd been tailored for her, a mauve designer tee, stylish sandals, and a buttery leather jacket that screamed money. She carried a grocery sack stuffed with the bikini and other finds, her expression one of gleeful triumph.

"Damn, J.P., some of your former girlfriends' castoffs are worth more than my entire wardrobe," she said, slinging the sack over her shoulder. "I have a question, though. If these are clothes your lady friends left behind, what were they wearing when they left?"

Alex burst out laughing, but J.P. just grinned, sidestepping the question. "You look great. Now, let's go see Jack."

"Who's Jack?" Trixie asked, falling into step beside them as they headed for the nearby cottage.

"Jack Wiesinski, the lighthouse keeper," J.P. said. "Lives in the stone house next door. He's a retired Merchant Marine and takes care of the island's trawler. We need him to take us out into the Gulf to look for your boat."

"The island has a trawler?" Trixie's eyes lit up.

"Came with the Majestic when Eddie acquired it," J.P. said. "Used to be a rumrunner back in the day."

"Eddie?" Trixie's brow furrowed.

"Former U.S. District Attorney in New Orleans," J.P. said. "Got canned for dating a mafia boss's daughter. Frankie Castellano —aka the Don of the South—owned the hotel and traded it to Eddie, hoping he'd patch things up with Josie."

"Frankie?" Trixie said, trying to keep up.

"Big-time mob boss," J.P. said. "Runs things down south, or at least he did until Eddie outmaneuvered him."

Trixie nodded, processing the tangled web of island politics. "Tell me about the trawler."

"Built in 1928, nearly a hundred years old," J.P. said. "Jack and Chief keep it in top shape. It's a beauty, still seaworthy enough to make a run to the Bahamas if we felt like it."

"Chief?" Trixie tilted her head.

"Gordon La Tortue," J.P. said. "Full-blood Atakapan Indian and the rightful owner of Oyster Island. He and Jack are partners in the dog training business.

Trixie's eyes widened. "You know the Atakapans were cannibals, right?"

J.P. chuckled. "Chief's no cannibal. He's a good guy. You'll see when you meet him."

"Do he and Jack live together?" Trixie asked.

"Nah," Alex cut in. "Chief lives in a teepee on La Tortue Mountain. Likes his space."

"A mountain in south Louisiana?" Trixie said.

"More like a hill," Alex said.

Trixie laughed, shaking her head. "Is there anyone on this island who isn't quirky?"

J.P. and Alex exchanged a look.

"Us," they said in unison, grinning.

"Relax," Alex added. "Jack and Chief are solid. You'll like them."

Jack's cottage was a reflection of the man himself—small, sturdy, and brimming with character. The interior was a love letter to the sea: framed nautical charts and maps lined the walls, their edges curling with age; a brass sextant gleamed on the mantle of a stone fireplace; and a bookshelf sagged under the weight of naval histories and maritime manuals. The air was thick with the savory aroma of gumbo simmering on the stove, a rich blend of shrimp, sausage, and spices that made Trixie's stomach rumble.

Jack, Chief, and a striking woman sat at a small table in the galley, a deck of cards scattered between them. Jack was wiry and compact, his weathered face suggesting he was in his sixties, though his sharp eyes and quick movements hinted at a younger spirit.

Chief, by contrast, was a giant—at least six-foot-six, with no trace of fat on his frame. His silver hair, held back by a turquoise headband, cascaded over his broad shoulders, and his presence filled the room like a quiet storm.

The woman, introduced as Renata Yatsenko, was a vision—tall, with ink-black hair, high cheekbones, and eyes that seemed to see straight through you. Trixie caught Alex's frown when he saw her, a flicker of tension that didn't go unnoticed.

"I'm cooking gumbo and wondered when you two troublemakers would show up," Jack said, his voice gravelly but warm. "Who's the attractive lady with you?"

"Trixie Kettler," J.P. said, making introductions. "Meet Jack, Chief, and Renata Yatsenko. Renata's the vet who keeps our dogs in fighting shape."

Renata stood, her height imposing at nearly six feet. She gave Trixie a polite nod, but her gaze lingered on Alex, cool and unreadable.

"Nice to meet you," she said, her voice carrying a faint Ukrainian accent. "Excuse me, I have work to do."

She slipped out, leaving a chill in her wake.

Jack broke the silence. "Anybody hungry?"

"I didn't think I was," Trixie said, "but that gumbo's calling my name."

Jack chuckled, tossing his cards on the table and heading for the stove. "Don't need to ask these rascals. They're always hungry for my rum and gumbo. Especially Chief—he's got a hollow leg."

Lucky, J.P.'s dog, had made himself at home, joining three other dogs sprawled in front of the fireplace. Their eyes tracked the newcomers, tails thumping lazily. Trixie knelt to pet them, her fingers sinking into their fur.

"Love your dogs," she said. "What are their names?"

"The bulldog's Oscar, my boy," Jack said. "Coco's the chihuahua, and Ol' Joe's the German shepherd. They're Chief's crew."

"Where's your dog, Alex?" Trixie asked.

"I have no pet," he said.

"Well, you do now," she said. "Squeaky."

"She's your cat, not mine," he said.

"I found her on the side of the road and intended to take her to an animal shelter, but she's so tiny and helpless that I didn't have the heart. I tried to make her my boat cat, but she hates the water. She likes you. Will you take her? Please?"

"Me?" Alex said.

When Alex turned to J.P., he said, "Don't look at me. White cats are lucky, and right now, with the trouble you're having with your new distillery and all, you need all the good luck you can get. Take the cat."

"Cats aren't lucky," Alex said.

"White cats are," Trixie said. "They're symbols of good luck, purity, and positive spiritual energy, representing prosperity, healing, inspiration, and divine protection. Squeaky will bring you good fortune, happiness, and spiritual guidance. Please?"

"Cats are good company," Jack said. "Just ask Chief."

"My teepee would be lonely without my calico, Buttercup," Chief said.

Alex didn't say no. Trixie glanced at him as he brooded in the corner.

"What's the deal with Renata? She has an accent I can't place, and she seemed... distant."

Jack's eyes flicked to Alex, but he didn't answer. J.P. stepped in. "Renata's Ukrainian. Came to the States with Alex."

Trixie caught the edge in Alex's posture, the way his jaw tightened. "Oh?" she said, pressing gently.

"Alex was a captain," J.P. said.

"Not by choice. I was conscripted into the Russian army and made an officer because of my degree. That's all you need to know."

The room grew heavy, the weight of unspoken history settling over them. Trixie sensed a story too raw to touch, so she let it go.

"Fair enough," she said softly.

"Let's eat," Jack said, breaking the tension. He ladled steaming gumbo into bowls, the rich broth studded with shrimp and andouille. The first bite was a revelation—spicy, soul-warming, with a hint of rum that lingered on the tongue. Trixie's smile lit up the room.

"I'll gain twenty pounds if I stay here much longer," she said, spooning up another bite.

"What brings you to the island, baby?" Jack asked, leaning back in his chair.

"My sailboat capsized in the storm last night," Trixie said. "Washed up on the beach, and these two"—she nodded at J.P. and Alex. "They pulled me out of a riptide that had me down for the count. J.P. said you might take us out in the trawler to look for my boat."

"You bet," Jack said, his eyes twinkling. "Chief and I have been itching to take the old lady for a spin."

"Old lady?" Trixie asked.

"The Argo," Jack said. "Built in '28 for running illegal booze. She's a smuggler's dream—old, but could still get us to the islands in the Caribbean."

Trixie grinned, her excitement infectious. "I'm ready. Let's go."

Jack winked, his weathered face creasing with mischief. "My kind of girl."

As they finished eating, the conversation shifted to logistics—tides, currents, the most likely spots to find Trixie's boat. Outside, the Gulf called out, its surface calm but misleading, hiding the storm's secrets. Trixie felt a surge of anticipation, balanced by the weight of the island's quirks and the shadows in Alex's eyes. Whatever lay ahead, Oyster Island was no ordinary place, and she was ready to dive in.

CHAPTER 5

The bar near the lobby of the old Majestic Hotel and Casino smelled of lemon oil and bourbon, the kind of scent that clung to the dark wood like a secret. A single brass lamp over the backbar threw a cone of light onto the bottles, leaving the rest of the room in velvet shadow. Paula Boutet sat on the stool closest to the service well, elbows on the rail, staring into the cloudy swirl of her martini as if it might speak. Odette Mouton wiped a highball glass with a bar towel, watching her friend.

"You look like somebody just told you the Saints traded Brees again."

Paula let out a short laugh. "Worse." She lifted the pick and let an olive fall back into the martini. "Father Guidry says I have to choose."

"Choose what, chère? Between gin and vodka?" Odette set the glass down, leaned in. "Talk to me."

Paula's voice came low, almost swallowed by the hum of the old refrigerator behind the bar.

"Between the craft and the gift. He says a traiteur works only by the hand of God. The other thing—" She flicked her fingers, the way you shoo a mosquito. "—that's the devil's shortcut."

Odette's blond brows lifted. "He told you that? Straight out?"

"After I laid hands on Mrs. Johnson's knee last week. Said he'd pray for my soul, but I couldn't keep 'mixing waters.' His words." Paula's mouth twisted. "Mama never drew a line. Gran'maman neither. They'd pull a fever with one hand and hex a lying husband with the other. Worked fine."

Odette poured herself a finger of rum, no ice. "Church always wants the world in neat boxes. You ever think maybe God's bigger than their filing system?"

Paula rolled the stem of the glass between her palms. "I think about the night Jimmie had the croup so bad his lips turned blue. I did both—prayer and the old words over a bowl of salt. He breathed easy by morning. Tell me which part saved him. Don't make much difference. Father Guidry says there's a thin line between faith healing and witchcraft."

Odette exhaled through her teeth. "You got a problem and I ain't the one to solve it for you." She capped the rum, Alex's rum, eyes narrowing in thought. "But Tante Félonise might. She's older than the levee and still pulls threads for half the parish. Lives out past the old sugar mill in that shotgun with the blue bottle tree."

Paula snorted. "The hoodoo lady? Father Guidry would have a stroke."

"Father Guidry ain't the one losing sleep." Odette reached across and tapped Paula's wrist. "Look, I'm not saying she'll hand you a tidy answer wrapped in a pretty yellow bow. But she's seen more than both of us and the priest put together. We'll bring her some of those pralines from the bakery —the ones with burnt sugar. She likes those."

"You know her?" Paula asked.

Odette said, "She helped me resolve some things."

Paula cast her a skeptical look and asked, "What things?"

"My love of nudity; getting high off of flashing my tits," Odette said.

"Honey, you flashed a lot more than just your tits when you worked as a nude dancer on Bourbon Street," Paula said. "What the hell does a voodoo woman know about exhibitionism, anyway?"

Odette let out a low laugh, the kind that started in her belly and rattled up like loose change in a tin cup.

"More than you'd think, cher. Tante Félonise don't waste words on shame—she talks in roots and rivers. Sat me down in her gallery one night, moon fat and low, cicadas screaming like they knew my secrets. Handed me a cup of something thick as motor oil, smelled like sassafras and regret.

"She said, 'Girl, you ain't sick. You just born with a hunger that don't fit in Sunday clothes.' Then she pulled out this little gris-gris bag, red flannel, tied with a snake vertebra. Told me my exhibitionism wasn't no devil whispering, wasn't no sin to confess. It was an ancestral echo. Said way back, before the boats and the chains, my people danced naked under the baobab, painted in clay, calling down storms with their bodies. That joy got buried under cotton rows and catechism, but it don't die—it just ferments.

"'You flashing ain't about the men watching,' she told me, eyes like river stones. 'It's about remembering you alive. Every time you bare yourself, you spill a little of that old power back into the dirt. But power gotta have direction, or it'll eat you hollow.'

"She made me sew a strip of my old stage thong into that bag —yeah, the sparkly one I wore the night I got arrested—along with a lock of my hair and a drop of rum. Said, 'Wear this when the urge come, let it choose the moment, not the moment choose you.'

"Didn't cure me, Paula. Don't want to be cured. But now, when I feel that itch under my skin, I touch the bag first. Ask if it's mine to give, or just the ghost of some plantation mistress laughing at me playing wild. Most times?" She grinned, sharp as a switchblade. "It's mine. And when it ain't, I keep my damn clothes on."

"Hell, girl!" Paula said with a laugh. "Maybe I should ask her why, even though I'm as comfortable as you are being nude, I've never let my own husband Jimmie see me naked."

"You'd need a team of shrinks, not Tante Félonise, to tackle that one," Odette said.

Paula studied the olive pick as if it were a tarot card. "And if she says the same thing about being a traiteur as Father Guidry? Pick a side or burn?"

"Then you'll know the rule's the same everywhere, and you can stop tearing yourself in half." Odette's voice softened. "Or maybe she'll tell you the line's only chalk, and the rain already washed it away."

Paula took a slow sip, the vermouth sharp on her tongue. "I don't even know what I want her to say."

"That's why we go." Odette plucked the pick from Paula's fingers and set it aside. "Drink up. Bar's empty, Eddie's not here, the tide's low enough to cross the bridge before the skeeters wake up."

They both turned when a voice said, "Someone call my name?"

Paula looked toward the door, where late-morning light leaked around the edges of the blinds.

Eddie Toledo stood in the doorway, the light behind him carving sharp angles across his face. Forty-three looked good on him—dark hair just tousled enough, the kind of five-o'clock shadow that cost money to maintain, and a linen shirt open at the collar like he'd dressed for a yacht that never showed. He flashed the smile that had once charmed juries and could just as easily charm tips out of high-rollers.

"Morning, ladies," he said, letting the door swing shut. "Or is it afternoon already? Time's slippery when you're up at dawn chasing ghosts."

Odette straightened, the bar towel forgotten in her hand. "Eddie. What in the world are you doing out of bed before the cocktail hour?"

He crossed the room in three easy strides, slid onto the stool beside Paula, and tapped the bar twice.

"Coffee. Black. And a splash of that Dominican rocket fuel Alex keeps bragging about." He glanced at Paula's half-empty martini. "Rough morning, Boutet?"

Paula lifted a shoulder, the motion small and tired. "Father Guidry's got opinions."

Eddie's eyebrows rose. "The priest? What'd you do, heal somebody on a Sunday?"

Odette poured his coffee, added a finger of rum without asking. "She healed Mrs. Johnson's knee. He says she can't do that and the other thing. Pick a lane or go to hell."

Eddie took the mug, inhaled the steam as if it were evidence. "Sounds like Guidry. Man's got a rule for everything except common sense." He sipped, winced at the heat, then fixed Paula with a look that could've cross-examined a mob boss. "You want my take?"

Paula met his eyes, dark and steady. "I want a lot of things."

"Fair." He set the mug down. "But you're not getting absolution from me. I'm the guy who traded a law career for a haunted hotel. My moral compass spins like a roulette wheel."

Odette leaned on the bar, elbows wide. "We were about to go see Tante Félonise. She might know—"

Eddie cut her off with a soft laugh. "The bottle-tree lady? She'll tell you the same thing your gran'maman did: the gift doesn't come with a warranty. You break it, you buy it."

"That's what I'm afraid of," Paula said.

He turned to Paula fully now, voice dropping. "But that's not why I'm here."

Paula's fingers tightened around her glass. "Then why?"

"A woman washed up on the beach last night near Alex's bungalow. He and J.P. rescued her."

"Washed up? What do you mean?" Paula asked.

"Her sailboat got caught up in last night's squall and washed her overboard. She almost made it to shore but got caught in a rip current," Eddie said. "She's lucky Alex and J.P. heard her yelling."

"What was she doing out last night in a sailboat, anyway?" Odette asked.

"She's a grad student in oceanography at L.S.U., and her dissertation has something to do with a man-made reef off of Oyster Island. She's been staying on her boat in a sheltered cove. Last night, the boat got loose in the storm."

"And?" Paula asked.

"I heard you and Jimmie were on the island for the weekend

and thought you might be able to help," Eddie said. "I thought I might find you here talking to Odette. We might need your help."

"Help for what?"

"Trixie Kettler," he said the name as if it tasted strange. "The woman who washed up last night. Her boat's gone—anchor line cut clean, not frayed. Jack, Chief, J.P., and Alex are taking the Argo out at high tide to hunt for it."

Odette's eyes widened. "Cut? You're saying someone meant for her to drift?"

"Or meant for her to disappear." Eddie drained his coffee and set the mug down with a click. "Either way, the reef she was studying? It's not on any chart I've got. And after what she babbled about burning it…"

He trailed off and glanced at Paula.

"Why do you need me?" she asked.

"Because of what we might find out there when we go looking for the boat."

"Like what?" Paula asked.

"Maybe something supernatural," Eddie said.

Paula's throat worked, and she said, "Maybe you'd better explain."

"J.P. and Alex saw something last night; something inexplicable," Eddie said.

Odette's elbows were still on the bar. "Damn it, Eddie!" she said. "Quit stalling. Tell us what they saw, for God's sake."

"They saw an image in the sky. They both saw the sailboat being tossed about by the storm, and the woman trying to unfurl the sail and getting washed into the water," Eddie said.

"A mirage," Paula said. "Mirages aren't supernatural."

"That wasn't all they saw," Eddie said. "The image morphed into a spirit; a spirit with a prophecy."

"Eddie—" Odette said.

"I'm getting there," Eddie said. "The spirit said, 'Beware the tides of January. They carry both good and evil. You must choose. The wrong choice leads to a horrible death.'"

"What the hell is that supposed to mean?" Odette asked.

"Don't know," Eddie said.

"You think we'll find out, out there on the water?" Paula asked.

"Maybe," Eddie said. "You coming or not?"

"Why not," Paula said. "It's a beautiful day to go for a cruise."

"Good. Because whatever's singing out there, it ain't dolphins." Eddie stood and smoothed his shirt. "I've got to change before the boys shove off. Odette, lock the till if you're coming. Paula—" He paused, something almost gentle in his voice. "Tante Félonise can wait. Some questions don't keep."

The brass lamp flickered, as if the room itself agreed. Paula stared into her martini, the olive bobbing like a tiny drowned moon. Odette was already reaching for her keys. Outside, the Gulf whispered against the pilings, patient and hungry.

CHAPTER 6

The Majestic Hotel's private dock jutted into Oyster Bay like a weathered finger, its pilings barnacle-crusted and slick from the morning's high tide. The water below was a murky teal, flecked with foam and the occasional flash of a mullet darting beneath the surface.

Gulls wheeled overhead, their cries sharp against the low hum of the Gulf breeze, while the air carried the briny bite of low tide mixed with diesel fumes from the idling engines of moored fishing boats. The storm's aftermath lingered in scattered debris —splintered planks, tangled fishing line, a lone flip-flop bobbing against a pier—reminders that the sea gave back what it took, but never cleanly.

Jack Wiesinski stood at the edge of the dock, one shoe propped on a coiled hawser, his wiry frame silhouetted against the glittering bay. The Argo, his pride and joy, rocked gently at her berth—an aging trawler with a hull of faded blue paint scarred by decades of salt and sun, her brass fittings polished to a defiant gleam. Built in '28 for bootleggers dodging Coast Guard cutters, she still bore the ghosts of rum crates in her holds and the faint scent of oak barrels in her timbers.

Jack ran a calloused hand along her rail, eyes soft with the affection of a man tending an old lover.

"Look at her," he said, voice gravelly from years of shouting over engines and waves. "Ninety-seven years old, and she'd outrun half the fancy yachts back in her day. Smoothed out more illicit hooch than a New Orleans speakeasy. Chief and I keep her heart beating—new planks here, fresh varnish there. Ain't no storm gonna claim my girl."

Chief Gordon La Tortue nodded beside him, his massive frame casting a long shadow over the planks. Silver hair tied back with a turquoise band, he squinted into the sun, his Atakapan features etched with the quiet wisdom of island blood.

"She's family," he said, voice deep as the Gulf's trenches. "Carried sailors through worse than last night's blow. We'll find that sailboat. Argo don't forget the water's debts."

Trixie Kettler leaned against a piling, the borrowed bikini peeking from beneath her leather jacket like a secret dare. The sun warmed her sun-kissed skin, but her blue-gray eyes scanned the horizon restlessly, fingers twitching at the memory of her lost boat.

J.P. and Alex flanked her, the former with his Stetson tipped low, the latter stocky and intense, both men exchanging glances heavy with the night's unspoken visions. Lucky panted at J.P.'s feet, tail thumping the dock in rhythmic anticipation.

"She's a beaut, Jack," Trixie said, pushing off the piling with a grin that didn't quite mask her worry. "If my little sloop's half as tough, she'll be floating out there waiting for me. Anchor line cut clean—someone wanted me gone. But why?"

Before Jack could answer, the dock creaked under new footsteps. Odette Mouton strode up first, her blond hair whipping in the breeze, curves hugged by a simple tank top and shorts that screamed unapologetic confidence. Paula Boutet followed, darker and more reserved, her eyes sharp with the weight of unspoken gifts. Eddie Toledo brought up the rear, linen shirt fluttering, his prosecutor's poise traded for the easy roll of a man who'd stared down mobsters and won.

"Room for a few more on this treasure hunt?" Eddie asked, flashing that jury-charming smile. He clapped Jack on the shoulder, then nodded to Chief. "Heard the Argo's the only lady fit for the job."

Jack's eyes lit up. "Eddie, you old dog. And Odette—Paula. Hell, the gang's all here." He made quick introductions, his gaze lingering on Trixie with a wink. "This here's Trixie Kettler, our damsel from the deep. Washed in with the storm, tougher than she looks."

Odette stepped forward, extending a hand to Trixie. Her grip was firm, her smile warm but knowing, like she'd spotted a mirror in a stranger.

"Odette Mouton. General Manager at the Majestic, part-time bartender, and full-time troublemaker. You got that fire in your eyes, cher—kindred spirits, you and me. Storm spit you out, but it didn't break you."

Trixie clasped her hand, a spark of recognition flickering. "Trixie. And yeah, the Gulf tried. Failed. Nice to meet someone who looks like they could handle a hurricane in heels."

Paula hung back a step, offering a quieter nod. "Paula Boutet. Eddie's dragooned me into this. Said there might be... more than a boat out there."

Chief grunted approvingly, already loosening the Argo's lines. "More hands make light work. Tide's turning—let's shove off before the reef starts its song again."

Alex shot Eddie a look. "You told them?"

"Enough," Eddie said, voice low. "The apparition, the warning. Trixie's ravings about burning the reef. Figured we need all eyes if we're chasing ghosts."

J.P. helped Trixie aboard, his hand lingering on her elbow a beat too long. "Watch your step. Argo's got character—uneven decks, hidden compartments from her rumrunning days."

As the group boarded, the trawler groaned to life under Jack's expert hand, engine thrumming like a contented beast. Chief cast off the lines with practiced ease, the dock receding as they nosed into the bay. The Majestic loomed behind them, its piers stretching over the water like skeletal arms where yachts once bobbed in their slips—now, little more than ghosts of Prohibition excess.

Trixie leaned on the rail, wind teasing her hair. "Out there," she pointed southeast, toward the open Gulf. "The reef's about a mile off. Man-made junk pile, but alive with fish and coral. If my boat drifted..."

Odette joined her, elbow to elbow. "We'll find it. Or what's left. You sense anything... off? Like last night?"

Trixie shivered despite the sun. "The reef. It hums sometimes, when I dive like it's breathing. Delirium, maybe. But after that thing in the sky..."

Paula overheard, her voice cutting in softly. "Tides of January. Good and evil. Sounds like a choice coming. My gran'maman would say the water remembers."

Jack throttled up, the Argo slicing through the chop. "Hold tight, folks. Gulf's calm now, but she don't forgive fools. Chief, eyes on the depth sounder—let's hunt us a sailboat."

The trawler surged forward, spray kicking up in salty arcs, the group falling into a tense rhythm—scanning the horizon, trading stories of storms and secrets. But beneath the banter, the apparition's words echoed like distant thunder: You must choose. Out in the Gulf, the water deepened to an inscrutable blue, and somewhere below, the reef waited, its song faint but rising.

The Argo knifed through the Gulf's glassy swell, her wake a clean white scar behind them. Jack stood at the helm, one hand on the wheel, the other shading his eyes under the brim of his salt-bleached cap. A mile out, the water shifted from bottle-green to a deeper indigo, and there—bobbing like a broken toy— rose the pale belly of Trixie's capsized sloop, sails shredded, mast snapped like a matchstick.

"Got her," Jack said, lifting binoculars. "Upside-down but afloat. Stubborn little thing."

Trixie crowded the rail, knuckles white. "That's Siren. My home, my lab, my everything." Her voice cracked on the last word, then steadied. "Reef's directly beneath her. I marked the GPS before the storm hit."

Behind them, Oyster Island shimmered like a mirage: sugar-white beaches, emerald scrub, the lighthouse a lone white needle on its promontory. The Majestic's spires glinted faintly in the haze, a toy palace on stilts. Chief leaned out, massive arm sweeping the view.

"See that rise yonder?" He pointed to a jungled hump. "La

Tortue Mountain."

Trixie snorted. "There are no mountains in south Louisiana."

Chief's laugh rumbled like distant thunder. "Not by Rocky standards, no. Hundred feet above the tide, give or take. From my teepee on the crest, I can spit and hit the Majestic, the bay, Jack's lighthouse, and the main beach. Best seat on the island."

"You live in a teepee?" Trixie asked, incredulous.

"Old ways are always best," Chief said. "Got my dogs, my chickens, my calico cat Buttercup. She bosses the roosters something fierce."

"Even a hundred feet is weird around here," Trixie pressed.

"Salt dome. Grandpa swore it," Chief said. "Whole island's a cork on a bottle of anomalies."

Alex, arms folded, stared at the water. "The limestone filters the aquifer. Best distilling water I've ever tested. Pure enough to shame Scottish highlands."

J.P. grinned. "Alex and his partners are resurrecting the old Baptiste distillery where you washed up, Trix. Gonna crown himself rum king of the Gulf."

The banter died as Jack eased the throttle. The Argo drifted alongside the sloop. Chief tossed a grappling hook; the prongs bit into the fiberglass hull with a hollow clunk. Jack winched the line taut, the trawler's diesel growling in protest.

"We'll tow her to the drydock," Jack said. "Patch the hull, step a new mast. Few days, maybe a week."

Trixie's shoulders sagged. "I've lived aboard for six months. Everything I own is in those lockers." She swallowed. "I've got nowhere to go."

Odette appeared at her elbow, sun glinting off her blond hair. "Stay with me—three-bedroom cottage on the north cove. Mudpuppy and Bruiser'll love the company. Meika, my roommate, skipped town for a Biloxi gig—plenty of room."

"You sure?" Trixie asked, voice small.

"Positive," Odette said. "We'll drink rum on the porch and scandalize the pelicans."

Eddie opened his mouth to speak when the sea beneath the sloop belched. A ring of fat bubbles erupted, each the size of a washtub, roiling the surface into a violent boil. The water darkened, as if ink bled from the depths. The Argo rocked hard; coffee sloshed from Alex's mug.

"Christ!" Eddie braced against the rail.

"Earthquake?"

"Gas vent," Alex said. "Storm must have fractured a fault line—"

Chief's headshake cut him off. "Horned Serpent." His voice carried the weight of centuries. "Storm tore the gate. It's waking."

Eddie barked a nervous laugh. "You're joking."

Chief's eyes, black and depthless, fixed on the churning circle. "Grandpa's bones are down there. I need to ask him what the serpent wants."

Paula stepped forward, skin prickling as if the air itself had teeth. "It's an omen," she whispered. "Not gas, not coincidence. The island's in danger. Everything we love."

The bubbles grew larger, each pop releasing a sulfur reek that stung the eyes. Beneath the surface, something moved—a shadow vast and coiling, sliding just beyond sight. The water bulged upward, a living dome, then collapsed with a sound like a sigh from the earth's core. Jack gunned the engine. The Argo lunged, towing the sloop clear of the circle. The towline sang with tension; the capsized boat skidded across the froth like a toy on a string.

"Whatever's down there," Jack said, "it don't want company."

Trixie stared back at the roiling patch, now spreading into a widening ring.

"The reef," she said. "It's directly under us. That's no gas. It's... singing."

Odette's hand found Trixie's, fingers interlaced. "If the reef is singing, we need to listen."

Jack eased the throttle, the Argo's engine dropping to a low growl as the capsized sloop trailed obediently behind on its towline. The circle of roiling water still churned a hundred yards astern, a dark wound in the Gulf's skin. The others crowded the rail, eyes fixed on the fading maelstrom, when something heaved upward from its center—a splintered chunk of fiberglass and teak, half a transom, spinning lazily like a leaf in a whirlpool.

"Wait," J.P. said, voice sharp enough to cut glass.

The debris broke the surface, bobbing in the dying froth. Protruding from a jagged hole in the wood was a waterlogged forearm, fingers curled like claws, skin sloughing in gray ribbons. A rusted brass button glinted on the cuff of a once-navy sleeve.

"Oh my God," Paula said, crossing herself.

"What's that sticking out?" Trixie asked, her voice cracking

"Hand," J.P. said grimly. "Or what's left of one."

Jack swore under his breath and spun the wheel. The Argo answered with a groan, swinging wide to avoid the towline tangling. Chief worked the stern hoist with steady hands, the cable whining as the block and tackle lowered. Eddie and Alex leaned out, gaffs ready, snagging the debris on the first pass.

The hoist creaked; the transom rose dripping, barnacles and seaweed streaming from its edges. They hauled it aboard in a rush of seawater that sluiced across the deck and down the scuppers. The arm flopped against the teak, bones visible through shredded flesh.

The uniform shirt—once crisp, now a rag—clung to a ribcage picked clean in places. A plastic nametag, miraculously intact, hung from a frayed epaulet: OLSEN.

Alex crouched, gloved fingers brushing the tag. "Casino security."

J.P. knelt beside the torso, clinical despite the stench. "Shipwreck bones don't wear polyester blends. This is fresh—three days, maybe a week. My guess is this is a murder scene."

Chief's eyes narrowed at the water. "Serpent don't care about time. Just takes what's offered."

Paula's voice was barely audible over the engine. "He was

guarding something. Or running from it."

The transom rocked gently under their feet, the skeletal hand seeming to point back toward the reef—toward the dark circle that had finally gone still, as if sated.

The Argo powered toward shore, the island growing larger, greener, deceptively serene. Behind them, the circle of disturbed water kept expanding, slow and deliberate, as if the Gulf itself were drawing a target around the spot where the Horned Serpent stirred.

CHAPTER 7

T he sun hung low over Oyster Bay, a bloated orange coin bleeding into the horizon, painting the water in molten copper and bruised purples. Not quite dusk yet —the light still sharp enough to etch every ripple on the bay's surface—but the day was bleeding out, the air cooling with the briny sigh of retreating tide.

Oyster Island's old marina clung to the shoreline like a stubborn barnacle, its weathered piers jutting into the shallows where mangroves twisted their roots into the muck, their leaves whispering secrets in the breeze. The drydock—a ramshackle affair of rusted cranes, splintered timbers, and oil-stained concrete—hummed with the low groan of winches and the slap of waves against hulls.

Gulls wheeled overhead, screeching like rusty hinges, while the distant hum of a generator mingled with the salty tang of low tide: fish guts, diesel, and the faint rot of seaweed baking on the pilings.

Trixie's sailboat, Siren, sat high and dry in the dock's cradle, right side up now, her hull patched with hasty fiberglass and tape, mast stepped but still swaying like a drunk on crutches. She looked battered but defiant, barnacles crusting her waterline, a jagged scar running along her keel where the reef had kissed her goodbye.

The Argo nestled at its usual berth nearby, the old trawler rocking gently, her blue paint flaking like old skin, brass fittings gleaming in the fading light. The skeletal remains—what the Gulf had spat up with that transom chunk—lay on the Argo's aft deck under a tarp, the air around it thick with the cloying reek of decay and formaldehyde from the investigator's kit.

J.P. leaned against the rail, Stetson pushed back on his dark Cajun curls, sleeves rolled high on his flannel shirt despite the chill creeping in. He poked at the bones with a gloved finger, careful-like, as if they might bite back. Beside him, two St. Bernard Parish homicide detectives—old buddies from his badge days—hunkered down, one chewing Red Man tobacco, the other nursing a Styrofoam cup of chicory coffee gone cold. Both were dressed in cheap suits and thrift store ties.

"What's the deal with the suits?" J.P. asked. "Ain't nobody here to impress except me."

"Comforts the victim's family. Separates us from the uniforms and makes questioning easier," the large man said. "I wore this to work, and I'm not taking it off until I get home."

The death investigator, a wiry guy named Thibodeaux with a mustache like a broom handle and a lab coat stained from too many "meat wagons," knelt nearby, his two assistants hovering like gulls over chum.

"Look at this poor bastard, at least what's left of him," J.P. said, his voice carrying that easy Gulf drawl, movie-star charm laced with cop grit. He nudged a rib bone with his boot. "Reef chewed him up good. And this button—casino issue, but which casino?"

Olsen, the tag said. Deputy Marcantel—big gut, bigger laugh —spat a stream of tobacco juice over the rail, wiping his chin with the back of a hairy hand.

"Least he ain't stinking. Hell, J.P., you always did have a nose for the stinking ones. Back when you were riding herd on us rookies, you'd sniff out a body in a bayou before the gators did. This fella looks like he been marinated in Gulf sauce—pickled and served with a side of mystery."

The other deputy, Johnnie Daigle, shorter and wirier, chuckled, slapping J.P. on the back hard enough to rattle teeth.

"Marinated? Boy, you making me hungry."

Marcantel shook his head. "My mama'd say it's rougarou work, but I say it's some fool dumped a body because the fish don't snitch."

J.P. grinned, his cowboy swagger kicking in as he straightened, thumbs hooked in his belt.

"Rougarou? Nah. Or hell, maybe he saw that Horned Serpent Chief's yammering about and got ate for his troubles."

Thibodeaux snorted, snapping photos with a digital camera that clicked like angry crabs. "Not much left but bones and gristle, boys. Flesh sloughed off like wet paper—three, four days in the drink, maybe more. No wallet, no watch, but that uniform's from some casino. Teeth'll tell the tale; dental records don't lie. Let y'all know soon as I carve out the truth in the lab."

"Three or four days?" Marcantel said. "That's all it takes for a body to decompose?"

Thibodeaux grinned. "Decomposition doesn't take long in highly oxygenated seawater, and that's what we're dealing with if it's genuinely a reef we're dealing with. Hell, Sam, the crabs and fish had a field day."

He waved his assistants over, who unzipped a black body bag with a rasp that cut the banter short. They lifted the remains—fragile as driftwood, vertebrae clicking like dice—into the bag, zipping it with a finality that hung in the air. One assistant, a kid fresh-faced and green, heaved a bit too hard; a loose femur slipped free, rolling across the deck with a hollow clatter.

"Shit—sorry, Doc!"

Daigle howled, doubling over. "Boy, you trying to start a bone dance? That's how you wake the dead—give 'em a jig!"

Marcantel roared along, slapping his knee. "J.P., remember that floater we pulled from Lake Borgne? Leg come off in my hands—thought it was a damn alligator tail!"

J.P. shook his head, chuckling as he scooped the bone back with a gloved hand, tossing it into the bag.

"Y'all ain't changed since I turned in the badge. Still clowning over corpses like it's Mardi Gras. But bag him gentle —this ain't no joke. Man's got family wondering, and that reef's still humming out there. Whatever took him ain't done singing."

Thibodeaux peeled off his gloves with a snap. "Not much

left of the body other than skeletal remains," he echoed to J.P. and the deputies, voice flat but eyes twinkling under bushy brows. "Storm must have torn him loose from wherever he was weighted. Let you know what I find out—tox screen, cause of death, the works."

He nodded to his assistants, who hefted the bag toward the gangplank, wheels rumbling on the dock as they loaded it into the awaiting transport van—the "meat wagon," as Marcantel whooped with a grin, ha ha, the joke landing like a familiar punchline in the fading light.

The van's doors slammed, engine coughing to life, taillights winking red as it pulled away, kicking up gravel and dust that swirled in the marina's sodium lamps, flickering on. J.P. watched it go, the jovial mask slipping just a hair, his dark eyes narrowing at the bay's darkening waters. The Siren creaked in her cradle overhead, the Argo rocking below, and somewhere out in the Gulf, the reef waited—silent now, but the island knew better. Tides of January were rising, and the bones were just the overture. J.P. realized as much as he left the Argo and headed toward the Majestic.

The sun had surrendered to a bruised horizon, the marina's sodium lamps buzzing to life like wary sentinels. The air had thickened, heavy with the promise of rain, and the first fat drops splattered the dock as he crossed the gravel lot toward the Majestic Hotel and Casino. Each step crunched with oyster shells, the sound swallowed by the rising wind that whipped the palms into a frantic dance.

Thunder growled low in the west. Oyster Island never let you forget who owned the night. The Majestic loomed ahead, its stilted silhouette a dark cutout against the storm-lit sky, neon sign flickering MAJESTIC in erratic pulses of pink and gold. The bar's entrance—a heavy oak door scarred by decades of salt and revelry—creaked as J.P. pushed through, the humid Gulf air chasing him inside like a bad omen.

The bar was a cave of polished mahogany and low amber light, the kind of place where secrets fermented alongside the bourbon. Brass rails gleamed under a single lamp, bottles behind the bar catching the glow like stained glass in a sinner's chapel.

The air was thick with lemon oil, cigar smoke, and the sweet rot of the bay seeping through the floorboards. A jukebox in the corner crooned a mournful zydeco tune, all accordion and heartache, barely audible over the rain now lashing the windows in sheets.

Eddie sat at the bar's curve, linen shirt unbuttoned to reveal a glint of gold chain, his prosecutor's charm dialed to eleven even in the gloom. Paula perched beside him, her dark eyes scanning a half-empty martini as if it held answers to questions she hadn't asked yet.

Alex Pavlovic hunched over a vodka neat, his stocky frame tense, knuckles white around the glass like he was strangling a ghost. Behind the bar, Odette moved with the grace of a woman who owned every inch of her domain, blond hair loose, tank top clinging to curves that didn't need permission to command attention.

And then there was Trixie Kettler, still in that polka-dot bikini that barely qualified as clothing, her sun-kissed skin glowing under the lamp as she polished a highball glass with a rag, her scrollwork tattoo peeking from the small of her back like a dare. The sight hit J.P. like a slug of rum—unexpected, warm, and trouble in a shot glass. He let out a low whistle, sharp enough to cut through the jukebox's wail, and slid onto a stool beside Eddie.

"Well, damn, Eddie," he said with a drawl, tipping his Stetson back, eyes locked on Trixie. "You hiring flash now to keep the high-rollers tipping?

Eddie's laugh was a quick bark, his smile flashing like a switchblade.

"J.P., you dog, if I could bottle Trixie's sparkle, I'd be richer than Frankie Castellano and twice as pretty as his daughter, Josie. But Odette's the real draw—Trixie's just the cherry on this hurricane."

"Keep talking, Eddie, and I'll serve you a hurricane with a

side of my boot," Odette said.

Trixie laughed, flipping the rag over her shoulder, her hips swaying just enough to keep every eye in the room tethered. Odette handed J.P. a rum— Dominican firewater—and leaned back, the stool creaking under his weight. The rain outside intensified, a relentless drum against the roof, each drop a hammer strike against the island's once fragile calm.

Thunder cracked closer now, shaking the bottles on the backbar, and the lights flickered, casting shadows that danced like the apparition's burning eyes. The zydeco cut out mid-wail, leaving a hollow silence broken only by the storm's roar.

"Coastal Louisiana weather," Eddie said, swirling his rum, eyes on the rain-streaked window where lightning stitched the sky in jagged white. "One minute it's all sunshine and pelican postcards, next it's Noah's flood with a side of wrath."

Paula's fingers tightened on her glass, her voice low, almost lost in the storm's din. "It's listening. The water. The reef. Whatever's out there, it's talking back tonight."

Alex grunted, draining his vodka in one gulp. "Talking or screaming. Same difference when the bones start rising."

J.P. took his rum from Trixie, his fingers brushing hers just long enough to spark a grin from her. He sipped, the liquor burning a clean path through the weight of the day, then set the glass down with a click.

"Speaking of bones," he said, voice dropping to that deputy's edge, "we don't know much yet. Thibodeaux's got the skeleton— Olsen, casino security uniform. Teeth'll confirm, but the single bullet hole in the skull? Sharks don't shoot pistols, and it's too precise for an accident."

J.P. nodded when Eddie said, "Professional hit?"

"Looks like it. My boys in St. Bernard Parish are the best —Marcantel and Daigle will turn over every rock from here to Chalmette."

"What about the reef?" Eddie asked.

"Sheriff's sending divers at first light tomorrow to scour for clues and evidence. Whoever or whatever dumped Olsen's carcass ain't just singing—it's burying secrets deeper than the Gulf's trenches."

Trixie stopped mid-wipe, the rag still in her hand, her blue-gray eyes wide. "My reef," she said, her words barely audible over a thunderclap that rattled the windows. "Siren flipped right over it. If someone cut my anchor, put me in that storm…"

She trailed off, the bikini suddenly looking less like armor and more like a target. Odette's hand found Trixie's shoulder, steadying.

"Easy, cher. Nobody's touching you here."

But the air in the bar had shifted, heavy as the storm outside. Lightning flashed again, illuminating the room in stark white, and for a split second, the shadows on the wall twisted —elongated, coiling like something alive. Paula's martini glass trembled in her grip, untouched now.

Alex's shoulders tightened, his eyes darting to the window where the rain blurred the world into a watercolor of dread. Eddie's charm had slipped, his face pale under the tan, the gold chain at his throat catching the light like a noose.

Another peal of thunder, closer, shook the floorboards, and the jukebox kicked back on with a crackle, spitting out a single note before dying again.

Eddie shook his head when Alex said, "You need to get that damn thing fixed or replaced."

"It's on my radar," Eddie said.

A clap of thunder shook the old Majestic. The storm wasn't just weather—it was a pulse, a warning, syncing with the reef's distant song. J.P. leaned forward, voice low, cutting through the tension like a blade. Outside, the rain became a roar, the Gulf clawing at the pilings beneath the Majestic, and somewhere in the dark, the island held its breath, waiting for the next bone to surface.

"Divers'll find more than fish."

"And the tides of January are just beginning," Paula said.

CHAPTER 8

The Majestic's oak door slammed shut behind J.P. and Alex, and the storm hit like a slap from God. Rain came sideways, needles of water driven by a wind that howled across the bay and rattled the stilts under the hotel. Lightning strobed the sky in magnesium-white, freezing the palm trees for an instant—black skeletons against a bruised violet sky—before plunging everything back into wet darkness.

Thunder followed so close it felt like artillery, shaking the ground and rattling their fillings. J.P. pulled his Stetson low and swore, the brim already sagging under the weight of the downpour.

"Lucky and your new cat are waiting for us at your place. We ride, or we swim."

Alex spat rainwater, the taste metallic on his tongue. "Ride."

J.P.'s tricked-out, four-door ATV sat parked under the dripping porte-cochère, its Mardi-Gras paint job—swirls of purple, green, and gold—already dulled by the deluge, running in muddy streaks down the fenders. He climbed into the fully-enclosed cab, the door sealing with a pneumatic hiss, and keyed the ignition; the engine snarled to life, a throaty growl that vibrated through the seats.

Headlights carved twin tunnels through the murk, illuminating sheets of rain that danced like ghosts in the beams. Alex climbed into the passenger seat, his coat flapping like a broken sail, shedding water onto the rubber mats. They shot out from under the shelter, tires spitting gravel, and the storm swallowed them whole. The trail across Oyster Island became a gauntlet of flooded ruts and whipping branches, the ATV bucking like a bronc on steroids. Alex had to raise his voice over the roar of the engine and the relentless drum of rain on the roof.

"Has Oyster Island ever taken a direct hit from a hurricane?"

"All around us but no direct hits," J.P. shouted back, hands white-knuckled on the wheel as he wrestled the vehicle around a submerged pothole. "Katrina, back in '05, skirted us close enough to taste. Ripped roofs off like tin cans, flooded the bayou up to the eaves. Folks still talk about the water moccasins swimming through living rooms. But the island held—barely."

"But you weren't on the island in '05, were you?" Alex asked.

"I lived in Chalmette at the time. St. Bernard was the parish that suffered the most damage. Katrina flooded nearly every building in the parish. The city is below sea level, and the hurricane affected everything. If I live to be a hundred, I'll never forget the smell of the dozens of portapotties FEMA brought in."

J.P. simply nodded when Alex said, "I'm sorry."

Palmettos lashed the windshield with wet slaps; puddles exploded under the tires, flinging sheets of brown water across the hood and splattering the side windows. Lightning flashed again, closer this time, and the Gulf lit up in a blinding tableau: whitecaps marching in relentless rows, each crest exploding into phosphorescent fire that glowed eerie blue-green against the black water.

The shoreline was a war zone—waves detonating against the dunes with concussive booms, hurling driftwood and tangled fishing nets like shrapnel. Alex caught a glimpse of a derelict crab trap tumbling end over end, its buoy light blinking forlornly before vanishing into the foam. Halfway to the island's far side, where the trail narrowed between thickets of scrub oak and sawgrass, J.P. braked hard.

The ATV fishtailed wildly, anti-lock brakes chattering, headlights sweeping a chaotic arc across the underbrush. Something had moved—something big, low, and impossibly fast —crashing through the foliage with a rustle that cut through even the storm's cacophony.

The beam caught a ripple of wet leaves shaking violently, a

shadow too bulky for a deer, then nothing but swaying fronds dripping like blood. J.P. grabbed his heavy-duty flashlight from beneath the dash—its beam a solid spear of LED white—and bounded into the rain without a word, boots splashing into the ankle-deep mud.

Alex cursed in Russian —a string of guttural syllables lost to the wind —and slammed the open door, but not before rain pelted his face like buckshot, soaking through his collar in seconds. Overhead, thunder rolled like a freight train derailing, the air thick with ozone and the salty tang of the Gulf.

The light jittered across tangled vines, broken palmetto fans, and pools of standing water that reflected the flashes like shattered mirrors. Ten yards in, J.P. crouched, one knee sinking into the muck, sweeping the flashlight in methodical arcs. The beam picked out trampled grass, bent stalks oozing sap, and then —there—a patch of earth gouged deep, as if by claws the size of garden rakes.

Nothing else. Only the relentless drip of water from leaves, the distant crash of waves, and that metallic smell lingering in the air, like crushed pennies mixed with low tide rot. Alex yelled out from the ATV, his voice cutting through the rain like a knife.

"What's out there? Bear? Gator?"

J.P. stood, water streaming off his hat brim in rivulets, and shouted back, his words whipping away on the gale.

"Something big. Bear-sized, but no bear moves like that— too fluid, too quiet under all this noise. Maybe Chief's Horned Serpent came ashore for a look-see, slithering up from the deep to see what the storm stirred."

When J.P. rejoined him, splashing back to the cab and shaking off like a dog, Alex barked a laugh that had no humor in it, echoing hollowly inside the enclosed space.

"You don't actually believe in that swamp fairy tale. Old Choctaw legend to scare tourists and kids."

"Don't know what I believe," J.P. said, wiping mud from his jeans as he slid behind the wheel. "Didn't use to believe in rougarous either, till one damn near took my scalp one full-moon night right here on Oyster Island."

"Everything has an explanation," Alex said, buckling in as the engine revved. "What we saw in the Gulf earlier? Earthquake. Submarine fault line shifting. I'd bet Lenin's lucky ushanka on it. Seismic waves, pressure release—boom, water boils."

"What the hell's a ushanka?" J.P. asked, throwing the ATV into gear with a lurch that sent them skidding forward.

"A warm Russian winter hat, fur-lined, ear flaps—like the one Dr. Zhivago wore in the snow. Practical. Keeps the brain from freezing when the world goes mad."

J.P. gunned the engine, tires biting into the mud. "This is Louisiana, Russkie. You ain't in Mother Russia anymore. Things here don't come with footnotes or rational explanations. They just bite."

The ATV lurched forward as lightning stitched the sky in a jagged seam, illuminating the dunes for a heartbeat—they looked like the surface of the moon, pockmarked with craters of shadow, silver water exploding upward in geysers from hidden cracks.

Then darkness swallowed them again, the headlights their only lifeline. They crested the last rise above Alex's bungalow, the trail dipping into a shallow valley where pines stood sentinel, their needles hissing in the wind. The little cedar house sat in its clearing like a ship foundering on a reef: front door yawning wide and banging on its hinges with each gust, every window lit from within by the strobing lightning that turned the interior into a flickering nightmare.

Shingles peeled from the roof like scales, clattering into the yard; the chimney belched smoke that the wind tore away in ragged plumes.

"What the hell!" Alex said, leaping out of the ATV before it fully stopped, his boots hitting the ground with a splash that soaked his cuffs. He sprinted through the downpour, skidding on wet pine needles and slick mud, heart pounding in his ears louder than the thunder.

J.P. wasn't far behind, flashlight beam bouncing ahead like a will-o'-the-wisp. They stopped in the open doorway, rain sheeting in across the threshold, assessing the damage in breathy bursts. Books lay scattered across the porch, pages fluttering; a rocking chair rocked itself in the gale, creaking a mournful rhythm. The living room was a battlefield of chaos: shelves toppled like fallen soldiers, Faulkner and Dostoevsky swimming in puddles that reflected the lightning; the chess table overturned, ivory pieces floating like tiny rafts on a brown sea.

The rug, Alex's thrift-store treasure with its faded Persian patterns, was bunched against the hearth where embers still glowed faintly, hissing and spitting when rain blew down the chimney in erratic gusts. A lamp lay shattered, its bulb flickering once before dying; the air smelled of wet paper, smoke, and something else—musky, primal, like a zoo after hours.

He didn't stop to gauge the damage further. Coat flapping wildly, shedding water in arcs, Alex bolted out the back door and down the muddy path to the distillery, his feet slipping on the incline. The unfinished building loomed ahead, half brick walls rising sturdy against the storm, half skeleton of exposed beams rattling under the corrugated roof like machine-gun fire.

The side door hung crooked on one hinge, banging insistently; inside, shadows danced wildly from the lightning bleeding through gaps in the walls. Copper pipes lay twisted like pretzels across the floor, hissing steam where hot mash met cold rain; the cloying stink of spilled rum hung heavy, mingling with the earthy reek of turned soil.

A jagged fissure split the concrete floor from wall to wall, black water welling up from below in lazy bubbles that carried flecks of sand and shell. The pride of his fleet, an antique brass pot still imported from Scotland, sat cracked open like a gutted fish, its belly leaking golden liquor that mixed with rainwater into amber rivers snaking toward the door. Alex stood in the doorway, fists clenched so tight his knuckles cracked audibly, the storm's roar drowning his curses.

"Fucking earthquake," he roared into the void, voice raw. "Salt dome collapse, pressure wave—nothing more!"

Alex slogged back to the bungalow, mud sucking at his boots, each step a labor. J.P. was inside the living room, righting the couch with grunts of effort, water dripping from his hat onto the floorboards in steady plinks. Lucky met Alex at the threshold, the chocolate Lab soaked to the skin, fur matted and dripping, tail thumping once in apologetic greeting.

His eyes, usually bright with mischief, were wide and watchful. Behind him, the bathroom door stood ajar, a slice of yellow light cutting through the chaos like a beacon. J.P. jerked his chin toward it, his face grim under the flickering shadows.

"That ain't all you got to worry about, comrade. Dog's been guarding something fierce."

Alex followed him down the short hallway, boots squelching on the runner rug. The bathroom was a sanctuary of steam and fur, the air thick with the scent of wet animal and milky warmth. Squeaky, the little white cat he'd rescued from the storm, lay on a nest of towels in the claw-foot tub, her sides heaving gently. Thirteen tiny kittens squeaked and squirmed against her belly, blind eyes shut tight, paws kneading in frantic rhythm.

Lucky had jumped into the tub and wedged his big body around them like a living breakwater, ears flat against his skull, eyes steady and unblinking despite the thunder. Every time thunder cracked overhead, shaking the foundations, the kittens mewled in high-pitched chorus; Lucky licked the nearest one—a tiny calico with a splash of orange—emitting a low whine in his throat that vibrated through the porcelain. Alex's anger drained out of him like the rum from his cracked still, leaving a hollow ache. He sank to his knees on the tile, water pooling around him, soaking his jeans.

"Thirteen," he said softly, voice cracking like the fissure in his distillery. "Unlucky number. In Russia, we skip it in buildings, like your American hotels."

J.P. crouched beside him, voice low under the storm's

relentless drum on the roof. "Or maybe the luckiest damn litter this side of the Mississippi. They're alive, Alex. The house is standing—creaking, but standing. We're standing."

"You're right," Alex said. "I should stop complaining."

J.P. rested a callused hand on Lucky's wet head, scratching behind the ears; the dog leaned into it briefly, then resumed his vigil.

"Whatever tore through here, earthquake, serpent, or pissed-off rougarou on a bender, it left us a message. That reef out in the Gulf? It's singing louder tonight, deeper notes. And it just changed key, like a warning shot across the bow."

Hours bled away in the small cedar house, the storm still hammering the roof like a drunk trying to break in, wind whistling through cracks in the walls with eerie moans. The two men had worked in grim silence at first, muscles aching from the adrenaline crash: books stacked in soggy towers on the kitchen table, pages bloated and ink running; the rug dragged to the porch to drip in heavy folds, leaving wet trails across the floor; the chess pieces corralled into a coffee can, kings and pawns mingling democratically.

The fire hissed and spat whenever wind drove rain down the chimney in sudden bursts, but it was alive again, throwing orange light across the walls, dancing shadows over the water-stained ceilings, and filling the room with the comforting smell of wet pine and burning oak.

Alex poured two fingers of his own rum—the last of a small test batch aged in charred barrels—into chipped enamel glasses that had survived the upheaval. The liquor glowed like liquid garnet in the firelight, its aroma cutting through the damp with notes of vanilla, molasses, and a hint of sea salt. They sat on opposite sides of the hearth, boots steaming by the flames, arguing in tired voices that rose and fell with the wind's gusts.

"Seismic shear," Alex said, jabbing a finger toward the floorboards, where a hairline crack had appeared near the baseboard. "Salt-dome fracture under the island. I felt the ground roll, J.P.—a longitudinal wave, then the shear. Not slither.

Not some mythical beast."

"Ground don't open doors and flip couches like they weigh nothing," J.P. shot back, his eyes reflecting the flames like polished stones. "And it sure as hell don't crack brass stills with one clean bite—look at the edges, smooth as a scalpel. Earthquake don't leave footprints in the mud out back, big as pie plates, with claw marks deep enough to plant okra."

Alex opened his mouth for a retort, closed it, and drank instead. The rum burned a clean line to his stomach, warming the chill that had settled in his bones. Outside, thunder rolled across the Gulf like artillery on the move, distant now but still menacing. J.P. tilted his head, listening intently, the fire crackling in counterpoint.

"Lucky's still in the bathroom. Not like him at all. Big dog likes his spot by the fire when the world's coming apart—usually sprawls out like he owns the place, snoring through storms."

He pushed up from the chair, joints popping like kindling, and disappeared down the short hallway, his footsteps muffled by the rug. Alex stared into the flames, counting heartbeats between lightning flashes, the bungalow creaking around him— old wood arguing with the wind, beams groaning like old men.

Somewhere in the bathroom, a kitten squeaked, high and frantic, followed by Squeaky's soft, reassuring purr. Then silence, thick and unnatural. J.P. returned slower than he'd left, his face the color of wet ash under the hall's dim bulb, shadows carving deep lines around his eyes. In his right hand dangled Lucky's collar, thick leather worn soft from years of bayou adventures, the brass nameplate bent like foil, the buckle sheared clean as if by tin snips—or something sharper.

A single thumb-sized scale, iridescent black-green with edges that gleamed like obsidian, was caught in the frayed stitching, crusted with dried blood that flaked off at a touch. Alex stood so fast his glass tipped, rum bleeding across the floorboards in a dark stain that soaked into the wood like an accusation.

"What the hell?" Alex asked.

"Something was in the house," J.P. said. His voice was flat, the kind of flat that comes after fear has already done its worst and left you hollow. "Something big. Slipped in while we were out chasing ghosts in the brush, maybe. Or it was waiting."

"How big?"

Alex's accent thickened, rolling the r's like gravel, the way it always did when the past clawed too close—Kyiv streets, betrayal, blood on snow. J.P. turned the collar so the torn edge faced Alex under the firelight. The leather was sliced, not chewed or frayed—one clean cut that gleamed wetly where fresh edges met. No teeth marks, no ragged tears.

"Lucky's a hundred and twenty pounds of pure Louisiana muscle—fought off gators in his younger days. Whatever came through here ripped this off him like it was tissue paper. He's got a gash along his ribs, deep but clean, like a fillet knife. Bleeding steadily, but he won't let me near it without growling. I called Renata from the sat phone. She's on her way—said she'd brave the creek if it killed her."

Alex's jaw worked soundlessly. Renata. The name hit like a fresh bruise, dragging up flashes he'd buried deep: a narrow alley slick with winter slush, muzzle flare blooming orange in the dark, her husband's body folding like a puppet with cut strings, her eyes wild and accusatory as she pressed a smoking pistol into his hand. J.P. stepped closer, the floorboards creaking under his weight, and opened his left hand. The scale lay in his palm, heavy as a coin from hell, its surface catching the firelight and throwing it back in oily rainbows that shifted from emerald to midnight blue. It was warm to the touch, unnaturally so, pulsing faintly like a heartbeat.

"Lucky got a piece of it while he was guarding the cats," J.P. said. "Must've latched on with those jaws of his. Dog's a hero, but he paid for it."

Alex took it between thumb and forefinger, the ridges pebbled and unyielding, like a snake's but thicker, armored plating that could turn a blade. A thin membrane of clear slime coated one side; when he tilted it, the slime slid like mercury, leaving a trail that evaporated with a faint hiss. The smell that rose—brine, sulfur, and something ancient, like the breath of deep ocean trenches—made his stomach lurch, bile rising in his throat.

"You believe in Chief's Horned Serpent now?" J.P. asked quietly, his gaze steady.

Alex's laugh came out cracked, brittle as the still's brass. "I believe in plate tectonics. Fault lines don't leave souvenirs."

"Then your plates just grew fangs, teeth, and a bad attitude."

From the bathroom came a pained whine—Lucky's voice, but thinner, edged with something that sounded disturbingly like fear, a sound Alex had never heard from the dog in all their years. A kitten answered with a mewl, tiny and plaintive. The fire popped loudly; a log collapsed, sending a shower of sparks dancing up the chimney.

Headlights swept the window suddenly, cutting through the rain like searchlights—Renata's Jeep, fishtailing up the muddy track, engine roaring defiance against the storm, wipers beating like frantic wings. The storm redoubled in fury, rain sheeting so hard the glass rattled in its frames, as if the night itself resented the intrusion. J.P. set the broken collar on the mantel like evidence in a trial, the scale beside it glinting ominously. He stared out at the approaching lights, then back to Alex.

"Whatever it was," he said, "it's still out there. Circling. And it knows where we live. Smelled us. Marked its territory."

CHAPTER 9

The vehicle's headlights cut two pale tunnels through the storm, tires hissing over wet pine needles and sheets of runoff before it lurched to a stop beside the porch, engine ticking like a cooling gun barrel. Renata Yatsenko stepped out without an umbrella, rain instantly plastering the escaped strands of her severe bun to her cheeks and neck.

She wore a black slicker open over jeans and a faded L.S.U. sweatshirt, the kind of clothes that tried to apologize for the face beneath them—practical, anonymous, forgettable. It didn't work. Even soaked and grim, she looked like a war poster come to life: tall, hair black as ink, cheekbones sharp enough to slice bread, eyes the color of winter steel. She moved with the deliberate economy of someone who had learned that hesitation cost blood, that a second's pause could mean a child's scream cut short or a lover's last breath rattling in a ditch.

The wind whipped her slicker like a flag in surrender, but she didn't flinch; storms were old acquaintances, lesser than the ones that still woke her at night. J.P. met her at the door with a towel, thick and threadbare from too many washes. She waved it off with a flick of her wrist—sharp, dismissive—and stepped inside, water streaming from her boots in rivulets that pooled on the worn pine floor.

The black medical bag in her left hand was old, inherited from her father, a battlefield surgeon who'd patched boys together with fishing line and hope. It was one of the few things she'd managed to smuggle out of Ukraine, zipped shut against memories that leaked like infected wounds.

Lucky lay in the tub, his chest rising slowly and raggedly,

one paw curled protectively over the smallest kitten—a calico mewling faintly. Blood matted his chocolate-colored fur, and a deep gash along his flank glistened in the firelight, the work of some predator that had mistaken him for easy prey. He didn't protest when Renata helped him out of the tub and laid him on a towel, the floorboards creaking under her weight like old bones.

She snapped on nitrile gloves with a crisp pop that cut through the storm's roar, and went to work: cleaning the wound with antiseptic that stung the air, probing with fingers that trembled only in her nightmares, murmuring in Ukrainian too soft for anyone else to catch—lullabies or curses, maybe both.

When the last suture was tied, black thread pulling ragged flesh neat, and the gauze taped secure, she shifted to the tub where Squeaky lay, exhausted but fierce, her white fur flocked with thirteen damp kittens, a writhing, squeaking litter that smelled of milk and rain-soaked earth. Renata's gloved fingers brushed the tiniest one—a calico wisp no bigger than a matchbox, its eyes still sealed shut—then checked the mother's eyes, ears, and belly with the precision of a sniper sighting down a scope.

Her touch was clinical, detached, but her shoulders loosened a fraction, the barest release of tension coiled since the day shells fell on her village. In the flicker of the fire, her mind flashed unbidden: Sveta at that age, small fists clutching a stuffed bear, sirens wailing overhead. She blinked it away, jaw tightening.

J.P. busied himself stacking the last of the books—water-warped volumes on distillation and island lore—giving her the room she never asked for but always took, a perimeter of silence he'd learned to respect from men who'd stared down barrels. He glanced at her once, noting the way her free hand hovered near her thigh, as if ready to draw a sidearm that wasn't there.

Pragmatism was his armor; he fixed what he could, stacked the rest for later. The earthquake had cracked his world too—his collarbone still ached from the tremor that shook Oyster Island like a dog with a rat—but he pushed it down, focused on the tangible: dry wood, strong rum, his dog breathing steadily.

Alex stood in the doorway, arms folded tight across his chest, feeling every inch the intruder in his own bungalow. The firelight painted harsh shadows across Renata's face, carving hollows under her eyes; she hadn't smiled once since arriving. She never did, not really. The war had taken that from her, the way it takes everything else—piece by piece until you forget what the whole felt like, until joy felt like a betrayal. Alex's own scars itched under his shirt, phantom pains from shrapnel long extracted, but deeper ones festered: the faces of men he'd led into fire, the echo of commands that ended in silence.

He shifted his weight, causing the floor to groan, and the sound grated like a misfired round. When Renata rose, snapping off her gloves with a sharp sound that echoed his cracking resolve, Alex couldn't hold back anymore. The words spilled out, sensitive and raw, layered with the vulnerability he masked behind smiles and rum.

"Why do you hate me?"

Renata didn't look up as she dropped the gloves into a biohazard bag, sealing it with a twist. "I don't hate you."

Her voice was flat, armored, but her fingers lingered on the bag a second too long, knuckles whitening.

"Then why do I feel that you do?"

His voice cracked on the last word, raw as the gash in Lucky's hide, exposing the boy beneath the soldier—the one still haunted by nightmares of mothers' cries and children's blood on his boots. She met his eyes at last, steel on storm-gray, and for a heartbeat, the room held its breath. The thunder outside rolled like distant artillery.

"My mother, Iryna Kalinichenko, and my daughter, Sveta Yatsenko, both love you. That is good enough for me."

The words were flat, final, like a door closing with the weight of a coffin lid. But beneath them, unspoken, was the burden: love twisted with hate, gratitude poisoned by memory. She handed J.P. an amber bottle, its label worn from handling.

"Tramadol. One every twelve hours. Fluids, rest, and bring him to the clinic in two days. Watch for infection—fever, swelling. If he stops eating, call immediately."

"Thanks, Renata," J.P. said, pocketing it with the efficiency of a man who'd triaged worse in back alleys. "You didn't have to come out in the storm. Roads are washing out; could've waited till morning."

"If it weren't serious, you wouldn't have called me," she said, her accent clipping the words. She glanced at Lucky, then the kittens, her gaze softening imperceptibly before hardening again.

"I was going to bring him to you," J.P. said.

"His injuries are severe, almost critically so," she said, voice rising just enough to carry over the wind's howl. "Shock, blood loss—there's a chance he wouldn't have survived the trip across the island. You know how these things go."

Her eyes flicked to Alex, then away, as if looking too long might reopen scars.

"I appreciate you," J.P. said, meeting her gaze. "I owe you one. Big one."

"You brought my mother and Sveta from Ukraine. It is I who owes you a debt that I'll never be able to repay."

The admission hung heavy, laced with the reticence of a woman who hated indebtedness, who'd learned debts were usually paid in blood or silence.

"I couldn't have done it without Alex," J.P. said, nodding toward his friend, bridging the chasm with facts, not feelings.

Renata started for the door, slicker rustling like dry leaves in a grave. At the threshold, she paused, rain lashing the porch in sheets, glancing back at the bathroom where Squeaky licked her calico runt with protective swipes. The slightest wisp of a smile —gone almost before it formed, a crack in granite—touched her mouth as she faced Alex. For a moment, the storm outside mirrored the one within her: wrathful, unrelenting, but with pockets of unexpected calm.

"You never quit saving mamas when they're caught in the storm," she said, voice softer than the rain, almost lost in the gale. It wasn't forgiveness, not yet, but a bridge—fragile, wind-tossed. "Bring mama cat and her kittens to see me when J.P. brings Lucky. Check the runt's weight daily; if it drops, formula supplement." She was halfway out, boots splashing into puddles that reflected the bungalow's warm glow, when she turned again, raindrops beading on her lashes like unshed tears. "Oh," she added, almost shy, the word catching in her throat, "and when they're weaned, I want the calico. She reminds me... of home."

Then the door shut with a thud that echoed like a salute, the ATV's engine coughed to life amid the downpour, and the storm swallowed her taillights whole, red eyes fading into the black. Later, the fire had settled into steady coals, glowing like embers in a spent battlefield. The bungalow smelled of wet dog, antiseptic sharp as iodine, and the ghost of spilled rum mingling with the salt tang of the sea.

Lucky slept in the bathroom, door ajar, kittens tucked against his belly like punctuation marks in a ragged sentence—periods of fur and faint purrs. J.P. and Alex sat with fresh glasses, the bottle between them down to its last inch of garnet, the keg's promise untapped but looming.

Alex grinned when J.P. said, "Guess I'm sleeping on your couch again tonight."

"You and Lucky are always welcome here, my friend. Couch is yours anytime you need it."

Alex's hospitality was genuine, but his eyes held the sensitivity of a man replaying Renata's words, searching for subtext in the thunder.

"We've almost gone through all of your rum," J.P. said, swirling his glass, his mind already inventorying supplies. "Now, with your only vessel cracked in the quake, we won't have any more until your new equipment arrives and is installed. Could be weeks—shipping delays, inspections."

"Not to worry," Alex said with a wave of his hand, though his smile didn't quite reach his eyes, shadowed by the distillery's ruin: copper coils twisted like broken spines, barrels split and leaking dreams into the sand. "I have a keg of rum that I have yet to tap. Even you and I, with our insatiable appetite for alcohol, won't deplete the keg anytime soon. Aged in oak, smooth as forgiveness."

"Thank God for that," J.P. said, the relief real, a small victory against the chaos. "Since you put it that way, I'll have another."

He watched Alex rise, movements fluid but edged with the subtle tremor of a man who'd seen too many dawns through crosshairs. The storm raged on, unabated, wind screaming around the eaves like banshees, rain hammering the tin roof in relentless barrages. Alex tapped the keg of rum with a practiced twist —the rich aroma blooming warm and spicy —filled a decanter, and set it on the table in front of J.P. The liquid caught the firelight, swirling like liquid amber.

"I saw you making eyes at Miss Trixie Kettler at the Majestic," Alex teased, pouring with a steady hand that belied the knot in his gut. "Is there the spark of romance there? Or just the rum talking?"

J.P. grinned, but it was wry, tempered by memories of stakeouts and lost partners. "I was going to ask you the same question. She's got that fire—reminds me of gals back in the precinct who could outshoot the boys."

"Odette has taken her under her wing, so I doubt either of us has a chance with her," Alex said, chuckling softly, though the sound carried the weight of unspoken longings, sensitivities bruised by war's indifference.

"I was thinking the same thing," J.P. said, sipping slowly. "How bad is the earthquake going to set back the distillery? Foundation cracks? Equipment salvageable?"

Alex shook his head, staring into his glass as if it held futures. "Don't know yet. Surveyors were coming tomorrow, but right now everything seems to be at a standstill. Barrels burst, stills buckled—months of work, gone in a rumble."

His voice dipped, his rational facade cracking to reveal the ache: the distillery was his rebirth, his attempt to brew something pure from the ashes.

"Keep the faith," J.P. said, clapping a hand on his shoulder, the gesture brotherly, grounding.

"Always," Alex said. "I'll start back on it tomorrow—clear debris, salvage what I can. What are your plans?"

"Working with the old gang today brought back lots of memories and made me realize how much I miss it," J.P. said, thumb tracing the rim of his glass.

The quake had unearthed more than rubble—flashes of raids, sirens, the copper tang of blood that no rum could wash away.

"You aren't thinking about rejoining the police department, are you?" Alex asked, leaning forward, his sensitivity picking up the undercurrent of unrest.

"I've gotten used to life on Oyster Island, and there are things about police work I don't miss."

"Like what?" Alex asked, voice gentle, probing the scars.

"Rolling out of bed at three in the morning to investigate a crime; reams of paperwork I never quite got caught up on; loose ends that never quite got tied."

He paused, eyes distant, the storm's fury outside echoing the tempests within—nights jolted awake by phantom calls, faces of the unsolved haunting quieter hours.

"There's a saying in Russia," Alex offered, his accent thickening with emotion. "To live out a life is not a field to cross."

"What the hell is that supposed to mean?" J.P. asked, brow furrowing, but a half-smile tugged at his lips.

"Just that life is a long and often arduous journey with many obstacles, not an easy walk across a field."

Alex's words hung, heavy with the PTSD they all carried unspoken: Renata's reticence a shield, J.P.'s busying a deflection, Alex's questions a plea for connection.

"Amen to that." J.P. turned the broken collar in his hands—Lucky's, torn in the fight—thumb worrying the torn edge like a worry stone. "Tell me, Alex. Ukraine. You and Renata. What the hell happened? You've danced around it long enough."

Alex stared into the coals for a long time, the fire popping like suppressed fire. When he spoke, his voice was low, each word measured like a round chambered, the telling ripping open wounds he'd cauterized with time and distance.

"I was the captain of an infantry group. We'd taken over the town. Two of my men—Petrenko and Lysenko—never came back from piss call. I went looking. Found them in a half-collapsed house. Husband already dead, throat opened ear to ear with a bayonet, blood pooling black on the dirt floor. Renata on the floor, clothes ripped to shreds, blood everywhere—hers, theirs, her husband's, mixing in the dust."

"You're shitting me!" J.P. leaned in, glass forgotten, his own memories surging: crime scenes that blurred into war zones.

Alex shook his head, knuckles whitening. "They'd finished with her and were kicking her, laughing, spitting like animals. Her mother—Iryna—was clawing at their legs, screaming in Ukrainian, nails raking flesh. Little Sveta ran out of the kitchen with a table knife, no bigger than a letter opener, and tried to stab Lysenko in the calf. He backhands her so hard she flew into the wall, crumpled like a rag doll, blood trickling from her lip."

"God almighty," J.P. said, his mind cataloging horrors, but the man recoiling.

Alex took a slow sip, eyes distant, the rum burning less than the recall.

"I lost it. Grabbed Petrenko by the throat, slammed him into the stove—cast iron, dented his skull. Lysenko came at me with a bayonet, grinning like a demon. I broke his arm at the elbow, bone snapping like dry wood, took the rifle, and beat him with it until the stock cracked and his face was pulp. Renata —she was bleeding from the mouth, one eye swollen shut, lip split—crawled across the floor through the gore, and picked up Lysenko's sidearm. Two shots. Center mass. Hands me the pistol like it's a relay baton, her hand shaking but steady on the trigger."

"Shit!" J.P. said, the word both a prayer and a curse.

Alex's knuckles went white around the glass, veins standing out like cords. "It wasn't long before more soldiers gathered outside, boots crunching glass, voices shouting. They took

Renata and me into custody."

"Why you?" J.P. asked, piecing it like a case file.

"I was holding the smoking gun, and it was apparent that it wasn't Renata or Sveta who'd bloodied Lysenko and Petrenko. Prints, blood spatter—clear as a confession."

"You could have talked your way out of it," J.P. said, ever the strategist.

"Our field commander was Lieutenant Colonel Viktor Morozov, the podpolkovnic. Cruel bastard, eyes like dead fish. He'd assessed the situation and had decided to execute me summarily—abetting the enemy, murder of comrades. He was pointing a pistol at my head, finger tightening, preparing to kill me, when Russian missiles hit our own position—friendly fire, wrong grid coordinates. Boom. Chaos. Dust, screams, fire everywhere. We run, Renata and me."

"How did Iryna and Sveta escape?" J.P. asked.

"Soldiers had already dragged them out of the house. They were safe, and we had no time to return for them, though I promised Renata I would."

"And you kept your promise," J.P. said.

Alex nodded and clinked J.P.'s glass with his own. "With your help. Renata and I escaped through the rubble, across no-man's-land, across the border, across the ocean on forged papers and favors owed. I thought we were square. Debts paid in blood."

J.P. let the silence sit, thick as the humid air, the storm outside easing to a steady drum on the roof, wind still howling, but the thunder receding like retreating troops.

"You saved her life," he said finally.

"She will barely even look at me," Alex said, his voice almost inaudible, his sensitivity raw, eyes glistening in the firelight. "To her, I'm Russian and she hates all Russians. The uniform, the accent—it's all the same monster."

"That's crazy," J.P. said, but gently, understanding the irrational grip of trauma. Alex slugged his rum and poured more, the decanter clinking.

"Is it? Every glance reminds her of that room, those laughs. I see it in her eyes—the flinch, the steel wall."

J.P. leaned forward, elbows on knees, his thoughts yielding to empathy forged in shared hells. "War's a gang rape gone bad, brother. Nothing good ever comes of it. Everybody walks away with scars—some on the skin, some carved so deep the light don't reach. Memory don't keep score. Sometimes, it gets stuck replaying the worst hits on loop."

Alex nodded slowly and gave J.P. a fist bump—solid, affirming, a pact against the dark.

"At least she spoke to me tonight," he said, a fragile hope flickering. "More than a grunt."

"And told you to bring the kittens and mama cat when I take Lucky to see her." J.P. tapped the scale on the coffee table —still warm from the fire, still gleaming like wet obsidian, a remnant of some island mystery. "Some folks block out the noise and soldier on. Some folks can't. And some folks—" he glanced toward the bathroom where Lucky's breathing had steadied, rhythmic now, the kittens' soft suckling audible— "fight like hell to protect the next litter."

Alex drained his glass and set it down with a soft thunk. The fire popped, sending up a single spark that died before it reached the ceiling, a brief life extinguished. In the hush that followed, the reef's song drifted in on the wind—low, hungry, and getting closer, waves crashing against the island's bones like unresolved echoes of the storm within.

CHAPTER 10

The Majestic's bar had gone from sanctuary to tomb in the space of a single thunderclap. Rain lashed the windows in horizontal sheets, turning the neon MAJESTIC sign into a bleeding watercolor of pink and gold. Odette killed the jukebox with a decisive flick of the breaker —enough zydeco for one apocalypse—and the silence that followed felt heavier than the storm.

Trixie wiped the last tumbler, her borrowed leather jacket creaking as she reached for the highest shelf. The polka-dot bikini beneath had long since dried into salt-stiff lace, but she hadn't bothered to change. Odette grinned and shook her head.

"Place is locked tighter than a gator's ass in a drought," she said, voice low, almost reverent. "Let's get the hell out before the Gulf decides it wants the bar back."

Paula Boutet stood at the door, fingers worrying the gris-gris bag hidden under her blouse. The storm smelled like pennies and low tide, the kind of scent that crawled under your skin and nested there. She hadn't seen Jimmie since breakfast—he'd stayed behind in Chalmette to wrestle inventory at the hardware store, promising to drive their RV to the island before the weather turned.

The RV would be parked by now, nose-to-nose with J.P.'s silver Airstream like old marrieds. She could almost hear the generator's familiar cough over the wind. Odette killed the lights. The three women stepped into the porte-cochère, where her ATV waited—a matte-black beast with roll cage, winch, and enough ground clearance to ford a bayou. Trixie climbed into the back, Paula shotgun.

The engine snarled to life, headlights carving tunnels through the murk as they shot out onto the shell road. The island had become a watercolor left in the rain. Palmettos bent double, fronds whipping like surrender flags. The low-water creek had swollen into a brown torrent, but the ATV plowed through, water sheeting off the fenders in silver arcs.

Lightning stitched the sky, freezing the dunes for an instant —sculpted waves of sand, each crest glowing like bone—before plunging everything back into wet darkness. They crested the rise above the lighthouse. Jack's stone cottage glowed amber through the downpour, a single defiant lantern against the night. The RV squatted beside J.P.'s Airstream, its awning flapping like a broken wing, generator chugging steady as a heartbeat.

Inside, the cottage was a pocket of warmth and smoke. The plank table had been dragged close to the hearth; cards lay scattered like fallen leaves. Jimmie Boutet looked up first, his Cajun grin splitting wide beneath a Saints cap gone dark with rain.

"There's my witchy woman," he said, voice warm as Cajun coffee laced with chicory. He pulled Paula into a damp hug, smelling of sawdust and motor oil. "Thought the storm done stole you."

"Takes more than a little weather," Paula said, the lie easy after twenty years.

She felt the weight of her secret like a second skin—never naked in the light, never letting him see the runes she traced on her thighs when the moon was fat. Their marriage worked in the dark, in the hush of breath and the creak of the RV's fold-out bed. Some truths were heavier than love.

Jack dealt another hand, his wiry frame dwarfed by Chief Gordon La Tortue, who sat stone-still at the table's head. The Atakapa's silver hair was unbound tonight, spilling over his shoulders like liquid mercury. His eyes—black and depthless— reflected the fire but gave nothing back.

The dogs had claimed the hearth rug: Oscar the bulldog, Coco the chihuahua, Ol' Joe the shepherd, and Buttercup the calico cat perched on the mantel like a tiny dictator surveying her kingdom. Odette kicked the door shut. The storm's roar dropped to a muffled thrum, as if the cottage itself had drawn a breath and held it.

"Deal us in," she said, peeling off her slicker. "Or are we interrupting a séance?"

Jack's laugh was gravel and rum. "Chief's been telling stories. The kind that makes the hair on your neck stand up and salute."

Chief didn't smile. He laid his cards face down, the movement deliberate. Outside, thunder cracked so close the windows rattled in their frames. The fire flared, casting his shadow huge against the wall—antlers, horns, something coiled and vast.

"My grandfather," he said, voice low, resonant as a drum struck underwater, "used to say the Horned Serpent never left. Just went deep. Waiting."

Paula's gris-gris bag burned against her sternum. She took the empty chair beside Jimmie, her thigh brushing his under the table—steady, familiar, safe. Trixie slid in opposite Chief, eyes bright with the hunger of a scientist who'd just realized folklore might be field notes.

"Tell it," Trixie said. "All of it."

Chief leaned forward. The firelight carved his face into cliffs and hollows, the story already living in the lines around his mouth.

"Long before the French, before the Spanish, before the sugar barons built their palaces of bone and rum, my people fished these waters. The Gulf was generous then—mullet thick as clouds, crabs scuttling in the shallows. But every seventh winter, when the January tides ran black under a new moon, the water would sing. Not fish. Not whales. Something older."

Chief nodded when Paula said, "The Horned Serpent?"

"It sang a note so low it rattled teeth in your skull, made the dogs howl, and the babies cry in their sleep. The elders called it Uktena—the Horned Serpent. Scales black as oil, horns like polished obsidian, eyes that burned with the cold fire of drowned stars. It rose from the trench where the continent ends, drawn by blood spilled carelessly on the water."

"You're scaring me," Trixie said.

"Sorry, baby," Chief said. "Want me to shut up?"

"No way," Trixie said. "Keep going. I'll try not to interupt."

"My grandfather, Tshu, was a man the first time he saw it. 1928. The night the rumrunners sank the Marie Laveau off the reef—cargo of molasses and bodies, payment for a debt the Gulf never forgot. Tshu was fishing when the water bulged. Not a wave. A breathing.

"The serpent broke the surface slowly, like it had all the time in the world. Coils thick as live oaks, barnacles crusting its hide like war medals. It looked at him and scared him so badly, he almost pissed himself right there in the pirogue." Chief crossed his arms. "It was the only time Grandfather ever admitted fear to me."

"What did he do?" Odette asked.

"The serpent opened its mouth, and the sound that came out wasn't a roar. It was a question. "'Why do you feed me your dead?'"

Chief paused again. The fire popped, sending up a shower of sparks that died before they touched the hearth. Jimmie's hand found Paula's under the table, calloused thumb tracing her knuckles. She squeezed back, hard.

"Continue," she said.

"Tshu paddled away, the serpent didn't chase. It just sank, slow as regret, leaving a circle of black water that stank of sulfur and rust. Three days later, the Marie Laveau washed up in pieces on the beach. No crew. Just bones picked clean, arranged in perfect spirals. Sound familiar?"

"Too damn familiar!" Odette said,

"The reef drank the ship, drank the men, and grew fat on their secrets. Every generation since, Uktena stirs when the tides run high, and the moon is dark. It doesn't want fish. It wants choice. Spill blood without meaning, sink your sins in its cradle, and it rises to ask again: Why? Refuse to answer, and it takes what's dearest."

"Are you suggesting the Horned Serpent is back because of Trixie?" Odette asked.

"I don't think so," Chief said. "The bones the reef belched up. Something else is at play here."

"Your story sounds so… mythical," Trixie said. "Are you sure your grandfather wasn't retelling a tribal fable?"

Chief shook his head. "It left something… a scale. Black-green, warm as a fevered brow. Proof it was real. Proof it was listening."

"And you've seen this scale?" Trixie asked.

Chief reached into his pocket and laid something on the table. The scale glinted—same iridescent black as the one Lucky had torn free, edges sharp enough to draw blood if you weren't careful. Trixie's breath caught. Paula's gris-gris bag pulsed like a second heart.

"What is it?" Odette asked.

"A scale from the Horned Serpent," Chief said. "Grandfather died, but he isn't gone. Shows up when the island's about to make mistakes it can't walk back. Tshu's out there now—walking the dunes, barefoot in the rain. I felt him pass the lighthouse not ten minutes ago. Cold as a grave, smelling of wet earth and chicory. He didn't speak. Just looked at me with those burning eyes and pointed toward the reef. Toward whatever we stirred up when we hauled bones out of the dark."

Jimmie's grip tightened on Paula's hand. "What's it want, Chief?"

Chief's smile was slow, sad, and ancient. "A choice. Burn the reef and everything it's guarding—secrets, bodies, the whole damn island if that's what it takes—or let Uktena finish its meal. January tides peak soon. After that, the question isn't what. It's who."

Outside, the wind shifted. The rain eased to a steady hiss, but the temperature dropped sharply enough to frost breath. The dogs whined, pressing closer to the fire. Buttercup's tail lashed once, then stilled. Trixie stared at the scale, her scientist's mind warring with the primal fear crawling up her spine.

Paula felt the gris-gris burn hotter, the knot loosening as if something inside it had decided to speak. Odette poured rum with a steady hand, but her eyes never left the window where the storm had gone eerily quiet. In the hush, they all heard it— a resonant note, felt more than heard, vibrating up through the floorboards and into their bones. The reef, singing its question into the night.

And somewhere out in the dark, Tshu's ghost walked on, barefoot and patient, waiting for an answer that hadn't come in a hundred years. The door hadn't even latched behind Paula and Jimmie before the room exhaled. The fire settled into a steady crackle, the dogs shifted on the rug, and the scale on the table caught one last flicker of orange before the shadows swallowed it whole. Paula had lingered at the threshold, fingers still tangled in Jimmie's, the storm's wet breath sneaking in around them.

"Chief," she said, voice low enough that only the hearth heard, "I need to talk to your grandfather."

Chief didn't blink. "Tomorrow night. La Tortue Mountain. Come alone."

Jimmie's laugh was half-hearted, half-worried. "You ain't serious, cher. Storm'll still be squatting like a drunk on Bourbon Street."

"I'll be there," Paula said, firm as the oak under their feet.

Jimmie tugged her out into the rain, the door banging shut behind them like punctuation. The RV's generator coughed once, then steadied, and the night swallowed their footsteps.

Silence pooled thick as roux. Trixie broke it first, rubbing her arms as if the chill had followed her inside.

"I'm a scientist. Facts. Data. Peer-reviewed journals. I'm not... equipped for this."

Jack snorted from the stove, lifting the lid on a cast-iron pot that released a cloud of heaven—shrimp, andouille, okra, a roux the color of midnight, and enough cayenne to make the devil sweat.

"Get used to it, kid. This is Oyster Island. More spirits here than live people, and half the live ones are half-spirits anyway." He stirred once, slow, the wooden spoon scraping the bottom like a confession. "Supper's ready. Serpent talk don't fill bellies."

The shift was instant. Cards were abandoned mid-hand; bowls appeared like magic. Jack ladled gumbo thick enough to stand a spoon in, passed around cornbread still steaming from the skillet. The dogs sat up, hopeful, tails thumping a lazy rhythm against the floorboards. Odette took her bowl to the hearth, legs stretched toward the fire.

"You put rum in this?"

"Two fingers," Jack said, winking. "Medicinal. Keeps the ghosts from souring the broth."

Trixie ate like a woman who'd forgotten food existed and had suddenly remembered. The gumbo was a revelation—smoky, spicy, with a pepper burn that bloomed into comfort. She chased it with cornbread slathered in mayhaw jelly, the sweet-tart bite cutting through the spice. Rum followed, smooth and warm, loosening the knot in her chest.

Conversation drifted to safer waters: Jack's years feeding hard men on rolling decks, the time a typhoon off Guam turned the galley into a soup cannon, the secret to a roux that never broke. Chief ate in silence, but his shoulders eased a fraction, the scale forgotten beside his elbow. When the bowls were scraped clean and the rum bottle stood half-empty, Odette pushed back her chair.

"We're out of here, gentlemen. Trix—let's roll."

Trixie followed Odette into the storm, the ATV's cab a warm cocoon against the rain. Headlights swept the muddy track, tires hissing through puddles that reflected the lightning like shattered mirrors. Trixie stared out the windshield, voice small.

"How the hell do I explain this to my thesis advisor? 'Chapter Four: The reef sings, the dead walk, and a Horned Serpent wants a sacrifice'?"

Odette laughed, the sound bright against the storm's growl. "Get used to it, Sister. Like Jack said—this ain't Kansas.

Write the data. The island'll handle the rest."

The ATV lurched forward, taillights swallowed by the rain, carrying them north toward Odette's cottage and whatever waited under the January moon.

when the dark. Then she said, "Handle the rest."

The A.V.s lurched forward, taillights swallowed by the rain, carrying them north, toward Odette's cottage and whatever waited under the January moon.

CHAPTER 11

Odette's cottage sat at the heart of the old bootlegger enclave, one of a dozen low-slung houses thrown up in the Roaring Twenties when the Majestic was a speakeasy's fever dream and Oyster Island was the middle of nowhere's nowhere. The Gulf had no mercy back then—no bridges, no ferries, just smugglers and their crews who needed roofs that could laugh at hurricanes.

The houses were Louisiana ranch style, long and low, built to take a beating: cypress floors that glowed like honey under bare feet, walls thick as a debtor's conscience, roofs pitched steep to shrug off rain like a duck's back—no air-conditioning in those days—just louvered shutters and the hope of a breeze. But when Eddie Toledo took over the Majestic and a movie crew rolled in to film some forgettable blockbuster, they'd wired the enclave for electricity, slapped in window units that hummed like lazy bees, and swapped out woodstoves for sleek appliances that gleamed like sin.

Odette's place wore her like a second skin. The covered porch ringed the house, its railings draped with pots of hibiscus and jasmine that fought the storm's tantrum with stubborn blooms. Every bedroom opened straight onto that porch, doors flung wide to let the night in. The living room was a riot of color —books stacked like drunks after Mardi Gras, throw pillows in every shade of a Gulf sunset, a velvet sofa that begged you to sink and stay.

Out back, the enclave's courtyard mimicked the French Quarter: a bubbling fountain at its heart, golden koi gliding through the water like lazy sunbeams, cobblestones slick with rain, and iron lanterns swaying in the wind, their glow soft as a whispered secret.

Odette killed the ATV's engine, and the storm rushed in to fill the silence—rain hammering the tin roof, wind rattling the palms like dice in a gambler's fist. Mudbug and Bruiser bounded out to greet them, shaking off water in joyful arcs, their barks swallowed by the gale.

Trixie followed Odette up the steps, the porch boards creaking a welcome under her borrowed sandals. Inside, the air was cool, scented with lavender and the faint bite of rum that never quite left Odette's skin.

"Heather and Meika used to keep this place loud," Odette said, tossing her keys into a bowl shaped like a pelican. "Heather up and married a lawyer who used to work for Eddie—moved to Chalmette. Meika's still slinging drinks at a casino in Biloxi, dark-haired Cajun siren with a wink that could bankrupt a man. Island gossip said half the bar was in love with her. Truth is, she was playing them for tips. Girl's gayer than a Mardi Gras float, but you let those boys dream—they tip better that way."

Trixie laughed, dropping onto the sofa, the leather jacket sliding off her shoulders. The cushions swallowed her like an old lover, and she let her head fall back, eyes half-closed against the soft lamp glow. For a moment, the storm outside felt distant, muffled by the thick walls that had stood against worse.

"Sounds like my kind of hustle," she said, voice lazy with exhaustion and rum's promise. "What's the word on J.P. and Alex? Spill."

Odette poured two fingers of rum into jelly jars—her good crystal was for company who didn't show up soaked. The liquid caught the light, dark as midnight swamp water. She handed one to Trixie, their fingers brushing, a spark of warmth lingering.

"Love 'em both, cher, but if you're hunting a husband, look elsewhere. J.P. was married to the badge too long—chasing criminals doesn't leave room for anything but ghosts and paperwork. Alex?" She shook her head, curls bouncing like they had a mind of their own. "He's still in Ukraine, fighting shadows in his head. Good men, both. Just not the settling kind."

"J.P. is good-looking enough to be a movie star. How does he keep women off of him?" Trixie asked, swirling her rum, watching the legs crawl down the glass like slow tears.

Odette grinned, a flash of white in the dim room. "He doesn't. Uses them and then dumps them. Leaves 'em with a smile and a story, but nothing more."

"That sucks," Trixie said, though her tone held a note of reluctant admiration, the kind that came from recognizing a fellow survivor in the game of hearts.

"One of these days, he'll meet a woman who'll turn the tables on him. Until then, he's the cock of the walk, and he knows it," Odette said, settling into an armchair across from Trixie, her legs tucked under her like a cat claiming territory.

Trixie sipped her rum, the burn blooming in her chest, chasing away the chill from the ride. "Have you two ever—"

Odette didn't let her finish, waving a hand sharp as a slap. "Never going to happen. He finally gave up trying, and now we have an understanding. Friends, nothing more. Keeps things simple."

"I'd do him," Trixie said, bold as brass, her grin wicked. "To see that great ass of his, if for nothing else."

"Trust me," Odette said, leaning forward, eyes sparkling with shared mischief. "Stay around Oyster Island long enough, and you'll get your chance. He does have a nice ass. Even Meika gave it a ten. Said it was sculpted by the gods themselves—or at least by years of chasing perps through the bayou."

Trixie let the comment drop, but the image lingered, a spark in the cozy haze. She took another sip, then shifted gears.

"Alex is a brooder. I can tell. Those eyes of his— like he's carrying the weight of the world and then some."

"You're right about that. He'd drive a wife crazy with the silence, the staring off into nothing. Comes back to the bar quieter each time, like pieces of him get left behind in the sand."

"He's smart and has a plan. Someday, he's going to be very wealthy. Men are easier to put up with when they're ultra-wealthy."

Trixie's voice held a cynical edge, honed from too many academia mixers where ambition masked emptiness.

"You wouldn't marry someone for money, would you?" Odette asked, tilting her head, studying Trixie like she was a puzzle worth solving.

"Nah!" Trixie said, laughing it off, but there was a flicker in her eyes—something raw, unguarded. "Lots of women do, though. Trade their fire for security. End up dimming themselves to fit someone else's lantern."

"And they end up getting what they deserve," Odette said, her tone softening, almost gentle. "A cage, even if it's gilded."

"Amen to that, sister," Trixie echoed, clinking her jar against the air in mock toast.

Odette disappeared into her bedroom, the floorboards sighing under her steps, and returned with a scrap of silk that barely qualified as a nighty—black, sheer, with lace that teased more than it covered. She dangled it from one finger, eyebrows raised in challenge.

"You're not sleeping in that salt-crusted bikini. Put this on. It'll feel like heaven after the day you've had."

Trixie didn't hesitate. She peeled off the bikini top, then the bottoms, standing unselfconscious in the lamplight, her runner's body lean and sun-kissed, the scrollwork tattoo at the small of her back catching the glow like ancient script come alive. The air kissed her skin, cool and electric, and she felt Odette's gaze—not judging, but appreciating, like one woman acknowledging another's strength.

She slipped into the nighty, the fabric clinging like a secret, whispering against her curves. A shiver ran through her, not from cold, but from the vulnerability of it all—the storm, the island, this stranger who felt like an old friend.

"Damn, girl," Odette said, whistling low, genuine awe in her voice. "That little wisp of nothing highlights that killer body of yours. You could've made a fortune shaking it on Bourbon Street. Hell, you still could."

"Might have to if I don't get this damn dissertation written," Trixie shot back, grinning as she snatched her rum and the bottle, sauntering into Odette's bedroom like she owned the place.

She flopped onto the bed, the mattress yielding with a sigh.

"There are two more bedrooms," Odette said, following with amusement, leaning against the doorframe.

"I'd rather sleep with you," Trixie said, patting the quilt beside her. "Do you mind? Feels safer, somehow. With the storm and all."

"No way," Odette said, but her smile said yes as she kicked off her shoes and joined her.

The bedroom was all open windows and flapping curtains, the storm's breath cool and wild, carrying the scent of wet earth and distant lightning. Lightning strobed, painting the cypress walls in stark white, thunder chasing it like a drunk with a grudge.

They lay side by side on Odette's quilt—patchwork bright as a juke joint—rum jars on the nightstand, the bottle within reach. The rain was a steady roar, a lullaby with teeth, drumming on the roof like impatient fingers. Mudbug and Bruiser had claimed spots at the foot of the bed, their snores a counterpoint to the gale. Trixie reached down to scratch Bruiser's ears, his tail thumping lazily against the floor.

"So," she said, voice soft against the wind's howl, "Meika had the barflies on a string. What else have I missed? Paint me the picture—I've been buried in books too long."

Odette propped herself on an elbow, eyes glinting with mischief, the lamplight carving shadows that danced across her face.

"Oh, cher, the stories could fill a bayou. Jack once cooked for a freighter full of smugglers—swears one of 'em was a pirate with a pet parrot that cussed in three languages. Bird called the captain a 'son of a gumbo pot' in English, French, and what sounded like pirate Spanish. Chief's got a teepee on La Tortue Mountain where he talks to ghosts and brews tea that'll make you see stars—literally. Drink too much, and the spirits start whispering your regrets back at you. And Renata? That Ukrainian vet could stitch a dog's heart and break yours with a look. Saved Bruiser once after he tangled with a gator. Tough as nails, soft as moss underneath."

Trixie sipped her rum, the burn grounding her, warming the hollow places the day had carved out.

"She's a looker, though she has a problem with Alex. I could tell," she said.

"PTSD. She's Ukrainian, and he's Russian."

Odette shook her head when Trixie asked, "What happened between them?"

"Don't know. They don't talk about it, and I'm afraid to ask," she said.

"What about Paula? She and Jimmie seem so different—like oil and water in the same bottle."

"As night and day," Odette said, her voice dropping to a conspiratorial hush. "Paula's my best friend. Not much about her that I don't know—or that she lets me know. She and Jimmie were high school sweethearts, back when the island was even wilder. He's a good provider, steady as the tide, and apparently good in bed—if you believe the whispers. They both like dogs. Other than that, he leads his life, and she leads hers. Separate orbits, same sky."

"Why?" Trixie asked, rolling onto her side to face Odette, the nightie shifting with a silken rustle. "That's not how it's supposed to work, is it? Marriage should be... shared. All of it."

Odette laughed, a rich sound that cut through the thunder. "If I knew, I'd be teaching psychology at some fancy university. Her marriage works for her. Maybe it's the mystery that keeps the spark—or kills it slowly. Who's to say?"

"Jimmie's never even seen Paula naked in the light of day. How does that work? Lights off, covers up—feels like hiding more than modesty."

Odette laughed again, shaking her head. "Obviously, neither one of us has an answer for that question. That's not the only secret she keeps from Jimmie. Not even the most important secret."

Trixie's eyes widened, the rum loosening her curiosity like a knot. "What is?"

"Paula calls herself a traiteur. Healer, folk magic, the old ways."

"She isn't?" Trixie leaned in, the storm's rhythm matching her pulse.

"Hell, girl, Paula's a witch. Full-on. She can cast spells, do magic, communicate with the dead, you name it. Brews potions that cure what doctors can't touch. But she hasn't yet come to grips with her powers. Fights 'em like a gator in a net—scared of what they mean, what they'll take from her."

"Damn! Is that the reason Eddie had her visit the reef? To... I don't know, commune with whatever's down there?"

Odette nodded, her expression turning serious, the mischief fading into something deeper, reverent. "Oyster Island doesn't have a mayor. If it did, Eddie would be it. Everyone on the island listens when he talks. Sees the threads others miss."

"Even you?" Trixie asked, searching Odette's face.

"Especially me," Odette said, admitting a rare vulnerability, cracking her voice. "Eddie saw beyond the fact that I'm pretty and have a great body. My mind is also pretty good—I have a degree from L.S.U., buried under years of pouring drinks and dodging hands. Eddie gave me my first chance to use my mind and not my body. Trusted me with the books at the Majestic, then more. Taught me to see the island's undercurrents, not just ride 'em."

"And the reef? The serpent? How do you live with that humming under everything? It's like the whole place is alive, waiting to swallow you."

Odette's laugh was low, warm, wrapping around Trixie like a quilt. "You don't live with it, sister. You dance with it. Island's got a pulse—salt and sugar, blood and rum. Ancient as the Gulf, hungry as sin. You learn the steps, or it steps on you."

"And Paula?"

"Paula's magic? It's part of the rhythm. The reef calls to her blood, same as it calls to Eddie's visions."

Lightning flashed again, closer, the thunder a gut-punch that rattled the windows and sent the dogs whimpering. The curtains billowed like sails in a ghost ship, and for a moment, the room felt like the belly of a beast caught in a squall.

Trixie's fingers tightened on her jar, her heart syncing with the storm's fury. Beneath it all, she felt it—the reef's distant thrum, a serpent's coil in her veins, pulling her toward truths she wasn't sure she wanted.

"Tomorrow," she said, voice steady despite the tremor, "I'm diving that reef. Data. Facts. Something to anchor this madness before it drags me under."

Odette clinked her jar against Trixie's, the glass singing a fragile note. "Good luck, Dorothy. Storm's got three days left in her, and the Gulf don't give up its secrets easy. But if anyone can wrestle 'em free, it's a stubborn scholar like you."

They drank, the rum a small fire against the night's chill, and talked on—gossip and ghosts, love and loss, the fragile threads binding people to places that could break them. Outside, the koi in the courtyard swam circles around their own reflections, waiting for the moon to remember its name, while the wind whispered warnings through the jasmine vines.

CHAPTER 12

The storm had yet to break, settling instead into a dark sulk. Gray light seeped through the clouds like dirty dishwater, and the wind still battered the palms as if it held a personal grudge. J.P. felt the gloom as he left Alex's bungalow with the taste of yesterday's rum still on his tongue and Trixie's laughter echoing in his ears.

His meeting with the homicide detectives the day before had reignited his old passion for the chase, the mystery, and the mental reward of solving a case and bringing it to a satisfying close. He had missed that feeling, even if he hadn't admitted it to himself. He wasn't planning to visit the St. Bernard Parish sheriff and beg for his old job back, but he was eager to take a boat out to the reef where the police department divers would be searching for clues.

J.P. took the ATV to Jack's place, tires slipping in the puddles deep enough to drown regrets. The little house sat back from the shell road, tin roof rattling like loose teeth. Inside, the air was thick with butter and cinnamon. Jack stood at his galley stove, flipping something that sizzled and popped in a black iron skillet.

"Where's Chief?" he asked, shaking rain off his jacket.

"Up on the mountain," Jack said without turning. "Hell-bent on summoning his granddad's ghost to ask about the Horned Serpent. Paula's with him."

J.P. grunted. "What about Jimmie?"

"Hardware store flooded. Drove back to Chalmette. Left Paula here by herself."

"Sounds like trouble."

"Paula don't need no help for that," Jack said, sliding a stack of pancakes on the plank table in front of J.P. "Hungry?"

"I am now," J.P. said.

Jack poured a cup of coffee and set it in front of J.P. as he spread butter and cane syrup on the steaming stack of pancakes. J.P. added a generous splash of rum to his coffee from the flask he always carried.

"Renata dropped by earlier. Said you and Alex had trouble last night," Jack said.

"Big trouble. Something visited his house while we were drinking at the Majestic last night."

"Like what?"

J.P. showed him the scale and said, "Maybe the Chief's Horned Serpent."

Jack turned the scale in his hand. "Chief has one just like it."

"Let me guess," J.P. said. "Chief's Horned Serpent."

"You got it," Jack said.

"Whatever it was, it gashed Lucky pretty bad. Renata sewed him up. He's recuperating at Alex's."

"I'm sure you didn't just come for breakfast. What brings you out on a stormy day like this?" Jack asked.

"Police divers hit the reef tomorrow. I wanted you to run me out in the Argo early—get eyes on it before they muddy the water."

Jack glanced over his shoulder, one eyebrow cocked. "Not in this blow, podna. Gulf's chewing boats like gum. You'd be chum."

"Dammit!" J.P. said.

"Stop worrying about it," Jack said. "No one's diving in this weather. It'll be at least two days before the police get a look at the reef."

J.P. swore under his breath. "Guess I'll work the dogs."

"Jimmie beat you to it. Kennels are good for a while. Eat your pancakes, drink some more rum, and chill."

"Chilling's not my strong suit."

"Sounds like a personal problem to me," Jack said.

Jack laughed when J.P. said, "And I'm getting no sympathy

from you."

"Pancakes and hot coffee, I have. Sympathy's in short supply around here."

Feeling like a spare part, J.P. finished his coffee and drove to the Majestic. The parking lot was a lake, his reserved spot sitting under several inches of water. He killed the engine and sat there a minute, watching raindrops streaking the windshield, trying to out-stare the storm. The lot was empty except for a flashy Cadillac Aviator with Mississippi tags. J.P. whistled low, wondering what someone had to pay for that pricey piece of machinery."

Inside the bar, the jukebox was off, the lights low. Odette was behind the counter, polishing a glass that didn't need it as she conversed with a woman sitting at the bar alone. She smiled and nodded when she saw J.P. and poured him two fingers of rum without asking. He took the stool beside the unknown woman, sipped the rum, and then let it sit on his tongue.

"Hi, beautiful. That your red Aviator?" he said.

"I'm the only one here. Whose else would it be?" she said.

"Good-looking vehicle," J.P. said, wondering what the woman did for a living that she could afford such an expensive car.

He looked at her for the first time when she said, "She's my baby."

Even seated, J.P. could tell she was tall, with legs that started at the floor and didn't quit, her perfectly tanned skin glowing against a silk blouse the color of storm clouds that showed more than a glimpse of her ample cleavage, and mahogany curls fighting a silver clasp and mostly winning. He guessed her age to be late thirties or early forties.

J.P. turned on the charm and said, "What's a gorgeous woman like you doing out on a day like today?"

She smiled, gave Odette a wink, and said, "Waiting for you to show."

"You know who I am?"

"John Pierre Saucier," she said, voice low, vowels stretched like taffy over broken glass. "Heard you pull bones out of the Gulf like it's a damn Cracker Jack box."

Odette smiled when J.P. frowned at her. "You know who I am. Who are you?"

"Evangeline LeBlanc," she said, offering a hand. "Most folks call me Vangie. Military police for a while. Now I chase paper trails and cheating husbands for beer money."

"Takes more than beer money to pay for that pussy wagon of yours in the parking lot, and I doubt you came all the way from Biloxi chasing a cheating husband. Why are you here, and how do you know who I am?"

"We have a mutual friend," Vangie said.

"Oh, and who would that be?"

"Meika's the bartender at the Golden Gulf, a Biloxi waterfront casino."

"And how did my name come up in the conversation?" J.P. asked.

"The bones you found. Meika and I were discussing them."

"That information isn't public yet. How did you know?"

"My client knows lots of things," she said.

"Yeah? Who's your client?"

Vangie didn't answer, pushing her empty coffee cup toward Odette for a refill. Odette glanced at J.P. as she poured hot coffee from the carafe.

"Coffee's for closers," he said. "You drink rum?"

"Only if it's older than my regrets."

She was sitting close enough to him that he caught the scent of jasmine, gunpowder, and the faint bite of bourbon on her breath. Her eyes were the color of the Gulf right before it turns mean—gray-green, unreadable. Odette set a fresh glass on the bar and filled it with Alex's rum. Vangie toasted the air, knocked back half in one go, and didn't flinch.

"Damn good!" she said. "Pleased to meet you, J.P."

Odette leaned in. "You're a long way from Howard Avenue."

"Evil doesn't respect zip codes, sugar." Vangie tapped ash from her Camel into a coaster shaped like a shrimp boat.

Odette grinned and said, "That's a fact. Say hi to Meika for me the next time you see her. She was my roomie here on the island."

"Was she now?" Vangie said, glancing up from her cigarette to give Odette an assessing glance.

"Yes, ma'am," Odette said.

Vangie grinned but didn't comment on the title Odette had bestowed on her. "Word is this island has more secrets than a confessional. Figured the man pulling bones out of the water might know a few."

J.P. studied her. The holster under the silk was a custom shoulder rig—meant for business but not obvious about it. The way she sat, with her weight on the left hip, suggested there was probably a .38 on her ankle, too. She wasn't there to flirt; she was there to hunt. The flirting was just lagniappe.

"The reef's locked down till this blow passes. You want in, you'll need to share with me who your client is," J.P. said.

"That could be an issue," Vangie said.

Odette wasn't missing much of the conversation, and it was apparent to J.P. that her presence was making Vangie uncomfortable.

"I'm looking for new wheels," he said. "Maybe you can give me a test drive in that pussy wagon of yours."

Vangie smiled and laid a hundred-dollar bill on the bar. When Odette started to make change, she held up a palm and said, "Keep it."

J.P. followed her out the door and to the covered parking lot. When she nodded to the passenger seat, he climbed into the Aviator beside her.

The storm hadn't let up, rain blowing sideways into the covered parking lot. The Aviator smelled of smoke and fresh purchase. J.P. didn't flinch when Vangie lit another Camel, took a deep drag, and then blew the smoke in his direction.

She smiled when he said, "Those cancer sticks will kill you."

"If a bullet doesn't catch me first," she said. "I have a client with deep pockets and deeper paranoia. They pay for silence and results," she said.

J.P. removed the silver flask from his shirt pocket, unscrewed the top, took a drink, and then handed it to Vangie. She smiled, drank from the flask, and handed it back to him.

She leaned closer, voice dropping to a conspiratorial rasp. "Good rum, but I prefer bourbon."

"I like bourbon," he said.

Vangie produced her own silver flask, took a drink, and handed it to J.P.

She smiled when he said, "Damn, girl! You don't scrimp on cars or whiskey."

"Or the people I ask to help me," she said. "We drink, we talk, maybe do some business. You interested?"

"I'm retired from the force. I live here on the island and train dogs for a living now."

"Some things you don't forget," she said.

"Maybe if you tell me who I'm working for and what the job entails," J.P. said.

Vangie took a last pull from her Camel, stubbed it out, and then drank more bourbon.

"Casinos are big business in Biloxi," she said. "They generate lots of money, and someone's always looking to dip their hand into the till."

"I can imagine," J.P. said.

"The Golden Gulf is equipped with all the latest high-tech security measures like high-definition cameras with facial recognition, AI-powered video analytics, license plate recognition, and biometric security to prevent theft. Still, they don't go it alone. They lean heavily on local, county, and state police, as well as the Mississippi Gaming Commission and the DOJ."

"Lots of fingers in the pie," J.P. said.

"That isn't all," Vangie said. "The casinos work together as a group to prevent theft. That's who I work for."

"What's the name of this group?" J.P. asked.

Vangie lit another Camel, blew a plume of smoke, and said, "Doesn't have a name."

"Who keeps track of what's going on?" J.P. asked.

"Harlan Roubideaux. Runs the operation from a back office in the Golden Gulf."

Vangie smiled when J.P. said, "General Harlan Roubideaux, Retired?"

"You've heard of him?"

"My nephew spent most of his duty in Biloxi at Keesler AFB," J.P. said. "It was General Roubideaux's last command."

"I'm impressed," Vangie said. "Kessler is primarily known as a high-technology training hub for the U.S. Air Force, with its 81st Training Wing specializing in electronics, cyber warfare, and weather forecasting."

"My nephew, Mark, told me the old man has a reputation," J.P. said.

"Yeah? Like what?"

"That he was a ball buster and no one crossed him without consequences," J.P. said.

J.P. laughed when Vangie asked, "Your nephew still in Biloxi?"

"You think I would have told you what he said about the general if he still was?"

"Smart man," Vangie said. "Kessler's so important to the Biloxi economy, Roubideaux's probably the only person in the world that everyone in the casino group trusts, and his knowledge of high-tech surveillance techniques has served him well."

"You trust him?"

"I don't trust anybody. "It's the reason I'm here now talking to you," Vangie said.

"What is it you need me to do?" J.P. asked. "Be your Oyster Island figurehead, or is there something else you expect of me?"

"The case I'm working on is complicated. I like working alone, but Meika convinced me I could use your help. That's good enough for me. You in or out?" Vangie said.

"In," J.P. said. "When do I start?"

Vangie smiled and lit another Camel. "The moment you said, 'Hi, beautiful.'"

CHAPTER 13

The storm continued to punish the island, rain drumming the Aviator's roof like a handful of gravel thrown against a tin sheet. After Vangie let him out at the edge of the covered parking, J.P. watched her red taillights bleed into the gray blur of the gale. The wind whipped his coat, stinging his face with salt spray. With the taste of her bourbon still on his lips —rich, oaky, and expensive—he ducked his head and returned to the Majestic. The heavy door shut out the howl of the wind, replacing it with the faint scent of spilled whiskey, lemon polish, and old wood. The bar was dim, lit by the amber glow of the back bar lights.

Odette stood behind the counter, arms crossed, watching the door like a cat watching a mouse hole. And there, atop the same stool Vangie had warmed earlier, was Eddie.

Eddie looked like money that didn't need to shout to be heard: a charcoal linen shirt open at the throat, sleeves rolled just enough to show a Rolex that cost more than J.P.'s truck, and linen trousers pressed sharp enough to draw blood. His dark hair, dusted with silver at the temples, was slicked back. He looked like he'd walked through the hurricane and told it to sit down and behave.

A single rocks glass sat in front of him—two fingers of Monkey Shoulder scotch, barely touched. He didn't turn when the door banged shut behind J.P., just spoke to the reflection in the mirror behind the bottles.

"John Pierre Saucier," he said, his voice smooth as the scotch he wasn't drinking. "Heard you were having a tête-à-tête in my parking lot."

Odette's eyes flicked to J.P.—a silent warning or perhaps an apology—and she reached for a clean glass without being asked.

J.P. slid onto the stool next to Eddie. "You have cameras in the parking lot now?"

"In this business, J.P., the question isn't if I have cameras," Eddie said, finally turning to face him. "It's whether I bother to turn the recording off."

"You might get some interesting videos that way."

"That's a fact," Eddie said, a cold smile playing on his lips. "Or maybe you could just save me the playback time and tell us."

"Miss LeBlanc wouldn't like it if I shared our conversation."

"Hell, J.P., you know you will," Eddie said.

It was J.P.'s turn to laugh. "You know me too well. The very reason why there ain't no Cajun spies in the CIA. We talk too much after two drinks." He accepted the glass from Odette. "But since you're asking, I have a few questions for you first."

"What makes you think I have the answers?"

"Because you were a D.A. with the DOJ in New Orleans before you wound up with the Majestic. You know where the bodies are buried, and more importantly, who dug the holes. I'm guessing there's not much you don't know about the mechanics of Biloxi gaming."

Eddie picked up his glass, swirling the amber liquid. "Privileged information."

"I'm not asking for names of your old indictments," J.P. said, leaning in. "I need to understand the ecosystem."

"Does this relate to Vangie LeBlanc?" Eddie asked.

J.P. glanced at Odette. She was polishing a glass, but her ears were practically twitching. "Hell, J.P.," she said. "I'm Cajun, too. The only thing I don't leak is a good gumbo recipe."

"There you go, Eddie," J.P. said. "We don't keep secrets on Oyster Island. Especially not when the wind is howling like a banshee."

Eddie took a slow sip. "Ask a specific question. I'll decide if the answer costs you."

"We all know organized crime covets the casinos," J.P. started.

"Hell, the Majestic was once a bootlegger's paradise. But I'm talking about the modern era. The corporate era."

"It's not about bootlegging anymore, J.P.," Eddie said, his tone shifting into lecture mode. "It's about volume. Casinos are financial wash cycles. They have no tangible product—just chips and hope. That makes them the perfect vehicle for cleaning dirty cash. You walk in with ten grand in drug money, buy chips, play a few hands of baccarat, lose a little, and cash out. Now you have a check from a legitimate casino. Clean money."

"Sounds simple."

"It's anything but. It's a constant high-tech war. The House watches the players, the Gaming Commission watches the House, and the Feds watch everybody."

"So, if someone was running a wash operation," J.P. said carefully, "they'd need help from the inside."

"High-level help," Eddie said. "Pit bosses can cheat a game, but to wash serious money? You need someone in the cage, someone in accounting, and probably someone looking the other way in security."

"What about cooperation? Between the casinos?"

Eddie snorted. "They hate each other, but they talk. If a card counter hits the Beau Rivage at noon, his picture is on the security screens at the Golden Gulf by twelve-fifteen. It's a shared immune system. If one catches a cold, they all get sick. They share intel on cheats, thieves, and... federal inquiries."

J.P. swirled his drink. "So if the Feds were looking into a wash operation at the Golden Gulf, the other casinos would know?"

"Within the hour," Eddie said. "And if the DOJ is sniffing around, the corruption isn't just in the casino. It's usually leaked by local law enforcement or the Commission itself. Too much money involved for people to keep their mouths shut."

"A problem," J.P. said.

"A problem with no easy answer," Eddie said. "Regulating this industry is like trying to hold water in your hands. Squeeze too tight, you lose the revenue. Too loose, and the sharks swim in."

"Why not just ban them?" Odette chimed in, pouring herself a shot of water.

"Because Biloxi would just be another humid beach town with bad traffic without them," J.P. said. "Jobs, taxes, infrastructure."

"Ask Meika if she wants to ban casinos," Eddie added. "The revenue built half the schools in Mississippi."

J.P. looked at Eddie dead-on. "What if the leak wasn't just information? What if an agent went dark inside the Golden Gulf and stopped reporting?"

Eddie's eyes narrowed. The playfulness vanished. "Then you're not talking about money laundering anymore. You're talking about murder."

"The skeleton on Trixie's reef," J.P. said softly. "He was undercover for General Roubideux. Tracking a wash through the Golden Gulf for six months. Someone made him, took him out, and fed him to the fishes. Vangie wants the who, the why, and the son of a bitch who signed the check."

"She works for the General?" Eddie asked.

"She didn't say," J.P. said, shaking his head.

Eddie went still. "And Vangie came to you."

"Because she thinks the leak came from inside the investigation. She can't trust the locals, and she can't trust the DOJ field office. She needs someone outside the ecosystem. Someone who doesn't owe anybody anything."

"Someone expendable," Eddie noted dryly.

"Someone capable," J.P. said, though he felt the weight of Eddie's words.

"One thing is for sure," Eddie said, raising his glass in a grim toast. "With a gale like this, nobody is going out into the Gulf to look for evidence. Whoever killed that agent thinks the storm will wash away the sins. They might be right."

"Maybe," J.P. said. "Or perhaps the storm just shakes things loose."

"Not to change the subject, but maybe we should advertise Oyster Island as a spring break destination. Our hotel bookings are at an all-time low," Odette said.

J.P. shook his head and said, "It takes a good-sized police force to deal with hundreds of hormone and alcohol-fueled teens. We don't even have a police force."

"Spring break isn't an option, though it wouldn't hurt to do some advertising to increase our occupancy rate," Eddie said.

Before Eddie could respond, the heavy oak door creaked open, fighting the wind pressure. A figure slipped inside, shaking off a wet umbrella.

"I can help with that," a voice said. "I'm pretty good at shaking things up. Or at least, using social media to do it."

It was Trixie. The tension in the room snapped like a rubber band. She looked striking in white shorts and an oversized purple-and-gold LSU sweatshirt, her hair damp and curling around her face. She seemed oblivious to the dark turn the conversation had taken.

Eddie blinked, shaking off the mood. He shifted gears instantly, the gracious host once more. "We could use some help," he said, forcing a smile. "We were just discussing... advertising. When can you start?"

"Right now, if you show me a computer I can use," Trixie said, hopping onto a stool.

"Basil's old office is empty," Eddie said.

"Basil?"

"Basil Doles. Young lawyer. Sharp kid. Worked for me until someone made him a better offer. He took it, along with his pregnant wife, Heather. His office has everything you'll need."

"Maybe you'd consider letting me use it to work on my dissertation, too?" Trixie asked.

"You bet. Consider yourself on the payroll. Office included."

"You don't have to pay me," Trixie said, looking earnest. "I already appreciate everything you've done for me. The room, the —"

"Nonsense," Eddie cut her off. "Nobody works for free on Oyster Island. Odette, show her the office."

"Yes, sir," Odette said. She shot J.P. a look that said we aren't done talking, then led Trixie toward the back hallway.

When they were gone, the silence rushed back in, heavier than before.

"Back to the casinos," J.P. said quietly.

"You're playing a dangerous game, J.P.," Eddie said, his voice low. "If General Roubideux is the liaison, he's the best man for the job. But if his man ended up as fish food, that means the corruption has teeth. Sharp ones."

"Exactly what Vangie said."

"What specifically is she looking for?"

"The tag on the skeleton was a casino marker. But the General thinks the money isn't just drug cash. He thinks someone is skimming the skimming. Stealing from the thieves. A double-cross like that gets people killed fast."

"And you're going to walk into the middle of it?"

"Money's right," J.P. said.

"Enough to pay for your funeral?" Eddie asked.

J.P. didn't answer; instead, he held up his flask. "Can you fill this for me? It's getting low."

Odette returned from the hallway just in time to hear the request. She didn't ask; she just grabbed the flask and the bottle of rum. After topping him off, she walked to the back of the room and slapped the side of the vintage Wurlitzer jukebox.

It whirred to life, mechanics clicking, before belting out Dr. John's "Right Place, Wrong Time." The funky, syncopated rhythm filled the room, a strange counterpoint to the thunder rocking the Majestic's timbers.

When Odette returned to the bar, Trixie was right behind her, phone in hand.

"Your office complex is impressive," she said, the perfect antidote to the gloom. "Internet's strong. I've already set up pages for the Majestic on three platforms. Do you have any promotional photos? The current online presence is... non-existent."

"Never knew I needed any," Eddie said. "I prefer word of mouth."

"In the digital age, silence is death," Trixie said dramatically. "As soon as the weather breaks, I'll take some pics with my cell phone. Until then, I can take some interior shots. The woodwork in here is amazing."

"I'll help," Odette said, grabbing a bar rag. "Let's get started. God knows this place needs some activity besides these two brooding over their drinks."

J.P. took a pull from his flask, the metal cool against his lips. He watched Trixie and Odette move away, snapping photos of the vintage bar.

"Right place, wrong time," J.P. muttered to the music.

"Let's hope so," Eddie said, watching the storm batter the windows. "Because if you're in the right place at the right time on this case, you might end up sharing a reef with that agent."

Eddie's words rang in J.P.'s ears as he left the Majestic and drove up the slight rise toward the lighthouse and his Airstream trailer. With the gale blowing full force, it was a white-knuckle crawl. J.P.'s ATV fought the wind for every inch of sand, the headlights reflecting off a wall of horizontal rain that made the world end five feet past the bumper.

He parked near Jack's stone cottage, the heavy masonry looking like the only thing on Oyster Island capable of winning an argument with this weather. The lighthouse beam above swung in a rhythmic strobe, slicing through the gloom like a prison searchlight.

J.P. grabbed his gear and made a run for it. His home was a thirty-foot Airstream Excella, a silver bullet he'd parked fifty yards from the lighthouse for the privacy and the view. Right now, the view was nonexistent, and the privacy felt like exposure.

He reached the metal steps, rain plastering his shirt to his back, and reached for the door handle.

He stopped.

J.P. was a former deputy from St. Bernard Parish, a detective where trouble usually announced itself with a shout or a shotgun blast—but years on the job had installed a distinct alarm system in his gut.

The door was latched, but the small strip of duct tape he'd placed near the bottom of the jamb—a trick an old narcotic officer had taught him to check for draft leaks—was peeled back.

Someone had opened the door. And recently. The adhesive was still tacky, not yet slick from the humidity.

J.P. didn't unlock the door. Instead, he reached under his rain slicker to the small of his back. His hand found the familiar grip of his Sig Sauer P226. He thumbed the safety, the click lost in the roar of the wind.

He took a breath, tasting salt and ozone, and yanked the door open, dropping low into a crouch as he swept the interior with the barrel of the gun.

"Sheriff's Department!" he barked, instinct overriding his current employment status.

The Airstream was dark, lit only by the intermittent sweep of the lighthouse beam through the rain-streaked windows. The interior sounded like the inside of a kettle drum, the rain hammering against the aluminum skin with deafening force.

Empty.

He moved forward, clearing the small space with practiced efficiency. Kitchenette: clear. Tiny bathroom: clear. Rear bedroom: clear.

He holstered the Sig but didn't snap the retention strap. The trailer was empty of people, but it was full of presence. The air, usually smelling of coffee and sea salt, held a foreign contaminant. It was faint, but distinct—the smell of stale cigar smoke and musk-heavy cologne.

J.P. hit the light switch. The overhead LEDs flickered to life, casting harsh shadows.

The place hadn't been tossed. The drawers were closed. His small TV was still bolted to the wall. It was a professional entry— in and out, leaving everything exactly as it was.

Almost everything.

J.P. walked to the small dinette table where he usually drank his morning coffee. He had left the file folder Vangie gave him in his truck, but his personal notebook, a beaten-up Moleskine he used for jotting down thoughts, was sitting on the table.

Resting squarely in the center of the black cover was a round object.

A poker chip.

J.P. picked it up. It had the heft of quality clay. It was gold and black, the edges crisp. In the center, the logo of a stylized sun setting over water was stamped in gold foil: The Golden Gulf Casino.

It wasn't a souvenir chip. The denomination printed on the face was $5,000.

J.P. turned it over in his fingers. It was a bribe, a warning, or a down payment on a funeral.

Eddie was right, he thought, a cold knot tightening in his stomach—the ecosystem leaks.

Vangie had hired him less than two hours ago. In that short time, someone had identified him, found his trailer, braved a tropical storm, and picked a lock to leave a piece of plastic on his table. A piece of plastic worth five grand, no less. They wanted either to buy him off or to make him realize that he wasn't the hunter; he was the prey.

J.P. peered out the window, into the black chaos of the storm. If someone were watching, they were doing it from hell's own weather. He returned to the table and poured two fingers of rum from his flask into a mug, his hand steady despite the adrenaline dumping into his system. He sat down, placed the Sig on the table next to the chip, and opened his notebook. On the first blank page, right beneath where the chip had sat, someone had written in block letters with a heavy black marker:

HOUSE ODDS.

J.P. stared at the words. In a casino, the House odds meant the player would eventually lose. It was a mathematical certainty.

The sudden trill of his cell phone made him jump. The sound was jarring against the relentless drumming of the rain.

He looked at the screen—unknown caller.

He let it ring twice, three times, debating whether to answer.

Finally, he swiped the screen and brought it to his ear.

"Saucier," he said, his voice an unrecognizable whisper.

Static crackled on the line, heavy with storm interference. For a moment, he thought the call had dropped. Then, a voice cut through the white noise—male, deep, and distorted, likely by a digital masker.

"Mr. Saucier," the voice said. "You found the amenities."

"Five grand," J.P. said, eyeing the chip. "That's a generous tip for housekeeping."

"Consider it a severance package," the voice said. "Before you've even started the job. Take the chip to the cashier at Golden Gulf and cash it out. Buy yourself a nice vacation. Go somewhere dry."

"And if I don't like vacations?"

"Then you should know that the forecast for Oyster Island has changed," the voice said. The menace was calm, almost bored. "The water is rising, J.P. Don't get swept away."

The line went dead.

J.P. lowered the phone. He looked at the chip, then at the gun.

He picked up the $5,000 chip and flipped it over his knuckles, a trick he'd learned from a card shark in a parish holding cell years ago.

"House odds," J.P. whispered to the empty trailer.

He reached for the Sig and checked the magazine. Full.

"I'll take the bet," he said out loud.

CHAPTER 14

The storm had come back meaner, as if it had regrouped offshore and decided its first punch wasn't enough. Rain fell in sheets so heavy they looked solid, hammering the Airstream until the aluminum sang in a high key. J.P. stood in the open doorway, slicker bleeding water onto the mat, the five-grand chip a cold coin against his heart.

After killing the interior lights, he let the lighthouse beam sweep through the trailer in slow blades before stepping outside and letting the gale slam the door behind him. Wind hit him like a shove, and he leaned into it, boots skidding on soaked sand, and started a slow circle around the trailer.

Lightning strobed—three quick photographs: the Airstream gleaming like a gutted fish, the lighthouse knifing the sky, the dunes beyond it rearing like breaking waves frozen mid-crash —no tire tracks. No footprints. The storm had scrubbed the island clean. He widened the circle anyway, face stinging from rain that felt like birdshot. Another flash, longer this time, and he saw them: one set of prints arrowing away from the trailer toward the little plank bridge that crossed to the mainland. Deep at the toe, shallow at the heel—someone running. By the time he reached the bridge, the prints were already drowning, edges collapsing.

J.P. dropped to a knee at the railing, flashlight carving a tunnel through the dark. Below, the water raged, whitecaps exploding every time the sky cracked open. No marks on the planks themselves; rain and wind had sanded them clean. On the far side, the sandy track to the mainland was flooded. If a truck had crossed, the storm had erased its tracks.

He swept the light along the railing, slow, methodical. Nothing. No torn cloth, no blood, no— There. Wedged tight between two planks where the railing met the decking, something pale caught the beam and held it. He worked it free with cold fingers. A slice of whelk shell, no bigger than a silver dollar, edges worn soft by centuries of tide or neck-cord. One side was polished to a dull glow; the other carried a carving so deep the flashlight beam seemed to fall into it—a mystical eye. It was as if the etching were staring at him. The shell was old. Older than the bridge. Older than the lighthouse. Maybe so old that the hand that carved it had never seen iron. He slipped it into the same pocket as the poker chip. The shell was warm— impossibly warm—against the cold plastic.

J.P. crossed the short bridge to the mainland and quickly picked up the prints again. Then they ended, as if the person wearing the gorget had been jerked straight up into the storm —or stepped sideways out of the world entirely. When the wind tried to take his hat, he clamped a hand on the brim and turned back toward the trailer, wishing Lucky were there with him.

If there were a trail, the big dog would have found it. Without him, there was no point chasing ghosts in this deluge. Whoever had left the calling card was long gone, laughing at him. J.P. stood there a moment longer, rain pouring off the brim of his Stetson, staring across the creek at the black line of the mainland road.

Somewhere out there, the house odds were stacking higher. He spat rainwater and started walking—not back to the Airstream, but down the shell path toward Jack's cottage. The smell hit him before he reached the porch: butter, cayenne, dark roux, and rum. Jack's gumbo, the real kind—the kind that took all day and most of a bottle. Jack opened the door before J.P. could knock, silhouetted against the orange glow of the hearth, Oscar the bulldog snoring like a broken chainsaw at his feet.

"Come in this house," he growled over the wind. "It's not a fit night out for mice or men."

J.P. stepped inside, water streaming from his slicker onto the flagstones. The warmth hit him like a living thing—woodsmoke, spices, the faint wet-dog odor of Oscar dreaming whatever bulldogs dream about.

"Something smells wonderful," he said, peeling off the slicker and hanging it on the peg by the door.

Jack stirred the pot with a wooden spoon the size of a canoe paddle. "Oyster and andouille gumbo. Haven't cooked this in three years. Figured the island owed us one decent meal before it tries to kill us all."

"Damn, man!" J.P. said. "You da one."

Jack ladled a bowl so dark it looked black in the firelight, slid it across the table with a chunk of cornbread the size of a fist. J.P. took the bowl with both hands as if it were holy. Jack poured two inches of rum into coffee mugs, no ice.

"Chief and Paula are still up on La Tortue Mountain getting soaked and talking to ghosts. Probably half-drowned by now." He chuckled, low and rough. "Sit. Eat. Then tell me why you look like you just swallowed a wasp."

J.P. sat. The first spoonful of gumbo detonated in his mouth —heat, smoke, the briny pop of oysters, the deep umami of roux that had been babied for hours. He closed his eyes for a second and just let it sit there, burning everything else away.

"You haven't told me why you ventured out on a stormy night like this," Jack said.

J.P. laid the poker chip on the table. "Someone visited my trailer while I was at the Majestic. Left me this."

Jack's eyes narrowed. He picked it up and turned it under the lamp.

"Golden Gulf," Jack said. "Biloxi?"

J.P. nodded. "Five grand. Left on my table."

"How'd they get in?" Jack asked.

"The door I taped to check for entry was peeled. Somebody picked the lock in this shitstorm just to leave me a calling card."

J.P. placed the gorget on the table, and Jack touched it, as if it might bite.

"Damn, J.P.," he said. "Sure you didn't steal that from a

museum?"

"I know," J.P. said. "It has to be old as hell and looks like some Indian talisman. Only thing the rain didn't wash away."

"Chief will know what it is," Jack said. "What else?"

"Footprints. They were all but washed away, though I managed to track them to the other side of the bridge until they disappeared."

"Washed away?" Jack said.

J.P. took a sip of the rum and shook his head. "Not exactly."

"What's that supposed to mean?" Jack asked.

"The prints didn't disappear. They changed," J.P. said.

"Changed? Into what?"

"Something that wasn't human; wolf prints, maybe."

Lightning flashed across the window, and thunder shaking the house quickly followed. "You mean like a rougarou?"

J.P. shook his head. "More like a real wolf. The prints disappeared into the brush on the side of the road. If I'd had Lucky with me, I would have tried to track it. With the rain, the wind, thick brush, and the darkness, I decided against it."

"Any ideas why someone would take the trouble to break into your trailer and leave you a poker chip?"

"A P.I. from Biloxi named Vangie LeBlanc hired me four hours ago," J.P. said. "Four hours. That's how fast word travels when the money's big enough."

Jack exhaled through his teeth. "You got somebody's attention real quick."

He told Jack the rest—Vangie, the General, the undercover agent now reduced to bones on a reef. Jack listened without interrupting, stirring the gumbo pot like it was the only thing keeping him calm.

When J.P. finished, Jack said, "Somebody doesn't want you to start digging."

"I know."

Jack pushed the rum bottle across the table. "First thing we need to do is show that piece of shell with the eye to Chief."

J.P. poured another two fingers, watched the liquid catch the firelight. "Then what?" he said.

"Hell, man, I don't know," Jack said. "Why did you take the job from the lady P.I., anyway? I thought you had that part of your life out of your system."

"I thought I did, but the kind of money Vangie LeBlanc is throwing around has made me think twice. One P.I. job won't kill me."

Jack chuckled. "At least let's hope not."

J.P. arranged the chip and the gorget on the table in front of him, as if his stares would somehow give him the answers to what they meant.

"Storm's got another day in her," he said. "After we see what else we can find on the reef, I'm going to Biloxi. Somebody there knows my name now. Time they learned I bite back."

Jack raised his glass. "To biting back."

They drank. Outside, the wind screamed around the cottage like it had heard them and didn't like the odds. The rain had settled into a drumming roar as Odette's headlight cut across the outside of Jack's little house. She killed the ATV's engine, and she and Trixie climbed the steps like two drowned cats, dripping on the planks. Jack looked up from the stove, wooden spoon in hand, and grinned.

"Thought you ladies were pulling a full house tonight at the Majestic," he said.

Trixie peeled off her jacket and hung it over the rail. "Full house of nobody."

Odette shook out her blond hair, sending droplets flying. "Smells like you've been busy, though. That gumbo?"

"Oysters fresh this morning and andouille I've been saving for a night exactly like this," Jack said. "Y'all sit. Bowls coming up."

J.P. nudged the chip toward Odette and Trixie. "Someone left this for me in the Airstream," he said.

Odette rolled the chip in her hand and said, "Is this from the casino Vangie was talking about?"

J.P. nodded. "Where the big wash took place."

"What does it mean?" Odette asked.

"A warning," J.P. said. "Someone doesn't want me on the case."

"Never seen anything like this," Odette said, rolling the gorget in her hand.

Jack, J.P., and Odette's attention turned to Trixie when she said, "I have."

"Well, don't keep us in suspense," Jack said.

"It's a gorget," Trixie said. "Crafted from a whelk shell. The symbol carved on it is the all-knowing eye. This piece is probably a thousand years old and likely came from the Poverty Point World Heritage Site right here in Louisiana."

"How do you know so much about it?" J.P. asked.

"I'm working on my PhD in Oceanography and Coastal Sciences. I've taken courses in archaeology and anthropology, among other sciences."

"Never heard of Poverty Point," Jack said.

"You kidding?" Trixie said. "It's a national historic landmark located right here in Louisiana. It's one of the most important archaeological sites in the world."

Trixie frowned and shook her head when Jack said, "Couldn't prove it by me."

They ate in comfortable silence, the storm battering the shutters, the gumbo pot gurgling on the stove. Outside, palms thrashed like they were trying to uproot themselves and leave town. Odette pushed her bowl aside.

"We're heading out," she said.

Trixie was already pulling her jacket back on.

"You boys stay dry. Call when it's time to dive."

Jack and J.P. watched as the door opened, rain needling sideways. Odette fired up the ATV. The headlights carved a tunnel through the dark; then they were gone, taillights shrinking to a red spark swallowed by the storm. Fifteen minutes of muddy tracks and flooded dips later, Odette nosed the ATV under the covered parking at the back of her house. The place sat on a low rise above the rest of the little settlement—twelve houses, maybe fifteen, all dark. Not a single light showed anywhere. Trixie climbed out and stared.

"Whole grid's out," Odette said.

She cut the engine, the sudden quiet feeling heavier than the rain had. She reached under the seat, pulled out a small flashlight, and clicked it on. The beam slid across the carport, across the door, which stood two inches ajar. They stepped out of the rain and into the waiting dark of the house.

The rain poured down in sheets, pounding the tin roof of Odette's small bungalow as if it had a vendetta. Trixie's boots squished on the porch as she followed Odette inside, both of them wet and cursing the storm that had chased them all the way back from the Majestic. The door slammed shut behind them with a wet slap, and darkness swallowed them whole.

"Power's out," Odette said, already moving by memory.

She scraped a match against the striker; sulfur flared, then the first candle caught. A second later, another. The weak glow pushed the shadows back just far enough to remind you they were still there, waiting. The dogs should have mobbed them by now. Two wet, stupidly happy mutts, hurling themselves at Odette's knees, the second the door cracked open. But the house was silent except for the rain. Odette froze, candle trembling in her hand.

"What are you looking for?" Trixie asked.

"My boys, Bruiser and Mudbug."

Trixie's pulse kicked up a notch. She watched Odette set the candles on the coffee table and head for the kitchen, bare feet slapping cold tile. The doggie door in the pantry was blocked from the outside. A plastic storage bin, a big sixty-gallon one that Odette used for feed, had been dragged across the opening and wedged tight. Rainwater sluiced off it in silver ropes. Odette's face went hard.

"Someone moved the bin."

She shoved it aside with a grunt. The second the gap opened, two soaked dogs shot through like cannonballs, whimpering, tails clamped. They didn't shake off. They didn't circle. They pressed against Odette's legs and stared back at the dark yard with the whites of their eyes showing.

Trixie grabbed towels from the laundry basket and tossed one to Odette. They knelt, rubbing fur in frantic circles. The dogs smelled like damp earth and something sharper, ozone, maybe, or fear. That's when Trixie saw the footprints. They started at the doggie door and crossed the kitchen in a perfect straight line. Bare feet. Too long. Too narrow. The water they'd tracked in had already started to dry at the edges, curling the prints into something almost delicate.

The prints stopped at the hallway threshold, then picked up again on the hardwood, fainter, but unmistakable, heading toward the bedrooms. Odette followed Trixie's stare. Her hands stilled on the brindle mutt trembling in her lap.

"Those prints aren't ours," she said.

The candle in the living room guttered in that second, casting its shadow up the wall. One of the dogs growled, not at the storm or the dark outside, but at the hallway. The sound that came back wasn't thunder. It was a single creak from the floorboard just past the bathroom door. The one that squeaked only when someone stepped on it.

Odette's eyes met Trixie's over the dogs' wet heads. Neither moved. The creak didn't repeat. But the air in the house shifted, the way it does when a room realizes it's being watched from within. And whatever was breathing in the hallway had just realized it wasn't alone.

CHAPTER 15

A top La Tortue Mountain, the storm had turned personal. It was no longer just raining; it was attacking. Sheets of water crashed against the palmetto scrub, bending the fronds until they screamed. Lightning flashed in magnesium-white, freezing every raindrop into a silver needle before thunder roared so loudly, it rattled teeth.

La Tortue Mountain, little more than a limestone blister rising a hundred feet above the Gulf, felt like the only solid thing left on earth. Chief Gordon La Tortue's teepee crowned the crest, a cone of weathered canvas glowing faint orange from the fire within. Smoke fought its way out of the smoke flaps only to be slapped down by the gale.

The chickens were locked tight in their coop, safe from the wind but clucking nervous hymns. The dogs, Ol' Joe and Coco, lay curled like a single breathing rug on Chief's pallet, ears twitching at every thunderclap. Buttercup, the calico, had claimed the exact center of the buffalo robe, tail wrapped around her nose, pretending the world wasn't ending.

Inside, the air was thick with cedar smoke, wet dog, and the copper tang of ceremonial ochre. A small fire crackled in the center ring, throwing shadows that crawled up the canvas walls like living things. Red candles, seven of them, burned in a half-circle behind the fire, their flames bowing but never breaking.

Paula stood barefoot in the center of the teepee, rain dripping from her hair, the hem of her soaked cotton dress clinging to her calves. Chief knelt opposite her, painting the last line of red ochre across her cheekbone with deliberate calm. The bowl between them held more blood than paint, and smelled of iron and storm.

Paula's voice was small against the roar outside. "What now?"

Chief didn't look up. He capped the ochre, set the bowl aside, and wiped his fingers on a square of buckskin.

"Storms don't bother spirits," he said.

"Only the living," Paula said.

She shivered, but not from the cold. The scent of the Majestic's lemon oil and Father Guidry's incense felt a million miles away. Didn't matter because the memory still registered. Here, there was only earth, blood, and fire. Chief looked at her, his dark eyes unreadable.

"Your hand is shaking," he said.

"I'm terrified," she admitted, her voice small against the roar outside. "Father Guidry said—"

When she hesitated, Chief said, "What did the priest say that has you so spooked?"

"He said there's a thin line between faith healing and witchcraft."

Chief glanced at the candle smoke wafting upward. "My guess is Father Guidry has never seen a spirit, and I doubt he'd know what to do if he did."

"He's a man of God," Paula said.

"Guidry isn't here," Chief cut her off, capping the ochre. "And neither is his God. Not tonight."

Chief rose, all six-foot-six of him unfolding like a redwood in slow motion, and handed her a rawhide pouch. Inside: a hawk feather, a shark's tooth, a single black-green scale, the twin of the one Lucky had torn loose the night before. Paula's fingers closed around it; the scale was fever-warm, pulsing faintly like a second heart.

"What now?" she asked.

"Grandfather is waiting. We go find him."

"What if he sees what I am?" Paula asked, the fear of the 'devil's shortcut' rising in her throat. "What if he sees my sin?"

"What he will see is the power you possess," Chief said. "Or he will see nothing at all."

Paula laughed, a cracked sound. "If we don't drown first."

"We might," he said.

They stepped into the storm. The wind nailed into them like a living fist, driving rain into their eyes, their mouths, their lungs. Paula staggered; Chief caught her elbow and leaned into the gale, a cliff refusing to erode. Together they fought their way to the eastern edge of the clearing, where the mountain fell away in a limestone escarpment.

From here, on a clear day, you could see the Majestic's neon crown, the white thread of beach, the Gulf beyond. Tonight, there was only darkness and water and the strobing rage of the sky. Chief planted his feet wide, raised both arms, and began to sing. Not words at first, sound, deep, guttural, older than French or English or even Atakapa. A note that seemed to rise from the stone itself.

The dogs inside the teepee answered with mournful howls that carried even over the storm. Paula felt the song in her breastbone, in the soles of her bare feet, in the roots of her teeth. Lightning answered. A bolt forked directly overhead, turning the world bone-white. In that frozen instant, Paula saw him.

An old man in buckskin, silver hair whipping like a war banner, standing ten feet away at the very edge of the drop. His eyes burned the same cold fire she'd seen in Chief's stories, twin embers in a face carved by a century of sun and grief. Tshu. Grandfather.

Then darkness swallowed him again. Chief never stopped singing. He reached back without looking, found Paula's hand, and pulled her forward until they stood shoulder to shoulder at the brink. Rain slashed their faces as the wind tried to blow them off the mountain. Paula tasted blood where she'd bitten her lip.

Tshu appeared again, this time only five feet away, untouched by the storm. Water ran off his buckskins as if they were oiled. His mouth didn't move, but she heard him as clearly as baptismal bells.

"You brought the witch-blood to my mountain, grandson." Chief's song faltered for the first time. His hand tightened on Paula's until bones creaked. Tshu's burning gaze shifted to her. "You carry both medicines, daughter. The prayer and the poison. Right and left hand. You fear the left will swallow the right."

Paula tried to speak; the wind stole her voice. She nodded instead, tears mixing with rain. Tshu lifted one arm. The storm quieted, not gone, but listening.

"We need your help, Grandfather," Chief said. "Something has awakened the Horn Serpent. Can you help us quiet the madness?"

Lightning, flashing behind the spirit's face, revealed his translucence and his eyes that were as intense as the storm.

"The Serpent wakes because the island forgot the bargain."

"What bargain, Grandfather?" Chief asked.

"Blood for blood. Secret for secret. You want to know what it wants? He stepped closer. The heat radiating from him steamed the rain around his body. It wants the witch to choose."

"Choose what?" Paula asked.

"Burn what must burn, or be burned. The reef is only the mouth. The casino is the belly. And something is coming up the throat wearing a smile men trust."

"You mean the Majestic?" Paula asked. "It hasn't been a casino in decades. The Horned Serpent... how do we stop it?"

Tshu smiled. It was not kind. "You don't stop Uktena. You pay the fare or you become the fare. January tides peak in three days. After that, the island chooses, or the island drowns."

"Can you be more specific?" Chief said.

"Tell the Russian his copper still cracked for a reason. The water under this island remembers every corpse ever sunk in it. Tell the Cajun with the movie-star face that the man who sent the golden chip is already dead. He just hasn't stopped breathing yet."

"Is that all, Grandfather?" Chief asked when Tshu fell silent.

"The answer lies with the reef, and the bones you'll find there," Tshu said.

Lightning flashed again, and the spirit was gone. The storm rushed back in twice as furious, as if offended at being silenced. Chief pulled Paula away from the edge. She was shaking so hard her teeth chattered. Together they stumbled back to the teepee, soaked to the marrow, the scale in her fist now hot enough to brand.

Inside, the dogs surged up to meet them, tails wagging in frantic relief. Buttercup blinked once, slow and regal, then went back to sleep. Chief peeled off his buckskin shirt over his head in one motion, skin gleaming like polished mahogany in the firelight. He tossed Paula a towel the size of a bedsheet.

"Dry off before you freeze."

She caught it, hands numb. Chief turned his back, giving her the illusion of privacy, and stripped out of the rest of his wet clothes without ceremony. Paula followed suit, peeling the sodden dress away from her skin, the chill raising gooseflesh on her arms, her breasts, her thighs. The fire's heat kissed her bare skin like a hesitant lover.

Chief handed her a plush terrycloth robe the color of storm clouds. It swallowed her, sleeves dangling past her fingertips, hem pooling at her ankles. She belted it tight and sank to the buffalo robe beside him. The dogs rearranged themselves around them, a living furnace. Buttercup climbed into Paula's lap without invitation and began to purr like a small engine. For a long time, they listened to the storm batter the canvas, the fire popping, the dogs breathing. Steam rose from their skin. Finally, Paula spoke, voice raw.

"'The casino is the belly.' What does that mean?"

Chief poked the fire, sending up a geyser of sparks.

"Grandfather never wasted words. Something rotten inside the Majestic, or coming for it. Someone feeding the Serpent on the sly."

"Maybe not," Paula said. "He could have been talking about another casino. What I don't understand is the part about me?" She pulled the robe tighter. "Burn what must burn, or be burned."

Chief met her eyes across the flames. "You've been standing with one foot in church and one foot in the crossroads, Paula. Afraid if you pick the left hand, you'll lose God, afraid if you pick the right hand, you'll lose yourself. Grandfather says the Serpent doesn't care about your fear. It cares about your power."

"But what does it mean?" she said.

"It means you hold the key to solving our riddle," Chief said.

Paula stared into the fire until the flames blurred. "Three days," she said in a whisper.

Chief nodded once and said, "Three days. That's how long we have."

Outside, thunder rolled like a closing gate. They sat in silence until the fire burned low and the candles guttered. The storm showed no sign of mercy, drumming the island like it meant to wear it down to bone. Paula's eyes grew heavy, the warmth, the robe, and the rhythmic breathing of the dogs pulling her toward sleep. Just before she slipped under, Chief spoke again, soft as falling ash.

"He also said one more thing. I didn't understand it."

Paula stirred. "What?"

Chief's gaze was fixed on the teepee's smoke hole, where rain still hissed against the flaps.

"Tell the witch-blood the Horned Serpent has a name now. And it learned to speak with a gambler's tongue."

"Maybe Eddie will know the answer," she said.

Paula's eyes snapped open. Somewhere far below, in the dark belly of the Majestic, a five-thousand-dollar chip spun across green felt and landed, gold sun glinting, on black—house odds. The storm laughed, and the mountain answered as Paula's eyes closed, though not for long.

"What is it?" Chief asked, seeing the strange look on her face.

"A dream that wasn't a dream," she said, sitting straight up like someone had jerked a string tied to her spine.

"You saw something," he said. "Tell me."

The air was damp, Chief's candles still burning, though the flame had gone tall and thin, bending toward the door flap.

Paula's mouth tasted like pennies. Chief was shirtless, rain still drying in his hair from the earlier dash through the storm. He felt the shift in her before she spoke. Unmindful of her nudity beneath the white bathrobe, she tossed it to the floor of the teepee and began pulling on her wet clothes.

"Get dressed," she said, voice flat, the way it got when the sight hit her hard. Chief didn't argue. He was stepping into the wet denim when she added, "Shotgun."

Chief froze with one boot on. "What'd you see?"

"Home invasion. Odette's house. Blood on the tile. Something wearing a man's shape but moving wrong."

Chief reached under an Indian blanket and grabbed the double-barreled shotgun that was once his grandfather's, cracked it open, and fed in two red shells thick as his thumb. The metallic snap sounded loud in the teepee. Paula was already pulling on her slicker as he began singing an ancient war chant, the sound melding with the outside storm. He stopped chanting long enough to nod toward Ol' Joe. The big shepherd was immediately responsive, moving to the tent flap and waiting there.

"We don't have much time," Paula said.

Chief racked the action. The sound was final. "Then let's not waste any."

CHAPTER 16

The creak from the hallway hung in the air like a held breath, and then the storm outside seemed to inhale, gathering itself for something worse. Odette rose slowly, her hand slipping into the drawer beside the sink, fingers closing around the grip of a small .38 revolver she kept there for nights like this. The metal was cold, reassuring.

Trixie stayed knelt by the dogs, one hand buried in Bruiser's wet fur, the other clutching a fireplace poker she'd snatched from the hearth. The mutts were rigid, hackles up, low growls vibrating through their chests like distant thunder.

"Stay here," Odette said.

Trixie was already standing, shaking her head. "Not a chance."

They moved together, bare feet and boots silent on the tile, following the fading prints down the hall. The candlelight from the living room stretched their shadows long and thin, twisting them into something monstrous on the walls. The bathroom door was ajar, a sliver of deeper black beyond. Odette nudged it open with the barrel of the .38.

Empty. The creak had come from farther down—the guest room, maybe, or her own bedroom at the end. Rain hammered the roof harder, as if trying to punch through. Lightning flashed through the window slats, illuminating the hallway in a stark white pulse. In that instant, they saw it: a shape at the end of the hall, hunched and too tall, limbs folded wrong, like a spider pretending to be a man.

Then darkness swallowed it again, but the afterimage burned—Trixie swore she saw scales glinting, a flicker of horns curving like sickles. Odette's breath caught.

"Out. We get out now."

They backed up, dogs pressing close, but the shape moved. Not toward them—away, crashing through the back door with a splintering crack that let the storm roar in. Wind howled down the hall, snuffing the candles in a single gust. Rain needled their faces as they spun, bolting for the front door. But the dogs broke ranks, charging after the intruder with furious barks that cut through the gale.

Odette shouted, but they were gone, vanishing into the black yard. "Bruiser! Mudbug!"

"Damn it," Trixie said, heart slamming.

They had no choice but to plunge out the back after them, into the deluge.

The yard was a swamp, ankle-deep mud sucking at their feet, rain falling so heavy it blurred the world into a gray smear. Lightning strobed again, and there it was: the Horned Serpent, no longer hiding in a man's shape.

It coiled in the center of the yard, massive and impossible, body thick as a fallen oak, scales iridescent black-green, slick with rain. Horns spiraled from its brow like twisted thorns, and its eyes—God, its eyes—burned with a hungry light, pupils slitted like a goat's.

The dogs circled it, snarling, but kept their distance, instincts screaming louder than the storm. Odette raised the .38, hands steady despite the cold.

"Bruiser, Mudbug! Get back in the house."

The dogs kept circling the beast, snarling and just out of its reach. The serpent's head swiveled, jaws parting in a hiss that vibrated the ground, revealing fangs dripping with something that steamed in the rain. Trixie swung the poker like a bat, but it felt ridiculous against this thing—a myth made flesh, Uktena from Chief's stories, the water monster that devoured islands and souls.

Terror clawed up her throat; she could taste bile. The beast lunged, not at them, but at the air, as if testing, its tail whipping through the mud and sending a spray that stung like shrapnel. Thunder cracked overhead, shaking the earth, and in the echo, headlights pierced the gloom—Paula's ATV skidding to a halt at the edge of the yard, doors flying open. Chief leaped out, shotgun shouldered, Paula right behind him, slicker flapping like wings. Ol' Joe and Coco exploded from the cab, joining Odette's dogs in a frenzy of barks, forming a loose ring around the serpent.

"Paula!" Odette yelled over the wind. "It's the Horned—"

"I see it," Paula said, voice steady but eyes wide with the same fear twisting in Trixie's gut.

Chief pumped the shotgun, the cha-chunk cutting through the rain.

"Back away, all of you!"

The serpent's gaze locked on Paula, and something shifted. Its form rippled, scales melting like wax in the downpour, horns retracting with a wet suck. The massive body shrank, contorting, bones cracking like lightning strikes. In seconds, it wasn't a serpent anymore—it was a woman, standing naked in the mud, wild and feral. Hair like tangled Spanish moss hung to her waist, skin pale as moonlit bone but marked with ochre runes that glowed faintly. Her face... it was Paula's, but not. The same sharp cheekbones, the same full lips, but twisted— eyes wilder, black as storm clouds, mouth curved in a smile that promised pain and ecstasy in equal measure. A spirit witch, shape-shifter, the left-hand path given form. Paula staggered back a step, breath hitching.

"What... what are you?"

The witch laughed, a sound like wind through hollow bones, cutting through the gale. "What are you, sister? The mirror doesn't lie. You've felt me in your veins, in the shortcuts you take when the prayers fall flat."

Chief leveled the shotgun. "Get back, Paula. This thing ain't natural. "But Paula held up a hand, stepping forward into the rain, robe plastered to her skin. The dogs fell silent, watching. Trixie gripped the poker tighter, glancing at Odette, who kept the .38 trained steady. The witch tilted her head, mirroring

Paula's posture, that disturbing smile widening. Paula began to recite, voice rising above the storm:

"I believe in God, the Father Almighty, Creator of Heaven and earth; and in Jesus Christ, His only Son, Our Lord..."

The Apostle's Creed, poured out like holy water. But the witch didn't flinch. She threw back her head and laughed again, louder, the sound weaving into the thunder.

"He cannot hear you here, child. The mud is too thick. Speak the language the mud understands."

Paula faltered, the words dying on her lips. Rain streamed down her face, mixing with tears. "This is faith. This is—"

"Lies," the witch hissed, stepping closer, bare feet leaving no prints in the mud. Her eyes bored into Paula's, twin voids pulling at something deep inside. "Your 'prayers' were always spells, disguised as devotion. Whispers to the roots, the bones, the blood. You've healed with them, haven't you? Commanded the fever to break, the wound to knit. Not asked—commanded. But you beg permission from a distant sky-god, afraid of what you are. Traiteur? Witch? The line is mud, sister, and you're drowning in it."

Paula shook her head, but her voice trembled. "Father Guidry said—"

"The priest fears what he can't control. But the land doesn't care for his crosses. The Serpent wakes because the bargain's broken—blood unpaid, secrets unearthed. To calm it, to heal this wound in the world, you must stop asking. Command the healing. Own the power. Burn what must burn, or be burned."

Lightning flashed, illuminating the witch's face—Paula's face, but untamed, alive with dark fire. Paula stared, seeing herself reflected: the conflict, the fear, the hidden strength she'd buried under rosaries and guilt. The storm raged on, wind tearing at her clothes, rain pounding like judgment, but in that moment, something cracked inside her. Not broken—freed.

Chief's finger tightened on the trigger. "Paula, say the word.

"But Paula lowered her hand, eyes never leaving the witch's. "I... I see you now."

The witch's smile softened, almost tender. "Good. Now see yourself."

The rain hammered down between them, a beaded curtain separating the real from the surreal. Paula wiped slick hair from her eyes, blinking against the downpour, trying to make the image snap into something rational. But the nightmare held its shape.

The woman—the creature—stood unaffected by the cold that was seeping into Paula's bones. The ochre runes pulsed on her pale skin, breathing with a light that seemed drawn from the lightning itself.

"It's rude to stare," the witch said. Her voice was a shock—it was Paula's voice, stripped of its warmth, sharpened into a blade of wet slate. It cut through the howling wind with impossible clarity. "Don't you recognize your own reflection?"

Chief shifted, the shotgun swinging nervously between the two identical faces. The dogs were losing their minds, a cacophony of panicked yaps and chest-rumbling growls, unsure which version of the scent to trust and which to attack.

"Chief, don't," Paula said, her voice cracking. She held a hand out, palm toward the gunman, eyes locked on the doppelgänger. "You might hit the wrong one."

The witch threw her head back and laughed, a sound like rising water in a cave. "Listen to her. So noble. So terrified." She took a step forward, mud sluicing off her bare calves. The movement was predatory, a hip-rolling stalk that belonged to a mountain cat, not a woman in a muddy yard. "You've been running from this side of you for a long time, Paula. All that polite smiling, all that helping. It must be exhausting."

"You aren't me," Paula said, finding a hard knot of anger beneath the fear. She planted her feet wide in the sucking mud, refusing to give another inch. "I don't know what you are, but you aren't me."

"Oh, but I am. I'm the part that remembers the old blood," the witch said. She raised a hand, fingers splayed. The Spanish moss hair lifted around her face, defying gravity, undulating as if underwater. "I'm the part that knows how to bite back."

Above them, the sky tore open with a deafening crack. Lightning struck a pine at the edge of the woods, the flash illuminating the witch in terrible silhouette. In that blinding instant, her eyes weren't just black; they were voids, swallowing the light.

The witch thrust her outstretched hand forward. It wasn't a physical blow, but Paula felt it like a hammer to the chest. The air pressure collapsed around her. A wave of psychic force, smelling of ozone and rot, slammed into her.

Paula gasped, her boots slipping in the slurry. She went down to one knee, mud splashing up her jeans. Her head swam, filled with a sudden impulse to tear, to shred, to run naked into the storm. It was an alien infection in her mind, a siren song calling her to let go.

"Feel that?" the witch said, stepping closer, looming over Paula's kneeling form. The rain hissed against the glowing runes on her skin. "It's freedom. Give in to it."

The witch dissolved, her body unraveling into mist the wind whipped away, leaving only the echo of her laugh mingling with the thunder. The yard fell silent, save for the relentless rain. The dogs whined, pressing close. Trixie exhaled, her poker dropping to her side. Odette lowered the .38, her eyes wide as she glanced at Paula.

"What the hell was that?" Trixie asked.

"Shapeshifter," Chief said.

Paula stood there, soaked and still, staring at the spot where the witch had been. The mud sucked at her feet. "The truth," she said softly. "And maybe the way forward."

Chief slung the shotgun over his shoulder, rain pouring off his hat. "Tides of January. You ready?"

All of Paula's bravado had disappeared, and she was crying, Odette and Trixie embracing and comforting her.

"Paula's going nowhere tonight," Odette said.

Chief shook his head, turned, and started away in the rain, Coco and Ol' Joe following him. The storm howled on, but something in the air had shifted—like the island itself was watching, waiting for Paula to choose.

CHAPTER 17

The storm had not let up; if anything, it had grown bored with mere rain and decided to throw the Gulf itself at the island. Wind screamed across the clearing like a living thing, ripping pine needles loose in green blizzards, driving sheets of water sideways so hard they stung bare skin.

Alex stood on the door in nothing but jeans and an unbuttoned shirt, staring at the lightning surging across the sky. The distillery lay broken behind him, copper entrails glinting whenever lightning strobed, and the taste of failure was sharper than the salt on the wind. He didn't hear the ATV until it was almost on him—small but powerful engine snarling, headlights cutting twin cones through the deluge. It fishtailed to a stop inches from the porch steps, tires spitting mud.

The driver's door flew open, and Renata stepped out, clutching the neck of her oiled slicker over her LSU sweatshirt. She brushed past Alex, handing him the wet slicker as she did.

Alex's heart lurched so hard it hurt. "Renata—J.P.'s not here."

"I'm here to check on Lucky, Squeaky, and her kittens," she said. "Not to see J.P."

"Can I fix you a cup of tea?" he asked.

Her hair strobed in the candlelight when she said, "No tea, but I'd take a mug of your rum."

"Of course," he said, not knowing what to make of her sudden friendliness.

Inside the bungalow, the air was thick with the scent of woodsmoke, rubbing alcohol, and the unspent electricity that seemed to arc permanently between Renata and Alex. Renata sprawled on the couch, waiting for Alex to present her with the mug of rum. Lucky was still in Alex's little bathroom, guarding Squeaky and her kittens ensconsed in the old four-legged bathtub. After sipping the rum, she joined them.

Renata knelt on the rug, her movements precise and economic as she peeled the soiled tape from Lucky's flank. She was a study in contradictions: the clinical detachment of a battlefield surgeon hiding a heart that beat too fast, too hard. Her face was a mask of cool porcelain, her eyes focused entirely on the wound.

"J.P. would die if something happened to his dog," Alex said.

Renata continued working, not looking up as she said, "Not to worry. "Granulation tissue is forming. No sign of sepsis. He is healing faster than I expected."

"Wonderful," Alex said.

"I hope your babies are doing as well," she said.

Alex stood a few feet away, watching her. He offered no reply, just a slow nod. He knew better than to interrupt her when she was working. He was resigned to the role of the observer—the ghost in his own house. He watched her capable hands apply fresh gauze and secure it with efficient strips of tape. Lucky thumped his tail once, a lazy acknowledgement, before drifting back into a drug-induced doze.

Finally, Renata stood, wiping her hands on a rag, and moved toward the claw-foot tub where Squeaky lay nestled in towels. The mother cat watched her with narrowed emerald eyes but didn't hiss. Renata checked the kittens one by one, weighing the calico runt in her palm for a long moment before setting it back against the warmth of its mother's belly.

"They survive," she said, more to herself than him. "Against the odds."

"They are resilient," Alex said. "Like the women of Ukraine."

Renata stiffened and turned slowly to face him. Alex was leaning forward, a glass of amber rum dangling loosely in one hand. His linen shirt was unbuttoned to the waist, a concession to the humidity of the stormy night. Averting her gaze, she packed away her medical instruments into her black satchel and returned to the living room.

Alex followed her, the firelight dancing across his chest, catching the dark hair and the jagged ridge of the scar that ran diagonally across his ribs. Renata saw it, feeling the pull—that magnetic gravity that dragged her toward him against her will. She hated him for who he was: the Russian officer, the man who gave orders to the beasts who had destroyed her life. And she hated him for who he had become: the savior, the man who had taken a bayonet through the chest to stop his own subordinate from finishing her off.

"You should have that looked at," she said, gesturing vaguely at his chest.

"It is an old wound, Renata. It requires no doctor."

"Scar tissue tightens," she said, stepping closer. "It restricts movement and anchors you to the past."

"I am anchored to the past by more than skin."

The air between them grew thin, difficult to breathe. Renata stopped just in front of him. She shouldn't be here. She should be back at the clinic, or with her mother and Sveta, safe behind the walls of resentment. But she reached out. Her fingertips, cool and calloused, brushed the center of his chest. Alex stopped breathing. She traced the line of the scar. It was raised and ugly, a violent punctuation mark on his body. She remembered the sound of the blade entering him—the wet thud, the grunt of surprise, the spray of blood that had mixed with the slush in the alleyway.

"It was cold that night," she said. "Like tonight."

The clinical mask was slipping. Her voice trembled.

"So cold," Alex said. He didn't move, didn't dare to touch her, afraid she would shatter. "I remember the steam rising from your husband's body. I remember the look in your eyes. Like a wolf caught in a trap." When she averted her gaze, he said, "I am so sorry to reopen old wounds."

"Wounds heal. You saved me," she said, the words tasting like bile and honey. "You risked your command to save me, and then you returned to Ukraine to save Sveta and my mother."

"I did not prevent your husband's death or those two cretins raping you in front of Sveta and your mother," Alex said, his voice cracking with an agonizing honesty. "I merely stopped the bleeding. I could not stop what they did. I could not bring him back."

"But you tried. You bled for me."

She pressed her palm flat against the scar, feeling the heavy thud of his heart beneath the disfigured skin.

"I would bleed every day," Alex said, his eyes searching hers, dark and tortured. "If it would scrub the memory from your mind, Renata, I would open every vein."

The dam broke.

It wasn't a slow leak; it was a collapse. A sob ripped from Renata's throat, harsh and jagged. Tears, hot and fast, spilled over her cheeks, washing away the stoicism she wore like armor.

Alex dropped the glass. It hit the rug with a dull thud, unnoticed. He reached up, his large hands cupping her face, his thumbs brushing away the salt. His own eyes were swimming, the stoic Russian façade crumbling into ruin.

"Renata," he choked out.

She collapsed against him, her knees hitting the floor between his legs. He pulled her close, burying his face in the crook of her neck, inhaling the scent of rain, antiseptic, and her. They held each other with the desperate grip of two people drowning in the same dark ocean.

Then, she pulled back, her hands framing his face. She looked at him—really looked at him—not as the enemy, not as the savior, but as the only other soul on earth who carried the weight of that night.

She kissed him.

It wasn't gentle. It wasn't sisterly. It was a collision of grief and need, a searing and almost desperate thing. She tasted the rum on his tongue and the salt of their shared tears.

Alex made a low sound in his throat, a growl of surrender, and pulled her down.

They wound up on the floor, the Persian rug bunching

beneath them. Hands fumbled with buttons and zippers, tearing at fabric that felt like an obstruction to survival. It was frantic, a fire burning out of control, fueled by too much silence and too much pain. There was no grace in it, only a raw hunger to feel something other than the ghost of death.

When the storm in the room finally broke, the silence that returned was different. It wasn't heavy anymore. They lay tangled together on the rug, limbs sprawled in a chaotic heap of half-undressed. Alex's shirt was torn at the shoulder; Renata's hair was wild, the severe bun completely undone, spreading like black ink across the floorboards.

Renata stared up at the ceiling, her bare chest heaving. A single laugh bubbled up, sounding foreign to her ears, rusty from disuse. But then it came again, louder.

Alex turned his head, looking at her with bewildered eyes. And then he started to laugh too. It began as a chuckle, deep in his chest, and spiraled into a resonant belly laugh.

They lay there in the wreckage of their clothes and their dignity, laughing uncontrollably, tears of mirth mixing with the drying tracks of grief. They laughed at the absurdity of it all—the stormy night, the bayonet, the kittens in the bathtub, the broken rum still, and the fact that despite everything the universe had thrown at them to break them, they were still here, warm and alive, half-naked on a thrift-store rug.

CHAPTER 18

It was late, and the storm had found its second wind, battering the coast with renewed fury, when Chief and his dogs pushed through the front door of Jack's cottage. A gust of rain-slicked wind followed them in, guttering the candles on the table before Chief shouldered the door shut against the gale.

J.P. and Jack were seated at the plank table, nursing rum and playing a sluggish game of gin. Jack didn't look up as he threw a towel at Chief's head.

Chief caught it mid-air, wiping his face as Ol' Joe and Coco shook themselves off and trotted over to the fireplace. They collapsed onto the rug beside Oscar, a tangled heap of wet fur and exhaustion. Chief disappeared into the bathroom, emerging moments later wrapped in a towering bathrobe, the towel draped over his damp hair. He pulled out a chair and sat heavily between J.P. and Jack, the wood groaning under his weight. His eyes landed immediately on the poker chip sitting in the center of the table.

"What's this?" he asked, picking up the chip. He turned it over in his large fingers. "You boys went gambling in Biloxi and didn't invite me?"

J.P. shot Jack a wink. "How do you know Jack didn't go without me, too?"

Chief's gaze flicked between them, his dark eyes narrowing, assessing the likelihood of a secret gambling junket.

Jack shook his head, pouring a generous measure of dark rum into a mug and sliding it across the wood to Chief. "Get your breechcloth out of a wad. No one's been gambling. Someone left that chip in J.P.'s Airstream while he was out."

"A chip worth five grand? Who leaves that behind?" Chief asked, taking a long pull of the rum, shuddering as the liquor hit his stomach.

"That's the sixty-four-dollar question," J.P. said, discarding a card. "We thought you were up on the mountain with Paula."

"I was. Until the call came in." Chief stared into his mug. "There was a disturbance at Odette's. We drove over to help. Paula stayed behind to secure the place."

"Odette and Trixie stopped here after work," J.P. said. "What kind of disturbance?"

Chief was silent for a moment, listening to the rain hammer the roof. "Something was in Odette's house when they got there. Her dogs were going crazy out on the back porch."

"What kind of something?"

Chief looked up, his expression grim. "The Horned Serpent."

Jack snorted, slapping his cards down. "You shitting us?"

"Why hell no!" Chief slammed his mug down hard enough to make the poker chip jump. "It was coiled in the yard when Paula and I arrived. Big... impossibly big. Body thick as a rum barrel, covered in scales that shone black-green in the lightning. And a mouth... a drooling mouth full of razor-sharp teeth." He traced a spiral in the air with his finger. "Two horns spiraled from its head, and its eyes burned red. Goat-slitted."

"Goat-slitted?" Jack frowned. "What's that supposed to mean?"

"Fucking city boy," Chief grunted. "You know what I mean, don't you, J.P.?"

"Nope. I grew up in Lafayette. Enlighten us."

Chief frowned, shaking his head as if trying to clear a blurry image. "Rectangular pupils. Horizontal slits. It gives a goat a panoramic view to spot predators." He shuddered. "But on this thing? They rotated. Kept level with the ground no matter how it moved its head. It was unnatural."

Jack chuckled nervously. "Didn't know you were such a fan of goats."

"Fuck you too, buddy! The monster wasn't a goat, Jack. It was a nightmare. And it didn't stick around long after Paula and I showed up."

"Where the hell did it go?" Jack asked.

"Nowhere," Chief said. "It transformed."

A crack of thunder shook the cottage foundation. The lights flickered, then held. J.P. reached for the bottle and topped off his own mug.

"Into what?" J.P. asked.

"A witch."

"You mean like the Wicked Witch of the West? Pointy hat, broomstick?" Jack asked, skepticism creeping back into his voice.

"This ain't Halloween, and real witches don't look like cartoons."

"How the hell do they look, then?"

Chief leaned in, his voice dropping an octave. "This one looked a hell of a lot like Paula. Except she was ten feet tall. And she was naked—not a stitch of clothing on her. Long black hair that had never seen a comb, matted with mud. She was wild, feral. Mud caked on her pale skin. She even had the same tattoo Paula has... right there on her breast, above the heart."

J.P. raised an eyebrow. "You've seen Paula's tits?"

"Well, yeah!" Chief said, defensively.

"Better not let Jimmie hear you say that," J.P. said. "He's never seen her tits."

Jack looked at J.P., confused. "How do you know?"

"Me and Jimmie always hit the bottle when we go duck hunting. Boy can't hold his liquor. When he's drunk, he gets weepy. He'll tell you anything."

Chief grunted. "Sounds like a personal problem."

"Maybe," J.P. said. "But most men wouldn't take kindly to another man knowing exactly what their wife looks like underneath her shirt. I'd keep that to myself if I were you."

"What does the tattoo look like?" Jack asked, leaning forward despite himself. Then he held up a hand. "Actually, stow that question. I don't want to know."

J.P. grinned. "What difference does it make? Jimmie doesn't even know she has a tattoo."

"And he's not going to find out from me," Jack said.

Jack covered his ears dramatically, but Chief ignored him. "It's a fleur-de-lis," Chief said quietly. "But with a twist. A serpent coiled beneath it."

The smile vanished from J.P.'s face. "Shit," he breathed. "That's... almost weird."

Chief nodded slowly. "I was thinking the same thing myself."

J.P. reached into his pocket and pulled out the whelk shell. Chief took it, twirling it in the firelight. The carved surface seemed to catch the shadows.

"You know what it is?" J.P. asked.

"A gorget. Probably a thousand years old," Chief said, running his thumb over the grooves.

J.P. nodded. "Same thing Trixie told us. She said the engraving is the all-seeing eye."

"The weeping eye," Chief corrected softly. "A gorget made of whelk shell, carved with a weeping eye."

J.P. stared at the engraving. "I swear I've seen this picture before. Not on a shell."

"You have," Chief said. "The Eye of Providence sitting atop an unfinished pyramid. It's on the back of every dollar bill in your wallet."

"What's the connection?"

Chief answered with a question of his own, his voice taking on a professorial tone. "Do you believe in the ether?"

J.P. grinned at Jack. They both knew where this was headed. Chief was about to get philosophical.

"No idea," J.P. said. "But I'm listening."

Chief pointed a thick index finger toward the ceiling, past the wooden beams, toward the storm outside. "Jung called it the Collective Unconscious. Thoughts are universal; our brains are just receivers of universal ideas."

"So there's no such thing as an original idea?" Jack asked.

"Not even close," Chief said. "The engraving on this gorget

—the weeping eye—is recognized in civilizations across history. Just like the Eye of Horus in Egypt."

"What I want to know," J.P. said, leaning over the table, "is what the hell does it mean, and why did I find it?"

"What does it have to do with the poker chip?" Chief asked.

"A P.I. from Biloxi tapped me wanting help on a case. Seems the skeleton we dredged up over Trixie's reef is related to a 'washing' case she's working on."

"Washing case?"

"Money laundering," J.P. said. "She hired me because I know the lay of the land. But when I got home tonight, I found someone had been there. They left the poker chip inside. I followed the tracks out to the bridge... found the gorget sitting right there. Someone either dropped it in a hurry, or they left it for me to find."

"Probably the latter," Chief said darkly.

"Because?"

"In native lore, the weeping eye means, 'I see clearly in both worlds'—this world and the spirit world. If the thief is a modern descendant who still knows the old protocols, leaving the gorget is an intentional message: 'We know what you took, and we're watching from the other side.'"

"Fuck me!" J.P. said.

"Tell him the rest of the story," Jack said.

J.P. nodded, taking a long swig of rum to steel himself. The dogs were twitching in their sleep by the fire, whimpering as the wind howled outside.

"I followed the tracks across the bridge," he said. "But halfway across... they changed."

Chief lowered his mug slowly. "Changed into what?"

"Wolf prints," J.P. said.

"A rougarou?" Chief asked, his eyes widening.

J.P. shook his head. "One big mama, but not a rougarou. The stride was different."

"A shapeshifter," Chief said, looking back at the fire. "Maybe... maybe Paula's witch."

"Tell me about the witch again," J.P. said. "Everything you saw."

Chief stared into the flames, his voice hollow. "A naked, muddy woman looking wild and feral. Hair like tangled Spanish moss hanging to her waist, and skin pale as moonlit bone but marked with faintly glowing ochre runes. Her face... it was Paula's, but not. The same sharp cheekbones, the same full lips, but twisted—eyes wilder, black as storm clouds, mouth curved in a smile that promised pain."

"And the same damned tattoo," Jack said.

Chief nodded and looked up at J.P., the firelight dancing in his eyes.

"A spirit witch," Chief said. "A shapeshifter. The left-hand path given form."

"You think it was Paula's witch who broke into J.P.'s trailer and left the poker chip?" Jack asked.

"And if it was, how is it related to the P.I. who hired him?" Chief asked.

J.P. nodded and said, "My question exactly. She said Meika told her about me."

"Meika?" Chief said. "Why was the P.I. discussing a washing case with Meika?"

"Hell, J.P.," Jack said. "You have Meika's cell number. Call and ask her."

J.P. pulled his phone out but hesitated, his thumb hovering over the contact list. He thought about Vangie LeBlanc—the way she moved, the way she looked at him. She was high-voltage, the kind of woman who used her sexuality like a loaded weapon. If she knew Meika well enough for the bartender to vouch for her, just how well did they know each other? Meika didn't play on J.P.'s team; she preferred women. If Vangie swung the same way, her sultry behavior toward J.P. wasn't just flirtation—it was a tactic—a manipulation.

And if she was willing to fake desire to hook him, what else was she faking?

"Well?" Jack asked. "You going to stare at it or dial it?"

J.P. tapped the screen. He was about to hang up when Meika answered, the background noise making reception poor.

"J.P., what's up?" she asked.

"Got a sec?" he asked.

"About all I got," she said. "This place never slows down."

The cacophonic ringing of slot machines jarred J.P.'s eardrums. "Damn, baby, how do you put up with the noise all day?"

"The casino pulses like a breathing creature," she said, her voice dropping a register, sounding more intimate than the noise allowed. "You get caught up in it. It's addictive."

"If you're gambling, maybe. I'd have to have a frontal lobotomy to work there," he said. He decided to skip the pleasantries. "I need a straight answer, Meika. Vangie LeBlanc."

There was a pause on the line, long enough for the slot machines to fill the silence.

"What about her?" Meika asked, her tone shifting from friendly to guarded.

"Is she a friend of yours?"

"You might say that," she said.

"She's hired me to help her in an investigation," J.P. said, leaning back in his chair, watching the firelight reflect in the dark rum. "But I need to know who I'm getting into bed with. Metaphorically speaking. Or maybe literally, if she has her way."

Meika laughed, a throaty sound. "She asked me the same thing about you."

"She's an attractive woman, Meika. Aggressively so," J.P. pressed, keeping his voice low so Jack and Chief wouldn't catch every word. "But birds of a feather tend to flock together. I know which way your compass points. Does her's point the same way?"

"Why?" Meika teased. "Afraid you can't handle the competition?"

"I'm afraid of being played," J.P. said flatly. "If she's batting for your team, then the eyes she's making at me are just a lure. I need to know if she's using the honey to trap the fly."

"Vangie is... complicated," Meika said, sidestepping the question with practiced ease. "She does what she has to do to get the job done. But I told her you were one of the good guys, J.P. That she could trust you."

"That's not an answer," J.P. said.

"It's the only one you're getting over the phone. "Are Chief and Jack with you?"

"Right behind me," he said. "I'm at Jack's."

"Put them on," she said.

Jack and Chief didn't have to be asked twice. "Hey, honey," Jack said. "We miss your sweet ass at the Majestic."

"Both of us," Chief said after wrestling the phone from Jack.

"Then come see me. I know all the pit bosses and can probably arrange a junket for a couple of high rollers."

"Love it!" Chief said. "Here's J.P."

J.P. gritted his teeth. "One more question. The General. Do you know him?"

The line went quiet instantly. Even the background noise seemed to dip.

"J.P.," she said, her voice devoid of its earlier playfulness. "The General's a powerful man."

"Eddie says he runs the consortium."

"He runs Biloxi," she said sharply. "He's not someone you ask about. He's someone you listen to. Is that who you're investigating?"

"I didn't say that."

"Good. Because if you were, I'd tell you to hang up and drive the other way."

"Does Vangie work for him?"

"How the hell would I know?" Meika asked.

Meika laughed when J.P. said, "Pillow talk?"

"I don't kiss and tell. You should know that by now," she said.

"Is there something about the General you aren't telling me?" J.P. asked.

"Gotta go," she said abruptly. "Come see for yourself. And bring Jack and Chief—you know, combine a little work with pleasure."

"Wait, Meika—"

The line went dead. J.P. stared at the phone for a moment, the unease in his gut twisting tighter than the knot in the storm outside. She hadn't denied Vangie's orientation, and her strong reaction to the General was unexpected.

"Did you get the answers you were after?" Jack asked, watching J.P.'s face closely.

J.P. shook his head, sliding the phone into his pocket. "I got a non-denial and a warning. Meika thinks Vangie is dangerous, and the General is worse."

"So, we're out?" Chief asked, though he was already reaching for the rum bottle.

J.P. sipped his rum and Jack and Chief saw a flash in his eyes they both recognized. "Not what I said. I'm going to take a little trip to Biloxi. I need to look Meika in the eye and see if she blinks."

"What about us?" Chief said. "Can we go with you?"

"I'm thinking this might be something I need to do alone," J.P. said.

"Don't be a spoilsport," Jack said. "We won't slow you down."

"That's not what I'm worried about," J.P. said.

"What the hell are you worried about?" Chief asked.

"If what Meika implied is true, it might be dangerous," J.P. said.

"Hell, J.P., you think because you were once a cop that you're the only person who has ever seen action? I was on a gunboat cruising up the Mekong and dodging AK-47 rounds when I was barely fifteen," Jack said.

"And there's no one better with a shotgun than me," Chief said.

J.P. laughed. "Hell, Chief, you can't take a shotgun into a casino."

"Maybe not," Chief said, "but my point is if it's danger you expect, you'll need backup."

"Maybe lots of it," Jack said.

"Hell, boys, I've been to battle before with you two, and there's no one I'd rather have my back," J.P. said.

"Does that mean we can go with you?" Jack asked.

As rain pounded on the house, J.P.'s smile and nod were all Jack and Chief needed to see. They quickly tapped their rum mugs, needing no verbal cue from him to know his answer was yes.

CHAPTER 19

The storm wasn't just outside; it was trying to get in, scratching at the shutters like a desperate animal. But inside Odette's cottage, the air was thick with the scent of lavender, damp wool, and the molasses sweetness of dark rum.

Paula sat deep in the velvet armchair, her legs tucked beneath her, nursing a mug of tea spiked heavily with Odette's private stock. She watched the two of them on the bed—Odette and Trixie—laughing as if the world wasn't ending just beyond the porch railing.

A flicker of something hot and ugly pricked at Paula's chest, and it wasn't the rum.

She watched Odette lean over and adjust the strap of the black silk nightie she'd lent Trixie. It was a scrap of a thing, a whisper of lace that Paula wouldn't have dared wear even ten years ago, let alone now. On Trixie, it looked like the gods had tailored it. The girl's skin was golden even in the low lamplight, her limbs long and firm, the scrollwork tattoo on her lower back flexing as she moved.

She was young. She was brilliant. And she was currently the center of Odette's universe.

"You have got to be kidding me," Odette howled, throwing her head back, her curls bouncing. "He said that? To a judge?"

"Swear to god," Trixie said, her voice raspy with exhaustion and liquor. "Told the judge that the dissertation wasn't plagiarism, it was 'intertextual homage.' I thought the bailiff was going to have a stroke."

Odette wiped a tear from her eye, beaming at Trixie. Paula

took a sip of tea, the ceramic hot against her palms. She and Odette were best friends running barefoot through the marsh, sharing secrets that would burn a priest's ears. They were the island's constants.

Now, watching Odette fuss over this newcomer, Paula felt the heavy weight of years settling onto her shoulders. She felt the gray in her hair, the softness of her belly, the secrets she was forced to keep even from Odette—especially the one about the fire currently running through her own veins, the magic she kept corked up like volatile spirits.

Trixie sat up, brushing a strand of damp hair from her face. She looked past Odette, her gaze landing squarely on Paula. The girl was sharp; she didn't miss much. The laughter died down in her eyes, replaced by a curious look.

"You're quiet over there, Paula," Trixie said.

"Just listening," Paula said, forcing a smile that felt tight. "Enjoying the show."

"She's always quiet when she's thinking," Odette chimed in, pouring more rum into Trixie's jar. "Paula's the deep water. I'm the babbling brook."

"You're the hurricane, Odette," Paula corrected gently.

Trixie shifted on the bed, swinging her legs over the side. She studied Paula for a beat too long. "You're in pain," she said.

It wasn't a question.

Paula stiffened. "I'm fine. Just the weather. My joints don't like the damp."

"It's not your joints. It's your fascia. You're holding yourself like you're waiting for a punch." Trixie stood up, the silk nightie rippling around her thighs. She didn't walk like a scholar; she walked like an athlete, balanced and sure-footed. She crossed the room and stopped in front of Paula's chair.

"Scoot forward," Trixie commanded softly.

"Excuse me?"

"I worked my way through my Master's as a massage therapist. You're wound tighter than a crab trap. Give me your foot."

Paula hesitated, glancing at Odette. Odette just grinned and took a sip of her drink. "Do it, cher. She's got magic hands. Fixed a crick in my neck earlier that's been there since I was a teenager."

Reluctantly, Paula extended her leg. Trixie dragged a pouf ottoman over, sat down, and took Paula's foot into her lap. Her hands were warm, strong, and unhesitating. She didn't ask for permission; she just went to work, her thumbs digging into the arch of Paula's foot with a precision that made Paula gasp.

"Breathe," Trixie said, not looking up. "Right there. That's your solar plexus reflex. You're carrying a lot of anxiety, Paula."

"Storms make me anxious," Paula lied.

"Mmm-hmm." Trixie worked the tension out of the heel, her touch firm but surprisingly gentle.

Paula watched the girl's head bent over her work. The jealousy that had flared earlier began to cool, replaced by a begrudging appreciation. It was intimate, this act. Women touching women, caring for the hurts they couldn't speak aloud. It was a language men didn't speak—Chief would offer a gun, Jimmie would offer silence, Jack would offer food. But this... this was grounding.

"You have a lot on your plate," Trixie said, her voice low, under the rumble of the thunder. "Odette told me you're the one everyone leans on. The Traiteur."

Paula shot Odette a look, who held up her hands in surrender. "I only said you know the old remedies, Paula. Nothing else."

Paula looked back at Trixie. "It's just folk medicine. Herbs and prayers."

Trixie looked up then, her eyes locking onto Paula's. They were intelligent eyes, lacking the judgment Paula usually saw in outsiders. "Whatever it is, it's heavy. I can feel it in the tissue. You spend so much time fixing everyone else, who fixes you?"

Paula didn't have an answer for that. She felt a lump rise in her throat and swallowed it down with a gulp of tea. The wind howled outside, rattling the windowpanes, but Trixie's hands were a steady anchor.

"Odette says you and Jimmie have been together forever," Trixie said, shifting the conversation as she switched to the other foot.

She sensed the wall Paula had hit and deftly steered around it.

"Since high school," Paula said, her voice softening. The physical relief was spreading up her calves, loosening the knot in her lower back.

"That's rare," Trixie said. "I can't keep a boyfriend for more than six months. Usually, about the time they realize I'm smarter than them, or when I prioritize a dead coral reef over their ego."

Odette snorted from the bed. "Men are fragile things, sugar. You gotta handle 'em like cheap china."

"Or," Paula said, surprising herself, "you just let them break and see if they can glue themselves back together. Jimmie... Jimmie didn't break."

"He's a lucky man," Trixie said. She applied pressure to Paula's toes. "And a blind one, if he doesn't see what he has. Odette told me about the separate lives thing. The mystery."

"It works for us," Paula said defensively.

"I bet it does," Trixie said, her tone devoid of sarcasm. "I think it's badass. You have your world, he has his. You meet in the middle. Most women lose themselves entirely. You... you've kept your edges sharp."

Paula looked at Trixie with new eyes. The girl wasn't trying to steal Odette. She wasn't trying to take Paula's place. She was just... searching like a moth looking for a light that wouldn't burn its wings.

"You're diving the reef tomorrow?" Paula asked.

"If the storm breaks. I need to see it. The skeletons, the formation. The data doesn't make sense."

"Be careful," Paula said, and she let a little of the knowledge slip into her voice, the tone she used when she was warning a patient about a fever that wouldn't break. "That water is old, Trixie. It remembers things. And it doesn't like to be poked."

Trixie stopped massaging for a second, her hands stilling on Paula's ankle. She looked up, and a shiver seemed to pass between them—not of fear, but of recognition.

"I'll be careful," she said.

"Good." Paula pulled her foot back, tucking it under her robe. "Because Odette likes you. And I'd hate to have to fish you out of trouble."

Trixie grinned, the tension breaking. "Is that an offer of rescue?"

"Let's call it insurance," Paula said, managing a genuine smile this time.

Odette clapped her hands. "All right, enough doom and gloom. Trixie, get your ass back over here. You promised to braid my hair before we pass out."

Trixie stood up, wiping her hands on a towel. She winked at Paula—a conspiratorial gesture that said we're good—before bounding back onto the bed.

As Trixie's fingers began to weave through Odette's dark curls, Paula sank back into the velvet chair. She watched them, the maiden and the mother, the scholar and the barmaid. The jealousy was gone, washed away by the storm and the touch.

But as the thunder cracked directly overhead, shaking the floorboards, Paula's hand drifted unconsciously to her chest, over her heart. Beneath the flannel of her robe, the tattoo of the fleur-de-lis and the serpent burned against her skin, hot and warning.

The men were drinking rum and telling war stories at Jack's. The women were braiding hair and sharing warmth at Odette's. But out there in the dark, something that wore Paula's face was walking through the rain, and Paula knew, with a sinking dread, that the storm was only just beginning.

As Trixie's fingers began to weave through Odette's dark curls, a sudden crack of thunder shook the cottage to its pilings. It was followed instantly by the pop of the enclave's transformer.

The lamps died. The hum of the refrigerator cut out. The cottage was plunged into a darkness so heavy it felt like velvet draped over their faces.

"Well," Odette's voice came from the dark, calm, and amused. "Eddie really needs to get this fixed."

The scratch of a match flared, harsh and bright. Odette held the flame to a cluster of beeswax candles on the nightstand, then two more on the dresser. The room filled with a dancing amber glow, throwing flickering shadows against the cypress walls.

"Come on, Paula," Odette said, patting the empty space on the King-sized mattress. "Stop lurking in the corner. If we're going to ride this out, we're doing it together. Like a sleepover. Only with better booze."

Paula hesitated, then sighed. She left the armchair and climbed onto the bed, settling against the headboard on Odette's other side. Trixie sat cross-legged at the foot, looking between them like a scout around a campfire.

The storm raged outside, rain lashing the tin roof like handfuls of gravel, but inside the circle of candlelight, the world shrank down to just the three of them.

"Chief was rattled when he left," Odette said softly, her eyes fixed on Paula. She wasn't smiling anymore. "The thing in my yard... the Serpent... knew you. Hell, Paula, the witch it transformed into could have been your twin and even had the same tattoo as you."

"Let me see," Trixie said.

Not waiting for permission, she opened Paula's robe until she saw the fleur-de-lis tattoo. She stroked it, resting her finger on the coiled serpent.

"There's a story here," she said. "Tell it."

Paula stared at the candle flame, watching the wick curl and blacken. She felt the pull of the secret, the weight of it, and looked at these two women—her oldest friend and this new, bright spark of a girl.

"I didn't just see it tonight," Paula said. The wind outside seemed to hold its breath to listen. "I've seen her my whole life. In the corner of my eye. In the space between waking and sleeping."

"Her?" Trixie asked, a chill that had nothing to do with the draft sliding down her spine.

"My grandmother, Grandmére Clotilde, was blind," Paula said, her voice drifting into the cadence of a memory. "She lost her sight to the pox before I was born. My mother... my mother wanted us to be modern. She hated the old stories and forbade us from speaking French in the house. But when Mama was at the market, I'd sit by Grandmére's knee while she shelled pecans."

When she paused, Trixie said, "Tell us."

Paula closed her eyes. "She smelled of dried sage and pipe tobacco. She used to grab my face with her papery hands and tell me, 'Ma petite, eyes are for the daylight, but the spirits see in the dark.'"

"What else?" Odette asked.

"She told me about the Ombre," Paula said. "The Shadow. She said every woman who carries the blood carries a shadow self. A twin made of everything we repress. Our rage, our wildness, the lust and the violence we aren't allowed to show. She said if you don't acknowledge the shadow, if you don't invite her to the table... she breaks the door down."

"The witch," Trixie said. "The thing we saw... it looked like you. Didn't it?"

Paula nodded slowly. "It looked like me if I had never learned to be polite. If I had never learned to be a wife or a nurse. It was naked and covered in the muck of the swamp, and it was beautiful and terrifying."

"Is it... is it real?" Trixie asked. "Or is it a projection?"

"Tonight, it was real enough to leave tracks," Paula said. "Real enough to scare a man like Chief."

She took a sip of her tea, her hand trembling slightly. "The veil is thin tonight, ladies. The storm has torn it wide open. It's not just my shadow walking the island."

"What do you mean?" Odette asked, pulling the quilt up higher around her shoulders.

"Before driving here, Chief and I were on his mountaintop. The rain was coming down in sheets, but I saw him standing there, clear as I see you now."

"Who?"

"Chief's grandfather," Paula said. "The Old Chief. He's been dead for decades. But there he was, standing in the storm, wearing his ceremonial leathers, holding a spear tipped with flint. He wasn't a memory, Odette. He was watching over us. Keeping guard."

The candle flickered violently, though there was no draft in the room.

"The ancestors are awake," Paula said, looking from Odette to Trixie. "The Serpent, the Witch, the Old Chief. They're all here. We aren't just fighting a storm or a mystery skeleton anymore. We're in a story that started a long time ago."

Trixie shivered and scooted closer to Odette. Odette reached out and took Paula's hand, interlacing their fingers.

"Well," Odette said, her voice trying for bravery but sounding small in the shifting shadows. "Then it's a good thing we have a witch of our own."

Paula squeezed her friend's hand, the fleur-de-lis tattoo on her chest throbbing in time with the thunder. "Let's hope," she said. "Let's hope it's enough."

CHAPTER 20

The phone jolted J.P. out of a rum-heavy sleep. He came awake all at once, the way a man does when he's spent too many years expecting trouble in the dark. For a second, he lay still in the narrow bed of the Airstream, listening to the silence—no rain hammering the aluminum roof, no wind trying to peel the skin off the island. The phone kept buzzing, crawling across the little fold-down table like it had somewhere better to be. He swung his legs over the side, bare feet hitting the cold floor, and snatched it up.

"Yeah."

"Did I wake you?"

Vangie's voice was amused, already dressed for the day even though the clock on the microwave read 6:17 a.m.

"Define wake," he said, rubbing the grit from his eyes.

He pushed the curtain aside an inch. The sky was the color of a fresh oyster shell, cloudless, innocent. The storm might never have happened if you hadn't looked too closely at the broken palm fronds and the debris tangled in the sawgrass.

"What are your plans?" she asked.

The endearment slid out smooth as cane syrup, but there was steel underneath.

"Sheriff's dive team is going out to Trixie's reef as soon as they're sure the surge is done. They're picking me up at the Majestic dock at eight. Invited me along for the ride."

A soft laugh. "I bet they didn't invite me."

"You'd win that bet."

"Exactly why I hired you," she said, not bothering to hide the satisfaction. "Though I do have some questions and a few concerns."

"Funny. So do I."

"Good. I'm sitting at the bar in the Majestic. Odette isn't in yet. Eddie Toledo's pouring. You got time for a cup of coffee before your boat leaves?"

J.P. peeked through the curtain, glancing at the dock down the hill from the lighthouse. The sheriff's Boston Whaler was already tied up down there, two deputies in dry suits hosing salt off gear.

"I have time," he said. "See you in ten."

She hung up before he could answer.

J.P. pulled on yesterday's jeans—still damp from the knees down—pulled on his cowboy boots, and shrugged into a faded gray T-shirt that smelled faintly of woodsmoke from Jack's fireplace. He tucked the whelk-shell gorget into his pocket out of habit now, the carved weeping eye pressing against his thigh like a warning that hadn't decided whether to speak yet.

The morning air outside the Airstream was cool and clean, the kind that comes after a storm has scrubbed the world raw. He walked the crushed-shell path to the Majestic, boots crunching, gulls screaming overhead like they were mad about the mess the storm had left them.

The bar was almost empty. Sunlight poured through the open French doors, laying bright bars across the old cypress floor. The smell was coffee, chicory, and lemon polish. Eddie —tall, thin, with hair a little too long—was wiping down the inside of the bar with a white rag, humming something unrecognizable.

Vangie LeBlanc sat alone on the customer side, legs crossed over the brass rail, wearing white linen trousers and a sleeveless black top that made her look like trouble on vacation. A white blazer was draped over the stool beside her, claiming territory. Her hair was pulled back, severe and sleek, with sunglasses pushed up like a headband. A porcelain café au lait cup sat untouched in front of her. She watched him cross the room without smiling, but her eyes tracked every step.

"Morning, handsome," she said when he was close enough. "You look like the storm chewed you up and spit you out."

"Feel like it, too."

He slid onto the stool next to her. Eddie was already pouring without being asked—black coffee, no cream, no sugar, the way J.P. had drunk it since he was old enough to drink coffee. Vangie turned her cup in small circles, studying him.

"So. Questions and concerns. You want to go first, or should I?"

J.P. wrapped both hands around the hot mug, letting it warm his palms. Outside, past the doors, the bay sparkled like shattered glass. Beneath the surface, bones were tangled in fresh coral. He twirled the $5000 poker chip. When it stopped spinning, it landed face up on the bar.

"Where'd you get the chip?" she asked.

"An intruder left it in my trailer last night," he said. "Any ideas who?"

Vangie's smile was small, sharp, and not particularly warm.

"Somebody broke into your trailer, left a five-thousand-dollar casino chip like a calling card, and you still got on the phone this morning, as if it hadn't happened?"

"I'm telling you now," J.P. said.

Eddie set a fresh bottle of Dominican rum and a squat bottle of Booker's on the bar between them like he was laying down offerings. He wiped his hands on the towel slung over his shoulder and gave them a knowing grin.

"Sounds like serious talk. I have stock to count in the back. Just keep a tally on the pad if you kill anything." He tapped the legal pad by the register. "And don't go stealing my limes."

Vangie's laugh was low and genuine. J.P.'s too, rusty but real. Even Eddie chuckled as he disappeared through the swinging door to the kitchen. When it clicked shut, the room felt suddenly bigger, the morning light louder. J.P. turned on the stool to face her.

"I'm working for you," he said, flat, no smile left. "That's not all I haven't told you. Someone called me after I found the chip."

"What?" she said.

J.P. could tell by the look in her eyes that she had no clue what he was talking about. "Someone who knew about the chip called. They also left me a message scrawled on the notes you gave me."

He opened his notebook. On the first blank page, right beneath where the chip had sat, someone had written in block letters with a heavy black marker:

HOUSE ODDS.

"What's it supposed to mean?" she asked.

"Hell, Vangie, you know exactly what it means. The House always wins, and the player eventually loses. It's a mathematical certainty. You know what else it means, don't you?"

J.P. nodded when she said, "We're compromised."

"Roger that," he said. "Whoever it was told me to consider the chip a severance package. Take the chip to the cashier at Golden Gulf tomorrow and cash it out. Buy yourself a nice vacation. Go somewhere dry."

Vangie lifted her cup, took the first sip of the café au lait she'd been ignoring, and set it down again. "That's a pretty direct threat. I'll understand if you want to back out of the job. You don't even have to return the retainer."

J.P. felt the heat crawl up his neck. "I took your money, and now I'm going to earn it."

"With a target on your back?" Vangie asked.

"I was in the infantry in Iraq and then on the police force for going on two decades. Trust me when I tell you that not a day went by that my asshole wasn't puckered. I'm used to living with danger."

"Meika told me you aren't afraid of anything."

Vangie nodded when J.P. said, "She told you that?"

Vangie drank half of her café au lait, opened her flask, and topped the glass with expensive bourbon.

"What about the B and E? Any clues other than the chip?"

"Whoever did it wiped the place down like a pro. I followed the tracks to the bridge. They disappeared into the underbrush on the other side."

"Did you follow the trail?" Vangie asked.

"There wasn't a trail, just thick underbrush," he said.

"You're confusing me," Vangie said.

Because I haven't told you everything. It was raining buckets when I left the trailer, and the prints were washing away pretty fast. They were still visible, so it means I just missed the intruder."

"Damn!" Vangie said. "I don't suppose you could tell anything by the prints?"

"I'm Cajun, but I have some Choctaw blood. My granddaddy taught me how to track."

"And?"

"The person who left the chip was a St. Bernard police officer," J.P. said.

Vangie took a swig of bourbon straight from her glass. "How do you know that?"

"Police departments issue uniforms. That's not always the case for shoes. Some PDs give you a shoe allowance and let you choose from several brands. Not so St. Bernard Parish. They have a brother-in-law deal with a particular shoe manufacturer, so everyone wears the same brand."

"Why hasn't someone complained?" Vangie asked.

"Because the tactical boots they issue are light, agile, give you great support, and most of all, the damn things are comfortable. The sole also features a tread made only for the St. Bernard Parish Police. Hell, I'm wearing a pair now."

J.P. crossed his legs and showed her.

"Why would a cop roll a place wearing readily-identifiable boots?" Vangie asked.

"Hell, Vangie, they're so damn comfortable I sometimes forget I have them on."

"You're still wearing your boots, and you are retired. Maybe the person who rolled your trailer doesn't work for the PD anymore."

"Maybe," he said. "Maybe not. Whoever it is wore a size thirteen and I'm betting there aren't many cops in the St.

Bernard Sheriff's Department with clodhoppers that big."

"Hope it's not one of your friends," Vangie said.

J.P. twirled the chip on the counter and waited until it stopped spinning. "No friend of mine would have broken into my trailer and left the chip. I don't like dirty cops, and neither does the Sheriff."

"What now?" Vangie asked.

J.P. glanced at the time on his cell phone. "Ride out to the reef on the police boat and keep my eyes peeled for a cop with big feet." He drained the glass, set it down hard enough to clack. "What happens after the dive?"

"Meet me tonight. Seven, seven-thirty. Place called Coops in Chalmette. Back booth. Terrible food, worse lighting, nobody remembers your face." She stood, slung the white blazer over one shoulder like armor. "We'll compare notes. And maybe..." Her smile came back, slow and crooked. "Maybe we can work something out that keeps everybody breathing."

She walked toward the French doors. Sunlight caught the gold in her earrings, which he hadn't noticed before, tiny coiled serpents. At the threshold, she paused, didn't turn.

"Leave the gorget in your trailer, cher. Whatever's watching you already knows you have it."

Then she was gone, white linen disappearing into the bright glare outside. J.P. sat there, staring at the two bottles Eddie had left, like loaded guns. Finally, he scrawled two coffees and one whiskey on the pad, added a twenty, and headed for the dock. The bay was flat and blue and Vangie was lying her ass off.

CHAPTER 21

Alex woke slowly, the way a man surfaces from deep water—disoriented, lungs burning with the need for air. For a moment, he thought he was still dreaming: the faint gray light of dawn filtering through the bungalow's shutters, the distant hush of the storm finally spent, and the warm weight of Renata curled against him.

Her head rested on his chest, one arm draped possessively across his waist, her breath soft and steady against his skin. He could feel the entire length of her pressed to his side—leg hooked over his thigh, breasts soft against his ribs—and the reality of it hit him like a second heartbeat. Not a dream. She was here. After everything, she was here.

He shifted just enough to look down at her. Her long hair spilled across his shoulder in wild tangles, the severe bun from last night long vanquished. In sleep, the sharp edges of her face had softened; she looked younger, almost fragile. But he knew better. He knew the steel beneath.

Renata stirred, sensing his movement. Her eyes opened—those piercing eyes—and locked on his. For a heartbeat, neither of them spoke. Then she smiled, small and wicked, and cradled his head in her arms as if he were something precious. She leaned in and kissed him.

It was slow this time. Deep. A kiss that tasted of rum and salt and the promise of more. Alex's hand came up to cup the back of her neck, thumb brushing the soft skin beneath her ear. When she finally pulled away, her lips were swollen, her eyes bright.

"Good morning, Russian," she said, voice husky with sleep and her faint Ukrainian lilt.

He exhaled a laugh that sounded more like surrender. "If this is how mornings begin with you, I may never leave this bed."

She kissed him once more—quick, teasing—then slipped from his arms and out of the bed. Alex watched, transfixed, as she padded naked across the room toward the bathroom. It was the first time he had seen her fully undressed in daylight, and the sight stole what little breath the kiss had left him.

Renata was breathtaking. Not delicate—never delicate—but powerfully built, every line of her body honed by hardship and survival. Shoulders strong from tending heavy animal patients, back tapered and muscular, legs long and athletic from years of running, when walking would not do. The curve of her waist, the flare of her hips, the small scars that mapped her skin like constellations—he wanted to trace every one with his mouth.

The bathroom door closed softly. Water ran. Alex lay there staring at the ceiling, trying to convince himself this was real. When he finally rose and pulled on the faded robe hanging from the bedpost, the scent of cooking already filled the bungalow—butter, onions, the faint sweetness of bread toasting. He stepped into the kitchen and stopped dead.

Renata stood at the stove, still gloriously naked, hair now twisted into a loose knot at her nape. She moved with easy confidence, flipping eggs in a cast-iron skillet, sliding thick slices of bread into the ancient toaster he rarely used. Her body caught the morning light streaming through the window—skin golden, muscles shifting beneath as she reached for a plate. He must have made some sound, because she glanced over her shoulder and smiled.

"Sit," she said, nodding toward the small breakfast table tucked in the corner. "You will need strength today."

Alex obeyed, but his eyes never left her. She plated the food with practiced motions: fluffy scrambled eggs flecked with herbs, golden toast, a small bowl of sliced tomatoes and cucumbers dressed with oil and dill. A traditional Ukrainian breakfast—syrnyky nowhere in sight, but close enough to home that his chest ached.

She carried the plates to the table and slid into the chair across from him, still naked, utterly unselfconscious. Alex stared openly, fork forgotten halfway to his mouth. Renata raised an eyebrow.

"You don't mind me staring at you?" he said, voice rough.

She laughed softly, the sound low and warm. "I worked as a dancer in clubs after we crossed the border. Men looked. Many looked. I learned to like it." She leaned forward, elbows on the table, chin in her hands. "Especially when the eyes belong to someone who sees more than skin."

Alex swallowed hard. "I'm sorry I wasn't there. That you had to—"

"It doesn't matter," she cut in gently, accent thickening with emotion. "I had amnesia for a long time after the border. Didn't remember who I was, where I came from. It was... a mercy, almost. A clean slate."

She reached across the table and touched his wrist. "Eat, Alex. Before it gets cold."

They ate in companionable silence for a while, the only sounds the scrape of forks and the occasional distant drip of water from the eaves. But Renata was watching him too closely.

"You are worried," she said finally. "I see it in your eyes."

He set his fork down. "The distillery. The storm took the roof off the old building. The copper vats I ordered—they're on backorder for months. I won't use stainless steel. It changes the soul of the rum."

Renata nodded, thoughtful. Then she leaned back in her chair, a movement that devastated his concentration.

"I can help," she said.

He frowned. "How?"

"There is an old rum distillery in New Orleans. Arcadia Distillery—abandoned since Katrina. The building is near the river, off Tchoupitoulas. Copper pot stills, original cypress fermenters, antique equipment. Some damage, but much of it salvageable. There is also an old brewery nearby—equipment that could be repurposed." She tilted her head. "Old equipment is best, yes? It has character."

Alex stared at her. "Old equipment is the best, unless it's ruined. But how do you know this place still exists? That it hasn't been gutted?"

Her smile turned mysterious. "I don't have to tell you all my secrets, do I?"

He laughed despite himself. "Take me there. Today. Show me."

Renata rose from her chair in one fluid motion and crossed to him. She slid into his lap, straddling him, arms looping around his neck. The robe parted beneath her; heat flared between them instantly.

"Right now?" she whispered against his mouth. "We have unfinished business, you and I."

Alex's hands settled on her hips, thumbs tracing the sharp bones. "With a body like yours, woman, I will never get anything done."

She arched against him, fingers sliding into his hair. "Good," she said. "Because you are built like some ancient warrior—broad and hard and impossible." Her palms skimmed down his chest, pushing the robe open, nails scraping lightly over muscle. "Like a Neanderthal. And I love every muscular inch."

He groaned, low and helpless, and pulled her mouth down to his. Outside, the island began to wake—birds calling, water dripping from battered palms—but inside the bungalow, time slowed to the rhythm of two people finally, fiercely, claiming what the years had stolen.

Renata stirred beneath the tangled sheets, reaching instinctively for the solid warmth that had been beside her in what seemed like only minutes before. Her hand met cool linen instead. She opened her eyes to an empty bed, the faint indentation of Alex's body the only proof he had ever been there.

The bungalow was quiet except for the insistent drum of rain against the tin roof—another storm front rolling in from the Gulf, turning the morning light the color of tarnished silver.

She sat up slowly, pulling Alex's faded bathrobe around her shoulders. It smelled of him: salt, rum, and something darker, like earth after lightning. The sleeves hung past her fingertips; the hem brushed mid-thigh. She cinched it tight and padded barefoot into the main room.

Alex sat at the small table he had long ago claimed as a desk, hunched over a sprawl of blueprints and scribbled notes. A single hurricane lamp burned beside him, throwing gold across the sharp angles of his face. His hair was disheveled, brows drawn together in concentration that bordered on anguish. A half-empty mug of coffee had gone cold at his elbow.

Renata paused in the doorway, watching the tension in his shoulders, the way his fingers drummed restlessly against the tabletop. Worry looked heavy on him.

"What is it?" she asked softly.

He looked up, startled, as though he hadn't heard her approach. For a moment, his expression softened at the sight of her swallowed in his robe, hair wild from sleep and from his hands, but the worry quickly reclaimed him.

"The old distillery building," he said, voice rough. "The one that survived a hundred years of storms on this island. It's… worse than I thought."

Renata crossed the room and stood behind him, resting her hands on his broad shoulders. She could feel the knots of muscle beneath her palms. Leaning down, she pressed her cheek to the top of his head.

"Forget it," she said.

He turned in the chair to look at her, incredulous. "Forget it? That building was the heart of this place. The history—"

"Is someone else's history," she interrupted gently but firmly. "Someone else's design, someone else's mistakes baked into every beam. Do you want to resurrect a ghost or build something perfect? Something that is yours?"

Alex exhaled, long and slow. "Renata, I know rum. I know sugarcane, fermentation, and fire. I know nothing about construction. Blueprints, load-bearing walls, permits—"

"You know people who do." She moved around the chair to face him fully, perched on the edge of the table amid the scattered plans. The robe parted slightly at her knees, revealing the smooth line of her thigh. His eyes flicked there, then back to her face, helpless. "Jack. Chief. J.P. They designed the dog training facility from nothing—drew every line, poured every slab, argued over every nail. They will help you. And so will I."

He frowned. "You?"

She smiled, small and fierce. "My minor at university was modern design. I am very good with AutoCAD, Alex. We will make something functional and beautiful—clean lines, open fermentation halls, natural light, airflow that kisses the vats instead of fighting them. No rotting cypress and shellcrete from the 1800s. Something worthy of your rum."

For a long moment, he stared at her, as if seeing her anew. Then he reached out, hands settling on her waist, thumbs brushing the soft terry cloth.

"You continually surprise me," he said.

Outside, thunder rumbled, closer now. The rain intensified, lashing the windows in sheets, turning the world beyond the glass into a gray blur. Renata leaned down, her lips grazing his ear.

"Mama is with Sveta. She practically pushed me out the door last night—told me to stay as long as I like. To have fun." A soft laugh escaped her. "She and my daughter have loved you since the night you carried them out of hell. They want you happy. They want us happy."

Alex's hands tightened on her waist. "We're going to New Orleans," he said, voice low. "As soon as this storm breaks. I want to see that old distillery you found. Touch the copper with my own hands."

Renata straightened just enough to meet his eyes. Rain hammered the roof like impatient fingers. Wind rattled the shutters.

"To hell with the storm," she said, and the words were half challenge, half promise. She slid off the table and into his lap, straddling him, the robe falling open as she framed his face with both hands. "Until then, we eat. We drink rum. And we make love till neither of us remembers what worry feels like."

His answer was a growl deep in his chest. He pulled her down into a kiss that tasted of coffee and desperation and gratitude, the blueprints forgotten beneath her thighs, the storm outside rising to match the one building between them once more.

CHAPTER 22

The St. Bernard Parish Marine Division's boat was a twenty-eight-foot Safe Boat with twin Yamaha 250s and more antennas than a shrimp boat had religion. Matte-gray gelcoat, black rubber gunwales thick enough to bounce a drunk deputy off, and the words SHERIFF in reverse block letters across the bow so helicopters could read them from the sky. Somebody had nicknamed her Miss Behavior; the vinyl was peeling, but the name still stuck.

Deputy Roland Guidry stood at the helm in a faded department dry-suit, mirrored shades, and a Saints cap turned backward. He gave a lazy two-finger salute as J.P. stepped off the Majestic dock.

"Morning, old man. Thought you were gonna sleep through your own party."

J.P. was smiling when he said, "This old man can still whip your young ass."

Guidry grinned. "New girlfriend?"

"Nah," J.P. said. "Had to kiss a few toads first."

Before anyone could answer, a low growl rolled down the dock—a brand-new Cadillac Escalade, pearl-white, chrome gleaming as if it had never seen road salt. The tinted windows reflected the morning sun. It eased to a stop at the very end of the pier, engine purring, then went silent.

The driver's door opened. Dr. Spivey Sonnier stepped out in crisp khakis, a starched white polo with the parish coroner's emblem embroidered over the heart, and aviators that looked too expensive for government pay. He was fifty-something, going on pampered, soft around the middle, but carrying himself like a man who'd just discovered he owned the room.

Trailing behind him, moving with the easy confidence of someone who knew every eye was on her, was a twenty-five-year-old brunette in tight white jeans and a low-cut red top. She leaned against the Cadillac's hood, legs crossed, one high heel dangling. Sonnier walked over, bent down, and kissed her—long enough, slow enough, that everyone on the boat pretended not to notice.

Then he murmured something in her ear; she laughed softly, got back behind the wheel, and pulled away with a throaty purr, leaving a faint scent of expensive perfume hanging in the humid air.

Tommy LeBoeuf let out a low whistle. "Well, damn. Coroner's got himself a new hobby."

Johnnie Daigle, leaning against the gunwale, muttered under his breath, "And a new ride to match."

Sonnier sauntered down the dock toward the boat, a black coroner's case swinging from one hand like it weighed nothing. He climbed aboard without waiting for an invitation, his deck shoes spotless.

Roland straightened. "Doc? Where's Thib?"

Sonnier waved a hand, dismissive. "Thibodeaux had a family thing come up last minute—granddaughter's birthday or some such. I told him I'd handle the scene myself. No sense dragging the boy out for what's probably just another floater."

J.P. studied him. Sonnier's smile was pleasant enough, but his eyes kept flicking toward J.P.—quick, assessing, irritated, like J.P. was a stain on an otherwise clean shirt.

"Saucier," Sonnier said, nodding once, the word flat. "Didn't expect to see you out here."

"Sheriff asked me to lend a hand," J.P. said.

Sonnier's smile tightened. "Of course he did."

Johnnie stepped forward, voice calm but firm. "Sheriff Comier cleared it, Doc. J.P.'s on the team for this one."

Sonnier's jaw worked for half a second before he shrugged. "Well, if the sheriff says so."

The words carried the faintest edge, like a man swallowing something bitter. He moved past them to the cooler, set his case down with exaggerated care, then popped the lid and pulled out a fresh pair of nitrile gloves. His hands were soft, manicured; the kind that had never scraped barnacles off a hull.

Sam Marcantel spat tobacco juice over the rail and wiped his chin. "Nice wheels you got there, Doc. Business must be good."

Sonnier chuckled, but it didn't reach his eyes. "Perks of the position. You know how it is—gotta keep up appearances in this parish."

Another low chuckle from Tommy. Nobody else joined in. The two St. Bernard Parish homicide detectives assigned to the case, Sam Marcantel and Johnnie Daigle, weren't diving but along for the ride—good thing, as there probably wasn't a wetsuit big enough for Marcantel's gut. At least neither man was in a suit and tie; both wore chinos and long-sleeved shirts.

Sam nodded his big head when J.P. said, "You boys got anything for me?"

"Thibodeaux identified the victim as Chris Olsen," he said.

"Cause of death?"

"Bullet through the brain. Close range. From the trajectory of the bullet, he was probably on his knees," Marcantel said.

"Execution style," J.P. said. "Professional hit. What do you have on him?"

"Born and raised in Biloxi. Enlisted in the military right after graduating high school."

"What branch?" J.P. asked.

"Air Force," Marcantel said. "ISR."

"What the hell's ISR?" J.P. asked.

"Intelligence, Surveillance, and Reconnaissance."

"What do they do?" J.P. asked.

"Lots of things: airborne, space, and cyberspace sensors for global intelligence. Hush hush shit."

Marcantel nodded when J.P. asked, "Was Kessler his home base?"

"You got it. Never left Biloxi."

"What about General Roubideaux? Was he the Kessler commander when Olsen was there?"

"Probably so, since he went to work for the General after mustering out of the service," Daigle said. "Security. Strange. Given his analytical background, it seems the General wouldn't have relegated him to a security job."

J.P. knew why. Olsen was working undercover. Vangie had told him. Based on the bootprints he'd seen outside his trailer, he decided to keep that juicy piece of information to himself. He'd already noticed that Tommy LeBoeuf had big feet. There were clothes lockers onboard, and J.P. planned to check LeBoeuf's boots when he had a chance.

Another man that J.P. didn't know sat on the cooler nursing a Red Bull. When no one introduced them, J.P. walked over and offered his hand.

"J.P. Saucier. Don't believe we've met."

"Bobbie Don Rooker," the man said. "Biloxi Police, homicide division. My chief thinks Olsen's murder was committed in Biloxi. I'm here to observe."

The hand that swallowed J.P.'s was callous-hard and hot, the knuckles swollen with old scar tissue that looked like what boxers called "breaks." Rooker didn't just shake hands; he engulfed them.

The man was a mountain of functional fat and muscle, standing at least six-four and taking up way too much oxygen on the cramped deck. He wore a short-sleeved button-down that was already sweat-stained at the collar and straining against a gut that looked solid enough to stop a shovel.

His face was a roadmap of broken capillaries, flushed a leathery red that suggested a lifetime of high blood pressure and Gulf Coast sun. Behind a pair of cheap, drug-store aviators, J.P. couldn't see the man's eyes, but he felt the weight of them. Rooker didn't look like the law; he looked like the kind of trouble you usually called the law on—a human roadblock that had decided to wear a badge. He also had big feet.

They idled out of the pass at quarter throttle, the twin props churning chocolate milk behind them. Once clear of the no-wake zone, Roland buried the sticks. The bow lifted, the hull slapped hard once, twice, then settled into a smooth run.

Wind whipped the salt spray over the console and into J.P.'s teeth. The sun was already fierce, turning the water into hammered metal. Twenty minutes out, the marsh fell away, and the Gulf opened wide and blue, innocent as a postcard. Roland throttled back two miles off the beach and let the GPS creep them the last half mile.

Trixie's reef was nothing you'd notice from the surface—just a darker patch of green where the bottom rose from sixty feet to twenty-two. But the fish knew. Mullet flickered silver under the boat like thrown coins.

"Bottom's clean," Tommy called from the sonar. "No debris field from the storm. Whatever's down there stayed put."

Roland killed the engines, and the sudden silence felt holy. The boat rocked gently, creaking, while the four men shrugged into tanks and checked regulators. J.P. pulled on a drysuit somebody had left aboard that almost fit. The January water was sixty-seven degrees. Not cold, but not exactly a warm bath either.

Johnnie and Sam stayed topside, Johnnie with a clipboard and a GoPro on a pole, saying he'd document from the surface. J.P. watched him fiddle with the camera. Roland handed J.P. a mask and fins.

"You still remember which end of the regulator the air comes out of?"

"I'll manage."

They giant-strided off the gunwale together. The water closed over J.P.'s head, not too cold and surprisingly clear—twenty-five, maybe thirty feet of visibility. Sunlight speared down in gold shafts, lighting up clouds of baitfish that parted like curtains.

The reef rose beneath them was a broken ridge of limestone and old iron, half-smothered in soft coral the color of a bruise. And there, tangled in a thicket of staghorn, lay the thing they'd come for: a human skeleton, still half-buried in sand, one arm stretching toward the surface light that would never reach it again.

It wasn't alone. Somebody had been here since the last storm. A second skeleton—this one fresh, flesh sliding off in gray ribbons, eyes already gone, a neat hole punched dead center in the forehead. And wedged between its teeth, glinting like a punchline, was a five-thousand-dollar casino chip. Same as the one sitting in J.P.'s pocket right now.

They hovered ten feet above the bottom, fins barely moving, suspended in the warm green light like men who'd just walked into church and found the altar on fire. The reef itself was a living thing, a jagged spine of brain coral and fire coral rose out of the sand in broken plates, attached to junker pickup trucks and car, their make and model no longer distinguishable, all furred with purple and rust-colored growth.

Snappers darted in and out of the shadows; a fat grouper the color of driftwood stared at them with stupid defiance from a cave. Everything looked peaceful until your eyes adjusted and you saw the bones.

One skeleton lay half-buried on its back, legs still tangled in the rusted remains of what might have been anchor chain. The skull was tilted toward the surface, jaw gaping in a silent scream that had lasted decades. Barnacles had colonized the ribcage like gray warts; a moray's head poked out between two ribs, thick as J.P.'s thigh, watching them with flat yellow eyes. One arm stretched upward, fingers long gone, as if the dead man had died trying to claw his way back to daylight. Somebody had been here within the last forty-eight hours since the storm, working fast, working alone.

Twenty feet away, floating just above the sand like a grotesque marionette, was a body. Fresh. Too fresh, a male, medium build, skin already slipping off in pale sheets, the way wet paper tears. Clouds of silt drifted from where the current had tugged at it. The hair, dark and longish, floated like ink. Both eyes were gone, pecked clean or eaten by crabs, leaving black sockets that stared straight at the divers.

A single bullet hole sat dead center in the forehead, edges beveled inward, powder burns still tattooed in a faint halo. Execution. The corpse wore the shredded remains of a charcoal suit jacket, white dress shirt now the color of old nicotine. The red silk tie, expensive, had snagged on a piece of staghorn and held the body almost upright, swaying gently with each surge. One loafer still clung to the left foot; the right was bare, toes already nibbled to the bone.

J.P. gently turned the dead man's head with two fingers. On the inside of the left wrist, lividity had already pooled purple-black, but above it was a tattoo: a fleur-de-lis with a serpent coiled beneath it. The ink was fresh enough that the skin around it was still raised. Same tattoo Paula wore over her heart. Same tattoo Chief had seen glowing on the naked witch in Odette's yard two nights ago. Beside the body, J.P. found something else: a whelkshell gorget complete with a weeping eye carving on it."

Thirty feet above, the Miss Behavior rocked innocently on the surface, sunlight flashing off her windshield. Daigle's silhouette leaned over the rail, filming everything with the GoPro. Someone else had been here first. Someone else had staged this horror show for them to find. J.P. felt the weeping eye gorget in his pocket press against his thigh like it had suddenly doubled in weight. He had seen enough. After motioning to Roland, he pointed toward the surface and began his ascent. Sam Marcantel and Johnnie Daigle helped him aboard, both men looking at him for answers, and Bobbie Don Rooker joined them.

"Where's Roland and Tommy?" Sam asked.

"Still have work to do," J.P. said. "Bodies to recover."

"Bodies?" Johnnie said.

"At least a half dozen," J.P. said. "Probably more is my guess. I'm also guessing they're not all from Biloxi."

"What makes you think that?" Sam asked.

"Just a hunch. Not all of the skulls had bullet holes. Most of the poor bastards were probably murdered somewhere else, brought here, and dumped. Not so for one of the bodies. It's fresh. My guess is someone brought him to Trixie's Reef last night, killed and dumped him."

"Who the hell would have been crazy or stupid enough to have a small boat out in last night's weather?" Sam asked.

"Don't know," J.P. said. "Maybe it wasn't small. Need to check the Coast Guard, though I'm betting whoever was here didn't alert them."

"Maybe not, but they probably have a record of all the boats that weren't in port last night," Johnnie said.

"Nearby ports," J.P. said. "If this is a commercial dumping site for dead bodies, criminals from all over the world likely know about it."

"Shouldn't be that hard to track down if this place is that well known," Sam said.

"You boys have your jobs cut out for you," J.P. said. "Especially Thib. He's going to have to bring in reinforcements to handle all the bodies."

Bobbie Don had heard all he needed to hear and was on the other side of the boat, making a cell phone call when Roland and Tommy popped out of the water. After they had climbed aboard, Sam tossed Roland a flask. He took a swig and passed it to Tommy.

"What, no bodies?" Sam asked.

"It's a crime scene cemetery down there," Roland said. "We're going to need a team of forensic archaeologists to document everything before we bring up the bodies."

"What about the fresh body?" J.P. asked.

"Photographed it, checked for clues as best we could, bagged it, and attached a line," Roland said. "This is a major crime scene now, and it's out of Tommy's and my league. Once we haul the body out of the drink, we can get the hell out of here."

A wind had picked up as Sam shielded his eyes and gazed to the south. "Good, because there's another storm heading our way, and the sky looks darker than it was last night.

The tides of January, J.P. thought to himself as he rolled the weeping-eye gorget in his palm, not bothering to tell the others.

Perhaps Chief's Horned Serpent was real. He didn't know. The only thing he knew for sure was that tonight, when he met Vangie for that drink in Chalmette, he would have quite a story to tell her.

CHAPTER 23

The storm came in hard and fast, the way Gulf weather does when it's got a grudge. By late afternoon, the sky over Oyster Island had turned the color of old pewter, and the wind began howling as if it wanted back inside the house. J.P. watched it build from the Airstream's little window, with rain already streaking the glass in sideways sheets, palms thrashing as if trying to tear themselves free of the ground.

Another front, colder this time, riding the back of the one that had just left. The island felt smaller under it, hemmed in and restless. He waited until full dark before he left. No point fighting the worst of it on the bridge; the blacktop to Chalmette would be slick as glass and twice as treacherous. But seven-thirty was coming, and Vangie didn't strike him as the kind of woman who liked to be kept waiting.

He pulled on his old oilskin coat, the one that still smelled faintly of diesel and cordite no matter how many times he washed it. He checked the Sig at the small of his back—habit, nothing more—then tucked the weeping-eye gorget into the inside pocket, right over his heart. It felt heavier tonight, as if it knew something he didn't. The casino chip he left behind was locked in the coffee can with the emergency cash. He wasn't carrying any more calling cards than he had to.

The pickup started on the second try, wipers slapping frantically against the windshield as he eased down the shell road. Lightning forked across the bay, lighting up the whitecaps for a frozen second—water boiling under the onslaught, the Majestic's lights blurred and trembling on the far shore. He'd wanted to visit Alex's house to check on Lucky and had called first. The big dog was doing well, and Renata was there, having just changed his bandage.

"He's in good hands," Alex said. "Go do what you have to do."

The muddy stretch to the main road was worse than he'd figured: wind rocking the truck hard, spray exploding over the hood like buckshot. Halfway to the turnoff, a gust hit broadside and shoved him into the wrong lane. He corrected without thinking, knuckles white on the wheel, and told himself this was nothing compared to Fallujah at night.

Chalmette was twenty minutes away if the roads stayed open. Tonight, they barely did. He hydroplaned twice on Judge Perez Drive, once badly enough that the rear end fishtailed and the ditch flashed hungry on the passenger side. Water stood in the low spots, black and shining under the streetlights, littered with palm fronds and somebody's overturned trash can. The radio spat static and dire warnings—flash flood alerts, tornado watch until midnight. With enough noise already rattling in his head, J.P. clicked it off.

Coops sat on a corner lot off Paris Road, a low cinder-block box with a faded red-and-white sign that had once said COOP'S PLACE but now just read OOPS in missing letters. The parking lot was half full, even in this mess—mostly pickups and a couple of parish units, lights off, drivers probably inside drinking off the overtime.

J.P. parked nose-out near the exit out of old habit, killed the engine, and sat a minute listening to the rain drum on the cab roof like impatient fingers. Inside, the place was exactly what Vangie had promised: terrible food, worse lighting, and the kind of anonymity money couldn't buy. Dim bulbs behind smoked glass, walls the color of old nicotine, a jukebox coughing up zydeco nobody was listening to. The air was thick with fryer grease, spilled beer, and the sour tang of too many wet bodies in too small a space.

Conversation was a low growl under the music—cops, roughnecks, a couple of casino dealers from New Orleans still in their vests. Nobody looked up when J.P. pushed through the door;

nobody ever did at Coops. He spotted her in the back booth, the one half-hidden by a fake ficus dying in a plastic pot. Vangie had claimed the corner that faced the room, back to the wall like she'd learned the same lessons he had.

A half-empty Hurricane glass sat in front of her, cherry stem floating like a tiny red flag of surrender. Her hair was loose tonight, dark waves brushing the shoulders of a black leather jacket that probably cost more than his truck. She was watching the door, and when she saw him, her mouth curved—not quite a smile, more like recognition of a shared secret.

J.P. threaded through the tables, rain dripping from his coat onto the sticky floor. A waitress in a Saints jersey gave him a tired nod; he lifted two fingers—beer, whatever's cold. By the time he slid into the booth across from Vangie, the waitress had already set a dripping Abita in front of him and vanished.

"You're late," Vangie said, but there was no heat in it.

Her voice was softer than he remembered, a little slurred at the edges. The Hurricane glass was her second, maybe third, and he understood why.

"Storm tried to kill me on the bridge," he said. "Figured you'd understand."

She laughed, low and throaty, and took another pull from the straw. Her eyes were bright, pupils wide in the dim light.

"I always understand, cher. That's my problem."

J.P. shrugged out of the wet coat and draped it on the seat beside him. The gorget shifted against his chest, cold even through the shirt. He leaned forward, elbows on the scarred table, and kept his voice low."

We need to talk about what I saw today."

Vangie's smile faded. She set the glass down carefully, as if it might explode. "I thought as much. You look like a man who's seen the bottom of something ugly."

"Bottom don't begin to cover it."

He started with the reef—told her about the old bones tangled in coral and rust, the fresh corpse swaying upright like a warning, the bullet hole neat as a period at the end of a sentence. Told her about the casino chip wedged between the dead man's teeth, identical to the one left in his trailer. When he got to the second gorget—the weeping eye carved exactly like the one in his pocket—her fingers tightened around the sweating glass. Outside, thunder cracked hard enough to rattle the bottles behind the bar. The lights flickered once, twice, then held. Nobody in the place even flinched.

"And the tattoo," he went on, voice barely above the rain. "Fleur-de-lis with the serpent coiled under it. Same as Paula's. Same as the woman Chief saw running naked through Odette's yard."

Vangie exhaled slowly, like she'd been holding her breath since he sat down. "You think it's all connected. The bodies, the… whatever the hell that serpent thing is."

"I know it is." He took a long pull of the beer, cold sliding down his throat like a small mercy. "And I'm wondering if Tommy LeBoeuf and that Biloxi detective—Bobbie Don Rooker—are knee-deep in it. Tommy's got size-thirteen feet and department-issue boots. Rooker's built like a refrigerator."

Vangie's eyes narrowed. She leaned in until he could smell the rum on her breath, sweet and dangerous. "Bobbie Don," she said softly. "I know him. Not well, but enough. He has a tab at the casino that would choke a horse. Always at the high-limit tables —baccarat, mostly. Loses big, wins bigger, then loses again. Word is he's into the wrong people for more than he'll ever earn honest."

"How does he get away with it?" J.P. asked.

"The General," Vangie said. "He protects him."

"Why?" J.P. asked. "Is the General using him for something?"

Vangie smiled. "They aren't brothers-in-law, if that's what you mean."

Lightning flashed again, turning her face stark white for an instant. In that frozen second, J.P. saw something raw in her expression—fear, maybe, or calculation.

"How deep is Rooker into the casinos?" he asked.

"Deep enough that people notice." She traced a wet ring on

the table with one fingertip. "Deep enough that somebody might decide a cop who gambles too much is more useful scared than honest."

"Deep enough to murder somebody to get out of his problem?"

"Hell, J.P., you met him. He has that vibe about him."

"What vibe?"

"Like someone who would cut his own mother's throat and not bother washing the blood off his hands."

The jukebox clicked over to a slow song, something mournful in French. Around them, the bar noise rose and fell like surf. J.P. felt the weight of too many eyes that weren't looking, too many conversations that stopped a beat too late when he glanced over. He reached across the table, covered her hand with his. Her skin was cool, trembling just slightly.

"We're in it now, Vangie. Both of us. Whoever staged that reef wants us to know they're watching. And they're not done."

She turned her hand palm-up under his, fingers curling to grip his wrist hard enough to bruise.

"I have a confession to make."

"Confession?"

Vangie didn't let go of his wrist. "I'm not a real P.I., just a wanna-be. It's the reason I hired you."

J.P. glanced at the bulge from her shoulder holster beneath her black leather jacket, smiled, and said, "Could have fooled me. You aren't working for the General?"

"That part's no lie. I work for the General, though not as a P.I. I'm his mistress, well... more like his whore."

"I wondered how you could afford that posh ride of yours, all your jewelry, and expensive clothes on a P.I.'s pay." When tears appeared in Vangie's eyes, J.P. clutched her hand. "Hey, it's okay. I have no leeway to judge anybody. Why are you playing detective?"

"The General is as dirty as they come. Chris Olsen worked for the casino. Chris is my brother."

Vangie shook her head when J.P. said, "Was he involved in the investigation of the wash?"

"I just made that part of the story up," she said.

J.P. squeezed Vangie's hand gently. "I'm so sorry. You think the General has something to do with his death?"

She took another drink of her Hurricane without answering J.P.'s question. The song on the jukebox ended, leaving the dark bar in silence until thunder shook the building, reminding everyone that the storm was still active.

"Chris was smart as a whip, but didn't have a lick of common sense. Mom wanted him to go to college. He joined the Air Force instead."

Vangie shook her head when J.P. asked, "Is your mom still alive?"

"Worked herself to death," she said. "The big bottle of Wellers she drank every week didn't help matters."

" What about your dad?"

"A worthless, skirt-chasing, alcoholic druggie," she said. "Mom finally managed to get us away from him, and she raised Chris and me on her own."

"I'm so sorry," J.P. said for the third time.

"Chris knew the General from Kessler and didn't know what he was getting into when he went to work for him. He was stubborn and short-sighted, but he wasn't stupid. He learned something that cost him his life."

"You didn't answer my question," J.P. asked. "Is the General responsible for your brother's death?"

"I think so, though I can't prove it," Vangie said. "I feel so... helpless."

Vangie nodded when J.P. asked, "Does the General know you're in Louisiana?"

"I told him I was going shopping in New Orleans. He said to have fun. Even if he doesn't know shopping isn't the real reason I'm here, I'm never going back to him."

Vangie grinned and sipped her Hurricane when J.P. said, "What about Meika?"

"I always thought I was bi until I met Meika. Now I'm leaning hard toward full-blown lesbian."

"Damn!" J.P. said. "You just shattered a whole batch of my fantasies."

Vangie grinned. "Hell, J.P., if you help me bring Chris's murderer to justice, I might just fulfill those fantasies. Maybe even convince Meika to help me."

"Well, hell, sweet talker. Now you got me thinking."

"Thinking's not good enough, sweetheart. I want to bring the big man down," she said.

The waitress interrupted them with another Abita and a fresh Hurricane for Vangie.

"How many Hurricanes is that?" he asked.

"Three," she said.

"Those babies are potent. You finish that one, and I'll be pouring you into bed tonight."

She laughed. "That's the General's favorite way to screw me, me practically comatose and him in total control. Maybe you can satisfy some of your fantasies tonight while I'm passed out."

"Not my style," J.P. said. "You're safe with me even if you are shit-faced snockered."

"Damn!" she said. "There goes one of my fantasies."

"Talking about sex isn't getting us anywhere. We need a plan."

"Meika told me if anyone can bring the General down, it's you. Help me."

"We need to talk with Eddie about this. He was an important man at the DOJ and likely knows more about the Biloxi casino scene than he was telling us. You okay with that?"

Vangie downed half the syrupy Hurricane while he was speaking, and her silly grin, drooping eyelids, and slurred words told him she was way beyond devising a plan to proceed."

"I'm staying at the Hilton. Will you take me there?"

Thunder shook the building as J.P. said, "Damn, girl! Guess I am pouring you into bed tonight."

CHAPTER 24

The rain came down in a steady pour as Alex eased his old Peugeot onto the blacktop off Oyster Island. The wipers beat a deliberate rhythm, pushing sheets of water aside just long enough for the headlights to catch the whitecaps churning in the bay. Renata sat beside him, legs tucked under her on the car's bucket seat, one hand resting lightly on his thigh as if to anchor him against the weather.

She wore a faded Saints hoodie he'd dug out of the bungalow closet—too big for her, sleeves rolled twice—and a pair of his jeans cinched tight with a belt. Her hair was twisted up under a baseball cap, a few damp curls escaping at her neck. They hadn't spoken much since leaving the island. The storm had knocked out the radio signal halfway down the muddy dirt road, leaving only the drum of rain on the roof and the low growl of the engine.

Alex kept his eyes on the road, one hand on the wheel, the other covering hers. Now and then, lightning flickered in the rearview mirror, turning the flooded marshes silver for an instant before the dark swallowed them again. Renata broke the silence first.

"You're quiet, Russian."

"Thinking," he said. "About copper. About fire. About how long it's been since I felt this... hopeful."

She squeezed his leg. "Good thoughts, then?"

He smiled without looking over. "The best."

The drive took just under an hour—up Judge Perez until it became N. Claiborne, then west through the sprawl of warehouses that always smelled faintly of sulfur even in the rain. Traffic was light; most sensible people had stayed home. Alex took the Tchoupitoulas exit, tires hissing on wet asphalt as he wound downriver past the port cranes standing like skeletal giants in the mist. Renata directed him with small gestures—left here, straight through the light, slow down. They turned onto a narrow side street paralleling the levee, where the pavement buckled, and the warehouses grew older, more forgotten.

Chain-link fences sagged under kudzu; broken windows stared like empty sockets. Finally, she pointed to a gap in the fencing half-hidden by overgrown oleander.

"There. Pull in."

Alex eased the agile French car through the opening, gravel crunching under the tires. The building loomed ahead: a long, three-story brick hulk with Arcadia Distillery in faded gold script across the façade. The roof was patched with mismatched tin, but the walls looked solid. A rolling steel door stood half open, just wide enough for a person to slip through.

Rain dripped steadily from the eaves, turning the ground into a shallow lake that reflected the gray sky. They sat a moment in the idling car, watching water stream off the windshield.

"You sure about this?" Alex asked. "Place looks like it's been empty since the flood, and I don't mean Katrina."

"It has," Renata said. "But the important parts are still inside. Come."

They dashed from the car together, shoes splashing through puddles, and ducked under the door into the dim interior. The air hit them immediately—cool, heavy with the ghosts of mash and yeast, charred oak and caramelized sugar. Even after twenty years abandoned, the smell of old rum lingered like a memory that refused to die.

Alex stopped just inside the threshold, water dripping from his jacket, and let out a slow breath that fogged in the damp chill.

"Mother of God."

The space opened up around them: high ceilings with exposed iron beams, rows of massive cypress fermenters thirty feet long, their staves swollen but intact. Brick arches supported the upper floors; shafts of weak light slanted through broken skylights, illuminating dust motes that danced like slow fireflies. And there, in the center of the main hall, stood the stills.

Copper. Beautiful, verdigris-kissed copper. Three pot stills in graduated sizes, swan necks thick as a man's thigh, lyne arms curving gracefully into worm tubs still coiled and waiting. Condenser tanks the size of small cars. Everything hand-hammered, riveted, and built to last centuries. A few valves were seized, some pipes furred with mineral deposits, but the bones were perfect.

Alex walked forward as if in a dream, shoes echoing on the concrete floor. He laid a reverent hand on the largest still, fingers tracing the patina like it was holy script.

"This... this is pre-Prohibition," he said. "Look at the rivets. The shape of the helmet. Louisiana sugar rum, maybe even earlier. They don't make them like this anymore."

Renata watched him from a few paces back, arms folded, a small smile playing at her lips. He moved from still to still, crouching to peer into the charge doors, running his palm over the smooth swell of the pots. In the far corner, he found a row of charred American oak barrels—some split, but many sound—stacked on their sides like sleeping soldiers.

A manual bottling line, glass jugs crated and waiting—even an old copper rectifier column, tall as a man, its trays still in place. Alex straightened, turned to her with eyes bright as a child's on Christmas morning.

"We have to have this—all of it. I don't care what it costs—we buy the equipment, move it to the island, rebuild around it. This is..." His voice cracked slightly. "This is the soul I thought the storm took from me."

Renata stepped closer, rain still beading on her cap. "The building too?"

"Everything that isn't nailed down. Hell, some of what is."

She reached out and brushed a wet strand of hair from his forehead. "I know who owns it, Alex."

He stilled. "Who?"

"Rockie LaSalle. Owner of Rockie's on Bourbon Street." Her voice was quiet, matter-of-fact. "The club where I danced. When I didn't remember my name. When I didn't remember you."

Alex's joy dimmed, replaced by something more complicated. He glanced around the vast space again, then back at her.

"The strip club."

"Yes." She met his eyes without flinching. "Rockie bought this place cheaply after Katrina, planned to turn it into lofts or a music venue. Never happened. The equipment's been sitting here ever since. He won't care who buys it, as long as the price is right."

Alex exhaled slowly, hands settling on her shoulders. "You're sure?"

"I'm sure." A faint smile. "I still know how to reach him. One phone call."

Outside, thunder rolled low over the river. Inside, the copper gleamed dully in the gray light, waiting. Alex pulled her close and rested his forehead against hers.

"Then make the call, love. Let's bring this beauty home."

Renata leaned against one of the massive cypress fermenters, arms crossed, watching Alex pace the dusty floor like a man possessed. The rain had eased to a steady patter on the tin roof patches overhead, but water still dripped from their clothes, pooling around their shoes.

"How do you plan to pay for it?" she asked, voice cutting through the echo. "Real estate is through the roof in New Orleans, even for a condemned, dilapidated building like this. The equipment alone—someone will strip it if they think there's money on the table."

Alex stopped, ran a hand through his wet hair. "I have a business partner. Jake Huntington—the Cryptid Hunter."

Renata's mouth curved into a slow smile. "I know about him. The reality TV show is Mama and Sveta's favorite program. They quote his catchphrases at dinner. And I know Mr. Huntington is a billionaire."

"I'll call him," Alex said, pulling out his phone. "He can deal directly with Rockie. Wire the money, handle the paperwork—"

Renata shook her head, stepping close enough that he could smell the rain on her skin.

"Rockie is street savvy. He'll smell blood in the water the second a billionaire's name comes up. The property will start being shopped around town before sunset. You must deal directly with Rockie."

"But…"

"Don't worry, my darling." She touched his cheek, thumb brushing his jaw. "He knows I hate Russians. Before I'm done with him, he'll think I'm setting you up as a vendetta—convincing some gullible foreigner to overpay for a money pit to watch him lose."

Alex searched her eyes, saw the steel there, and nodded slowly. "All right. Your lead."

They locked the rolling door behind them and drove into the Quarter, the streets slick and shining under the storm's aftermath. Parking was a miracle—a tight spot off Bienville, half a block from Bourbon. By the time they splashed through the puddles and pushed open the heavy door of Rockie's, they were soaked through again.

The place hit them like a fever dream: throbbing bass, neon bleeding pink and blue across bare skin, the sharp tang of perfume, bourbon, and sweat. Beautiful women in varying states of undress moved through the crowd like bright fish in dark water. Men clustered around stages and tables, eyes hungry, wallets open.

At the center of the main room was the circular bar—the pussy bar, they called it—ringed by stools where dancers perched and posed, legs spread for the encircling admirers, tips tucked into garters and thongs. A waitress in glittering pasties immediately spotted Renata.

"Vixen!" she squealed, throwing arms around her in a fierce hug that ignored the wet clothes. "Girl, where you been?"

More dancers drifted over, cooing and touching Renata's arm, calling her Vixen like it was still her name. The bartender —a burly guy with a gold tooth—grinned widely and slid a pitcher of draft beer across to Alex without asking, then mixed something tall and virgin for Renata, heavy on the fruit and expensive syrups.

"On the mister's tab," he said with a wink, ringing it up loud enough for half the bar to hear.

Word traveled fast. Rockie appeared from a back hallway like a king summoned to his court. Mid-fifties, flashy suit straining at the belly, gold chains nestled in chest hair, a diamond pinky ring catching the neon. His eyes lit on Renata and stayed there, hungry and proprietary. He'd always carried a torch for her— everyone knew it.

"Vixen, baby!" He swept her up in a twirl that made her borrowed hoodie ride up, exposing the curve of her waist. His gaze raked over the oversized shirt and jeans, lingering. "Look at you, all covered up. What's this bullshit?"

She laughed, low and throaty, playing him from the first note. "Miss me, Rockie?"

"Every damn night."

He led them to a back table, velvet rope parted by a bouncer the size of a refrigerator. Drinks appeared unbidden. Renata leaned in, conspiratorial, whispering just loud enough for Rockie to strain closer. She painted the picture: this Russian mark she'd hooked, desperate for the old distillery, convinced it was a steal. She'd talked him into it out of spite—let the dumb foreigner sink his money into Rockie's headache.

Alex sat quietly, jaw tight, as she conducted the orchestra. Rockie named his price: one million, cash.

"Bullshit," Renata shot back, eyes flashing. "The building's condemned. The roof leaks like a sieve. City's gonna make you tear it down or restore it—either way, it'll cost you a fortune. You'll be lucky to get half that on the open market."

"What difference to you how much he pays?" Rocky asked.

"I want you to take all of his money. He has a half-million, though not much more than that," she said.

"He's lying to you," Rocky said.

Rocky smiled when she said, "All men are liars."

They went back and forth, voices rising over the music, Rockie's face flushing deeper red with every counter. Finally, he leaned back, spread his hands.

"Half a million. But only if Vixen gives me a table dance. Like the old days and not a half-ass peepshow.."

Renata didn't hesitate. She stood, peeled off the soaked hoodie, then the jeans, moving slowly to the beat pulsing through the floor. The oversized clothes hit the floor; beneath, she wore only simple black underwear that came off just as deliberately.

The club went electric—heads turning, conversations dying, every eye in the place suddenly fixed on the gorgeous statuesque woman who'd once been their queen. Alex gripped his beer glass hard enough to whiten his knuckles, temper a hot coil in his gut. He bit the inside of his cheek until he tasted blood, forcing himself to stay seated, to trust her play.

Renata—Vixen—danced for Rockie alone at first, body fluid and commanding, hips rolling inches from his face. Sweat gleamed on her skin under the lights. The crowd pressed closer, lathered, chanting her old stage name. When she finished the table dance and straightened, glistening and triumphant, the roar went up.

"Pussy bar! Pussy bar!"

Her eyes met Alex's across the table—dark, fierce, a flash of something wild and exhibitionist waking after years asleep. She smiled wickedly and bounded onto the circular stage. One sultry dance bled into another. Bills rained onto the bar around her. She owned the room the way she once had, her body moving like liquid sin, the storm outside forgotten.

While the music thumped and the crowd howled, Alex slipped his phone under the table and dialed Jake.

"Tell me you've got good news," Jake said, his voice crackling with excitement.

Alex explained, keeping his voice low. "The building's perfect. But we're at Rockie's now, negotiating. Need you to cover half a million, maybe more."

"Done," Jake said without hesitation. "Mama and I are already headed your way—figured you'd need backup.

"Keep it low profile," Alex said.

"Too late, buddy. Word is the city's been holding up sales because they want full historic restoration. Millions in compliance."

Alex glanced at Renata on the stage, powerful and untouchable amid the frenzy. "Oh no! What will you do?"

"Don't worry," Jake said. "I'll make it work."

CHAPTER 25

J.P. came awake slowly, the bed beneath him too soft, the sheets smelling of cheap motel soap and something sweeter, floral, that clung to his skin. Not his Airstream. Not Oyster Island. He opened his eyes to dim light filtering through heavy curtains, the faint hum of an air conditioner rattling in the window. Vangie was curled against him, one arm draped possessively over his chest, her breath warm and steady against his neck, her dark hair cascading across the pillow like spilled ink.

For a moment, he let himself feel it—the weight of her, the heat—then memory slammed back in: Coops, the storm, three Hurricanes down her throat, her confession about Chris, about the General. He eased away carefully, untangling her arm. She stirred anyway, murmuring something incoherent as he sat on the edge of the bed.

His clothes lay in a damp heap on the chair—jeans stiff with dried rainwater, shirt wrinkled and sour. He pulled them on, the fabric cold against his skin. Vangie's eyes fluttered open. She watched him dress, a lazy smile curving her lips despite the hangover he knew was already clawing at her skull.

"I had a hard time controlling myself last night," he said quietly, buckling his belt.

She pushed up on one elbow, the sheet slipping to her waist —no shame in her, just that frank, challenging gaze.

"Why didn't you give in?"

"I ain't the General, sweet thing."

She laughed softly, then winced, pressing fingers to her temple. "God, my head."

"Hair of the dog," he said. "It's the only thing that really works."

Vangie reached for her flask on the nightstand, unscrewed the cap, and drank.

"You're right," she said.

J.P. checked his phone—6:47 a.m. Battery low, one missed call from an unknown number. No voicemail.

"I'm heading back to the island. Can you meet me at the Majestic around noon? I'll buy you lunch. We can talk to Eddie—get his take on the General, the casinos, all of it."

"Maybe," she said, voice rough. "If a long shower and my flask can resurrect me from the dead.

"Three Hurricanes," he said, shaking his head. "Most people would be in the ER."

"Trust me, cher. I couldn't feel any worse than I do right now."

As he pulled on his boots, the room felt smaller, the walls pressing in. Outside, the storm had passed, but the sky visible through the curtains was still bruised and heavy, promising more trouble later. He glanced back at her—beautiful, broken, deadly as hell.

"Watch yourself," he said. "Whoever killed Chris... they're dangerous and know we're digging."

Vangie's smile faded. "You too, baby. Watch your back."

J.P. nodded, slipped out the door into the damp Chalmette morning. The parking lot was pocked with puddles reflecting the gray sky. His pickup sat where he'd left it, driver's side mirror cracked—storm debris, probably. Or not. He scanned the lot anyway, old habit. Nothing moved except a stray cat slinking around a dumpster.

The drive to Oyster Island was quiet, the roads slick but empty. Spanish moss hung in wet ropes from the oaks along the highway, dripping like mourning veils. Halfway there, his phone buzzed in the console. Unknown number again. He thumbed accept.

It was Sam Marcantel, his voice thick with coffee and

tobacco. "Where you at?"

"Just left Chalmette. Halfway home."

"Well, turn your ass around." Sam's tone was flat, but J.P. caught the edge under it—something sharp and urgent. "Meet me at the Bayou Café on Paris Road."

J.P.'s grip tightened on the wheel. "What's up?"

"Trouble."

The line went dead.

J.P. stared at the phone a second, pulse kicking up. Sam didn't spook easily. Whatever the big detective had to tell him was bad enough to drag him out before the sun was fully up. He yanked the wheel hard, tires squealing as he swung into a U-turn across the median. Gravel pinged the undercarriage. The sky darkened further, clouds boiling in from the Gulf like they'd heard Sam's warning too.

His mind raced ahead to the café. Sam would be in a back booth, nursing black coffee and chewing Red Man, eyes scanning every face that walked in. Whatever he had to say, it wasn't good news. Maybe about the reef. Maybe about Chris Olsen. Or maybe —his gut twisted—about Vangie. Or about him. The weeping-eye gorget shifted in his pocket as he accelerated back toward Chalmette, heavy as a bullet. He had a cold certainty that the storm last night hadn't been the worst thing coming his way.

J.P. pushed the pickup harder than he should have, the engine growling as he blew past the speed limit back toward Chalmette. The sky hung low and sullen, a lid on the world, and every mile felt like borrowed time. Sam's voice kept looping in his head— short, clipped, the way the big man got when something had gone sideways bad.

The Bayou Café sat at the corner of Paris Road and St. Bernard Highway, a squat brick box with a hand-painted sign, half-washed away by years of storms. The gravel lot was already crowded with parish units, rusted pickups, and a couple of eighteen-wheelers idling like sleeping beasts.

J.P. nosed in between two patrol cars, killed the engine, and jogged through the drizzle to the door. The place was loud with morning rush—forks scraping plates, waitresses barking orders to the kitchen, the sizzle of bacon, and the rich smell of chicory coffee thick enough to chew. Locals hunched over their food as if it might run off the plate. Nobody looked up when the bell over the door jingled.

Sam Marcantel sat in the far back booth, the one under the flickering fluorescent that made everybody look half dead. He was alone, staring into a cup of cold coffee, his big shoulders slumped. A half-eaten plate of eggs and grillades sat pushed away like it had personally offended him. When he saw J.P., he lifted a hand heavy as a wrecking ball.

J.P. slid in across from him. A waitress—Miss Rita, hair teased high and a Saints lanyard around her neck—appeared like magic, setting a mug of black coffee in front of him without asking.

"Morning, cher," she said, voice smoky from a lifetime of Camels. "Haven't seen you in a while. You want the usual?"

"Just coffee for now, Rita. Thanks."

She nodded and vanished into the clatter. J.P. leaned in. "Where's Johnnie?"

Sam's jaw worked, chewing on something that wasn't tobacco this time.

"Jail."

J.P. felt the words hit him like a gut punch.

"Jail? What the hell for?"

"Tommy LeBoeuf's dead." Sam's voice was low, almost lost under the café noise. "They're saying Johnnie killed him."

J.P. sat back, the vinyl seat creaking. "Tommy?"

Sam shook his head slowly.

"Somebody put two in his chest and one in the head last night, in his own garage. The neighbor heard the shots around one a.m. and called it in. Johnnie's prints on the weapon—a throw-down .38 found in the azalea bushes. His cruiser was parked two doors down, engine still warm."

"Jesus." J.P. took a swallow of coffee; it burned going down. "What does Johnnie say?"

"They got him on ice at the parish lockup. Won't let anybody near him till the F.O.P. lawyer shows. Feelings are... mixed."

"Why mixed?"

Sam's eyes flicked up, red-rimmed. "Cop on cop, J.P. That's the third rail. Some of the old guard think Johnnie finally snapped."

"What the hell do you mean?"

"Tommy was riding him pretty hard lately, talking shit about Johnnie's divorce, money troubles. Others figure it's too neat. Too many loose ends."

"Like why Johnnie would be dumb enough to leave the gun in the bushes."

"Exactly." Sam rubbed a thick hand over his face. "Johnnie called me late—after midnight. Got my wife instead. Told her it was urgent, life or death. By the time I called back, his phone was off. Then the call-out came for the shooting."

"Shit," J.P. said.

Sam reached into his shirt pocket and pulled out a folded sheet torn from a message pad—yellow paper, parish sheriff logo faint at the top. He slid it across the table, as if it might bite.

"Sara at dispatch gave me this twenty minutes ago. Johnnie slipped it to her when they brought him in for booking. Told her it was for my eyes only."

J.P. unfolded it carefully. The handwriting was Johnnie's —hurried, ballpoint digging into the paper: Setup. Bayou Mortuary.

"The reef," J.P. said. "Someone never intended for its discovery."

"And no way to hide the bodies now," Sam said.

"Damn!" J.P. said. "So they're changing the narrative to shift the blame, and Tommy was expendable."

"Or someone thought his mouth was too big," Sam said.

"What's the reference to Bayou Mortuary mean?" J.P. asked. "You think it's the body disposal entity?"

"Maybe," Sam said. "Johnnie was probably on to something, the reason he was targeted. I'll check it out. Suggestions?"

"Hide the note and play things close to the vest. If Tommy was dirty, there are probably others in the department who are too."

"Who do you suspect?"

"Spivey Sonnier, for one," J.P. said.

"Man's as mean as a water moccasin. I wouldn't put it past him to take money under the table. Hell, I was wondering how he afforded his new house."

"He's no friend of either of us," J.P. said. "That's for sure."

"I'm going to talk to Johnnie as soon as I can," Sam said.

J.P. shook his head. "No. We won't catch anybody if they know that we know. Be cool, or they'll come for you next."

J.P. read Johnnie's note twice, the café noise fading to a dull roar in his ears.

"You sure?" Sam asked.

"Somebody killed Tommy to shut him up, then framed Johnnie to keep the rest of us chasing our tails. The reef keeps its secrets a little longer."

Sam drained his cold coffee like it was whiskey. "Question is, who's next on the cleaning list?"

J.P. folded the note and tucked it into his pocket next to the weeping-eye gorget. The weight of both felt suddenly heavier. Outside, thunder rumbled again, low and mean, like something big waking up hungry.

"I'm spooked, J.P.," Sam said.

"Me too," J.P. said. "Sheriff Comier's not a part of this. I worked with him for way too many years. He's not dirty. I'd stake my life on it."

"Maybe not, but Comier's retiring next week, before the end of his term."

"You're shitting me!" J.P. said. "I haven't heard anything about him retiring. There's no election until next August. Who is going to take his place until then?"

"The Chief Deputy," Sam said.

"Who is that?" J.P. asked.

"Johnnie," Sam said.

"Bullshit!" J.P. said. "He can't be a homicide detective and Chief Deputy, too, can he?"

"He can, and Johnnie would be the interim sheriff, except for one thing."

"What one thing?" J.P. asked.

"If he's indicted for a crime, the position goes to the coroner."

"Fuck me running!" J.P. said. "Spivey Sonnier is going to be sheriff?"

Sam nodded. "Johnnie's fucked. I'm fucked, you're fucked, our whole damn case is fucked."

"Someone needs to talk the sheriff into staying on for another couple of months," J.P. said.

"Good luck with that. His mind is pretty well made up."

"Someone needs to tell him what's going on," J.P. said. "Maybe he'll change his mind."

"Sounds like a good way to put our head on the chopping block," Sam said. "You have no standing, and if I accuse Sonnier of malfeasance without proof, I'll be out the door faster than you can say squat."

The windows of the little café shook when thunder rocked the old wood-framed building. J.P. shook his head and put his Stetson back on.

"Hang in there, Sam. I know someone who can help us, and I'm on my way to see him now."

CHAPTER 26

The storm had finally spent itself sometime before dawn, leaving behind a sky the color of wet slate and air so thick it felt like breathing through damp cotton. Odette's cottage smelled of rain-soaked jasmine, beeswax, and the lingering musk of three women who had slept tangled together under one quilt like sisters who'd forgotten how to be anything else.

Paula woke first. She lay still, eyes tracing the familiar cracks in the cypress ceiling while the other two breathed slow and deep beside her. Odette was curled on her side, one arm flung across Trixie's waist, mouth slightly open, a faint snore escaping every third breath. Trixie slept on her back, one leg hooked over the edge of the mattress, the black silk nightie twisted around her hips, exposing the long runner's curve of her thigh and the scrollwork tattoo that seemed to move in the soft gray light.

Paula felt the weight of the night before settle on her chest like a stone smoothed by the river. The witch's words still echoed in her skull: Burn what must burn, or be burned. She touched the fleur-de-lis on her breast through the thin cotton of her sleep shirt. The serpent beneath it felt alive, coiled tighter than ever as she slipped from the bed without waking them, bare feet silent on the cool planks.

The robe Odette had lent her hung on the back of the door. She pulled it on, cinched the belt, and stepped out onto the porch. The world was quiet in the way only post-storm mornings can be. Spanish moss hung in wet ropes from the live oaks. Puddles reflected a sky that hadn't yet decided whether to stay gray or try for blue. The air tasted clean, almost sweet, as though the Gulf had finally rinsed its mouth after vomiting up everything it had swallowed.

Paula leaned against the railing, arms folded tight across her ribs. She closed her eyes and let the quiet seep into her. For the first time in years, the silence didn't feel like judgment. It felt like permission.

Inside, the bed creaked. Odette appeared in the doorway, hair a wild halo, wearing nothing but an oversized Saints jersey that hit mid-thigh. She yawned, stretched, then came up behind Paula and wrapped both arms around her waist, chin resting on her shoulder.

"Morning, witchy woman," she said, voice still thick with sleep.

Paula leaned back into the embrace. "Morning, hurricane."

They stood like that a long time, watching the light change on the water. Then Odette's arms tightened.

"You're different this morning."

Paula let out a breath she hadn't realized she was holding. "I feel... unmoored. Like something inside me finally let go of the dock and drifted."

Odette kissed the side of her neck, soft, no heat, just comfort. "Good. You been holding that line too long."

Trixie padded out barefoot, rubbing sleep from her eyes, the silk nightie slipping off one shoulder. She saw them and smiled —small, private, without jealousy.

"Coffee?" she asked.

"On it," Odette said, but she didn't move right away.

Paula turned in her arms and met her oldest friend's eyes. "I need to see Tante Félonise. Today."

Odette nodded once. "Then we go. All three of us."

Trixie leaned against the doorframe, arms crossed loosely. "Who is Tante Félonise?"

"Voodoo woman," Odette said.

Trixie grinned and said, "I'm in."

Paula looked between them—Odette's steady warmth, Trixie's fearless curiosity—and felt something loosen in her chest.

"Breakfast first," she said. "Then we drive."

Odette kissed her forehead, quick and fierce.

"Damn right."

Inside, the smell of chicory coffee soon mingled with butter sizzling in a cast-iron skillet. Odette scrambled eggs with tasso and green onion while Trixie sliced tomatoes and set out mayhaw jelly. Paula moved between them, pouring coffee, setting plates, feeling—for the first time in a long time—like she belonged exactly where she stood. When the plates were cleared and the last of the coffee poured, Odette grabbed her keys.

"Lincoln's gassed up," she said. "Let's go see the old mambo before the next squall decides to park itself over us."

They stepped into the damp morning. The Lincoln Continental waited under the live oak like a sleeping panther —old, its chrome gleaming through the patina, white sidewall tires spotless. Odette slid behind the wheel, Trixie took shotgun, and Paula sat in the back, the gris-gris bag resting heavy in her lap.

The engine turned over with a throaty purr. Odette pulled onto the shell road, tires crunching, and pointed the big car toward Chalmette. The sky stayed gray, clouds low and restless, but the rain held off. Spanish moss dripped from the oaks like slow tears. Paula watched the landscape slide past—marsh, bayou, the occasional shotgun house with blue bottle trees clinking in the breeze—and felt the pull of something older than any church.

Tante Félonise was waiting. They all knew it. The road curved, the trees thickened, and the little shack came into view—gray weathered boards, tin roof patched with tar paper, a bottle tree glittering in the yard like a chandelier made of secrets. Odette killed the engine. Silence settled, broken only by the drip of water from the eaves. Paula opened her door first.

"Showtime," she said, voice steady.

The three women stepped out of the Lincoln into air so heavy it felt like breathing through wet silk. The bottle tree in

Tante Félonise's yard clinked softly, hundreds of blue, green, and clear bottles catching the muted daylight like trapped stars. Each one was supposed to hold a restless spirit, trapping it inside the glass so it couldn't wander and cause mischief.

Today, the bottles seemed to hum faintly, as though the spirits inside were listening. The shack itself was small, shotgun-style, raised on cypress piers against the flood-prone ground. Weathered gray boards, patched here and there with tin and mismatched planks, leaned slightly toward the bayou as if tired after a hundred years of standing watch.

A narrow porch sagged under the weight of hanging ferns and drying herbs—sweet Annie, rue, hyssop, and something sharper that made the back of the throat tighten. A single red door, chipped but freshly painted, stood open. From inside came the low pulse of a hand-drum, slow and deliberate, like a heartbeat heard through water.

Tante Félonise waited just beyond the threshold. She was tiny, barely five feet, but the room seemed to shrink around her. Skin the color of dark honey, wrinkled like river-washed parchment. Hair white as egret feathers, wrapped in a scarlet tignon tied high and proud. She wore a long dress of deep indigo cotton, sleeves rolled to the elbows, hem brushing the tops of bare feet that looked strong enough to root her to the earth itself. Around her neck hung a necklace of cowrie shells and tiny black river pearls; on her left wrist, a copper bracelet etched with serpents eating their own tails. Her eyes were pale milky blue, almost blind, yet they tracked each woman the moment she crossed the sill.

"Been expecting y'all," she said. Her voice was low, smoky, carrying the old patois that mainly had died out in the parish. "Storm woke everything up. Even the ones who sleep deep."

She didn't smile, but there was warmth in the way she gestured them inside with one gnarled hand. The single room was a temple disguised as a parlor. No electricity—only candles. Red ones burned in the corners for the Petro spirits, black ones on the small brick altar for Baron Samedi and Maman Brigitte.

A long table against the far wall held the veves: intricate cornmeal designs drawn fresh that morning—Damballah's double serpent, Erzulie's heart pierced with swords, Ogoun's machete crossed with a rifle. Offerings lay everywhere: rum in cracked porcelain cups, white flowers wilting in mason jars, a half-eaten plate of fried plantains, a raw egg cracked into a bowl for the dead.

The air was warm, damp, thick with incense—copal, frankincense, and something sharper, like crushed cloves and gunpowder. A low table stood in the center of the room, round, covered in a white cloth. Three chairs waited.

Above it hung a single bare bulb, unlit; instead, a hurricane lamp burned low, throwing golden light across the walls where old photographs and chromolithographs of the saints hung beside veve drawings and a framed chromo of St. Michael spearing the dragon. Tante Félonise moved to the altar, slow but sure, and lit a fresh black candle with a wooden match. The flame caught and steadied.

"Sit," she said.

"Yes, ma'am," Odette said.

They sat—Paula in the center, Odette on her left, Trixie on her right. The chairs were old ladder-backs, worn smooth by decades of supplicants. The mambo regarded them for a long moment, milky eyes seeming to see straight through skin.

"You come for answers," she said, "but answers cost. First, you pay the price of knowing." She reached behind the altar and brought out a shallow clay bowl, black as midnight, filled with water from the bayou. She set it in front of Paula. "Look."

Paula leaned forward. The surface of the water was still at first, then began to ripple without wind. Images formed in the dark mirror: the reef, bones tangled in staghorn coral, the fresh corpse with the chip between its teeth. Then the witch in Odette's yard—naked, feral, wearing Paula's face. Then the weeping eye gorget, glowing against black velvet. Finally, a casino floor at night, green felt tables stretching into shadow, and a man in a crisp uniform turning slowly, bullet hole blooming in his forehead like a dark flower.

Paula jerked back. The water went still. Tante Félonise nodded once.

"The Serpent is awake and hungry. Been fed secrets and blood for too long. Now it wants payment in full." She looked at Paula. "You carry both hands—the right that prays, the left that commands. You been afraid to hold both at the same time. Afraid one will burn the other."

Paula swallowed. "I don't know how to choose."

"You don't choose," the mambo said. "You marry them. You let the left hand hold the rosary while the right draws the veve. You stop asking permission and start remembering who you are."

"Yes, ma'am," Paula said.

The little mambo turned to Odette. "You carry fire. You burn bright, but you burn alone. Time to share the flame before it consumes you." Then to Trixie. "You carry questions. The reef calls you because you listen. But listening ain't enough. Sometimes you got to answer back."

Tante Félonise stood. She took a small bottle of rum from the altar, poured three drops into the bowl, and three more onto the floor for the ancestors. Then she began to sing—low, wordless, a melody older than the bayou itself. The hand-drum in the corner seemed to beat on its own, slow and deep.

She moved to each woman in turn, touching forehead, heart, hands—marking them with a paste of white clay and ground herbs. When she reached Paula, she lingered, pressing the clay between her brows until it felt like a third eye opening.

"Tonight," she said, "you dream. Tomorrow, you act. The tides of January wait for no one."

"Yes, ma'am," Paula said.

Tante Félonise stepped back. The candles flared high, then settled. The drumming faded.

"That's all," she said. "Now go. The island is listening."

They rose without speaking. Paula felt something shift inside her chest—like a door that had been locked for decades finally creaking open. Outside, the sky had cleared to a bruised lavender. The bottle tree chimed softly as they walked back to the Lincoln. None of them spoke until Odette started the engine.

Then Paula, very quietly, said, "I think I know what I have to burn."

Odette glanced at her in the rearview mirror. "And what's that, cher?"

Paula touched the serpent tattoo over her heart. "Everything I've been afraid to be."

Trixie reached back from the front seat and squeezed her hand as Odette put the car in gear. The Lincoln rolled down the shell road, headed back toward Oyster Island, carrying three women who were no longer quite the same people who had arrived.

CHAPTER 27

The Majestic smelled of lemon oil, old wood, and the faint ghost of last night's rain still clinging to the pilings beneath the building. Mid-afternoon light slanted through the tall windows, turning the bar into a cathedral of dust motes and amber reflections.

The place was empty except for the three of them: Eddie Toledo behind the mahogany rail, polishing a highball glass that didn't need it; Vangie LeBlanc perched on a stool like she owned the room, legs crossed, white linen trousers pristine despite the morning's humidity.

She looked impossibly fresh—hair sleek, makeup flawless, hangover apparently burned away by sheer force of will, a very long shower, and hair of the dog. J.P. paused just inside the door, letting his eyes adjust from the glare outside. The storm had scrubbed the island clean, leaving the sky hard and clear blue, but the air still felt bruised. Eddie glanced up first.

"You look like you slept in the truck."

"Close enough," J.P. said, walking over. He tipped his Stetson back and slid onto the stool beside Vangie. "Morning, beautiful. You're looking a damn sight better than when I poured you into bed."

Vangie's smile was slow, wicked. "I'm resilient. Also, I have a perfect concealer." She lifted her glass and saluted him. "Eddie's been kind enough to let me bend his ear about my brother, the reef, and the fact that somebody's trying to buy you off with casino chips."

Eddie set the glass down with a soft clink. "She has a hell of a story, and I've heard worse from better liars."

J.P. took the black coffee Eddie slid across the bar. "So we're all caught up?"

"Pretty much," Eddie said. "Except the part where we figure out who's watching us and why they're moving so fast." Vangie tapped a manicured nail on the bar. "That's why we're moving to the back booth. Old habits."

J.P. raised an eyebrow. "Why the intrigue? There's nobody here except us."

Eddie gave him a look that had once made mob lawyers sweat on the stand.

"The walls have ears, and old habits die hard. All the worn-out platitudes that are still around because of the truth they contain."

He jerked his head toward the far corner, where a high-backed booth sat half-hidden behind a real palm.

"Fine," J.P. said, "but let's ditch the coffee and tea and start on the hard stuff."

"Amen to that," Vangie said.

Eddie grinned and grabbed some bottles behind the bar. "Thought you'd never ask."

They slid in—Eddie first, back to the wall; Vangie beside him, facing the door; J.P. across from them, keeping the entrance in his peripheral. The booth smelled faintly of old cigar smoke and spilled bourbon. Eddie leaned forward, elbows on the scarred table.

"Talk," he said to J.P. "Start with the reef and work backward. I want to know what you saw that made you look like you'd swallowed a live grenade."

"Things are moving faster than that," J.P. said. "There was a murder in Chalmette last night, a deputy with the St. Bernard Sheriff's department named Tommy LeBoeuf. Tommy's a diver and was on the Miss Behavior with me when we started fishing bodies out of the water."

Eddie leaned in. "Tell me more," he said.

"They have a suspect in custody; Johnnie Daigle, a homicide detective and a close friend of mine working the reef case."

"I can see why that has you worried," Eddie said.

"It seems the reef is a commercial dumping ground for murder victims run by someone in Chalmette. Criminals from Biloxi and elsewhere, maybe as far away as Florida and the Bahamas, are dumping bodies there. The unexpected discovery of Vangie's brother's body has exposed many murders."

"And?" Eddie said.

"The criminal element has a mess on their hands. They can't clean it up, so they're trying to cover it up."

"How?" Eddie asked.

"Tommy was a dirty cop, maybe with a big mouth. He was expendable. Someone killed him and made it look as if Johnnie Daigle did it."

"Why would they frame Daigle?" Eddie asked.

"Because Sheriff Comier is an honest cop and would see through the mob's plan. Problem is he's retiring before the end of his term. Johnnie is the Chief Deputy and would normally serve as interim sheriff until next fall, when the next election will be held. He can't serve in that position if he's being indicted."

"So, by Louisiana law, the next person in line is the coroner," Eddie said.

J.P. nodded. "Correct, and therein lies the problem."

"The coroner's dirty?"

"As an old boar hog rolling in slop," J.P. said.

"I've lost track," Eddie said. "Who is the parish coroner now?"

"Dr. Spivey Sonnier."

"What's his claim to fame?"

"Peddled ED and hair-loss medication on a website. Son of a wealthy donor to our current governor. Ran unopposed," J.P. said.

"What makes you think he's dirty?" Eddie asked.

"He's living well above his pay grade to afford his new house and yacht club membership. And, his new flashy girlfriend is half his age and drives the new Cadillac he bought her and lives in a fancy condo on the river he's bankrolling."

Eddie grinned. "I'd say he's complicit."

"Complicit, my ass!" J.P. said. "Somebody owns his soul, lock, stock, and barrel."

"Any idea who's running the body disposal operation?"

"Johnnie Daigle was apparently doing some investigating on his own. The note he managed to pass to his partner, Sam Marcantel, said, Setup. Bayou Mortuary."

"So Bayou Mortuary is the front for the body dumping business?"

"Sounds like it," J.P. said.

"Wait a minute," Vangie said. "Why wouldn't they simply bury the bodies, or cremate them instead of going to the trouble of dumping them offshore?"

"Not that easy," Eddie said. "In Louisiana, crematory owners are legally required to maintain detailed cremation records, including authorization forms, permits, identification, and tracking logs, creating a crucial paper trail for accountability and ensuring transparency and compliance. The same goes for burying bodies."

"So they just dumped them at Trixie's Reef instead," J.P. said.

"I have someone who might be able to convince Sheriff Comier to remain with the department until your investigation is over.

"What's our Plan B if that idea turns to shit?" J.P. asked.

"General Roubideaux. Nothing much illegal happens in Biloxi without General Roubideaux having a finger in the pie," Eddie said.

Vangie says he's up to his neck in every crime imaginable."

Eddie took a drink straight from the scotch bottle. "We had our eyes on the General the entire time I was in the DOJ. He's slippery. We never got close."

"What about a plant?" J.P. said.

Eddie took a drink and looked at Vangie. "Your brother, Chris, was working for the DOJ. He came closer than anyone to nailing General Roubideaux. It's what got him killed."

Eddie nodded when Vangie said, "Chris worked for the DOJ? That explains everything."

"Roubideaux apparently keeps detailed records of everything he does and keeps them in the safe in his hotel suite. His goons caught Chris accessing the safe. I'm sorry to have to be the one to tell you," Eddie said.

"It's okay," Vangie said. "Knowing how and why he died somehow eases my soul."

"If it means anything to you, Chris came as close as anyone to bringing down General Roubideaux. At least because of him, we now know about the safe."

"I know someone who can access General's safe," J.P. said.

"Who?" Eddie said.

"Vangie."

"Pardon me?"

J.P. looked at Vangie and said, "Tell him."

"Tell me what?" Eddie said.

"I'm going to need another Hurricane to tell the story," she said.

"I can fix that," Eddie said with a grin.

He slid out of the booth, returning shortly with a colorful drink in a tall Hurricane glass with a picture of a dying sunset and the words: Majestic Hotel & Casino, Oyster Island, Louisiana. Vangie smiled when she took a sip through the multicolored straw.

"The new house specialty," he said. "How is it?"

"A lifeline to a drowning woman," she said.

Eddie waited until half the Hurricane was gone, and then said, "Now tell me about the General."

"I'm not a real P.I. I was the General's mistress." As her story poured forth, she began to cry. "When Chris was murdered, I couldn't take it any longer."

"Were you an insider and privy to what he was doing?"

Vangie shook her head. "He has never told me anything about his business. You're right, though. He keeps detailed records in his safe. I've seen him put documents he's working on there many times."

"Did you have access to the safe?" Eddie asked.

"Only the General has access," she said.

Eddie took another drink straight from the bottle of scotch. "I still have friends at the DOJ. If you can get your hands on some of the information, we can bring him down."

"Not happening," Vangie said. "I'm never spending another night with that cretin."

"Then you need to resign yourself that you're never going to get payback for your brother's murder," Eddie said.

"There must be another way," she said.

"There's not," Eddie said.

Before J.P. or Eddie could reply, the front door banged open. Odette stormed in first, blond hair wild, eyes flashing. Trixie was right behind her, cheeks flushed, scrollwork tattoo peeking above the neckline of a cropped LSU hoodie. Paula brought up the rear, moving more slowly, but her face was set in the same determined line. Odette didn't break stride. She vaulted the bar like she'd done it a thousand times, grabbed a shaker, and started measuring rum without looking at the bottles.

Eddie called over, "It's your day off, Odette."

"I'm off the clock, so don't worry," she shot back. "You don't have to pay me."

Eddie's mouth quirked. "Then knock yourself out."

Odette finished mixing Hurricanes for everybody—dark, red, and wicked-looking—poured them into Eddie's Majestic souvenir glasses, stuck in straws, and carried them over. She slid one in front of each of the booth's occupants, then dropped into the seat beside J.P. without asking.

Trixie and Paula dragged extra chairs over, forming a loose circle around the scarred table. The Hurricanes sat untouched for a moment, condensation already beading on the glasses.

Odette broke the silence. "Paula had a visitor last night that wasn't exactly human."

All eyes turned to Paula. She met them steadily, fingers tracing the rim of her glass.

"The witch," she said quietly. "The one that looked like me. She came back."

Eddie leaned forward. "And?"

"And she told me the same thing Tante Félonise did this morning." Paula's voice was calm, but there was steel in it now. "The Serpent is awake. It's been fed secrets and blood for too long. It's demanding payment in full. And it wants me to deliver it."

Eddie's eyes narrowed. "Payment how?"

Paula touched the place over her heart where the tattoo lay hidden beneath her shirt. "Burn what must burn. Or be burned."

The booth went quiet except for the low hum of the air conditioner and the distant slap of water against the pilings. J.P. broke the silence first.

"We're talking about the reef. The bodies. The chip in the dead man's teeth. All of it."

Paula nodded. "The reef is the mouth. The casino is the belly. Something's coming up the throat wearing a smile men trust."

Eddie's face went very still. "The Golden Gulf."

"Where Meika works and the name on the chip left in J.P.'s Airstream," Paula said.

Eddie leaned back, arms crossed. "So we've got a mythic snake that wants a human sacrifice, a dead undercover agent, a dirty cop leaving five-grand calling cards, and a shapeshifting witch who looks like Paula. All converging on Oyster Island in the middle of January."

"That about covers it," J.P. said dryly.

Trixie spoke up, voice steady despite the tremor in her hands. "I'm diving tomorrow. I need to see the reef myself. If there's more down there—more bodies, more evidence—I want to document it before the sheriff's team turns it into a circus."

"Not going to happen," J.P. said. "Your reef is now officially a crime scene. Consider yourself out of work for a while."

"No way!" Trixie said. "I have a professorship awaiting me when I complete my dissertation. I have just enough money to last until summer. After that, I'm broke."

"I thought you were helping me," Eddie said. "I told you, I pay well."

Odette reached over and squeezed her shoulder. "We won't let you starve, baby."

"Now, if we could just solve Vangie's problem," J.P. said.

"I'll do it," Vangie said. "I can't let Chris's life end for nothing."

"Do what?" Eddie asked.

"Take over where he left off," she said.

CHAPTER 28

The Arcadia Distillery smelled of old brick, damp cypress, and the lingering ghost of rum that had soaked into the walls for a century. Afternoon light slanted through the high windows, turning dust motes into lazy gold fireflies. The copper stills stood like silent sentinels in the center of the vast main hall, verdigris-kissed and proud, waiting to be awakened.

Alex walked ahead, one hand trailing along the curve of the largest pot still as if it were the flank of a sleeping horse. Renata stayed close beside him, dressed again, finally, and her hair pulled back in a loose knot. She moved with the same quiet confidence she brought to everything, but there was a new softness in the way she glanced at Alex, as if the morning had rewritten something fundamental between them.

Behind them came Mama Mulate and Jake Huntington. Mama—tall, regal, dark hair braided into a thick rope down her back—wore a flowing purple caftan and carried herself like someone who had already seen the end of the story and was merely waiting for the rest of the cast to catch up.

Jake, by contrast, looked like a man who had stepped out of a television screen: expensive boots, a black Cryptid Hunter windbreaker, aviators pushed up into his salt-and-pepper hair. He was grinning like a kid who'd just found the best treehouse in the world.

Alex stopped beside the tallest still and turned to face them. "This is it," he said, spreading his arms. "The heart of the operation. Three copper pot stills—pre-Prohibition, hand-hammered. The lyne arms are original. The worm tubs are intact. Even the rectifier column is here, trays and all."

Mama stepped forward, laying a palm against the cool copper. She closed her eyes for a moment, as if listening.

"Old," she said. "And wise. This metal remembers sugar and fire. It remembers men who loved what they made."

Jake circled the stills, inspecting the rivets, the seams, the graceful swan necks. "This is museum-quality," he said. "You could sell tickets just to stand here and look at it."

Alex's smile was tight. "So sorry it's going to cost you so much to renovate the building. Roof's damaged, foundation's cracked in places, and I suspect the city's been itching to condemn it since Katrina."

Jake waved a hand. "Don't worry about it. I renovated my Cryptid Hunter property in the Central Business District, know all the complex New Orleans laws, and which backs to scratch. I intend to turn this building into upscale condos. I'll ultimately triple my investment." He turned to Alex, his grin fading into something more serious. "It's you I'm worried about."

"Me?" Alex said.

"You have all the beautiful equipment for our distillery and no place to put it," Jake said.

"Renata and I have been discussing a building. J.P., Chief, and Jack can help us. They have experience."

Jake nodded, but his expression stayed skeptical. "Even with all the money you need and all the experience in the world, it'll still take months, maybe a year, to erect and finish out a building."

Alex shrugged. "The Chinese can build an entire hospital in a weekend."

"You're not Chinese," Jake said.

"There's plenty of clean sand on Oyster Island," Alex said. "We can construct the building in record time using concrete blocks. We can lay the foundation as soon as the storms abate."

Jake held up a hand. "Better stow that idea until you survey to make sure the soil and bedrock are compatible."

"How long does that take?" Alex asked.

"For as long as the engineering company wants it to take,"

Jake said.

Renata held up a hand. "We're not Chinese, but there's a Chinese construction company in New Orleans. Dragonfly Construction uses recyclable Styrofoam to form their concrete blocks, and there's plenty of clean sand available on the island."

Jake's tone was skeptical when he said, "Styrofoam?"

"Just as strong as regular concrete blocks but seventy to eighty percent lighter," Renata said.

"What about code?" Jake asked.

Renata grinned. "Oyster Island has no codes."

"How long will it take this Dragonfly Construction to complete your building?" Jake asked.

"Don't know," Renata said, "but way shorter than a year."

Jake smiled, the old TV charm flickering back on. "I like your enthusiasm. I'll have Angie, my assistant, call Dragonfly and set up a meeting. We'll get it done. What do you plan to do in the meantime?"

Alex turned in a slow circle, taking in the vast space again —the high ceilings, the brick arches, the rows of empty cypress fermenters waiting like patient giants. He had no answer and glanced at Renata.

"Start producing rum from this facility," Renata said. "All the needed equipment is here, and Alex can have it working in a week."

Jake cast Alex a skeptical glance. "Alex?"

"I can get the vats and fermenters in working order," Alex said. "I can't control how long it might take to get the building in shape. "It needs repairs."

"And brought up to hurricane standards," Mama said.

"They construct buildings in China to survive an earthquake. If they can withstand a major earthquake, they'll also withstand a hurricane.

"You need to renovate this building and bring it up to code anyway, dearest. Why not get started?" Mama said.

"I'll get Angie on it now."

Mama Mulate raised one perfectly arched brow. "With water

from the Mississippi River?"

Jake laughed. "There's artesian water on the other side of Lake Pontchartrain. Maybe we can pipe it in. Hell, there might be a whole new revenue source there. I'll make it work."

As Jake dialed Angie, Mama stepped closer to Renata, her voice dropping so only the two women could hear. "You're sure about this man?"

Renata glanced at Alex, who was running his hand along the swan neck of the still again, lost in thought.

"I wasn't sure about anything until this morning," she said. "Now I'm sure about him."

Mama studied her for a long moment. Then she nodded once, a small, satisfied gesture.

"Good," she said. "Because the spirits are watching this place. They've been waiting a long time for someone to remember how to listen to them."

Outside, the rain began again—soft at first, then steady. The copper stills gleamed in the gray light, patient, ancient, and ready. Alex looked at Jake. "How soon can we start?"

Jake pulled out his phone. "Yesterday. But tomorrow will do. Angie is already calling back."

Jake was smiling when he hung up the phone. "What?" Alex said.

"Jimmy and Bruce Chen, the owners of Dragonfly Construction, are on their way here." Mama smiled, slow and knowing. "The ancestors are impatient. They've waited long enough."

Renata slipped her hand into Alex's. He squeezed back, hard. The distillery waited, copper hearts beating in the quiet, while outside the rain fell like a promise kept. Less than forty minutes later, the heavy front doors creaked open, and two young men stepped inside, shaking water from lightweight rain jackets.

They carried themselves with the easy confidence of people who had already solved harder problems than this one. Both were in their early thirties, dark hair clipped short, wearing identical navy polos embroidered with a small silver dragonfly above the breast pocket.

Jimmy was slightly taller, with a quick, assessing gaze; Bruce carried a slim tablet and moved with the deliberate calm of someone who trusted his numbers.

Mama Mulate straightened. "Jimmy. Bruce." Mama turned to Jake and said, "I've known these two since they were teens. Their mom teaches at Tulane."

Jimmy grinned, stepping forward to offer her a respectful hug. "Professor Mulate. Mother's favorite show is Cryptid Hunter, and she answered the phone when Angie called. She said you'd be here and that you'd probably already have the spirits negotiating the contract terms."

Mama laughed, low and rich. "Tell Dr. Chen she owes me lunch for keeping her boys out of trouble."

Bruce gave a small nod, polite but already scanning the high ceiling, the cracked brick arches, the water stains blooming like dark flowers along the walls.

"We've seen the preliminary photos Angie sent," he said. "We also pulled the original 1890s blueprints from the city archives. Good bones. Very good bones."

Jake extended a hand. "Jake Huntington. Thanks for coming so fast."

Jimmy shook it firmly. "We don't waste time when the clock's ticking, especially when it involves Cryptid Hunter and our mother still wields a mean switch."

Alex laughed as he stepped forward, offering his hand. "Alex. This is Renata. We're the ones who'll be running rum out of here —assuming the roof stays on long enough."

Bruce's eyes flicked to the stills, then back to Alex. "We've done distilleries before. Small-batch in Baton Rouge, full-scale in Guangzhou, before we came back stateside. We know what high humidity and sugar residue do to concrete and steel."

Renata tilted her head. "You were both born here?"

"In Metairie," Jimmy said. "Mom came over for grad school, stayed for the tenure track at Tulane. Dad's from Fujian. We grew up with dim sum on Sundays and crawfish boils on Saturdays."

Jake crossed his arms. "So what's the verdict? Can you save this place before the next named storm decides to use it for target practice?"

The brothers exchanged a glance—the kind that didn't need words. Bruce tapped his tablet awake.

"We can have a crew here this afternoon: thirty men, minimum. Demo, shoring, and roof tear-off start today. We'll stage materials on the wharf lot across the street—Angie's already clearing permits for emergency access."

Alex blinked. "Today?"

"Today," Jimmy confirmed. "We keep two full crews on perpetual standby for storm-damage jobs. They're already mobilized from a warehouse rebuild in the Ninth Ward that finished early. As for Oyster Island..." He glanced at Renata. "We can have the second crew there tomorrow morning. Soil tests are preliminary, but the sand you've got out there is clean. We'll use our ICF system—recycled Styrofoam forms, poured-in-place concrete. Lighter, faster, stronger in shear. Hurricane-rated to Cat 5."

Jake raised an eyebrow. "No waiting on engineering stamps? No six-month permitting dance?"

Bruce smiled for the first time, small but genuine. "We're licensed in Louisiana, Mississippi, and Texas. We pre-file for emergency reconstruction under the state's disaster-recovery ordinance. The city knows us. They fast-track because we don't screw up inspections."

Renata looked between them. "How fast are we really talking?"

Jimmy considered the question like a man adding figures in his head. "This building—full structural rehab, new roof, seismic/hurricane upgrades, MEP rough-in, and interior fit-out for distillery use? 90 to 120 days if we run double shifts and there are no major surprises in the foundation. Oyster Island build —from foundation to turnkey shell, including on-site block production—we're looking at 45 to 60 days. Faster if the weather cooperates."

Jake let out a low whistle. "You're telling me you can give us a functional distillery and a new production facility in under six months total?"

"Better than that," Bruce said. "We can sequence them. Start pulling permits and pouring footings on the island while we stabilize this place. You'll have rum fermenting here, and bottling capability on Oyster Island by summer."

Alex stared at the brothers, then at the silent copper stills, then back again. For once, the engineer in him had nothing skeptical left to say.

"You're serious." Jimmy shrugged. "We don't bid jobs we can't deliver. And we like working with people who respect the old stuff." He nodded toward the stills. "Those pots deserve to run again."

Mama laid a hand on Alex's shoulder, her voice soft. "See? The ancestors sent engineers, not bureaucrats."

Jake laughed, the sound bouncing off the high brick walls. "All right. You two have sold me. What do you need from us right now?"

"Access," Bruce said simply. "Full access, twenty-four-seven. Keys, alarm codes, and a point person who can make decisions fast."

"That's me," Alex said without hesitation."

And me," Renata added.

Jimmy pulled a slim folder from his jacket. "Then we'll start with these. Non-disclosure, scope of work summary, and emergency mobilization agreement. We'll have the full contract drafted by tomorrow morning, but we can begin under letter of intent today."

Jake glanced at Alex and Renata. Both nodded.

"We're in."

The brothers moved as one, efficient and unhurried. Within minutes they were walking the perimeter with Alex, pointing out load-bearing points, water intrusion paths, and places where the old cypress beams could be sistered rather than replaced.

Outside, the first work truck rolled up, rain beading on its silver roof. Men in bright vests began unloading equipment, voices low and purposeful. Renata watched them for a moment, then turned to Alex.

"You ready for this?"

He looked at the stills, gleaming softly in the returning light, then at her. "I've been ready since the first time I touched one of these."

Mama Mulate smiled, slow and satisfied, as the sound of hammers and the whine of saws began to fill the old brick hall. The distillery was waking up. And this time, it would never sleep again.

CHAPTER 29

J.P. pushed through the heavy door of Jack's stone cottage, bringing the damp smell of salt air and wet pine with him. The room was warm, lit by the low fire and a single lamp. Jack sat at the plank table, dealing solitaire with a worn deck, while Chief lounged in the big armchair by the hearth, long legs stretched toward the flames, a bottle of dark rum and three mugs already waiting. Both men looked up when he entered.

Jack's eyes flicked to the tension in J.P.'s shoulders; Chief raised one silver eyebrow.

"Trouble?" Jack asked, sliding the cards aside.

"Always," J.P. said. He hung his damp coat on the peg by the door, shook rain from his Stetson, and dropped into the empty chair. "Vangie's on her way back to Biloxi. She's going to try to get inside General's safe—see if she can pull anything that ties him to the bodies on the reef."

"How's she going to do that?" Chief said.

"Seems she's the General's mistress and not a real P.I. She has an in, and we're taking advantage of it."

"Brave girl," Chief said.

"Or crazy," Jack said.

J.P. poured three fingers of rum into each mug. "She's scared, and General Roubideaux repulses her, but she's got no choice. Her brother was down there in the coral with a bullet in his head because of him. She's not walking away."

Jack took his glass and swirled it. "And you're letting her go alone?"

"I'll be there," J.P. said. "I'm heading to Biloxi tomorrow. Need to alert Meika, and be there if Vangie gets in over her head."

Chief leaned forward, elbows on knees. "You're not going alone."

J.P. started to protest, but Jack cut him off. "It's our island too, podna. Whatever's feeding that reef, whatever's got the General's fingerprints on it—it's touching all of us. You think we're going to sit here playing cards while you have all the fun?"

J.P. opened his mouth, closed it. He looked from Jack's stubborn jaw to Chief's steady gaze.

"This ain't a pleasure trip," he said finally. "It's business. Dangerous business. I don't need you two tagging along, drawing attention."

Chief's laugh was low and dry. "You think we're going to draw more attention than you? A retired deputy sheriff with a movie-star face walking into Biloxi casinos asking questions about the General? Hell, J.P., you're a neon sign."

Jack nodded. "We have different skill sets. Chief can read a room like he reads the weather. I know boats, back channels, and how to move without being seen. And neither one of us is afraid to get our hands dirty."

J.P. rubbed a hand over his face. "Y'all are serious?"

"Dead serious," Chief said.

The room went quiet except for the crackle of the fire and the soft patter of lingering rain on the tin roof. J.P. looked at his mug, then at the two men who'd stood with him through worse than this. He exhaled, long and slow.

"Fine," he said. "But we do it my way. No cowboy shit. We go quiet, we stay quiet, and we come back breathing."

Jack raised his glass. "Sounds like a plan."

They drank. The rum burned clean and warm. J.P. set his glass down.

"We leave tomorrow. I'll drive. Chief, bring the shotgun. Jack, pack light. We're not going to be there a week."

Chief nodded once. "Already got my go-bag ready."

Jack grinned, small and sharp. "I'll bring the good coffee."

They were still mapping out the route—Biloxi casinos, back roads, places to watch and be watched—when J.P.'s phone buzzed on the table. It was homicide detective Sam Marcantel.

"Where you at?" he asked.

"Oyster Island," J.P. said.

"How fast can you get your ass to Chalmette?"

"Thirty minutes if I speed."

"You know where the Bayou Mortuary is? There's a shopping center down the street. Park your truck and walk toward the mortuary. I'm in an unmarked black Ford sedan. I'll be waiting."

"Who was that?" Chief asked.

"Sam Marcantel, St. Bernard Parish homicide detective. He's staking out the Bayou Mortuary."

"For what reason?" Jack asked.

"I'll have plenty of time tomorrow on the road trip to bring you up to speed. Right now, I gotta go," J.P. said.

J.P. left Jack's cottage, the heavy door slapping shut behind him like a punctuation mark. Rain still misted the air, fine as gnats, and the gravel crunched under his boots as he crossed to the truck. He didn't look back. Chief and Jack were already moving—quiet, practiced, the way men who've hunted together for years move when the quarry turns dangerous.

The drive to Chalmette was a wet blur of low beams and windshield wipers. Thirty-two minutes door to door. He took the back way, avoiding the interstate cameras that had started feeling too attentive lately. The shopping center was dark except for the drugstore, its blue-and-red neon pharmacy sign buzzing like a dying insect.

J.P. killed the headlights, coasted into the farthest corner slot beneath a broken security light, and sat for a moment listening to the engine tick down. Then he stepped out, pulled the collar of his jacket up, and started walking. The two blocks felt longer in the dark. Lightning flickered through the live oaks, turning the broken sidewalk into a strobe of roots and puddles.

Thunder rolled low, somewhere over the river. When he reached the unmarked Ford, the passenger window was already down. The Bayou Mortuary squatted low and unassuming along the cracked asphalt road, a single-story brick building the color of dried river mud, its facade weathered by decades of humidity, salt air, and the occasional hurricane aftermath.

In the ordinary daylight, it might have passed for just another small-town funeral home in St. Bernard Parish— functional, modestly maintained, with a flat roof, narrow windows shuttered against prying eyes, and a discreet side driveway leading to a covered loading area for deliveries. But on a night like this—dark, rainy, with lightning slashing through the thick canopy of live oaks and cypress trees—it looked ominous, almost predatory.

The rain, sheeting down in relentless curtains, turned the parking lot into a shallow black mirror, reflecting the building's pale sodium lights at itself in distorted ripples. Water streamed off the eaves in steady ropes, drumming against the metal canopy over the side delivery door like impatient fingers.

The few security lights that remained on cast a sickly yellow glow, barely penetrating the mist and Spanish moss that hung limply and dripped from the branches overhead. A simple rectangular sign hung above the front entrance, its white letters once crisp but now faded and ghosted by time, read Bayou Mortuary – Compassionate Care in Life's Final Passage.

The neon tube outlining the words flickered in the wet, buzzing faintly when the lightning flashed, making the letters strobe on and off like a failing heartbeat. Below the main text, in much smaller script, was the tagline: Resting in the Bayou's Gentle Embrace—meant to be soothing, but tonight it read like a threat.

Most passersby wouldn't notice the subtle logo tucked into the lower corner of the sign: a lotus flower rising from stylized wavy lines meant to represent water, its petals slightly asymmetrical, almost like they were wilting.

To the casual observer, it was just generic funeral-home symbolism—rebirth, peace, the cycle of life. J.P. saw something different: in the storm's strobing light, with rain streaking across it, the flower looked more like something dredged up from the muck, petals curling inward as if hiding secrets—that unmistakable sense of something watchful in the dark.

Sam Marcantel filled the driver's seat of the sedan like a sack of wet cement. The car sagged noticeably on that side. A Styrofoam spit cup sat on the dash, same as the last time J.P. had ridden with him. The smell inside was equal parts tobacco juice, old coffee, and the faint metallic tang of a man who hadn't been home to shower in a day and a half.

J.P. slid in and closed the door softly. "What's up?"

"The body disposal business is booming," Sam said, voice gravelly from too many cigarettes he'd quit long ago. "This place has had two deliveries since I got here, and I think it's safe to say you won't see any of the deceased's names in a local obituary."

J.P. stared through the windshield at the mortuary's low brick silhouette. "Don't they know the reef's shut down?"

"Guess not." Sam shifted, the seat creaking under him. "Or they don't care. Either way, they're still accepting new customers."

"Who owns the Bayou Mortuary?" J.P. asked, though he already suspected the answer.

"Our very own Dr. Spivey Sonnier," Sam said. "St. Bernard Parish's illustrious coroner."

J.P. let out a slow breath. "I had a feeling it might be him, though I wasn't sure."

"Greedy bastard," Sam said after a beat.

"Maybe a good thing for us," J.P. said. "Greedy people tend to cut corners and make mistakes."

"He's damn sure showing no discretion about the way he's bringing them in," Sam said. He patted his digital camera. "I already have some interesting pictures he'll have a hard time explaining."

Lightning lit the darkness, followed by thunder that shook the sedan's weak shocks.

"Wonder how he intends to dispose of the bodies?" J.P. asked.

"He's apparently stacking them up in the freezer until he figures it out." Sam nodded toward the building. "Refrigeration unit's been running nonstop. You can hear the compressors from the sidewalk if you stand close enough."

J.P. rubbed his jaw. "Have you talked to Johnnie yet?"

Sam shook his head. "They aren't letting anyone near him. Suicide watch, they say."

"Johnnie would never commit suicide," J.P. said.

"I was thinking more of the assisted variety," Sam said quietly. "It would be real convenient if Johnnie were out of the picture."

Lightning cracked again, closer this time, bleaching the trees white for an instant. J.P. felt the old familiar tightening in his gut —the one that came right before everything went sideways.

"What about you?" he asked.

"I haven't been home in twenty-four hours. Called you on a burner. I've got a target on my back, podna. I'm a dead man if they catch up to me."

"Don't get caught," J.P. said.

They sat in silence for a moment, watching the mortuary's side door. Then headlights swept the driveway. A dark Suburban rolled under the delivery canopy. Two men got out, moving with the practiced economy of people who'd done this before.

Trunk open. Black body bag. One knock, two knocks on the metal door. It opened from the inside. The bag disappeared. The men climbed back in and drove off without lights. Sam raised a small digital camera, snapped three quick frames.

"Did that look like a normal delivery to you?" he asked, lowering the lens.

J.P. stared at the now-empty driveway. "And did you notice one of them was Bobbie Don Rooker?"

Sam gave a grim nod. "We've got enough to take this operation down. You game?"

"Not yet," J.P. said. "I don't just want to cut off the rattler. I want the damn snake's head."

Sam studied him. "General Roubideaux?" J.P. didn't answer. "How do you plan to do that?" Sam asked, then immediately raised a hand. "Never mind. Don't tell me. I don't want to know in case they catch up with me."

J.P. reached over and patted the big man's shoulder—once, firm. "Watch your ass."

Sam grunted. "You too, podna. And tell Chief and Jack I said hello."

J.P. flashed a tired smile, opened the door, and stepped back into the rain. Lightning flashed again as he walked away, throwing his shadow long and jagged across the broken sidewalk. Behind him, the mortuary lights stayed on, cold and steady, like eyes that never blinked.

Tomorrow was Biloxi. But tonight, the bodies were still stacking up. And General Roubideaux was fishing somewhere in Mississippi with Sheriff Comier. J.P. hoped he wasn't in on the ongoing crime. He kept walking, the drizzling rain following him all the way back to the truck.

CHAPTER 30

The floor of the Golden Gulf was a living, breathing beast of noise and neon. It was a cacophony of desperation and dopamine—the rhythmic chime of slot machines, the sharp clatter of roulette balls, and the low hum of a thousand conversations fueled by free alcohol and bad odds. General Harlan Roubideaux moved through the chaos like a shark parting a school of fish.

He was a man who understood the value of packaging. At fifty-something, he carried himself with the deliberate gravity of a monarch. His suit was Italian, a charcoal silk that didn't ripple so much as flow over his frame. On his left wrist sat a diamond-encrusted Rolex that cost more than most of the gamblers in the room would earn in a decade; on his right pinky, a heavy gold ring caught the overhead lights. But it was the shoes—gleaming, thousand-dollar oxfords—that announced his approach with an authoritative click against the marble floors.

He was never alone. Flanking him were the twin shadows of his authority, the men he humiliated with the names Scruffy and Pinkie.

They were a study in grotesque contrasts. Scruffy was a mountain of a man, wide as a vending machine, with knuckles that looked like they had been broken and reset by a blind doctor. Pinkie was the opposite—small, wiry, and vibrating with a coiled energy. Despite the infantile nicknames, no one looked them in the eye. They were visibly armed, the bulges under their jackets poorly concealed, a deliberate warning to anyone watching. And everyone was watching.

The General smiled as he walked. It was a practiced

politician's smile.

"Good evening, General," a pit boss said, bowing his head slightly. The General merely tapped his gold bracelet against the velvet rope in acknowledgment.

He paused at the center bar. The bartender, a man named Clive who knew better than to ask for an order, immediately reached for the top-shelf bourbon. He poured a straight shot—no ice, no chaser.

General Roubideaux lifted the glass, saluted the room, and swallowed the amber liquid in one smooth motion. He set the glass down with a clink, turned on his heel, and headed for the private elevators.

The ride up was silent. The noise of the casino floor was severed the moment the brass doors slid shut. As the numbers climbed, the air grew thinner, colder. The General adjusted his cuffs.

"She's upstairs," Pinkie said. His voice was high and reedy, like a rusty hinge. "Miss LeBlanc. Just got in."

The General's eyebrows, manicured and grey, twitched. "Is she, now?"

When the elevator opened directly into the penthouse, the silence was absolute. The suite was a sprawling expanse of white leather, chrome, and floor-to-ceiling glass overlooking the black void of the Gulf of Mexico. It was a space fit for an emperor, designed to make human beings feel small.

"Wait outside," the General commanded. Scruffy and Pinkie retreated to the hallway.

He walked into the sunken living room. Vangie was standing by the window, her back to him, staring out at the dark water. She turned as he approached. She was wearing a slip of black silk that clung to her like a second skin, ending high on her thighs. It was scanty, provocative, and precisely what he liked. But beneath the makeup and the perfume, her heart was hammering against her ribs like a trapped bird. She knew the danger. She knew that despite the jewelry and the suits, Harlan Roubideaux was a man who solved problems with his fists, or worse.

"You're back," he said. It wasn't a greeting; it was an accusation. He stopped five feet from her, his eyes scanning her face for cracks. "I thought you were shopping in New Orleans. You weren't due back for two days."

Vangie forced her lips into a pout, closing the distance between them. She placed a hand on the lapel of his expensive suit, feeling the heat of his chest underneath. "I got lonely, Harlan."

He stiffened, suspicious. "Lonely?"

"New Orleans is just noise and tourists," she lied, her voice dropping to a husky whisper. She traced the line of his gold bracelet with her finger. "I was walking down Royal Street, and I realized... I didn't want to be there. I wanted to be here. With you." She looked up at him through her lashes, praying he wouldn't see the terror behind her eyes. "Did you miss me? Or did you find someone else to keep your bed warm?"

The General stared at her for an agonizing second. Then, the suspicion in his eyes dissolved into lust. A smirk touched his lips.

"There's no one else, Vangie," he said, his voice thick. He gripped her waist, his fingers digging in hard enough to bruise. "You know you're my girl."

"Show me," she said, her voice a whisper.

An hour later, the suite was dim, lit only by the glow of the city below. The General was in the bathroom, showering off the day. Vangie sat on the edge of the massive white leather sofa, her hands trembling as she reached into her purse.

She pulled out the document she had forged with Eddie's help. It was thick, stamped with official-looking seals—a copy of an intestate succession regarding her mother's estate. It was boring, dense legalese. Perfect camouflage.

The bathroom door opened. The General walked out, a towel wrapped around his waist, smelling of expensive soap and steam. He saw her on the couch and frowned.

What is that?" he asked, toweling his hair.

Vangie looked up, keeping her face open and innocent. "Shopping wasn't the only reason I went to New Orleans," she said, waving the papers. "My mom died without a will. You know how messy that gets. The courts finally finished with her estate."

The General lost interest immediately. "Bureaucracy. A waste of time."

"I know," she sighed. "But it's done. This is the final succession. I don't want to leave it lying around where the maid might throw it out." She stood up and walked toward him, holding the papers out. "Will you keep it for me? Just until I can get a safety deposit box?"

General looked at the papers, then at her. He shrugged. "Sure, doll. Give it here."

He took the stack of papers and walked toward the wall behind the wet bar. Vangie stayed where she was, her breath held in her lungs.

He pushed a panel in the mahogany wall, revealing a steel safe embedded in the structure. It was digital.

Vangie didn't blink. She watched his hand.

One.

Nine.

Seven.

Five.

Zero.

The red LED numbers flashed briefly with each press of his finger. 1-9-7-5-0.

A mechanical whir, and the heavy door popped open. He tossed her mother's fake legal papers inside, right on top of a stack of black ledgers and hard drives. He slammed the door shut and spun the handle.

"Safe and sound," he said, turning back to her with a grin.

Vangie smiled back. It was the hardest thing she had ever done.

"Thank you, Harlan," she said softly. "You take such good care of me."

Inside her head, she was screaming the numbers over and over again. 19750. 19750. 19750.

She had him.

CHAPTER 31

The storm had blown itself out by dawn, leaving the sky scrubbed raw and a brilliant blue. By the time J.P., Jack, and Chief hit the final stretch of Highway 90, the afternoon sun was turning the Gulf of Mexico into a blinding sheet of hammered copper.

J.P. was behind the wheel of his truck, humming along to a muddy blues track on the radio, while Chief took up the entire back seat of the crew cab, dozing intermittently. Jack rode shotgun, his arm hanging out the open window, watching the "Redneck Riviera" slide by.

Biloxi rose from the horizon like a mirage made of concrete and neon. To their right, the man-made white sand beaches stretched out, dotted with tourists who had emerged post-storm to take pictures and search for seashells. The old city fought a losing war against the new; ancient live oaks draped in Spanish moss stood guard over historic antebellum homes, but the towering monoliths of the gaming industry dwarfed them.

"Look at that," Jack said, gesturing toward the skyline where the casinos clustered like jeweled knuckles along the water's edge. "Smell the money, boys? The scent of desperation and bad math."

"It smells like dead shrimp and diesel," Chief said from the back seat, sitting up and rubbing his face.

He peered out the window as they passed the Biloxi Lighthouse, the cast-iron landmark standing stoic in the median, splitting the traffic.

"And history," Jack said. "I'll never forget the first time I saw this place. This peninsula used to be nothing but cannery

233

wharves and boat builders before the gambling lobby moved in."

"The only thing I remember from my first visit to Biloxi was the inside of a stinking jail cell," Chief said.

J.P. laughed and said, "Sounds like a personal problem."

They rolled past the Small Craft Harbor, where the trawlers were docked three deep. The riggings clanged against masts in the stiff breeze, a forest of steel and netting. Weather-beaten shrimpers were hosing down decks, prepping for the next run, oblivious to the gleaming glass towers just a half-mile down the road.

"Right about that," Jack said, his eyes scanning the crowds. "It's two worlds: the people who work the water, and the people who play on it."

"And we're headed for the playground," J.P. said, changing lanes to bypass a slow-moving RV with Florida plates. "There she is. The Golden Gulf."

The building was impossible to miss. In a city of flashy architecture, the Golden Gulf Casino screamed the loudest for attention. It sat on a massive barge permanently moored to the shore, integrated into a hotel tower that soared thirty stories into the air. The entire façade was mirrored in gold-tinted glass that caught the sun and threw it back with an arrogant glare.

"Subtle," Chief said with a grunt.

"About as subtle as a kick to the crotch," J.P. said.

As they drew closer, J.P. felt the knot in his stomach tighten again. The structure looked like a fortress. Valets in white uniforms scurried like ants around the porte-cochère, opening doors to limos and luxury SUVs. It was a monument to excess, controlled by a man called "The General"—a man Meika couldn't stand.

"Meika wasn't kidding," Jack said, watching the security cameras that dotted the perimeter fence like roosting birds. "Place is locked down tight. You really think a wash is happening in there?"

"If you wanted to hide a dirty dollar," J.P. said, slowing the truck as they approached the entrance ramp, "that's exactly where you'd put it. Amid millions of clean ones, moving so fast nobody can count 'em."

J.P. looked up at the gold tower looming over them. Somewhere inside was Meika, pouring drinks and looking over her shoulder. And somewhere in the penthouse, or the back rooms, was Vangie LeBlanc—either the damsel in distress or the spider spinning the web.

"This is it, boys," J.P. said, putting his sunglasses back on to hide the skepticism in his eyes. "Let's go see if the house really always wins."

"I got a feeling that the house doesn't like visitors who ask questions," Chief said.

J.P. steered the truck into the shadows of the parking garage, the bright sun vanishing, replaced by the underground's cool gloom.

"Game on," Jack said.

The casino floor was a pulsating cavern where light died, and sound was amplified. J.P. felt the familiar sensory assault: the synthetic chime of slot machines, the constant murmur of voices, and the recycled air that smelled of expensive cologne, cheap whiskey, and stale cigars.

They found Meika behind a grand bar, just past the bank of high-limit slots, a beacon in her crisp black-and-white Golden Gulf uniform. She looked tired, but her eyes held a spark of wicked excitement. Her hair was dark, like her eyes, and fell to her shoulders. She was drop-dead gorgeous, even by Biloxi standards, and her bar was almost always surrounded by admiring men.

"Look at you three," she said, her voice a little breathless as she leaned over the bar and hugged J.P. "Chief, you're going to break the bank, I can feel it."

Chief, looking uncharacteristically scrubbed and wearing the one dress shirt he owned, puffed out his chest. "We're here to bleed 'em dry, Meika-girl."

The sale of an expensive dog was the perfect cover story and a convenient way to fund their little investigation.

"Thanks for the hook-up, Meika," Jack said. "What exactly did you tell them?"

Meika grinned, pulling a key card from her apron pocket. "I told them you were a legendary Gulf Coast charter captain who hit it big with a side hustle training very specialized animals. And that your friend, the big one, is a retired Choctaw chief who loves high-stakes Blackjack and buys the table when he's drunk. They didn't ask for specific details; they just saw the numbers on the comps I wrote up."

"Comped?" J.P. said, his eyebrows practically disappearing into his hairline. "Everything?"

"Suite, food, booze, the works. Just remember you are high rollers," she said, handing the card to J.P. "Act the part. Flash the cash. And whatever you do, do not mention Vangie LeBlanc or the word 'wash' to anyone who isn't me."

"What about Vangie?" J.P. asked.

"Scared shitless," Meika said. "I told her I'd do anything to help, and I meant it. Anything."

"Understood," J.P. said. "Where are we?"

"Thirty-first floor. Penthouse Suite, Gulf-side view. They're calling it the Admiral's Quarters." Meika leaned in conspiratorially. "It's usually reserved for whales who drop six figures a night. Enjoy the show."

She gave them a quick wave before hurrying away to fill her backlog of orders from her many male admirers, leaving the three men blinking at the key card and wondering what was coming next.

They took the private elevator up, the ascent so fast it made Chief's ears pop. When the doors whispered open on the thirty-first floor, the difference from the casino was immediate. It was quiet, carpeted in deep blue wool, and smelled faintly of ozone and lemon polish.

J.P. slid the card into the reader. There was a quiet chime, and the massive mahogany doors swung inward. Jack and Chief stopped dead in their tracks, rendered temporarily speechless. The suite was vast, stretching out toward a wall of floor-to-ceiling glass that offered an uninterrupted panorama of the Gulf of Mexico. The setting sun was beginning its descent, painting the water and the sky in violent shades of orange, pink, and gold.

The living space alone was at least twice the size of Jack's cottage back on Oyster Island, featuring pristine white leather furniture, a massive flat-screen television that looked permanently out of scale, and a wet bar stocked with every high-end spirit imaginable.

"Sweet Lord above," Jack said, dropping his duffel bag instantly. He walked straight toward the windows, his hand pressed against the cool glass. "You can see for fifty miles! Look, J.P. That's the curve of the whole coast!"

Chief, who spent most of his life sleeping in a teepee, wandered into the master bedroom. It was a study in excess, centered around a King bed with white linens and seven perfectly plumped pillows. He didn't touch anything, just stood in the middle of the room, looking around like a ghost who'd wandered into a palace.

"They got a jacuzzi in the bathroom," he said, his voice echoing slightly off the marble tile. "And it's big enough for a whole damn hog."

Jack was already tearing through the complimentary bar. He pulled out a bottle of top-shelf Irish whisky.

"No rum tonight, boys. We are drinking like gentlemen of leisure!"

He poured three generous tumblers.

J.P. wasn't focused on the luxury. He walked slowly around the perimeter of the room, his eyes sharp and analytical, scanning the edges of the walls and the ceiling fixtures. He was looking for seams, for cameras, for anything that hinted at surveillance. A suite this nice, given to someone they knew nothing about, wasn't a gift; it was an investment. He picked up the expensive glass of whiskey Jack offered him.

"Don't get too comfortable," he said, walking back to the window and looking down at the tiny figures milling around the docks below. "This is a golden cage, boys. And someone wants to see exactly how we behave inside it."

He took a slow sip of the whiskey, the heat spreading through his chest. It was the best damn whiskey he'd ever had.

"We're hip," Jack said.

"Good, I want you on that casino floor tonight. Drop five or ten grand like it's pocket change. Make some noise. Chief, you're hitting the buffet and keeping your eyes open. This is our ticket in, but it's also our spotlight. We make one wrong move, and they'll see it from the moon."

"What about you?" Jack asked.

"I'm meeting Vangie."

"Kind of risky, don't you think?" Jack said.

"If anyone sees us and reports it back to the General, she's going to tell him I was the Louisiana lawyer who helped with her mother's succession," J.P. said.

"That'll never hold water if they check," Chief said.

"A chance I have to take. The bar where we're meeting is secluded, and she says Roubideaux rarely goes there."

"Watch yourself," Jack said. "There are security cameras all over this damn place."

"Don't worry. I'm on it," he said. "Are we meeting up later on?"

"I'll find you after meeting with Vangie," J.P. said.

J.P. watched Jack and Chief practically sprint for the elevator, their eyes glazed over with the dual promise of high-stakes gambling and an all-you-can-eat buffet. Chief, now wearing a slightly wrinkled sports jacket over his dress shirt, had an almost predatory grin, looking like a mountain come to town. Jack, jingling a massive wad of cash, was already humming a victory tune. They were perfect distractions.

Alone in the vast suite, J.P. allowed himself a slow smile. The silence was restorative. He spent the next thirty minutes conducting a meticulous sweep of the suite, not letting the luxury lull his senses. He checked behind the artwork, inside the heavy phone handsets, and beneath the lip of the marble bar counter.

Everything was clean—or at least, clean of anything that a quick visual check could reveal. If they were listening, they were using professional gear far beyond his current ability to detect. He moved to the closet and pulled out the garment bag he'd brought. Most of his clothes were functional, built for the bayou—canvas, denim, and waterproof everything. But he kept one specific suit for jobs that required an entrance. The tuxedo was midnight black, custom-tailored, and still smelling faintly of cedar and dry cleaner solvent. Putting it on, he transformed.

J.P. had inherited his looks from his mother, a long-ago beauty queen, and his features were sharp, chiseled, and cinematic. The tux didn't just fit him; it molded to him, giving him the sleek and dangerous silhouette of an apex predator dressed for a gala. When he checked the mirror, he saw not the rugged charter captain, but the kind of man the Golden Gulf Casino was built to attract—or to fleece.

He took a final breath, smoothing the satin lapel, and headed out.

CHAPTER 32

J.P. found Vangie where she said she would be: at The Gilded Cage, a tiny cocktail bar tucked away upstairs, away from the main casino noise, near the high-limit poker room. It was hushed, lit only by amber lamps, and lined with velvet banquettes. The only people there looked like they owned the place, or wished they did.

He spotted her sitting at a small table beside a glass wall that offered a view of the Gulf. She was dressed in a sleek emerald silk gown that clung to her figure, creating a striking contrast with her raven hair and smooth olive skin. She held a delicate martini glass, her gaze contemplative as she watched the moonlight cast a silvery glow over the water.

When J.P. appeared in the arched doorway, the room seemed to pause. The maître d' stiffened, and a nearby couple stopped talking. He walked across the room with a deliberate stride, every inch the character he was playing.

Vangie saw him, and her glass-smooth façade cracked. Her eyes widened, tracking him from the moment he left the doorway until he reached her table. It wasn't simple appreciation; it was a visible jolt, a flash of unedited admiration.

"J.P.," she said, her voice a husky whisper that barely broke the silence of the bar.

She slowly pushed back her chair, rising to meet him. She had expected a man in a damp shirt and jeans from the swamp, not a Greek statue wrapped in Armani.

"It's me," he said with a grin, taking her hand.

He raised it to his lips, brushing a light kiss across her knuckles, his eyes never leaving hers, as he searched for the flicker of fear that Meika had warned him about.

Vangie pulled her hand away, a faint blush rising beneath her cheekbones, and pointed to the seat across from her.

"I'm sorry," she laughed, a genuinely surprised sound. "You look... so handsome. I didn't know you kept a tux in your Airstream."

"I clean up pretty good," he said, his voice a smooth register of controlled confidence.

He settled into the banquette, letting the silence hang between them. A waiter appeared instantly. "A martini for the gentleman?" he asked.

J.P. nodded. "Extremely dry. Olive on the side."

"A tux," Vangie repeated, leaning forward, resting her chin on her hand. "You went all-in on this"

"This could be life or death, and you can never be too prepared," he said. "Is everything on track?"

"General Roubideaux wouldn't trust his own mother, but the succession ruse Eddie thought of worked. He barely glanced at the stack of documents."

"Wouldn't have mattered if he did. Eddie never does anything half-ass," J.P. said.

"When he put them in his safe, I memorized the code."

"What about...?"

"I had to fuck the bastard, if that's what you were going to ask," she said.

"Vangie, I'm sorry."

Vangie didn't reply, handing J.P. a slip of paper. "What's this?" he asked.

"The code to General's safe," she said.

The waiter delivered his martini. J.P. took a sip—it was perfectly chilled, impeccably dry.

"What now?" he asked.

"Give the code to Meika."

"Meika?"

"She's my best friend. She said she would do anything to help me. What I've asked her to do goes beyond friendship."

Vangie shook her head when J.P. said, "What else?"

"At exactly midnight, whenever General is in town, room service brings dinner to his room. It's always something special: lobster thermidor, Oysters Rockefeller, or maybe chateaubriand, along with a bottle of the best champagne."

Vangie smiled when J.P. said, "Must be nice."

"One of the few things I've had to look forward to," she said. Server Tina will leave the dinner on the dining room table and take the serving cart down the main elevator to the basement. The hallway connects to the kitchen, where they prepare room service."

"Tina?"

"Sweet, red-headed girl working her way through college. A friend of mine. You need to be at the elevator door when she arrives with the serving cart. She'll have something for you."

"You trust her?"

"Next to Meika, she's my best friend. You'll know what to do with what she gives you."

"I'll be waiting for her," J.P. said.

Vangie glanced around the dark little bar, as if someone might be overhearing their conversation.

"General has two dangerous goons, Scruffy and Pinkie, who are never far away. You'll know if you see them."

Vangie finished her martini and started to leave. J.P. clutched her hand. "Good luck," he said.

Vangie's gaze dropped to the glass in her hand, the lights reflecting in the liquid.

"I'm scared out of my wits, J.P.," she said. "General deals in certainties. My plan has none. It's messy, wrapped up in... "

Vangie's voice trailed off.

"Keep the faith. Loose plans are sometimes the best," he said.

Her emotional kiss lasted but an instant before she hurried away toward the entrance.

J.P. waited until he was sure Vangie was gone before clearing the tab and returning to the cacophony of the Golden Gulf Casino. He descended the curved staircase from The Gilded Cage, the hushed atmosphere of the high-end bar instantly replaced by the sonic assault of the main floor. He navigated the labyrinth of slot machines, the air thick with smoke and desperation, until he spotted the beacon of the center bar.

Meika was furiously mixing a mojito, her movements efficient but tight. When she saw J.P. approach, she wiped her hands on a towel and leaned over the polished mahogany, her eyes darting left and right.

J.P. ordered a club soda, loud enough for the patrons nearby to hear, and slid a folded napkin across the wood. Inside was the slip of paper Vangie had given him.

"You're on," J.P. said, his voice dropping to a murmur. "That's the code. Vangie said you'd know what to do."

Meika palmed the napkin, her hand trembling slightly. "I guess I'm involved up to my neck in our little caper now, aren't I?"

"Just keep your head," J.P. said. "Chief, Jack, and I won't be far away."

"I'm scared, J.P.," she said in a whisper, her eyes flicking toward a pair of men standing near the entrance to the high-limit pit. "General has two thugs, Scruffy and Pinkie. They probably eat glass for breakfast."

J.P. glanced over his shoulder. He saw them—one with a patchy beard that looked like mange, the other with a complexion like raw hamburger meat. They were watching the floor with dead eyes.

"You're beautiful, and you know how to work men," J.P. said, turning back to her with a reassuring smile. "If something goes sideways, you'll know how to handle it."

She laughed, a brittle sound that didn't reach her eyes. "I don't know about Scruffy, but Pinkie would rather fuck you than me. The way he looks at me makes my skin crawl."

"Good luck, Meika," J.P. said, tapping the bar.

Her expression hardened into something tragic. "I'll need more than luck. I've never been with a man, J.P. Not really. And if I ever had, it would definitely not be a man as utterly repulsive as

General Roubideaux."

"I'm sorry, Meika," he said.

"I'm doing this for Vangie. I need you to make sure it counts."

"I won't let you down," he said. "I promise."

When she turned away to serve a customer, J.P. felt a cold knot of guilt in his gut. He pushed off the bar and headed for the poker room.

ᖴᑎᕼᑐ

J.P. found Jack and Chief at a Texas Hold'em table. Jack had a mountain of chips in front of him, and a cigar clamped between his teeth. Chief sat stone-faced, wearing sunglasses indoors, looking as if he were about to scalp somebody and terrifying the other players into folding.

He walked up behind Jack and squeezed his shoulder. "Party's over. Cash out, gentlemen."

Jack protested. "I'm up four grand!"

"I need your help," J.P. said.

Jack heard the tone and instantly racked his chips. Minutes later, they were huddled in a quiet alcove near the restrooms. J.P. laid it out fast.

"Vangie is in. Meika has the code. She's going up to the penthouse to… distract General. She's going to fake a need to use the bathroom or get ice to gain access to the safe while Vangie keeps General occupied."

"Poor girls," Chief said.

"A young woman named Tina, a friend of Vangie who works for the hotel, is bringing the room-service cart down to the basement kitchen about ten minutes after midnight," J.P. said. "She'll have the package. But here's the kicker: Two of General's goons, Scruffy and Pinkie, might be shadowing the food cart. If so, I may need a distraction. A big one."

Chief cracked his knuckles. "Distraction is my middle name."

ᖴᑎᕼᑐ

Hours had passed since Vangie had left J.P. at the Gilded Cage, and still there was no sign of General Roubidoux. Something had disrupted his predictable routine, and the thought of what it might be terrified her. She was reaching for her cell phone when the door opened, and he appeared. Dropping the phone, she put her arms around his neck and kissed him.

He smiled—slowly, satisfied—the smile of a man who had never lost. "You always did know how to please me."

"I try." She stepped closer again, fingers tracing the lapels of his shirt. "Shall we continue this conversation in the bedroom?"

She took his hand and led him down the hall. The master suite was dark except for the glow of the city lights through the floor-to-ceiling windows. The bed was enormous, draped in white Egyptian cotton. Vangie let him undress her slowly, piece by piece, her movements languid and practiced. When she stood naked before him, she looked like something carved from moonlight and sin.

He reached for her, but she caught his wrists gently, guiding his hands to her waist instead.

"Wait," she said. "I have a surprise."

"I love surprises," he said. "At least when they aren't the gotcha variety."

Vangie smiled as he crossed to the nightstand, opened a drawer, and pressed a button. The room's hidden speakers came to life—slow jazz, the same track that had been playing in the living room. But underneath it, barely audible, was something else: the faint sound of breathing, of fabric rustling, of a woman's low moan.

"I thought you might enjoy... company."

She stepped aside as Meika emerged from the shadows of the adjoining dressing room, wearing nothing but black lace and a wicked smile. Her dark hair was loose, skin glowing in the low light. She moved with the same effortless grace she brought to the casino floor, hips swaying, eyes locked on General.

"Evening, General," she said, voice like honey over gravel. "Vangie thought you might like... a threesome."

General's smile widened. He looked from one woman to the other, then back again.

"Well," he said softly, "this is unexpected."

Vangie stepped close, pressing herself against his side, lips brushing his ear. "I told you I missed you."

Meika moved to his other side, fingers trailing down his chest. "And we thought you might enjoy... options."

General laughed—low, rich, satisfied. "Ladies," he said, "you have my full attention."

Vangie's hands were gentle, almost tender; Meika's were bolder, hungrier. They undressed him with practiced efficiency, their touches coordinated, complementary. He closed his eyes, letting himself sink into the sensation. Vangie glanced at Meika over his shoulder. A quick nod passed between them—silent, certain.

As General's hands moved over their bodies, Vangie's heart raced. Too busy enjoying his surprise, he never noticed. General Harlan Roubideaux surrendered to pleasure, unaware that every moan, every whispered endearment, every moment of vulnerability was orchestrated.

Vangie's eyes met Meika's across the expanse of his body. The look they shared was not one of desire, though Meika knew what it meant. She was naked when she rolled off the bed.

"Gotta pee," she said. "Be right back."

Vangie made sure General didn't notice that Meika left the bedroom.

Vangie had dimmed the lights. Now, the moonlight reflected through the floor-to-ceiling window cast the room in furtive shadows that moved in slow motion.

Meika's heart raced as she found the cell phone Vangie had planted, then opened the cabinet to reveal the safe. When she punched in the combination and the lights flashed open, she issued a big sigh of relief. She'd taken dozens of pictures with the phone's camera when someone knocked on the door, not bothering to pull on a robe when she answered it because she knew who it would be.

"Meika...," the young redheaded woman said when she pushed the serving cart into the room.

"It's okay, baby," Meika said, embracing her, kissing her

forehead, then stepping away to see what was in the stainless serving trays. "Smells good."

"I only brought two champagne flutes," Tina said, already pouring the bubbly liquid.

"No problem," Meika said. "Vangie and I can share."

Tina grinned as Meika handed her the cell phone wrapped in a hundred-dollar bill. She slipped it into the pocket of her white smock and then disappeared out the door with the serving cart. Meika took the two glasses of champagne and returned to the bedroom.

"Surprise!" she said.

The service elevator lobby in the basement was a stark contrast to the gold-plated world above. It was concrete, cold, and smelled of commercial sanitizer and grease. J.P. waited in the shadows of a linen closet while Jack and Chief lounged near the vending machines, looking like two drunks who had gotten lost searching for the buffet.

The elevator indicator light pinged, and the doors slid open.

Tina, a petite redhead in a server's uniform, pushed a stainless steel cart out. She looked terrified. And for good reason. Standing right behind her in the elevator car were Scruffy and Pinkie.

"I need to check the cart," Scruffy growled, stepping out."

"What for?" she asked.

Scruffy and Pinkie were pawing through the stainless steel serving trays and containers and didn't bother to answer her.

Visibly shaken, Tina scanned the hallway until she locked eyes with J.P. in the shadows. He gave her a microscopic nod.

J.P. tensed to move, but Pinkie stepped out, spotting Jack and Chief instantly.

"Hey!" Pinkie barked. "Staff only down here. Get lost."

"Whoa, hold on now, partner," Jack said, slurring his words and stumbling forward. He waved a half-empty beer bottle he'd snagged from somewhere. "We're just looking for the little boys' room. My large friend here has a bladder the size of a thimble."

"Upstairs," Scruffy said, moving to block them. "Beat it."

"You don't have to be rude," Chief said, his voice deep and menacing. He took a heavy step toward Pinkie. "I don't like rude."

"I said move!" Pinkie reached for his jacket, presumably for a weapon or a radio.

"Hey! Is that a gun?" Jack said, suddenly feigning panic and lurching forward, effectively tripping over his own feet and crashing directly into the smaller bodyguard. It was a beautiful mess. Jack was bigger than Pinkie and sent the smaller man stumbling back into the elevator door frame. Seizing the moment, he grabbed Pinkie by the lapels and spun him around, slamming him against the elevator wall with a metallic clang.

"You spilled my beer!" Jack said.

Chief and Scruffy jumped into the fray to help. In the split second that the goons were occupied, Tina shoved the room service cart hard to the left. As she passed J.P.'s hiding spot, she didn't stop, but her hand flashed as she handed him the phone.

J.P. reached out and snatched the hard plastic of a cell phone from her hand.

"I have to go!" she said, terrified, pushing the cart faster down the hall toward the kitchen.

J.P. slipped the phone into his tuxedo pocket and melted back into the shadows.

Down the hall, Chief helped Scruffy to his feet and patted Pinkie on the chest. "My mistake. I see the exit sign now. Come on, Jack."

"Sorry, fellas!" Jack called out. "We're going, now."

Jack and Chief retreated toward the stairwell, leaving the confused and angry bodyguards dusting themselves off.

J.P. waited until the heavy stairwell door clicked shut behind his friends looking at the phone. On the screen was a gallery of photos: deeds, ledgers, and bank routing numbers.

"Gotcha," he said under his breath.

CHAPTER 33

It was less than ninety miles from Biloxi to Chalmette, and J.P. made the drive in record time. He'd come alone, leaving Jack and Chief at the Golden Gulf Casino so as not to draw unnecessary attention on his departure. His cell phone rang as he approached the outskirts of town. It was Detective Sam Marcantel.

"What's up, Sam? You sound kind of hoarse."

"I'm in front of the Bayou Mortuary. Where you at?"

"About twenty miles out," J.P. said. "I got something to do first, and then I'll join you."

"Come now. I need you," Sam said before the line disconnected.

J.P. dialed Eddie, who answered on the first ring. "I have the package," he said.

"Where are you?" Eddie asked.

"Closing in on Chalmette. About twenty miles away."

"Good, see you when you get here."

"It'll be a while," J.P. said. "Sam Marcantel just called. From the sound of his voice, I think he's in trouble."

"Where is he?" Eddie asked.

"Staking out the Bayou Mortuary. Call you after I see what he wants."

The drive to Chalmette was a wet blur of low beams and windshield wipers. J.P. had taken the back way, avoiding the interstate cameras. He killed the headlights as he rolled into the shopping center, coasting into the farthest corner slot beneath a broken security light. The only illumination came from the drugstore, its blue-and-red neon pharmacy sign buzzing like a dying insect.

J.P. sat for a moment, listening to the engine tick down. The rain turned the parking lot into a shallow black mirror, reflecting the world in distorted ripples. He stepped out, pulling his collar up against the damp chill.

The two blocks to Sam's stakeout felt longer in the dark. Lightning flickered through the live oaks, turning the broken sidewalk into a strobe of roots and puddles. As before, he found the unmarked black Ford sedan parked in the shadows of a cypress tree. He approached the passenger side, expecting the window to roll down, expecting the smell of stale tobacco and old coffee.

Nothing happened.

He leaned in, cupping his hands against the glass. The car was empty, his hand on the hood told him the engine was cold. A warning bell went off in the base of his skull—primitive and urgent.

Sam had sounded breathless on the phone. Scared. Now he was gone, and his ride was cold. J.P. scanned the perimeter. The Bayou Mortuary squatted low and unassuming fifty yards away, a single-story brick building the color of dried river mud.

In the daylight, it was just a business. Tonight, under the slashing rain, it looked predatory. The neon sign above the entrance flickered: Bayou Mortuary – Compassionate Care in Life's Final Passage. The "P" in Passage was burnt out, leaving a dark gap like a missing tooth.

J.P. reached under his jacket and unclipped the Sig Sauer. He thumbed the safety off, the click lost in a roll of thunder.

He moved off the sidewalk, sticking to the deeper shadows of the landscaping, boots sinking into the sodden mulch. He bypassed the front entrance and circled toward the side delivery driveway. The metal canopy drummed under the rain like impatient fingers.

The side door was unlocked. It shouldn't have been. He nudged it open with the toe of his boot and slipped inside, the heavy door sealing out the noise of the storm.

The silence that followed was heavy, suffocating. Then, he heard it.

Music.

It was faint, piping through the ceiling speakers—a funeral organ rendition of "Rock of Ages," slow and mournful. It was playing to an empty house.

The hallway was a tunnel of gloom. The lighting, usually muted out of respect for the grieving, had been dimmed to almost nothing. The carpet runners muffled his footsteps. The air was frigid and smelled of lilies and antiseptic, a cloying sweetness meant to mask rot.

J.P. moved with practiced stealth, the Sig held close to his chest. He cleared the first room—an office, empty. He cleared the viewing parlor—rows of empty chairs staring at an empty dais. The shadows seemed to detach themselves from the corners, dancing in the periphery of his vision.

The organ music swelled slightly, a discordant bass note vibrating in the floorboards. It felt less like a comfort and more like a taunt. When he reached the rear of the building, the décor shifted from plush carpet to linoleum and stainless steel. This was the prep area. The embalming suite.

At the end of the hall, a heavy door stood slightly ajar. A low and mechanical hum emanated from within—the aggressive drone of heavy-duty compressors working overtime. J.P. stopped. The smell here was different. sharper. The chemical tang of formaldehyde couldn't quite cover the underlying scent of organic decay. He pushed the heavy insulated door open with his shoulder, raising the gun, ready for Sam, ready for a guard, ready for anything.

He lowered the weapon slowly, his breath catching in his throat.

It was the refrigerated storage. But there was no order here. No respectful rows of drawers.

The bodies were everywhere. Wrapped in black plastic, shrouded in white sheets, some just partially covered. They weren't laid out side-by-side. They were stacked. Like cordwood.

Like trash bags awaiting a curbside pickup. Limbs jutted out at unnatural angles from the pile, stiff and gray in the harsh fluorescent light of the cooler. He stared at the macabre mound of human debris. The compressors roared, struggling to keep the temperature down against the mass of heat, but they were losing the battle.

Sam wasn't here but a lot of bodies were. And business, apparently, was booming.

J.P. stepped carefully around the grisly mound of human refuse, his boots sticking slightly to the fluid leaking onto the concrete floor. He tracked the source of the freshest blood—a dark trail that didn't belong to the frozen dead. It led past the stacks, toward a utility sink in the back corner.

He found Sam there.

The big detective was slumped against the plumbing pipes, legs splayed, chin resting on his chest. His face was a ruin of purple bruising and lacerations, his shirt sodden with red.

"Sam," he said, holstering the Sig to check for a pulse, he pressed two fingers to Sam's neck.

It was there. Threadbare and thready, fluttering like a trapped moth, but there.

"Hang on, podna," he said.

When he slid his arm under Sam's shoulders to hoist him up, a blow came from nowhere.

It wasn't a sound, but a feeling—a sudden displacement of air behind him. Before he could pivot, something heavy and unyielding connected with the base of his skull. A white-hot starburst exploded behind his eyes. The smell of formaldehyde and rot rushed up to meet him, and then the floor dropped away into absolute black.

Consciousness didn't return all at once. It leaked in, cold and sharp.

J.P. was staring at a drop ceiling. A water stain in the shape of a continent spread across the acoustic tile directly above him. A fluorescent tube buzzed angrily, flickering with a strobe effect that sent spikes of pain through his skull.

He tried to sit up.

Nothing happened.

He tried to turn his head, attempted to clench a fist. Struggled to twitch a toe.

Nothing.

Panic, cold and primal, flooded his chest. He wasn't bound. He could feel the lack of straps. But his body was heavy, dead weight, completely disconnected from the commands his brain was screaming. He was in a chemical straitjacket, his growing desperation palpable.

J.P. was naked, the stainless steel beneath him biting into his bare back, leeching the heat from his skin. The curved channels of the metal table pressed into his flesh—grooves designed to carry away fluids. Blood. Water. Embalming waste. The thought was unnerving.

He was on the prep table.

A face leaned into his field of vision, blocking out the water-stained ceiling.

It was a face J.P. knew from the police dive boat, though now it was splattered with microscopic red speckles. Dr. Spivey Sonnier. The Coroner.

Sonnier wore surgical scrubs that might once have been blue but were now dark and wet across the chest. He looked calm, clinical, like a man deciding where to make the first incision on a Sunday roast.

"I see you're with us," Sonnier said. His voice was smooth, a stark contrast to the butchery surrounding them. "Don't bother trying to struggle. It's a paralytic cocktail I usually reserve for... difficult cases. You can blink, and you can breathe. That's about all the luxury you get right now."

J.P. blinked. It was the only defiance he had left.

Sonnier smiled, thin and cold. He held up his left hand. In it was the burner cell phone—the package.

J.P.'s heart hammered against his ribs, a trapped bird in a cage he couldn't open. The evidence.

"Had yourself a real prize here," Sonnier said, turning the phone over in his gloved fingers. "Documents, photos. Very thorough. The DOJ would have had a field day with this."

He slipped the phone into the pocket of his bloody scrubs and raised his right hand. The overhead light glinted off a number ten scalpel blade.

"Too bad it's never going to see the light of day," Sonnier said softly, lowering the blade until the tip hovered inches from J.P.'s throat. "Or you either."

A shadow moved in the periphery of J.P.'s vision. A mountain of a man stepped into the light, arms crossed over a massive chest. Bobbie Don Rooker. He looked down at J.P.'s naked and paralyzed form with a sneer of pure contempt.

"Boss wants it clean," he said, his voice like grinding stones. "Don't make a mess we gotta clean up later."

"I'm the embalmer, Bobbie Don," Sonnier said, his eyes never leaving J.P.'s. "I don't make messes. I make the dead presentable."

He tapped the flat of the cold blade against J.P.'s chest.

"Now," he said. "Let's embalm him."

The storm that was drenching Chalmette was just as violent over Oyster Island. Thunder rattled the sash windows of the Majestic Hotel bar, shaking the old cypress beams in the ceiling and making the floorboards tremble beneath the stools. The vintage chandeliers overhead buzzed and dimmed, casting the room into momentary gloom before flickering back to a nervous brightness.

It was very late. The bar was empty of patrons, leaving only the core group huddled against the weather.

Eddie sat at the polished mahogany counter, staring at his cell phone as the screen went black. He placed it face down on the bar top with a heavy click, his hand lingering over it for a second too long. Next to him, Paula sat motionless, staring into the amber depths of her untouched drink.

Behind the bar, Odette and Trixie were taking advantage of the lull to wipe down the taps and arrange the glassware.

"Who was that?" Odette asked, tossing a rag into the sink.

Eddie picked up his scotch, swirling the ice. "J.P. He's on his way here to deliver a package."

Trixie perked up, flashing a red-lipped smile as she leaned over the counter. "Love it! J.P. knows how to liven up a party. Maybe he'll bring some decent music with him, too."

Odette chuckled, pouring herself a splash of wine. "Lord knows we need it. This storm is putting everyone in a mood."

The two women continued to banter, their voices light and oblivious, rising above the drumming of the rain against the roof. They joked about the leaks in the ceiling and the ghost stories the storm always seemed to dredge up at the Majestic.

Paula didn't join in. She didn't even blink.

She sat rigid on her stool, her head bowed low. Her hands were pressed hard against her temples, fingers massaging the skin in tight circles as if trying to push back a migraine that had come on like a freight train.

Odette stopped mid-laugh. The silence coming from Paula's side of the bar was louder than the thunder. She leaned in, her expression softening from amusement to concern.

"What's the matter, girlfriend?" Odette asked. "You look like you just walked over your own grave."

Paula didn't look up immediately. She took a ragged breath, the kind that shudders in the chest. When she finally raised her head, her eyes were wide and unfocused, fixed on something a hundred miles away.

"J.P.'s in danger," she said.

The lights flickered again, plunging the bar into darkness for a heart-stopping second. When they buzzed back on, Paula hadn't moved.

"He's in trouble," she said, her voice trembling. "We need to do something, or he's going to die."

CHAPTER 34

The air inside the Golden Gulf Casino in Biloxi was thick with the scent of expensive cigars, stale perfume, and the desperate electricity of high-stakes gambling. Jack and Chief sat at the Texas Hold 'em table, their faces masks of professional indifference. They were playing their parts, blending into the neon-lit excess to keep General Roubideaux from realizing J.P. had already slipped away toward Chalmette.

The dealer was mid-shuffle, the cards clicking like a rapid-fire heartbeat, when the world at the table shifted.

Chief's massive frame suddenly went rigid. His head snapped back with a violent jerk, as if an invisible fist had struck him. The stacks of chips in front of him rattled, and his breath caught in a guttural wheeze.

Jack's eyes narrowed, his hand hovering over his own cards. "Chief? What the hell?"

Chief didn't look at him. His jaw was clenched so tight the muscles in his neck stood out like corded steel. "J.P.," he said, the name sounding like it was being dragged over gravel. "He's in trouble."

Jack glanced at the security cameras overhead, then leaned in close, his voice a low hiss. "Keep it together. We're ninety miles from Chalmette. There's not a damn thing we can do about it from here."

"I have to... contact Grandpa," Chief said with a groan.

Then, the transformation began.

Chief's eyes rolled back, revealing nothing but the veined whites. His upper body began to sway—not with the rhythm of the room, but to a pulse only he could hear. A rhythmic chant started deep in his chest, a vibration of ancient vowels that seemed to push back against the pinging of the slot machines and the upbeat lounge music.

"Hey, what the hell is the crazy Indian doing?" a player at the end of the table barked, shoving his chair back. "Is he having a fit?"

"Sir, please remain still," the dealer said, his hand already moving toward the silent alarm beneath the table.

Chief didn't hear them. His swaying grew more violent, his hands gripping the edge of the felt table so hard the wood began to groan. The chant grew louder, a haunting drone that cut through the casino's artificial atmosphere like a jagged blade.

"Chief, stop it," Jack said, reaching out to grab his arm.

Chief's skin was hot to the touch, vibrating with kinetic energy.

"Grandpa... see him... help him..." Chief's voice rose to a shout, the words blurring into a language that predated the casino, the state, and the country.

The floor manager arrived first, followed by three burly security guards in dark blazers. "Sir! You need to leave the table immediately!"

Chief didn't blink. He was somewhere else—somewhere dark, damp, and smelling of formaldehyde.

"Get him out of here!" the manager yelled.

As Jack tried to intercede, shouting that it was a medical emergency, the guards moved in. They grabbed Chief's shoulders, but he was like an unrooted oak. Finally, with a coordinated heave, they rolled him out of his chair.

Chief hit the patterned carpet hard, but his body never stopped its frantic twitching. He curled into a fetal position, the chanting turning into a guttural roar that echoed off the vaulted ceilings.

"Back off!" Jack said, shoving a guard away. "He's in the throes of an epileptic fit."

Nearby, women began to scream as the sheer intensity of Chief's episode radiated outward. Gamblers scrambled away from the table, chips scattering like plastic hail. The lights above the table flickered and died, and for a heartbeat, the only sound was Chief's voice, calling out to a spirit world that didn't care about the laws of man or the distance of miles.

Then, the heavy weight of a dozen hands bore down on Jack, and the screaming madness of the casino floor faded into a suffocating black.

Back at the Majestic, the air in the bar had turned electric with a different kind of storm. The playful banter of moments ago had vanished, replaced by jagged panic. Paula remained hunched over her drink, her face pale and her eyes fixed on a terrifying internal vision.

"J.P.'s going to die," she said, her words cutting through the roar of the thunder. "I feel the chill."

Odette slammed her palms onto the mahogany bar. "Don't you say that! Not J.P." She turned her fiery gaze toward Eddie, her voice cracking with urgency. "Eddie, do something! Call the Sheriff's office. They've got sirens, they've got the authority—they can get to that mortuary way before we can even get the truck out of covered parking."

Eddie already had his phone in his hand, his thumb hovering over the keypad, but he shook his head grimly.

"I can't call the Sheriff's office," he said, his voice tight with frustration.

"Why the hell not?" Trixie asked, her usual bubbly persona replaced by raw fear. "He was a deputy, for God's sake!"

"Because some of the department is dirty and answer to the same people J.P. is trying to put away," Eddie said, his eyes darting to the window as a bolt of lightning illuminated the marsh. "General Roubideaux's reach is long, and Sonnier is the Parish Coroner. If I call the wrong deputy, I'm just giving them the order to finish the job."

Odette grabbed Eddie's forearm, her grip like a vice. "Then who? Who are you calling? We can't just sit here and watch Paula go into a trance while he gets slaughtered!"

Eddie's jaw set into a hard line as he finished dialing a number he'd kept in his private directory for years.

"The Chalmette Police," he said. "They aren't connected, and I know a few guys on the night shift who still care about the badge. They can't be more than five minutes away from the mortuary."

He pressed the phone to his ear, pacing the space behind the barstools.

"Pick up, pick up," he said.

Outside, a tree limb snapped like a gunshot, and the Majestic's lights gave a dying flicker before plunging them all into an oppressive darkness.

Eddie's voice was a jagged bark into the receiver, shouting over the thunder to a contact at the Chalmette PD. "Bayou Mortuary! Breach it now, or you're going to be collecting a deputy's head in a bucket! Just go!"

He slammed the phone down and bolted toward his office. A moment later, he emerged, checking the action on the heavy .45 he kept in his desk drawer.

Behind the bar, the women weren't waiting for instructions. Odette reached into the shadows beneath the brass rail and pulled out a sawed-off shotgun, its twin barrels gleaming dull and mean. Trixie, her face set in a mask of terrifying resolve, snatched a serrated butcher knife from the lemon-slicing station.

"We're coming with you," Odette said.

They started for the door, but stopped dead. Paula hadn't moved from her stool, but she was no longer present. Her body was rigid, her head thrown back, and a guttural humming vibrated from her throat. Her eyes were rolled back, and a faint purple haze began to bleed out of the shadows, swirling around her like incense smoke.

"Paula!"

Trixie reached out, but Eddie caught her arm.

"Leave her," Eddie said, his voice tight. "She's somewhere we can't follow. She'll be okay, but J.P. won't. We gotta go. Now!"

They burst out into the torrential rain, leaving the Majestic behind.

Inside the bar, the world dissolved. The hotel's walls seemed to liquefy, the darkness turning into a violet mist that pulsed with the beat of a heavy heart. From the center of the haze, an old man stepped forward. He was translucent, dressed in buckskin and ancient beads, his face a map of a thousand years of swamp history.

It was Chief's grandfather.

Reaching out, he took Paula's hand, his touch a jolt of static lightning.

Instantly, the floor of the Majestic vanished. Paula gasped as she was jerked upward, the ceiling dissolving into the stormy sky. They were aloft, soaring through the lashing rain, hundreds of feet above the jagged canopy of Oyster Island. The wind should have been freezing, but the purple aura kept her warm.

"Where are we going?" she said over the roar of the gale, looking down at the white-capped waves of the Gulf below.

"To see the Swamp Witch," the old man replied, his voice echoing inside her skull rather than through the air.

"Oh my God! We're going to die," Paula said, her terror peaking as she saw the black expanse of the marsh rushing beneath them. "I need to pray! I need to ask God."

"Save your prayers, child," the spirit said, his grip tightening. "The Heavens are silent tonight. Only the witch can intervene for us with the Horned Serpent to save J.P."

Below them, the prehistoric rot of the deep swamp rose to meet them, a place where the laws of man and the light of the church had never reached. The violet mist thinned as the spirit dropped Paula into the sucking black mud of the deep swamp. She gasped and struggled, the smell of sulfur and ancient decay filling her lungs.

From the cypress knees, a figure emerged—naked, slick with moss and river silt, her hair a wild silver mane. As the woman stepped into a shaft of moonlight, Paula's breath hitched. It was like looking into a distorted mirror. The woman was her—older, harder, stripped of the veneer of civilization.

The witch lunged.

They collided in the muck, a frantic tangle of limbs. She pinned Paula down, her fingers digging into her shoulders. With a snarl, she ripped open Paula's rain-soaked blouse, baring her chest. There, in the strobing light of the storm, the identical tattoos pulsed: a fleur-de-lis entwined with a coiled snake. Paula tried to free herself from the witch's grasp, closing her eyes and saying The Apostle's Creed.

"Your god cannot hear you here. The mud is too thick," she said. "Speak the language the mud understands. Stop asking for permission to heal; command the healing yourself. Choose, or he dies!"

Paula looked at the tattoo—the symbol of her lineage, the traiteur's gift, and the witch's curse. The shame she had carried, the fear of the Parish priest's wagging finger, evaporated in the heat of the struggle. She stopped fighting the mud and started feeling the pull of the earth.

"I am both," she said, her voice echoing with a power that stilled the wind. "I am what I was born to be! Will you help me?"

"You don't need my help. You possess the power. Use it."

When Paula nodded, the Swamp Witch's terrifying expression morphed into a knowing grin, and she vanished into a cloud of dragonflies.

In Chalmette, the silence of the Bayou Mortuary was shattered by a mechanical roar.

Blue and red strobes sliced through the rain as three Chalmette PD cruisers drifted into the parking lot, tires screaming on the wet asphalt. They didn't knock. A heavy battering ram took the side door off its hinges with a crack like a thunderclap.

"POLICE! DROP THE BLADE!"

Inside the prep room, Sonnier was frozen, the scalpel's tip having already drawn a single bead of blood from J.P.'s sternum. Rooker had reached for a sidearm, but he was staring down the barrels of four service weapons.

The chaos escalated within seconds. The fire department arrived, their sirens adding a high-pitched wail to the night. Neighbors peered from windows as the sleepy street was transformed into a crime scene.

Eddie, Odette, and Trixie burst through the shattered door just as the officers were slamming Sonnier and Rooker against the cold brick walls, the metallic clack of handcuffs signaling the end of their reign.

Eddie took advantage of the confusion and bounded for the table.

J.P. lay there, pale and unmoving, his eyes open but vacant, staring at the ceiling. The single drop of blood on his chest looked like a ruby against the sterile stainless steel. Odette dropped her sawed-off, her hands shaking as she reached for his cold hand. Trixie stood back, the butcher knife trembling in her grip, her face wet with a mix of rain and tears.

Eddie stood at the head of the table, looking at the paralyzed and naked form of the man who had risked everything for a "package." When he saw the surgical tools laid out, the industrial drains, and the clinical coldness of the room, he realized what Sonnier was about to do to J.P.

"Holy Mother of God," he said, his voice thick with a horror that even the arrest couldn't wash away. "We almost lost him to the butcher."

The fluorescent lights overhead seemed to settle into a steady hum as the chemical fog in J.P.'s brain began to lift. It started as a pins-and-needles fire in his fingertips, a slow and agonizing thaw that crawled up his limbs. At last, he emitted a rattling breath—the first one that felt like his own. His fingers twitched against the cold steel of the table, and then his elbow buckled as he tried to push himself up.

"Easy, J.P., easy!" Odette said.

She and Trixie didn't care about the police, the sirens, or the gore-spattered room. They draped their coats over J.P.'s shivering frame, pulling him into a frantic, three-way embrace. The scent of rain, perfume, and gunpowder on the women acted like smelling salts, dragging him the rest of the way back to the world of the living.

J.P. coughed, his throat raw. His eyes darted around the room, scanning the chaos. Sonnier was being shoved toward the door in zip-ties, screaming about his rights, while Rooker was pinned to the floor by two patrolmen. In the scuffle, the "package"—the burner phone—found its way to Eddie's pocket.

"The package," J.P. said.

"Got it," Eddie said, patting his pocket. "General Roubideaux's not just cooked. He's well-done."

CHAPTER 35

The drive back to the Majestic was a blur of hydroplaning tires and the metallic scent of spent adrenaline. J.P. sat in the passenger seat of Eddie's Miata, wrapped in a coarse wool blanket, his skin still humming from the remnants of the paralytic. Trixie and Odette followed in J.P.'s truck. He felt raw, like he'd been scrubbed down with lye, but the weight of the burner phone in Eddie's jacket pocket acted as an anchor to the real world.

Inside the hotel bar, the storm had moved into a more rhythmic rumble. Eddie stood by the mahogany counter, the "package" laid out before him like a holy relic. He flipped through the digital gallery Meika had captured—ledger sheets, offshore routing numbers, and the GPS coordinates of the body drops.

"J.P., you don't even know," Eddie said, his voice thick with a triumphant awe. "This isn't just a smoking gun. It's the whole damn arsenal. It's everything I wanted and more. We didn't just catch them in the act; we caught the architecture of the whole operation."

J.P. leaned against the bar, his hand trembling slightly as he reached for a glass of water. "Just make sure the Feds get the originals. No middlemen, Eddie. No local heroes."

"I know, I know," Eddie said, looking at J.P. with a newfound gravity. "You did it, podna. You really did it."

"Not just me," J.P. said. "We all pulled together on this one."

The celebration was cut short by a strangled cry from the back of the room.

Odette and Trixie had gone to check on Paula, who they assumed was still in her trance. Instead, they found her sprawled on the floorboards behind the far table.

"Eddie! J.P.! Help me!" Odette shouted.

They rushed over to find Paula in a state that defied the logic of a woman who had been sitting in a locked room. Her clothes were shredded as if she'd been dragged through a thicket of briars. Her hair was a matted nest of swamp mud and Spanish moss, and her skin was coated in a sulphurous silt.

Most unsettling was her chest. Her blouse had been torn away, exposing the tattoo over her heart. The fleur-de-lis and the serpent weren't just ink on skin; they were glowing with a rhythmic heat. The serpent seemed to be constricting, its black scales shimmering with a metallic-green light, pulsating in time with a heartbeat that wasn't entirely human.

"She's like ice," Trixie said, rubbing Paula's muddy hands.

It took ten minutes of frantic warming and the scent of ammonia to drag Paula back. When her eyes finally snapped open, they weren't the eyes of the woman who had left for the mortuary. They were deep, dark, and filled with the reflection of a place that didn't appear on any map.

"I'm here," she said.

Odette and Trixie hovered over her, eventually hoisting her up and leading her toward the hotel suites. "We're getting you cleaned up, sugar," Odette murmured. "No arguments."

An hour later, the atmosphere in the bar had shifted from horror to a fragile and exhausted peace. A bottle of vintage champagne sat on the bar—Eddie's private reserve—its cork popped with a muffled thud that felt like a celebratory gunshot. Paula returned to the group, her hair damp and smelling of lavender soap, wrapped in a thick white terry-cloth bathrobe. She looked fragile, but there was a new stillness in her posture, a lack of the nervous fidgeting that had defined her for years.

Eddie poured five glasses, the bubbles hissing in the quiet room. "To being alive," he said. "And to General Roubideaux's downfall."

They drank deeply, the cold wine cutting through the

lingering taste of the swamp and the mortuary. Odette leaned against the bar, her eyes settling on the collar of Paula's robe, where the tip of the fleur-de-lis peeked through. The adrenaline of the night had stripped away her filter.

"Paula," Odette said softly. "I saw it. The snake... it was moving. It was like it was breathing for you. I've known you a long time, but I've never seen it do that. What does that tattoo really mean?"

Paula glanced at her chest, her fingers tracing the outline of the ink through the fabric. She didn't flinch or look away.

"I didn't know yesterday," she said. "I spent my whole life trying to keep the two halves of myself from meeting. The Church told me I was a healer, a traiteur, as long as I only used the prayers they gave me. They told me the roots, the voices, the power in the mud—was the devil.

She pulled the collar of the robe aside slightly. In the candlelight, the serpent's head rested near the junction of the lily petals, its tiny tongue seemingly tasting the air.

"The fleur-de-lis is the life I was supposed to have. The purity. The 'right' way," Paula said. "But the serpent... he's the foundation. He's the wisdom that lives in the dark. For years, I thought he was trying to swallow the flower. I thought he was the enemy.

She looked at J.P., then back to Odette.

"Last night, in the mud, I realized the serpent isn't eating the flower. He's protecting it. He's the root. You can't have the healing without the sting. You can't have the light of the prayer without the power of the shadow.

Paula took a slow sip of her champagne, a knowing smile touching her lips.

"It means I'm done apologizing for who I am," she said. "The Priest won't like it. The neighbors won't understand it. But J.P. is alive because I finally let the snake move."

J.P. raised his glass to her, his "well-done" grin returning. For the first time in a long time, the shadows in the corner of the Majestic didn't feel threatening. They felt like home.

EPILOGUE

The Majestic's main ballroom glittered under a constellation of crystal chandeliers, their light refracting through champagne flutes and the polished copper of Oyster Bay Rumworks' first bottled batch. The room thrummed with laughter, the low pulse of a country swing band, and the warm scent of fresh oak, molasses, and sea air carried in on the guests' clothes.

The Chalmette Playboys held court on the raised stage, fiddles and steel guitar weaving through the old Prohibition-era space like a river finding its way home. Couples two-stepped across the wide floor, boots and heels clicking in time, while others clustered around high-top tables, toasting with the new rum—smooth, rich, and unmistakably of the Gulf.

Alex Pavlovic stood near the center of it all, one arm around Renata Yatsenko, the other cradling a glass of the first pour. His suit was crisp, his smile unguarded for once. Renata's mother, Iryna, and daughter, Sveta, were also present. Renata leaned into him, her dark hair loose, wearing a deep emerald dress that caught the light like the scales of something ancient and proud. She looked at him the way a woman looks at a man she has finally decided to keep. From the smiles on her mother and daughter's faces, it was clear they approved of her decision.

Mama Mulate and Jake Huntington stood nearby, Mama in flowing purple, Jake in a black blazer and the easy grin of a man who'd just watched a very large bet pay off. Mama raised her glass.

"To the water that remembers," she said, voice carrying without effort, "and to the people who finally listened."

The toast rippled outward. Glasses lifted. The band shifted into a slower tune. Alex clinked his glass against Renata's.

"To new beginnings," he said.

She smiled, soft and sure. "And not letting the past drown them."

Across the room, J.P. Saucier leaned against a pillar, watching the dance floor with a half-smile. Lucky sat at his feet, tail thumping lazily. Vangie LeBlanc stood beside him in a simple black dress that somehow made her look both dangerous and at peace. Meika, radiant in red, laughed at something Vangie said, then pulled her onto the floor.

The two women moved together easily, drawing eyes and smiles. J.P. didn't mind. He raised his glass to them from across the room. Eddie Toledo moved through the crowd like the host he was born to be, shaking hands, kissing cheeks, making sure every glass stayed full. He paused beside Sheriff Comier, who had postponed retirement long enough to see this night through. The old lawman looked tired but satisfied.

"We couldn't have done it without J.P.," he said, voice rough with emotion.

Eddie nodded. "To J.P."

They drank. On the dance floor, J.P. had found Vangie again. She stepped close, her hand sliding into his.

"You kept your promise," she said.

He raised an eyebrow. "Which one?"

"That you would make sure I survived my ordeal," she said,

"Seems I remember that you made a promise to me if we succeeded in bringing General down," he said,

"The three-way?" she said, nodding toward Meika, who was already dancing with Chief.

"Uh-huh!" he said.

Vangie laughed, low and easy. "Dream on, cowboy."

J.P. smiled as she rested her head against his shoulder and the band slid into a slow two-step.

Odette stood near the bar with Trixie Kettler, who had traded her dissertation stress for a glass of rum and a quiet glow of accomplishment. Jack was also there. The reef was closed to diving now—federal jurisdiction—but the data she'd gathered before the shutdown had already started conversations in Baton Rouge and Washington. She leaned against Jack, watching the room.

"I finished my dissertation," she said. "Graduating in the spring."

Jack raised his glass. "To the girl who washed up in a storm and stayed to change the tide."

Trixie clinked her glass against his. "To the island that wouldn't let me leave."

At a quiet table near the windows, Paula Boutet sat with Jimmie. He'd driven in from Chalmette, still in his work boots, still looking a little dazed by everything that had happened. Paula's hand rested on his.

For the first time in years, she wasn't hiding. The fleur-de-lis and serpent tattoo was visible at the neckline of her dress. She didn't cover it. Jimmie looked at it, then at her. He didn't speak for a long time. Then he lifted her hand and kissed the knuckles.

"I always knew there was more to you," he said. "I just didn't know how to ask."

Paula smiled, tears shining in her eyes. "You never had to."

They sat in silence, hands linked, watching the room spin around them. The band finished the song. A hush fell over the ballroom. Alex stepped to the microphone. Renata stood beside him, her hand in his. He cleared his throat.

"Ladies and gentlemen... thank you for being here tonight. This rum—" he lifted the bottle, amber liquid catching the light —"this is the first batch from Oyster Bay Rumworks. It's made with water from our island, sugarcane from the Gulf, and more than a little stubbornness." Laughter rippled through the crowd." But mostly," he continued, voice thickening, "it's made with love. For this place. For these people. And for the woman who reminded me that some things are worth fighting for, even when the storm tries to take them away.

He turned to Renata. She smiled up at him, eyes shining. "So if you'll all raise your glasses... "Every hand lifted, "To Oyster Bay Rumworks," he said.

The room answered in one voice: "To Oyster Bay Rumworks!"

The band struck up again. The dance floor filled. Glasses clinked. Laughter rose. And somewhere out in the Gulf, beneath the dark water where the reef still slumbered, the Horned Serpent stirred once, sighed, and sank back into sleep. The January tides had come. And they had chosen.

End

BOOK NOTES

I finished writing Oyster Bay Boogaloo on the last day of 2025, a year that began poorly for me, though ended on a positive note. The tone of the book, like the year, was stormy and moody. Storms are inevitable, but they never last forever.

Oyster Bay Boogaloo wasn't the only book I wrote in 2025. I also penned Tsisdetsi's Shadow, the fourth book in my *Paranormal Cowboy Series*. Writing both books immersed me in a world of mystery, justice, and the supernatural and took me away from the reality that haunted me.

Fans of my *French Quarter Mystery Series* will recognize familiar faces in *Tsisdetsi's Shadow*. Mama Mulate and Jake Huntington, the charismatic Cryptid Hunter, are spinoffs from the moody, haunted streets of New Orleans, where my primary character, Wyatt Thomas, operates as a private investigator.

In 2025, Wyatt visited Oyster Island in *Oyster Bay Mambo*, a standalone mystery that bridges both series with recurring characters. And for those who love the French Quarter's blend of mystery and hauntings, mark your calendars: *Blood and Ashes, Book 15* of the *French Quarter Mystery Series*, arrives in February 2026.

To my readers, thank you. Your support breathes life into my stories, keeping them from fading like morning fog over a forgotten lawn. Without you, my words would vanish into the Great Unknown. Here's to shared adventures and the stories yet to come.

ABOUT THE AUTHOR

Eric Wilder is an American author known for his gripping mystery novels set in New Orleans. He was born and raised in Louisiana, where he discovered his love for storytelling at a young age. After completing his education, Wilder spent several years in the oil and gas industry before pursuing a career as a writer.

Wilder's breakthrough came with the publication of Big Easy, which introduced readers to his signature blend of suspense, action, and local color. The book was an instant success, drawing critical acclaim and a devoted following. Wilder followed up with a collection of thrillers set in the heart of New Orleans.

Wilder's writing is characterized by his deep knowledge of the city and its unique culture and his skillful use of suspense and plot twists to keep readers on the edge of their seats. His books have been praised for their authenticity, vivid descriptions, and compelling characters.

Eric Wilder has a reputation for delivering top-notch thrillers that transport readers to the heart of New Orleans. He's the author of twenty-eight novels. His series features characters who often find themselves involved in the paranormal. He lives in Oklahoma near historic Route 66 with his two dogs, Moe and Buddy.

OTHER BOOKS BY ERIC WILDER

<u>French Quarter Mystery Series</u>
Big Easy, Book 1
City of Spirits, Book 2
Primal Creatures, Book 3
Black Magic Woman, Book 4
River Road, Book 5
Sisters of the Mist, Book 6
Garden of Forbidden Secrets, Book 7
New Orleans Dangerous, Book 8
Cycles of the Moon, Book 9
Half Past Midnight, Book 10
Thief of Souls, Book 11
Krewe of Illusion, Book 12
Wild Magnolias, Book 13
Night People, Book 14
Blood and Ashes, Book 15
Paranormal Cowboy Series
Ghost of a Chance, Book 1
Bones of Skeleton Creek, Book 2
Blink of an Eye, Book 3
Tsisdetsi's Shadow, Book 4
Adobe Moon, Book 5
Oyster Bay Mystery Series
Oyster Bay Boogie, Book 1
Oyster Bay Tango, Book 2
Oyster Bay Two Step, Book 3
Oyster Bay Limbo, Book 4
Oyster Bay Mambo, Book 5
Standalone Novels
Of Love and Magic

Diamonds in the Rough
Ben's Magical Midnight Garden
Anthologies and Cookbooks
Murder Etouffée – out of print
Over the Rainbow – out of print
Lily's Little Cajun Cookbook

ERIC'S LINKS

Twitter: EricWilderOk
Blog: Murky Bayou Blogspot
Blog: Eric Wilder Blogspot
Facebook: Louisiana Mystery Writer
Instagram: Louisiana Mystery Writer
Website: Eric Wilder Books

www.ingramcontent.com/pod-product-compliance
Lightning Source LLC
Chambersburg PA
CBHW011516240626
47154CB00010B/3046